Code Blue in Cell 52:
A Legal and Recovery Journey

Gary M. Lang

This novel is dedicated to the men and women who are committed to seeing that our rights are protected and who often toil for inadequate compensation.

Acknowledgements

My Stepdaughter Shauna and my friend John, both of whom provided their respective skills.

Contents

CHAPTER 1–CHRISTMAS AT THE COALTON JAIL

Franklin and Kim approached what he sometimes called the first line of defense in the Coalton County Jail. They had already stashed their personal belongings in a locker, and would pass through a magnetometer as soon as they were IDed.

The guard who sat at the entrance to the jail behind a desk that was protected by a wire mesh screen, Sergeant First Line of Defense, asked: "Franklin, who's your lady friend?"

"Actually," Franklin lied, "she's my wife." Although Franklin detected the slightest sign of bewilderment on Kim's face, she didn't correct him.

"Whatcha got there? Smells like cookies." The Sergeant motioned toward the aluminum foil wrapped mounded circle that Franklin was carrying.

"Well, we have clearance to pass them out at the meeting and to Cell Block C, the old timers. We cleared it through the Warden."

"Well, I will have to taste them to see if there is any contraband inside." He then motioned them through the magnetometer, stepped out of the cage – like office, and, when Franklin had uncovered the cookies, devoured a couple.

"Merry Christmas, Sarge," Franklin grunted with a touch of sarcasm which he hoped went unrecognized as he pressed the elevator button that would take them to the jail's gym.

He would run the jail's AA/NA meeting from the gym, as he had done for months now, and then he and Kim would pass out the cookies to the "old timers", who were actually reaching near the end of their sentences. The jail only housed those sentenced up to five years; if the sentence was greater than five years, you went to a state pen.

When they stepped out of the elevator, immediately in front of them was another guard sitting behind a desk. He spoke:

"If it isn't my favorite Savior of alchies and addicts. Frankie baby, who's your lady friend?"

Franklin, deciding not to press his luck, responded, "She's a friend, and she made these cookies," he said as he presented the cookie tray.

"Who are they for, besides me?"

"They're for the old timers in Cellblock C, it's our effort to bring a little Christmas cheer to this sorry ass place."

"You got that right."

"Hey Al, since I can't have my friend Kim here present during the meeting, could she sit by you until I'm done with the meeting and then we'll go to C and pass out the cookies."

"Sure, and the lady will be safe with me."

Franklin kissed the obviously confused Kim on the cheek and walked into the gym, where the folding chairs had already been placed in a circle. While he waited for customers, they had to sign up in advance, he reviewed what had brought him to the Coalton County jail this Christmas season.

When he had gone to the hospital after damn near becoming a homeless corpse, Sam Wright, an attorney who he had helped with a case, paid for him to go to a halfway house called the Phoenix. There he stayed for six months, and then found work as a copier repair man and moved into the cheap housing available to the homeless in Pittsburgh. He was happily sober for almost three years now, and was semi-dating his ex-wife, Kim, and going to night school to become a drug and alcohol counselor. He believed what they said about staying sober by helping other alcoholics, so here he was.

As was typical at his jail meetings, most of the inmates who attended were only interested in the diversion to the boring jail routine which these meetings represented, and tonight was no different. When no one offered to share, he told his abbreviated story for the umpteenth time. A few attendees had heard it before. He was about to adjourn the meeting with the Lord's prayer when a hand suddenly shot up. It was connected to the body of a skinny young man who he knew only as "Slim."

"Yes, Slim, what do you have to offer today?"

"Well, I hope to stay clean and sober once I get out of this fuckin' hell hole, but I heard the jail lady shrink talking to a guard and she said that ninety percent of us with drug or alcohol problems would be back."

He knew that Slim must be talking about the jail psychologist, a rather dour looking, nondescript fiftyish woman who he had met once or twice. She didn't seem very empathetic for a jail psychologist.

"I don't know where she got that statistic," Franklin countered, "but I know from my own experience that there is hope to turn your life around. Will you be here next week, Slim?"

Slim nodded.

"Then I'll do a little research, and I think that it's an excellent topic for next week's meeting."

With that, he ended the meeting with the "Our Father," and went to the guard station to collect Kim and the cookies.

When they were in the elevator and going down to the area populated by the "old timers," Franklin asked Kim about what the guard and she talked about when he was running the meeting.

"Not a lot; mostly he just did paperwork. He seemed like a nice enough guy, and seemed to be concerned about the welfare of the prisoners."

Franklin muttered something about that being good when the elevator doors opened into the common area. A miasma of decades–old cigarette smoke and despair permeated the common area. There were twenty-five or thirty circular steel tables bolted into the floor around which were steel benches, also bolted into the floor, which could accommodate three or four inmates per bench. There were three benches per table. The tables and benches reminded Franklin of a picnic area, but there would be no carving of initials in these benches.

There were two TVs mounted ten feet or so up and opposite each other, one of which in Franklin's experience was always tuned to ESPN. Rimming the common area were two tiers of cells, in which the prisoners would be locked at 9:00 PM. Unless they were subject to discipline, a prisoner's out–of–cell time was mostly spent in this common area, excluding time in the dining area for meals and half an hour in the gym or the yard, weather permitting, for exercise.

It was Kim's first trip "inside" as the residents called it, and she wondered aloud why the place reeked of cigarette smoke, since, she grumbled, "They banned cigarettes in all government buildings a few years ago."

His ex–wife was vehemently against smoking, because, he surmised, her father was a prodigious smoker, and died of lung cancer.

Franklin chuckled. "They did, but each county agency had to come up with a plan of enforcement, and I suspect that since eighty percent of the inmates, and over half of the guards smoked, the plan is in bureaucratic purgatory." Kim looked horrified, and announced that she would, "have to wash these clothes when we get home."

Franklin asked one of the guards how many prisoners were present in the common area, and he was told that there were forty-five. Good thing, he thought, all because in addition to maybe a dozen loose cookies, they had packaged five cookies per baggie, and there were fifty baggies. They would have enough.

Through an arrangement with the jail's chaplain office, when they arrived with the cookies, a guard was supposed to pass out a sheet with the words to a couple of Christmas carols to the inmates. Not surprisingly, the guards that were present in the common area weren't informed of this, and one of them went to the chaplain's office to secure the handouts. Meanwhile, the presence of Franklin and Kim had piqued the interest of a number of inmates; mostly the presence of Kim, Franklin thought. They had a number of questions for Kim, the most tame of which was, "Did you bake the cookies?" when Kim told them of their mission at the jail.

When the guard arrived with the song sheets, and passed them out to those that desired them, it became obvious during this scene of joy to the world that there was an outstanding baritone voice emanating from a pudgy inmate with very thick glasses. Franklin asked him if he wouldn't sing Hark! The Herald Angels Sing by himself, and he was glad to comply. At the conclusion of his a cappella performance, he was treated to raucous applause and cheers.

After everyone sang Silent Night, it was time for the cookie distribution. The guards had the inmates line up single file to score (as one of the residents referred to the issuance of the cookies as), and then lapsed into a rather laissez-faire attitude. As a result, there was much cutting in line, and more than a few inmates collected two bags of cookies. It was during the ruckus caused by the dearth of available cookie baggies that the lock down order came.

As prisoners were returning to their cells, a guard told Franklin and Kim that they had to leave the facility. They had heard the words over the loudspeaker 'Code Blue'.

As they made their way down on the elevator and approached the entrance, Franklin asked Guard First Line of Defense what was going on. "Some new guy hung himself in his cell," was the reply.

CHAPTER 2–SAM AND HIS SHORT-SKIRTED CLIENT

As he was walking back to his office from the courthouse, Sam was still obsessing over this morning's goings on. First of all, his client, a woman in her late twenties, showed up for the first day of trial late. He had been afraid that he would need to give his opening statement without her being present, and that would not have been a fortuitous start to the trial in his experience.

And then, he had told her to dress like she was going to church. When she did show up, minutes before the judge called on him to give his opening remarks to the jury, she was dressed in a short skirt and a low cut blouse. When he questioned her as to why she was dressed that way, she responded that this was the way she dressed for church. Ah well, that's memoir material when he retires, he thought.

As he went up in the elevator after completing the short, two block trip to his office, he expected to find that Rhonda had gone to lunch, but instead he found her gnawing on the crust of a piece of pizza and sitting at her computer. She glanced up from her screen, and reported: " Your next wife called because she couldn't reach you on your cell. I told her that you were in court. She said to tell you that you should look for your own dinner tonight, because she promised Tyler and the boys a home — cooked meal. Can you tell me why in heaven's name that man will not hire someone a couple of days a week to care for those kids?"

He had settled Tyler Hatcher's medical malpractice case on behalf of his dead wife for a substantial amount, and he had met Becca, to whom he was engaged as soon as his divorce became final, when he was working on Tyler's case. Becca was Tyler's sister – in – law, and she had helped out upon her sister's death. Tyler and his deceased wife, Alice, had three kids, Nicole, Josh and Jake. Josh and Jake were school – aged, and Nicole was a junior at Pitt.

"Well, I guess the boys may want to see their aunt."

"How did it go over there this morning?" Rhonda asked.

"She showed up late to court, and in a very short skirt and a low cut blouse."

"She's an airhead that's for sure. What's your jury look like?"

"Eight men and four women, oddly enough. Six of the men are between twenty and forty."

"They certainly won't mind short skirts and low cut blouses."

"No, they won't. And there's no doubt but that she wasn't at fault in the accident. It's only a matter of how much her injury is worth. Can you spare a couple of pieces of pizza, it'll save me from ordering."

With two pieces of Rhonda's pizza in hand, he went into his office, and turned on his cell phone. He had two calls. Curiously, they were both from people that he had met through his work on the Hatcher case: Nicole Hatcher, Tyler and Alice's daughter, and Franklin, a homeless man who he discovered in the office basement the same day as he became aware of the Hatcher matter, and had given him preternatural advice on the case. Now that he had gotten sober, Franklin had returned to his old job as a copier repairman, and was going to night school at Duquesne to become a drug and alcohol counselor.

He started with Nicole. During their preliminary pleasantries, in which she referred to Sam as her uncle, because her aunt Becca and he were planning on getting married as soon as his divorce became final, he asked her how college was going.

"It's going just fine. I think that I'm going to make the Dean's list for the seventh time in a row."

"Congratulations! And why is my only niece checking in with me now?"

"Well, as you know I'm a journalism major, and I got a part – time job writing for the Greene Gazette."

"Congratulations young lady," Sam interrupted, sensing that the punchline was to come.

"You remember that my mother used to write for the Greene Gazette?"

"Indeed, I do." Alice Hatcher was, in his estimation, a talented writer. In fact, he was going to introduce several of her poems and writings into evidence at the medical malpractice trial regarding the death of her mother to humanize her, but the case ended up settling during trial.

"Then you'll remember that it was only published once a week, but now it has a daily online presence. It's certainly not the New York Times, but a page or two every day online. I'm going to write an article every two weeks or so to be included in the paper edition and/or online."

"That's great! I hope they're paying you well."

He could hear her laughing. "They're not the New York Times. It will barely cover my weekly Starbucks tab, but it's journalism. Which brings me to the purpose for this call, besides the pleasure of hearing your voice."

"Yes," Sam really had no idea what this had to do with him.

"I thought that I might interview you regarding some cases that you found interesting or significant. We could make it a monthly feature. It would be free advertising for you for what it's worth."

"That's a great idea, as long as I don't have to write anything. I can talk with the best of them." Sam was smiling. "When do we start?"

"How about next week I stop by your office. Why don't you let me know what would be convenient.Be thinking about the case that you want to discuss."

When he hung up and glanced at his watch, he decided to end his lunch hour on a productive note. He would eat his pizza and mentally review his direct examination of Ms. low-cut blouse and short skirt, who he would call as a witness right after lunch. Franklin could wait.

CHAPTER 3– EDITOR TIM BLACK HIRES A REPORTER

When Mr. Black arrived at the office from lunch shortly after Becca had picked Nicole up from her Oakland apartment and dropped her off at the Greene Gazette, he welcomed her with enthusiasm:

"Hello there young lady. I trust that you have introduced yourself to your coworkers in my absence."

She had indeed: There was Mary, a rotund woman in her late fifties who seemed very friendly and served as Mr. Black's girl Friday and "distribution manager", and Scotty, a recent Pitt journalism graduate who was confined to a wheelchair, and was, along with Mr. Black, a writer/ reporter.

Mr. Black continued, "I suppose that I don't need to tell you what a hit print journalism has taken since the advent of the computer and the Internet. I am afraid that print newspapers are on their last legs. We barely make enough on advertising to keep the doors open. Thank God that my father left me this building. That's why I will be paying you such a handsome salary; to see if we can make a go of it by publishing a print newspaper as well as having an online presence. That, and my having a strong suspicion that you are as good a writer as your mother, having seen the obituary that you wrote for her."

"I want to thank you, Mr. Black, for hiring me since it's been three years since you saw me."

"From now on, my name is Tim, since we are working together. Let me show you around the pond and provide you with colorful commentary on what you will see."

With that, Tim lit up a cigarette, and proceeded to show Nicole around the office, and provide a somewhat cynical but detailed history of the Gazette: How it was founded by Tim's father in 1954, the year Tim was born, how it was one of the earliest community papers to come out against the war in Vietnam, and how, in 1968, when Tim was fourteen, the office used by escaped prisoners in the jail, which was right down the street, to "hole up" in. Luckily, Phil related, an "accommodation" was reached with the escapees after two days, and they were returned to jail.

When Tim had finished the tour, he asked Nicole if she had any questions about her role at the paper. Nicole hesitated, and then responded, "I do have some ideas about a feature which I think would be of interest to our readers."

"I am always interested in hearing new ideas, especially from the generation who grew up with computers and social media."

"I talked with Sam Wright, you know, the attorney who handled my mother's case, and he would be willing to share some of his thoughts regarding interesting cases that he had handled."

"He's not going to do some bullshit like 'who needs I will' or 'what to do if you are in an accident', is he? "

Nicole smiled, "Of course not, and I would be writing the article based on my interview with him. Of course, as editor, you would have the final say."

Tim took a long drag off his cigarette, and observed, "That sounds like it might be a good idea. Let's see what you come up with. Now come with me, young lady, and I will show you how we used to typeset and print the paper. But we need to go into the basement to see the antiques of publishing."

He lit a fresh cigarette off the other, and descended the stairs.

CHAPTER 4–FRANKLIN AND SAM DISCUSS JAIL HANGINGS

Franklin was just finishing his dinner of franks and beans when Sam called him.

"I am sorry for taking a couple of days to get back to you, Franklin, but I was in trial. But it's over now."

"That's okay, it was nothing earth – shattering. How did your trial turn out?"

"The jury handsomely rewarded my client in her short skirt and low cut blouse."

"What was the case about?"

"It was a multi-car accident, and it began when my gal was rear – ended."

Franklin was never much good at small talk, but he owed it to the man who may have literally saved his life. After all, three years ago he was a homeless and hopeless alcoholic when he essentially squatted in the basement of Sam's office building to get out of the cold. But by asking Sam how his trial had turned out he had fulfilled any small talk requirement he figured.

"Sam, do you remember that I told you that I ran an AA/NA meeting on Monday night at the Coalton County lockup?"

"Yes, I do. How many months have you been doing that now?"

"About six months or so. They say the only way that you can keep it, is by giving it away. As the French say, 'it is better to prevent than to heal' .At this point in my life, I would rather prevent than heal."

"So you think that helping others with their addiction will prevent you from slipping back. That's undoubtedly true and very noble."

"Well, thank you Sam. And I suppose this call is to see if you can help another person like you helped me."

"You mean help a homeless guy who spouts quotations from French philosophers and has squatted in the office basement?" Franklin knew Sam was referring to him.

Franklin chuckled into the phone, both because he thought it deserved a chuckle and because Sam expected it.

"No, there's one guy at my Monday jail meetings who I think is serious about getting clean and sober. I don't think he has anywhere to go once his sentence is up, and I was wondering…"

Sam interrupted, "Whether I could pull some strings and get him into The Vulture, as you guys call the halfway house. I assume he doesn't have any money."

"I would guess not." The Vulture was officially known as The Phoenix.

"I think that you and I together might be able to get him a 'scholarship' when he gets out."

"What could I do? You're the guy with the connections."

"Franklin, you are a big success story at The Vulture. I'm sure that between the two of us we could do something. How's Kim?"

"She's fine" was his only response. He didn't need to know that the relationship was on again, off again, despite the fact that they had shared an apartment for three months now." She baked Christmas cookies and we passed them out to the 'old timers' at the jail."

"How did that go?"

"It went as well as could be expected. But we had to leave because some guy tried to hang himself, and the jail went on lockdown."

"I didn't see anything online about a jail hanging."

"Hopefully, that means he wasn't successful. Didn't you handle a jail hanging case?"

"I handled two of them. Two deaths. They are very difficult cases. In order to hold any government responsible, you have to prove deliberate indifference, which is a much tougher standard than negligence."

"Then why did you take the cases? Did you get any money?"

"I took the cases because both involved basically holding cells, where the arrested people were held only until they could be transferred to the Allegheny County Jail. Both hangings happened in the early morning hours. There were only a handful of cells in the lockups of each borough. In one case, there was a video camera in the cell where a young woman hung herself that was to be monitored by the desk cop. He didn't monitor it. In the other, they didn't take the man's belt from him, and that's what he used to hang himself. The defense lawyers must have thought in both cases that we might be able to prove deliberate indifference, and the cases settled."

"For a lot of money?"

"Not enough to retire on, certainly. And you have to remember that a settlement in this type of case is an educated guess as to what a jury would do, and there is a sizable percentage of our citizenry who are unsympathetic to people in jail. Surprise, surprise."

"Why were they arrested?"

"The young woman was a heroin addict, and she was charged with possession with intent to sell. She was dealing just to maintain her habit. The man was arrested on drunk and disorderly charges, and he was screaming obscenities at his neighbor at 2 o'clock in the morning. His neighbor happened to be a councilman."

Franklin, who was obviously sympathetic to people with drug or alcohol problems, winced, and said, "I hope that they got to that Coalton County guy in time."

"I do too, and it's a good sign that they did because I didn't see anything in the papers or on- line about it." Sam paused, and then enthused: "Franklin, I am really impressed that you are giving back by holding the jail meetings."

"I have a lot to be grateful for, not the least of which is what you did for me."

"I had a little self-interest involved." Sam teased, referring to Franklin's "visions" about the Hatcher woman's medical malpractice case, "you haven't had any hallucinations involving me or any of my cases lately, have you?"

"No", Franklin responded flatly, although he had contemplated many times these last three years why the "dreams" or premonitions were restricted to the Hatcher case. Maybe that had something to do with getting sober?

"We have to get together for dinner sometime, you and Kim and Becca and I."

"Yeah, we do", Franklin faking enthusiasm because his relationship with Kim was tenuous at best.

Once he had signed off with Sam, he got himself an oatmeal raisin cookie for his dessert.

CHAPTER 5—SAM CONFRONTS A MEMORY

When he had gotten off the phone with Franklin, Sam walked out of his office and saw that Rhonda was just preparing to leave for the day. Darkness would quickly descend at this time of year.

"So, the young men on your jury rewarded Ms. Short Skirt and Low Cut Blouse. Will you celebrate with Becca?"

"No, right now she is helping her niece, Nicole, pick out a car."

"So Nicole is going to spend some of that money that you got for her."

"Yeah, she'll be a second semester junior at Pitt, and she has an apartment and a part time job with the local newspaper."

"I always thought that that girl was going places. So what's up this evening with you?"

"Right now, I am going to go to the basement and get the Christmas decorations for the lobby."

"Night, Sam."

"Good night, Rhonda."

Sam, in what might, or might not prove to be a reckless use of the money which he got for the firm, and for which he got a substantial bonus, purchased the building from the firm. The firm was looking to sell the building since downtown properties had taken a hit since the pandemic, and he got what he thought was a good price. Now he was the firm's landlord.

He went down to the basement, where seasonal decorations had been stored for years. Every time he stepped from the elevator into the basement since that January day almost three years ago when he discovered Franklin, the thought that he might find another homeless person with their bedroll stashed in some of the way corner of the basement was intrusive. He smiled at the thought.

Since Franklin had referenced it, as he slung the wreath over his shoulder and grabbed the lights which would go on the wreath in the lobby, he couldn't help but think about his most recent jail hanging case, a twenty-two year old woman, what was her name? He was lousy with names, but wasn't his forgetting her name illustrative of her short life. He was certain that only her immediate family remembered her.

She had hung herself in a lockup with only two cells, where arrestees were housed until they could be transferred to County. Because the borough had installed video cameras in the cells to guard against this very occurrence, and they had been advised not to destroy evidence, there was a videotape of her preparations and actual death by hanging.

At 2 o'clock in the morning, when she hung herself, the Corporal charged with monitoring the cell via video monitor had either gone to the bathroom or abandoned his desk for some other reason. In his deposition, he was unclear. In any event, he was absent from his desk where a video screen, similar to a small TV, would have allowed his early intervention, and prevented the young woman's death. The corporal's life was irretrievably affected.

Of course, he had watched the video; it was his duty to his clients, the family, to do so. The young woman had fashioned a noose from her blouse, tied it to an overhead bar, using a cot to reach it, and slipped the blouse – noose over her head. He watched the rest of the video with gruesome fascination: the young woman's twitching, the evacuation of bodily fluids, and finally the stillness of death.

Since the young woman wasn't married, and had no children, her parents were the only legal heirs. He wondered how they had spent the not insubstantial settlement; how they felt in acquiring things with their new – found wealth from their daughter's death. She was a heroin addict, and undoubtedly put them through hell. She had been a cheerleader in high school. He remembered that the parents shared with him a picture of her in her cheerleader's outfit. Pretty girl, which her addiction had only minimally damaged.

As he got off on the first floor to rig up the lights on the wreath, he scolded himself for such morbid thoughts, 'Tis the season to be jolly!

CHAPTER 6–NICOLE COUNSELS BROTHER JAKE

When Nicole pulled into the driveway of her childhood home, followed closely by Becca, she blew the horn, and her father, Jake and Josh all wandered out of the house and onto the porch. As Nicole got out of the car, she practically shouted, although there was really no need for her to shout to be heard, "Look at my new car!" She then swept her hand in a magician – like gesture toward a Ruby red Honda Elantra.

"Year?", her father gushed, obviously picking up on her excitement.

"2019."

"I am happy that you are using your mother's settlement money so wisely."

"Well, I think that's what she would have wanted; she wasn't frugal, but she wasn't a spendthrift either."

"Are you implying that I am?"

"No, of course not," she replied with a sarcasm that he didn't catch. Since word got out in their small community that her father had come into money as a result of his lawsuit against the hospital,he had taken advantage of that perception: he bought himself a huge black pickup; she understood that he frequently bought rounds of drinks at his favorite watering hole; and, he had taken out all of the single ladies that would have him. Some were around his age, and some were single. In the short, he had become a big man in town.

"It's been weeks since we saw you. You will be home for Christmas, won't you. Doesn't Pitt have like a two week break for Christmas."

"Yes, and I will spend a couple of days here, but I am going to spend time at my apartment. I want to see these guys." With that, she hugged both Josh and then Jake as Becca ascended the porch steps.

"What do you guys have in here to eat," Becca squawked, "we spent a couple of hours at the dealership and I am starved."

As they convened over leftover pizza on the dining room table, the small talk eventually turned to her brothers. She learned that Jake had been suspended from school for selling blunts to other students.

"Becca", she asked, "did you know anything about this?"

"Yes, I learned about it a few days ago."

"Are there any criminal charges?" Nicole was not naïve enough to think that her brothers wouldn't experiment with booze or weed, but she had hoped that that investigation would be closer to when they were sixteen or seventeen. Jake was only fourteen.

"No", her father growled, "the principal said that they wouldn't pursue criminal charges unless it happens again, although he did have the police examine the marijuana cigarettes. The police said that it appears that they were commercially manufactured in a state which has legalized marijuana."

"Jake, are you insane? Selling blunts to kids at school. Where are you getting them?"

Jake, obviously chagrined, replied in a barely audible voice, "It was the first time, honest Nicole. I bought them from a guy who I don't know. He was just driving by my friends and I, and he wound down the window and asked if we wanted to buy some blunts, and like none of my friends had any money and I did, so I bought six."

"And you sold them at school?"

"Only two before Mr. Cross caught me."

Her father interjected, "Since the settlement, I had been giving both of the boys more of an allowance than I fucking should have been. No more."

"Becca, you knew about this?"

"Like I said, I only found out about it a couple of days ago."

"Listen, honey, I will discipline Jake. You're not his fuckin' parent, you're his sister."

"Like you disciplined me right after my mother's death?" They both knew that she was referencing the incident where he had slapped her shortly after their first meeting with Sam on her mother's case.

"You're never going to let me Goddamn forget that, are you?"

Becca cautioned, "Not around the boys, please."

With this reproach, her father became silent and sullen. Becca attempted to foreclose further discussion of the subject, and asked, "So, what do you boys think of Nicole's new car?" After receiving the "it's nices" from her brothers, Nicole excused herself, and slid her chair out from the table.

"It's getting late, and you and I ought to be getting back," Becca said.

"No, I think that I will spend the night here, and drive back to the city in the morning."

After saying goodbye to Becca, Nicole walked down the hallway to what she still thought of as her room, although it had been nearly three years since she had occupied it full-time. She went into her chest of drawers, and under a pile of her underwear and night clothes (to assure that her father wouldn't find them),she came upon her "stash" of her mother's writing. She sorted through the papers until she came upon a poem entitled," To Jake", and written several days after his birthday in March:

Pine frame the portrait of spring,

Water straining toward bright wood of dream,

Brown grass in an endless ring,

In a sea of hopeful green.

Life moves as a tendril of grass,

Reaching toward the golden grasp,

Of brilliant rays and the birth of a son,

The story of our life together has just begun.

Having found what she wanted, she went across the hall and into the bedroom shared by Jake and Josh. She was relieved that Josh was apparently in the living room with his father; she wanted to talk to Jake alone.

As soon as she walked in the boys' bedroom door, she could see him wince. He spoke first:

"I suppose that you're going to tell me you are disappointed in me."

"No, I was just going to give you some sisterly advice, but first, I want you to read this."

She handed him the poem, and clarified: "It was written by mommy a few days after your birth."

He read it, and looked for all the world as if he would begin crying at any moment, but he didn't. He tried to hand it back to Nicole, but she motioned for him to keep it, directing him to read it whenever he was contemplating doing something stupid. She got the expected smile from him.

"God knows, I can't stop you from being curious, although curiosity about marijuana shouldn't include selling it. I just read about marijuana being cut with fentanyl. If one of the blunts which you sold contained fentanyl, you can be charged with murder."

"I didn't know about the fentanyl thing."

"Well, it's true. And why in the hell were you selling blunts? Doesn't dad give you enough of an allowance?"

"I suppose so, but I wanted to buy you guys a really nice Christmas presents, and there is this girl…."

Just then, Josh walked in the bedroom.

"Just read the poem and realize how much mommy loved you before you do something stupid."

With that, she concluded her sisterly admonition.

CHAPTER 7–FRANKLIN AND SLIM

When Franklin came to convene his regular Monday meeting of AA/NA, the first thing he did was ask Sergeant First Line of Defense whatever happened to the prisoner who hung himself last week.

"We were told by the warden not to discuss that, but I suppose I can tell you because you will hear it from other prisoners. The guy survived, and was no worse for the wear, at least physically. He's in the jail infirmary until a shrink clears him."

"Glad to hear it", Franklin offered.

"I guess that was one that the questionnaire didn't catch."

"What questionnaire?"

"The suicide assessment questionnaire. It's a questionnaire that we are supposed to fill out for all new admittees until the jail psychologist can do a full interview. It's supposed to predict who is going to do himself in, so we can keep an eye on him. It obviously didn't work in this kid's case."

"I'm glad that he's still with us."

"Maybe you'll eventually see him at one of your meetings."

"Does he have a drug or alcohol problem?"

"I don't really know, but almost everyone in here does. You should know that."

"I do. Merry Christmas, Sarge."

He ended up presiding over a meeting of four listless and uncommunicative inmates and an enthusiastic and energetic one – Slim. It didn't take long for Sam to ascertain the source of Slim's zeal.

After the opening prayer, Slim abruptly announced, "I'm due to get out in January".

"Congratulations, Slim, and I would like to talk with you after the meeting about an option that you might have."

The meeting was very short: he supposed that pre-Christmas ennui affected the prison population too. He motioned for Slim to sit beside him. Slim settled his 6 foot plus frame into the folding chair. Slim was, as his nickname implied, skinny, with longish brown hair and brown eyes.

Although Franklin wasn't accustomed to evaluating the looks of males, after all he had spent years with a rag – tag crew of the homeless, but it occurred to him nonetheless that Slim would be found to be handsome by the opposite sex. He smiled, and thought that Slim reminded him of himself.

"You know Slim, once you get out of here you may face the toughest challenge in keeping your sobriety. As I understand it, and from what you have said, I understand that your primary problem has been with alcohol."

"Yeah, mostly, but I have been known to take some of my mother's hillbilly heroin."

"I thought I had heard all of the nicknames for drugs, but hillbilly heroin is a new one on me. What is it?"

"It's oxy."

"Is your mother prescribed oxycodone?"

Slim laughed. "I guess you could call it that. She is prescribed it, and she gets what ain't prescribed from her boyfriend who owns a pharmacy. She's addicted to that shit. And she will probably get my little brother addicted too."

Franklin had been around alcoholics and drug addicts for many years, but he had only run into a handful of families composed entirely of abusers. It was time to collect some vital statistics he thought.

"What's your real name, Slim?"

"It's Jeff. Jeff Moran."

"And you are in here for stealing a car?"

"Yep, that's me. I took that game grand theft auto one step too far," Slim cackled.

"And where is your home, Jeff?"

"I live with my mother and younger brother in the projects in Coalton."

"I am familiar. What if I were to tell you that I think I could get you into a halfway house once you leave here."

"I would say that it sounds good, but I need to get home and look after my mom and little brother."

"You will be a lot more help to them clean and sober, don't you think? Going to the halfway house, The Phoenix, will help with your early recovery. It did mine."

"I am sure that it would, but I have got to get home. There's fuckin' bad shit about to go down if I don't get home. I can just feel it."

Franklin knew a lost cause when he saw one, and he concluded that it was no use trying to convince Slim that he should go to a halfway house. Fully expecting that he might not ever see Slim again, he wished him good luck and offered him the standard advice to take one day at a time.

As Slim was shuffling out of the gym, Franklin felt a sudden, inexplicable desire to see Slim again, which he translated into a question: "How are you getting home when you are released, Slim?"

"My brother is supposed to pick me up, and he doesn't have a license. I hope he doesn't get pulled over on his trip here."

"Here's my cell phone number. You call me when you're getting released, and I will arrange my schedule, pick you up and take you home."

Slim looked at Franklin incredulously, and stammered, "You would do that for me?"

"As Voltaire said, 'It is up to us to cultivate our garden.'"

Franklin could see that Slim was struggling to understand what Franklin meant, but eventually he merely mumbled, "Okay, see you in January."

As Franklin pulled his coat more tightly around his body in deference to the late December wind in the jail parking lot, he was still wondering what role fate might have for him and Jeff.

CHAPTER 8—SAM READS A LETTER TO NICOLE

Just as Sam was about to tell Rhonda that she could leave at around 3 o'clock on December 23, the elevator doors opened and Nicole stepped out.

As Sam watched from the door to his office, Rhonda exclaimed, "Look what the cat dragged in, to what do we owe this visit?"

"I just bought a car, and I'm staying with my father and the boys over Christmas. I went out for a drive, found myself in Pittsburgh, and decided to drop in."

"I am glad you did," Sam said genuinely, "come here, and let me give you a great big Christmas hug!"

While Nicole was making her way the short distance from the elevator to Sam's office, Rhonda intervened, "Would you please give this to huggy bear?"

"Sure, Rhonda."

Sam could see that it was a handwritten letter with the envelope paper clipped to it. She gave the letter to Sam before receiving his embrace.

"I heard that you just bought a car."

"I did. A 2019 Honda Elantra."

"Good choice. A nice reliable car. Are you here to interview me for an article for the paper?"

"No, I'm just here to see you guys, but come January, I will need to interview you regarding an interesting case of your choosing."

"I have given it some thought, and I have a few cases picked out. If you want to interview me now, I am game."

"Nah, I'm not in the mood right now, besides I have a long ride home to look forward to."

"If you don't mind my asking, what is the letter that I gave you about. I didn't even know that they made pencils anymore, and the letter was written in pencil. If you can't discuss it because of attorney-client privilege, I understand."

"No, it's not privileged. It's just one of the many letters that I periodically get from inmates from jails in the area."

"Oh, that's interesting. I suppose they want you to represent them in appeals of their convictions."

"Surprisingly, that's not what most of them have to deal with. They mostly concern conditions in the jail."

"What sort of conditions?"

"Well, let's see what this one has to do with. It's from an inmate at the Coalton County Jail." Sam began to read the letter:

"To whom it may concern, we are writing you as a group 3B to let you know about the conditions in the Coalton County Jail. At the time there is no heat on the pod we have to wear double clothing to keep warm especially in the cell where some of them you can actually see your own breath people are walking around shivering and causing people to be out of character and irritable and also health concerns and even the food is coming up cold everything in this place is cold there are cockroaches in the food some of the guards are Nazis and make it tough for those of us who are different please help this letter is from all of us on 3B. Once again we would like to stress the conditions in here. It ain't human.'"

"Sounds horrid. Do you think it's true what he says?"

"It may be partially an exaggeration, but I wouldn't be surprised if it's mostly true."

"Why can't something be done about it then?"

"Easier said than done. It's partially due to the standard applied to a government, and jails are a part of the government. It's not enough to prove negligence, you have to prove willful or deliberate indifference to the rights of prisoners to be successful in most cases. That's a difficult standard to meet."

"Have you ever sued a jail?"

"A couple of times in jail hanging cases, and I once sued an independent contractor that provided medical services to the jail, and that medical provider was negligent. I tried that case."

"What happened?"

"My client, who was a heroin addict, ended up losing his leg due to the negligence of the jail's doctor. The jury returned a verdict that the doctor was negligent, but refused to give him any money. They thought he would spend it on heroin. That taught me a tough lesson that some people view inmates as deserving whatever they get."

"What about the jail hanging cases?"

Sam winked, and suggested, "Those might make a good subject for your columns. I think that I will hold those stories in abeyance until you have your reporter's pad with you. Enough about jails, it is the most wonderful time of the year!"

Nicole frowned, and he could see that the subject of jails had affected her mood. "What's up Nicole, and don't tell me nothing, an old trial attorney like me can sometimes read faces."

"I wanted to talk to you about it, although I doubt you can do anything. My fourteen year old brother Jake was suspended from school for three days for selling blunts."

"What is his story? Becca never said anything to me about it." Becca regularly spent time with her sister's kids, and she spoke of them often.

"Apparently, she just found out about it. He said that some dude sold him half a dozen blunts that apparently this guy had bought in a state where marijuana was legal. He attempted to unload them at a profit in school, stupid kid, and he was caught by the teacher in the midst of the transaction. He was suspended for three days."

"Was he charged with any crime?"

"He says he wasn't."

"You know, I used to take my two boys to the jail on take your child to work day. The Allegheny County Jail had a program on that day where they had three inmates talk to the kids about how horrible jail was. It made quite an impression on the boys. Sounds like Jake could benefit from a visit to a jail. I think I know who could make that happen."

"Do I know him?"

"Yeah, you have met him. Why don't you let me see what I can do." Sam was wondering whether Franklin could arrange something at the Coalton County Jail that would scare the shit out of Jake.

Nicole sat for a brief moment looking pensive, and then asked Sam, "Would you still represent the heroin addict?"

"You mean the one who lost his leg?"

"Yeah, knowing that you would lose?"

"That's a very existential question, young lady. Sartre said that existentialism examines man's search for meaning and a meaningless universe. Have you ever wondered why you were born into that family that you were born into, and not to our family that is starving and lives in a cardboard box in India?"

"I have wondered something along those lines."

"And have you ever wondered why you have the brain chemistry that you have, rather than, say, the brain chemistry of an addict?"

"I guess I have. Not everyone's the same, and I suppose some people are more prone to do antisocial things more than other people. We are certainly not all Mother Teresas, and that I suppose is somewhat a reflection of our brain chemistries."

"Well, that's why I hope that I would represent that guy who lost his leg as a result of the gross negligence of the doctor even today. There are just some things that are just wrong, no matter who they happen to."

Sam thought he saw a fleeting emotion register on Nicole's face: Could it conceivably have been admiration? Whatever it was, the conversation morphed into a discussion of Christmas plans. Apparently, Nicole was going to spend part of the Christmas holidays at her father's house, rather than her apartment. She approached this arrangement with some apprehension, because, as she put it, "you know my father."

"I certainly do". He did, in part, because Sam had met Becca, Nicole's aunt and her father's deceased wife, while handling a medical malpractice case on behalf of the estate of Nicole. She, her father, whose name was Tyler, and her brothers were all heirs to her mother's estate.

"I think he harbors some animosity toward me because I am now engaged to Becca." Sam was sure that Nicole knew exactly what he meant: her father had thought he would replace her deceased mother with her mother's sister. But it was not to be; Becca found Tyler, Nicole's father, to be a boor.

Eventually, Nicole excused herself, saying she had a long drive in the dark, and Sam went down in the elevator, past the Christmas decorations that he had put up in the lobby and exited the now nearly empty office building. He would go home to Becca, because he didn't have his boys until Christmas Day.

CHAPTER 9—NICOLE'S CHRISTMAS GIFT TO JAKE

Nicole awoke on Christmas Day to the clatter of pots and pans and her father singing "It's Beginning To Look a Lot Like Christmas", which she was surprised he knew. She assumed from the noise of the cookware and her father's off – key rendition of the song that her father was in a good mood, and that his latest girlfriend, Phyllis, was making their Christmas dinner. Phyllis was the most recent in a long line of "girlfriends" that her father had captivated, or should she say captured, since the death of her mother nearly 3 years ago. She smiled wryly at the thought that these women must have perceived her father as wealthy since the settlement, and he had done nothing to disabuse the community at large of this perception. But Phyllis seemed like a good egg.

Having exchanged presents the night before, she and her brothers played Monopoly until Christmas dinner was served. It was traditional in every sense except the apple cobbler that Phyllis made for dessert. They watched Die Hard halfheartedly, and then her father and Phyllis excused themselves, Josh announced he was tired and going to bed, and she fortuitously had Jake to herself. She decided to broach the subject of Sam's proposed intervention delicately:

"So, you told me that you're interested in a girl in your class?"

"Yeah, her name is Ruth. I think that she is very pretty."

"Oh you do, do you?" She struck her most coquettish pose, and asked, "is she as pretty as me."

"Nobody is as pretty as you, you're the original foxy lady."

"Thanks." Nicole got up from her seat, and slanted a kiss on Jake's forehead. The time was right, she thought, to broach the subject of his education regarding crime and punishment.

"You remember Sam, who handled our mother's malpractice case, don't you?"

"Yeah, he's been here picking up Becca, and has stopped in a few times since the case."

"Well, he and I both think that you could benefit from education on how our criminal justice system works."

"Because I sold a blunt to some kid?" She could see that this wasn't going to be easy.

"Jake, don't you realize that selling drugs could conceivably put you in jail on a murder rap. You don't know what could have fentanyl in it."

"First, they looked like professionally rolled blunts, and secondly, there are a few fuckin' assholes in my class that I would like to kill with fentanyl."

"There will always be people that you don't get along with." She decided to ignore his use of profanity and his wish to see some of his classmates dead, although she was nonplussed by the glibness which both of them seemed to roll off his tongue.

"Yeah, but being called a fag by half the class is not just not getting along with some people."

Nicole was stunned by Jake's disclosure. Of course, she could have cared less about her brother's sexual orientation, but true or not, she was greatly disturbed to think that her Jake was being subjected to bullying.

"Have you told dad about this?"

"No, because he's part of the problem, with his screwing around with all of the old women in town. He's a laughing stock. I guess it's because I'm one of the shortest kids in my class, and I have a high voice. I'm not gay."

"It would make any difference to me if you were."

"That's one of the reasons that I bought the blunts, better to have a rep as a dealer rather than a fag."

"Jake, I really don't know what to do about you being called that hateful name, but I do think that you seeing what the consequences could be of your selling drugs would be of benefit. Would you be willing to visit a jail with Sam's friend? It might be interesting."

"I already have to go to three hours of what they call drug education. It's an afterschool program, like detention, where they basically bitch at you for three hours. I was sentenced to that."

"Maybe if you go with Sam's friend, it will count as drug education. Let me talk to Sam and see what I can do."

"Okay, I ain't saying that I'll go, but if I could get out of the drug education program, I would seriously consider it."

"Who's in charge of discipline at the high school these days."

"Mr. Coates."

She remembered Mr. Coates. He was a big, burly man with a shaved head. He looked rather like a professional wrestler.

"Then I'll see what Sam can do."

The conversation wasn't as bad as it could have been, she thought, but she was troubled by the realization that Jake was being bullied. She momentarily thought about telling her father, but rejected it. There was a good chance that he might urge an action which would result in a physical confrontation with the bullies, and Jake didn't need that. She might seek Sam's advice since she would be talking with him anyway.

Shortly after her conversation with Jake, she went to her "old" bedroom, and reviewed her mental "to do list". She would have the apartment to herself beginning tomorrow, when she planned on traveling back to Pittsburgh, and would finish a paper that was due after Christmas. And, she needed to check in with Sam on the Jake thing and her initial installment for the paper.

As she lay there, she could almost hear her mother reciting the words of a bedtime prayer, which her mother said her grandmother had taught her: "Now I lay me down to sleep…."

CHAPTER 10– SAM RECRUITS FRANKLIN FOR NICOLE'S PLAN

On the drive to their favorite restaurant, Calabria's, Franklin grinned. When Kim asked him why, he responded, "oh no reason." In fact, he did have multiple reasons to grin. They had had a wonderful Christmas, and the season wasn't even over yet, it was only the 27th. Kim and he had been getting along famously, so much so that Kim wondered out loud on Christmas day about the possibility of having a child.

Moreover, school was going very well, and he suspected that with all of his AA connections plus the people that he had met at the Vulture, the halfway house where he had resided after he damn near killed himself with booze, he could secure a position in one of the alcohol and drug treatment facilities that seemed to be springing up like weeds, pun intended. The Fentanyl craze was devastatingly crazy. Once he had gotten his degree and had a job at a rehab, he could say goodbye forever to photocopier toner fumes.

Just as they were pulling into the Calabria's parking lot, the phone started to play Rollin' on the River, his ring tone; it was Sam. He told Kim to go in and get them a table, and answered the phone.

"Hello Sam, do you know it's December 27th, you're supposed to be still celebrating Christmas."

"What can I say? There is no rest for the weary or wicked."

"What can I do for you? We just got to our restaurant."

"Then I will be quick. I have somebody that I would like you to take to the AA/NA meeting that you run at the Coalton County jail within the next couple of weeks."

"I think that I can swing that. He would have to be thoroughly searched but I think I could get him in. Who is it?"

"Well, remember when I got you out of the halfway house to serve as my gopher during the Hatcher trial? It's one of Alice Hatcher's boys. He was caught selling blunts in school, and I thought that it might do him some good to see how the caged half lives."

"Sure, I remember the boys. I assume that he is the older one. How old is he now? He must be a teenager."

"His name is Jake, and he's 14."

"As a matter of fact, I'm supposed to drive a guy named Slim to his house; he's due to be released. I will see if I can't take him to the regular meeting in the jail, and then we can take Slim home after he is released. I know where Slim lives in the projects so he will get a real education on how the other half lives."

"Wasn't Slim the guy that you were asking me about getting into the halfway house?"

"Yeah, but he says he has to get home and look after his mother and younger brother."

"I know you have got to go and have dinner, but how's night school going? We haven't talked about that in a while."

"I've got an A- average. Within a couple of years I expect to be doing drug and alcohol counseling. Goodbye photocopier smell."

"One thing I forgot to mention, but the Josh kid's sister, Nicole, says he's being verbally bullied by his classmates."

"I remember Nicole. I'll talk to him about that."

"Thanks Franklin. I'll call you with the particulars as soon as I get it set up. Happy New Year!"

"Yeah, Happy New Year to you too." As Franklin hung up the phone he had a disturbing feeling; something he could only identify as a premonition. Sam was going to have a very significant year, and he would be tested by it.

CHAPTER 11– SAM MEETS MR. COATES

Since Franklin had brought up the subject of school bullying, when Sam was taking his two sons to school after their Wednesday overnight a few days after the Christmas break, he decided to explore the subject with them. He had just had a telephone conversation with Nicole on New Year's Day, the primary purpose of which, in addition to a perfunctory New Years well wishes, was to set up Jake's jail meeting with Franklin as well as to serve as a reminder to Sam that they had to work on the initial column for the paper.

During the course of that conversation, Nicole had apprised Sam of Josh's reluctance to go to the jail with Franklin unless he could be excused from his mandatory drug reeducation session that the high school had sentenced him to. Nicole wondered whether Sam might be able to call the vice principal in charge of meting out discipline, a Mr. Shaw, and see if Sam might be able to make a waiver of that requirement happen if Josh went to the jail with Franklin during that conversation. She had echoed Franklin's offhand remark that she suspected that Josh was being bullied at school.

Sam began, "Do you remember the case I tried where the woman in her early thirties died because the radiologist missed pneumonia?"

Marcus responded, "Yes, I do. Wasn't that the case that the homeless guy helped you with?"

"Yes, it was. And do you remember that the woman had two sons right around your age?"

Sam got a positive response from both boys. "Well, the 14 year old has been bullied by a number of kids in his class. I just wondered whether you guys thought that bullying was a problem in your school."

Sean requested elaboration: "How was he bullied? Online? What did they call him?"

"Apparently, they called him a faggot and other vicious names for homosexuals."

"Online," Marcus asked.

"I guess online and in person."

"I told my French teacher that I had overheard a kid calling another kid in the class that name."

"And what did the French teacher do," Sam asked.

"I don't know but he must have done something because he called the kid up and made him stay after everybody else left the class."

"And what did you think about that, Marcus?"

"I am glad that the kid got in trouble."

"Why?" Sam was testing Marcus, and besides he was curious to hear Marcus' response.

"So what if the kid were gay? That's an awful name to call him. And the way I figure, we are all different, and life would be Goddamn boring if we weren't."

Almost reflexively, Sam opened his mouth and was going to chastise his son for his use of the word Goddamn, but thought better of it. After all, he was sure that his son's language could be much more "colorful" than that when he was around his friends.

Besides, he was taking a mental victory lap because of Marcus' answer to his question; he must be doing something right.

He dropped off his sons at school, and headed to the office. His first order of business was to call the assistant principal of Jake Hatcher's school to see if he could obtain for Jake a special dispensation which would allow him to go to the Coalton County Jail with Franklin in lieu of the drug reeducation program that he had been sentenced to.

He placed a call to Mr. Coates, the vice principal in charge of discipline, and left him a message. Rhonda buzzed him, and he took a call from Joy Osgood, an attorney who referred him cases. Joy called him frequently because she thought every minuscule incident where someone was hurt was a case. He had to frequently disabuse her of that mindset. Joy had two children in Ivy League schools so she was interested in every little case in which she could garner a referral fee from Sam.

Today's non-case du jour was a situation in which a twelve year old boy was bitten by a dog while he was in a neighbor's home. The boy was teasing the dog, and had sustained an inch and a half laceration to his neck which required some stitches. The dog, a miniature French poodle, was a little bitty thing, and he had to explain to Joy for the umpteenth time why he wasn't interested in a case of such insignificant injuries. Joy was obviously disappointed, he could tell by her voice, but pledged to get him a multimillion dollar case next time.

When he hung up with Joy, he walked out of his office and Rhonda questioned him about his call with Petunia, her nickname for Joy because of her overly floral smell when she visited Sam's office. He told her the story of the vicious miniature French poodle, and they both cackled.

Rhonda commented on the new Joy for Justice billboard featuring a fiery automobile crash, which had been recently installed on a billboard within a block of their office.

"Where does she get the money to advertise like she does?" Rhonda wondered out loud.

"She gets a lot of automobile accident cases, and she handles ninety five percent of them herself. The rest she spreads around to various attorneys in town, including me. She refers all of the medical malpractice cases to me."

"I know but she has got to be spending a fortune on advertising. You can't watch TV during the afternoon without seeing a Joy for Justice ad especially during the local news. I wonder if any of her clients' eyes tear like mine do from her perfume when she is in your office."

Sam grinned, and Rhonda picked up the line that was ringing. Then she punched the hold button, and said to Sam, "are you expecting a call from a Mr. Coates."

"Yeah, he's the vice principal at the high school of one of the Hatcher kids." He then explained briefly to Rhonda why this Coates fellow was calling.

"If nothing else it sounds like Jake is going to need lessons in how to be circumspect if he wants to be dealing in weed."

Sam nodded, walked into his office and hit the blinking light on his phone connecting him to the deep, almost guttural voice identifying itself as Lloyd Coates.

"Hello Mr. Wright, I understand from your message that you're calling regarding the Hatcher boy."

"Yes, I am. I promised Nicole that I would talk to you. I told Nicole when she told me about the Jake situation that I had an associate who ran a meeting for alcoholics and drug addicts in the Coalton County Jail. I thought that Jake might benefit from attending the meeting with Franklin. It seems that Jake was more agreeable to doing that if he could be excused from the drug reeducation program that school would require."

"Nicole," Lloyd Coates growled, although his growl had a note of affection, "nice kid, and smart too. I'll tell you what, I am in downtown Pittsburgh for a school administrators conference, and I could stop in and see you during my lunch hour and we can discuss Jake and the possibility that we might be able to do this with other kids in the future."

Sam frowned, he didn't want to be the point person for a program for delinquent teenagers, and if he wasn't careful that's what he would become, but meeting with the vice principal over a piece of pizza wouldn't necessarily involve a lifetime commitment.

"Sure, we could do that. I'll order a pizza and we can meet in my office and talk." Sam proceeded to give him the office address. He dictated some letters while he waited for Mr. Coates. When the vice principal stepped off the elevator at about 12:10, he saw a huge totally bald man, who looked like a professional wrestler.

"Mr. Coates I presume."

"Please call me Lloyd." Then unnecessarily but, Sam thought, in an effort to build some rapport, he added, "The kids call me Q Ball behind my back but I prefer Lloyd."

After Rhonda had distributed a couple of pieces of pizza each on paper plates, and the small talk was concluded, Lloyd initiated the business portion of their meeting with the following question:

"So, how did a big city lawyer like you become interested in Jake Hatcher?"

"Well, long story made short, I represented the estate of his mother in a medical malpractice case. Through that case, I met my soon – to – be wife, who is his mother's sister."

"So, he is like your nephew?"

"Yeah, something like that." Sam was embarrassed that he had never put that together, but he supposed that it was, or would be accurate.

"As Jake's uncle and a respected member of the legal community, if you can vouch that Jake attended a drug education meeting at the Coalton County Jail, I will excuse him from the mandatory drug reeducation program at the school."

But, Lloyd continued, "I will need his father's authorization too, of course."

"Of course."

"What's your associate's background? The one who runs the jail meetings."

"He's a recovering person, and is studying to become a drug and alcohol counselor at Duquesne."

"Maybe I can set something up with him, you know, to show 'at risk' kids what is in store for them in jail. Would you mind talking to him for me and seeing if he would be interested?" Almost as an afterthought, he added parenthetically, "Of course, he would have to get state certification that he is not a Chester the molester."

"No, I wouldn't mind, and the certification should not be a problem. I think he would be interested. There's an additional problem with Jake that I almost hesitate to mention. I'm not sure what you can do about it. I think Jake is being bullied."

"Oh yeah, tell me about it."

"He's being called disgusting names for gay people, you know, fag and I assume other pejorative things."

"Is he gay?"

"No, I don't think so, and what if he was."

Lloyd gave him a look that he couldn't quite interpret, and asked, "Is there any allegation that he has been physically assaulted?"

"No, not that I am aware of. But, I am getting it all third hand."

"I will see if his teachers have noticed anything. Of course, if he reads the wrong stuff on the Internet it could turn him into a homosexual."

Sam couldn't hide his astonishment: "You don't honestly believe that you, Lloyd?"

Lloyd didn't answer the question, but instead offered, "You know what a lot of these boys need is a stint in the military. Were you ever in the military?"

Trying to disguise his discomfort at the tack which this conversation had taken, Sam replied with a negative shake of his head.

"Well I have. United States Marine Corps. Oorah! That will make a man out of you. That's what some of these kids need."

As Sam was trying to fabricate a graceful exit from the conversation, Lloyd continued: "Why don't you tell Jake that he should join the junior ROTC. I am the faculty advisor, and I have the boys march around the parking lot. Teaches them self – discipline."

"I will certainly mention that to Jake when I see him. I enjoyed our little chat, but I do have a client that I need to prepare for."

Lloyd took the hint, and after their awkward goodbyes, he waited for the elevator and Sam stood in his office doorway. When the elevator came, Lloyd smiled and said, "Oorah!"

"What was that all about?" Rhonda wondered out loud. In response, Sam began humming, "From the halls of Montezuma, to the shores of Tripoli…."

CHAPTER 12–NICOLE INTERVIEWS SAM

Nicole was parked in the cemetery with her mother's grave in sight when she decided to call Sam about her brother. She pushed the button for Sam (he was on speed dial) and, surprisingly, he picked up after a few rings.

"Hi, Sam."

"Hi Nicole. Well, I understand that it's a sad day for you."

"It is. It was three years ago today that my mother passed."

"I know, Becca told me."

"I'm sitting in the cemetery now by her grave."

"You know I am so sorry. Although I didn't know her in life, I feel like I got to know her from your and your family's memories of her."

"Thank you Sam. The main reason for my call is Jake. Have you had a chance to talk with Mr. Coates?"

"Yes, I have. He has waived the requirement that your brother has to attend drug reeducation provided I certify that he has attended a meeting with Franklin at the Coalton County jail."

"Franklin. I haven't seen him since that lunch after my mom's case settled."

"Your mother's case was, in some ways, the weirdest case I ever handled. Thanks, in no small part, because of Franklin's input."

"Someday, you'll have to tell me the full story of my mother's case. I'm not ready yet. We ought to do my first column about weird cases that you handled."

"Do you have time now? Do you have your recorder with you?"

"I guess that it's fitting to do my first article from my mother's grave since she used to write for the paper." With that, she fished her pocket recorder out of her purse, and told Sam to fire away.

"You will find this interesting. I once represented the parents of a Chatham student who died of misdiagnosis of meningitis."

"Sounds tragic, what happened?"

"It was still September, and the girl was an 18 year old freshman who was going to major in architecture. It was during the third week of school, and she came back to the dorm from some campus function, and told her roommate, who she didn't know very well because it was only the third week of school, that she didn't feel well and was going to bed early."

Nicole wished that she had not acceded to Sam's story hour now, she could see where this was going, but she took no action to interrupt it. It was clearly going to be a medical malpractice story that ended in death, like her mother's.

Sam continued, "The girl, or more precisely young lady, went to the ER of a Pittsburgh hospital, and was told that it was only the flu, and she was sent back to her dorm in Chatham."

"Didn't they have an infirmary?"

"Yeah, I forgot that part of the story. She first went to the infirmary and they sent her to the emergency room, where she was told to go back to her dorm, drink plenty of fluids and take Tylenol. It was the flu."

"She languished there for two days getting progressively worse. Eventually, she was found by her roommate in a semi-delirious state and an ambulance was called."

"Where were her parents during all of this?"

"They lived in Boston, and she contacted them every day. Well, when she went to the ER the second time by ambulance, the hospital called her parents and told them their daughter was in fairly serious condition. The young lady had two school–aged brothers, and the mother hopped on the first plane that she could get to Pittsburgh, while dad waited for a later flight and got the brothers off to school."

Nicole couldn't help but be drawn into the story; after all, she was away at college and had two school – age brothers.

"So, mom got to the hospital in the morning, and dad was on an afternoon flight from Boston to Pittsburgh. He suddenly had a feeling of abject sorrow and hopelessness. He looked at his watch and it was 3:18 in the afternoon."

Sam continued, "The hospital had sent a car to pick dad up at the airport. When he got to the hospital, the doctors met with him in a conference room, and told him that his daughter had passed away."

"Time of death," Nicole finished Sam's story, "3:18."

"This was a medical malpractice case?"

"Yep, the ER doctor on her original trip to the ER, the doctor who advised that it was only the flu, misdiagnosed her. She was actually suffering from meningitis."

"Could she have been saved had he recognized it as meningitis?"

"We had an expert testify that she almost definitely could have been."

"So the jury must have given her, or her parents, a lot of money."

"No, they didn't."

Having now become invested in the story, she pressed Sam: "Why didn't they?"

"That's a long story, but the bottom line is this: We tried the case twice to conclusion. In the first trial, the ER doc came off as a real prick, excuse my language."

Nicole laughed, and said, "That's all right Sam I have heard that expression before. In fact I have used a lot worse." She could hear Sam chuckle. He continued:

"He was a young guy, as I said just out of his residency, and he was arrogant. At the time, juries in civil cases had to be unanimous as in criminal cases. There was one holdout juror, it was 11 to 1 in favor of finding the doctor liable when the judge finally declared a hung jury."

"I talked to a juror afterwards, and if that one juror hadn't been a holdout, he said that they were about to start discussing damages at two million."

"You had to try it again; what happened?"

"About six months later, we tried the case a second time. Almost the same witnesses and experts for both sides. The difference was the defendant, the ER doc right out of residency. The defense had worked on him. He came off as a caring young man. He even cried when appropriate over the loss of, as he called her 'his beautiful young patient'."

"And the jury found him not guilty", Nicole finished the account for Sam.

"The technical term is not negligent, but, yes, the jury found him not responsible for her death."

"Sounds like what you guys call a miscarriage of justice."

"Welcome to my world."

She then spent a couple of minutes discussing the logistics of Josh's visit to the jail and hung up. Not lost on her was that she had composed an obituary for the Greene County Gazette, a copy of which was buried in a peanut butter jar at her mother's grave, and now, three years later, was composing her first article for the Gazette for which she was getting paid. Interesting.

CHAPTER 13–FRANKLIN AND JAKE

When Sam pulled into the Hatcher driveway in the late afternoon light, he could barely discern two shadowy figures on the front stoop. They approached, and he recognized one as Tyler, and the other looked vaguely like Jake, but he had a peach fuzz beard–like growth on his face.

Franklin rolled down the window in spite of the cold, and Tyler stuck his hand in the open window and shook Franklin's hand. "The last time I saw you, you were cleaning my clock in a poker game at our house right before my wife's case settled."

Tyler was making reference to Sam's temporary liberation from the halfway house in which he had been staying and the one night that he had spent at Tyler and his kid's house. Sam had "employed" him as his gopher during the trial of Alice Hatcher, and he had spent the evening after court with Tyler playing poker.

Franklin smiled in acknowledgment of what obviously was an affable introductory comment. Tyler continued, "I want to thank you for agreeing to take Jake here to the jail; hopefully, it will do him some fuckin' good." He swept his hand in the direction of his son, and Franklin saw a diminutive kid of average looks. The only things distinguishing him from a totally ordinary 14-year-old were his reddish chin hair and an earring.

"Pay attention to what this guy can teach you; he has had a helluva life." With that, Jake opened the passenger side door and took his seat sullenly. Tyler brightly chirped his goodbyes and Franklin and Josh were off.

They drove for a while in silence; after all, it had been many years since Franklin was 14, and he hadn't had any exposure to 14-year-olds since. Finally, at the risk of spending an hour in the car in uncomfortable noiselessness, Franklin asked a stupid question, "What do teenage kids do for recreation these days? Play video games?" This elicited a shrug.

Having made an effort to engage Jake in conversation, silence reigned until Jake asked the question, which should have been self–evident, "Do you have any kids?"

Franklin responded solemnly, "I don't. I would have had a little boy that would have been Josh's age, but my wife had a miscarriage on the day that Josh was born."

"How do you know that?"

"Your mother wrote an article about his birth in the Greene Gazette. I read the article that she wrote online, and it so happened that it was the very same date at the very same hospital that my wife and I went to when our baby was declared dead."

"Is that what made you a drunk? My dad said that you were a homeless drunk."

Franklin smiled. "Well, I think that it's a little more complicated than that but that certainly contributed to it."

"What was that like?"

"You mean being a drunk?"

"No, being homeless."

"'Man is free at the moment he wishes to be.' That's what Voltaire said."

"Who is he and what does that mean?"

"Voltaire was a French philosopher, and the question you asked reminded me of that quote."

"You still haven't answered my question about what it is like being homeless."

"Most of the time it sucks. It's cold and wet in the winter and sometimes unbearably hot in the summer. You are always worried about your next meal or where your next bottle is coming from. But, occasionally, you revel in the freedom that it brings."

A long silence followed. Finally, Franklin solicited some information of his own from Jake: "So…why were you selling weed?"

"For the money, of course."

"That's not all of the reason, is it?"

"No, it isn't."

"So, what's the reason?"

Franklin saw Jake look out of the window, and he could sense that Jake didn't know whether he could trust Franklin or not. Franklin did not press him. Eventually, Jake spoke, "I wanted to buy this girl in my class diamond earrings. That's why I needed the money. And I thought that by buying her the earrings and having her tell everyone that I bought them for her, it would prove that I'm not a fag."

Franklin knew he was seriously out of his league. After all, he definitely wasn't an adolescent psychologist. But, the kid had proven that he trusted Franklin, at least to a certain extent.

"How often are you called that name, and do these kids ever get physical with you?"

"So often that you would think it was my fuckin' name. If physical includes shovin' and being bumped into, I guess you could say that it gets physical."

Despite being uncomfortable even asking the question, Franklin knew that whatever help he could be to the kid required an answer, "Are you gay?"

"No, do I look like I'm fuckin' gay? They call me the little gay kid because of my size."

"What does gay look like? It's not a choice, like blue or brown eyes are something you're born with."

"Yeah, yeah, I have heard that from Nicole. She knows many gay guys at school, and one of her roommates was gay. She says they are no different but I say this is a shit–kicking town, not the University of Pittsburgh."

"I will take it that the answer is no."

"And you would be right, dude."

Franklin next explored with Jake what he had learned in college which was called chemical history. He determined that Jake had only smoked weed three or four times, all at parties. No reason to conclude that he had a problem.

Next came his consumption of alcohol. He had drunk a few beers, mostly at parties. The first time he ever drank a beer was in what he called the bunker.

"Why was it called the bunker?"

"Well, this kid who was a friend of mine, his parents owned like 40 acres. They raised cows and chickens and shit. He and his older brothers dug a pit about 6 feet deep where his parents wouldn't see it, put plywood over the top of it, and got a couple of powerful, battery-operated lights. They called that their bunker, and they used to go down there and drink beer and shit."

"Sounds ingenious."

"Yeah, until a cow walked over the plywood and fell in. I understand that his parents were pissed. Anyway, that's where I had my first beer."

Franklin laughed out loud at his mental image of a cow disappearing into the earth, although in deference to animal rights groups, he hoped the cow wasn't injured. The remainder of their right to jail covered the standard topics: your favorite subject in school, what you do in your spare time, do you play any sports, etc.

When the Coaton County Jail materialized in the twilight, Franklin parked the car, and the two of them trudged through the slush and into the jail.

CHAPTER 14– SAM AND BECCA ORDER IN

When Sam left the office at 6:30 pm to drive home, he was exhausted. He could not pinpoint a reason for his fatigue but he didn't dwell on it. He figured that it was just his age catching up with him.

But, simultaneously descending upon him like a death shawl was his occasional preoccupation with death. It had its genesis in Franklin's reminder of the couple of jail hanging cases that he had handled, and he had not been able to shake this feeling of doom since. And the Pittsburgh winters didn't help much, especially in January.

As he pulled into the driveway, he considered taking Becca out to eat, maybe at their favorite seafood restaurant. That might lighten his mood, but when he got into the house and proposed that to Becca, his suggestion was not met with very much enthusiasm. She reminded him that it was her day to serve as a reading advisor to the school district, and she had gone from there straight to the animal shelter where she was a volunteer. She was tired. She suggested that they order something from DoorDash. He knew that Becca sensed his dark mood and, in an apparent effort to redirect him, reminded him that his divorce could be finalized as early as April.

"We could have a June wedding like it was our first time and we were virgins, well, marital virgins at least," she giggled.

Sam smiled and countered, "I already feel like I have one foot in the grave."

Becca gave him a kiss on the cheek and cooed, "What's the matter, honey? Did you have a bad day?"

"Ever since Franklin told me about the attempted hanging in the Coalton County Jail, it reminded me of the one case especially; you know, the one where the young woman addict who was barely out of her teens hung herself in the municipal lockup."

"Yes, I know the one. I had only just met you when you were working on that case."

"Those Goddamn pictures still haunt me."

"Pictures?"

"Yeah, the coroner's pictures."

Sam went on, "I guess it reminds me of how we are all mortal. "Therefore, 'ask not to know for whom the bell tolls, it tolls for thee.'"

"John Donne's poem starts, *No man is an island, entire of itself.*"

"Yeah, so what are you trying to say?"

"Just thank you for sharing your fears with me. I'm not used to that. My ex was so…taciturn and uncommunicative."

Sam embraced and kissed Becca. She certainly made him feel better; maybe his feeling of gloom and doom would pass. It always had.

"What if we order something from the Red Lobster?"

Sam wanted their Seafood Fettuccine Alfredo, and probably because Becca felt sorry for him, he thought, she acceded to his highly caloric request, although she was always watching her weight. After dinner, Sam fell asleep on the couch. He reasoned that it was because he had a fearfully tough day although he could not point to anything which was unusually tiring.

CHAPTER 15– NICOLE GETS A PRESS BADGE

When Nicole presented to the offices of the Greene County Gazette unexpectedly, Tim, the editor and owner, asked, his words cutting through the ever-present pall of cigarette smoke that surrounded him, "To what do we owe this visit from our cub reporter? Are you going to help us get out the paper tomorrow?"

She hadn't really remembered that the paper came out on Wednesdays and responded with a smile, "No, I just wanted to be home and visit with my brothers." This was a half-truth. She actually wanted to be there when Jake got home from his trip to the jail with Franklin.

"Besides, my roommate has a meeting in our apartment, something about removing the statue of a Confederate General. from the front of the courthouse in Clarksburg, West Virginia."

Tim took the cigarette out of his mouth, where one typically resided, and commented, almost to himself, "They're still screwing around with that statue of Stonewall Jackson in Clarksburg. I thought that had been resolved years ago. Why's your roommate so interested?"

"He's from West Virginia."

"Oh, your roommate is a he?"

"Yeah, but we're not involved romantically. We just split the cost of the apartment."

"Hmmm… back in my day, it was called living together and, by our elders, 'living in sin.'"

"My roommate wants me to go with him to the rally. Hey, maybe I could write a column about it. Clarksburg is only about forty miles from here."

"I don't know about that. I wouldn't want to be responsible for you getting tear-gassed or worse."

"My roommate is a second-string offensive lineman for Pitt. He will protect me."

"Well, if you're going to go anyway, and if your roommate is over six feet tall and 225 pounds, you can be our representative at this so-called rally. There is probably interest in it anyway, given how close we are to Clarksburg and West Virginia."

"He is massive," Nicole said with a grin, anticipating that Tim would assign her her first newsworthy event.

"When is this rally supposed to take place?"

"Next week, on Tuesday at 7 o'clock."

"It's going to be cold. Why not in the summer?"

"Because the county commissioners are supposed to take up the issue in their January meeting."

"Well, I have a press credential that you can hang from your neck. You make sure that it is visible all the time."

"Is that, you know, legal?"

"Yes, anyone can hang a press credential from their person and it's legal. Don't tell anyone that, though," Phil said with a wink, "because everyone with intent to riot will be sporting a press credential." He added, in as commanding a voice as he was capable of, "And you get the fuck out of there at the first sign of trouble."

Nicole feigned shock and teased, "Why, Phil, I have never heard such language."

"Don't you forget, it was the boomers that made that word acceptable in polite discourse? Have you ever heard of the fish cheer at Woodstock?"

Nicole just grinned and shook her head.

"No, I suppose you haven't. Sorry if I offended you."

Nicole giggled and said, "I am sure I will hear a lot worse when I work on a paper."

Inadvertently, she had set up Tim, who replied, "You are fuckin' right you will."

CHAPTER 16—FRANKLIN TAKES JAKE TO JAIL AND JEFF IS FREED

When Franklin presented to the check-in Sargeant with Jake in tow, as expected, it brought a smart-ass comment, "So, Franklin, you're bringing children to the jail now."

"This is Jake Hatcher, and he's been okayed by the warden."

"Not that I don't believe you but I had better check, and I will need to see some identification, young man."

"Well, you'll have to take my word on the identification because he's not of driving age yet and he doesn't have a license."

"Better let me talk to the warden. "

Franklin noted that upon entrance to the jail, his charge got wider and wider-eyed. The start of an accomplished mission. When the authorizations and searches were complete, and Franklin and Jake were going in the elevator to the gym, Jake wondered about the jail's distinctive odor. Franklin explained: "That's the smell of stale cigarette smoke, human sweat and desperation." *Not original, but effective,* he thought.

When they finally got to the gym and the residents had settled into their folding chairs for the meeting, he began with the serenity prayer as was standard. Then, he was going to announce Slim's imminent departure when a relatively new inmate whose name he had forgotten started in, "This place sucks. It's always cold, they don't give you enough blankets and the food is crunchy because of the roaches. It's fuckin' inhuman."

Franklin had heard these complaints many times before, and he didn't entirely discount them. As usual, he would commonly suggest a potential solution and then attempt to bring the discussion back to recovery.

"I'm no lawyer but I'm sure that if your complaints have merit, and I'm sure that they do, letters to prisoners' rights attorneys might bring some action."

"Hell, I have written letters to most of the lawyers in this part of the state who I thought might be interested and I've gotten not a single fuckin' response."

"Sometimes these things take time," Franklin offered. Although he was anxious to redirect the conversation, he inwardly smiled because of the impact that he thought it must be having on Jake.

"Who is your sidekick?" the forgotten-name inmate asked.

"His name is Jake, and he just wanted to check out what life in jail was like."

Looking at Jake, the forgotten name inmate announced, "This is no place you want to be, especially a young kid like yourself." And then, continuing to eye Jake, he gave an exaggerated wink. He was uncertain whether Josh had fully processed the forgotten name's comment until he saw Josh's face redden. He opted not to elevate its salacious nature by acting shocked, so he posited a question, "So, what will be the biggest threat to your sobriety once you get out?"

Slim, who had taken to identifying himself by his given name, Jeff, in what Franklin assumed to be an attempt to jettison his prisoner persona, waved his hand enthusiastically, and Franklin called on him to share.

"My mother and brother will test my sobriety."

"How so, Jeff?"

"Well, as you know, since you agreed to take me home, today is my last day here." Then, he addressed the group, "In fact, I will be leaving you assholes right after this meeting."

After the expected laughter had dissipated, Jeff/Slim continued, "My mother is addicted to percs and my brother fucks around with booze and occasionally my mother's percs. And I'm walking into this shit when I get out."

"How old is your brother?" one of the other attendees asked.

"He's eighteen but he's still in high school. It's not that he's stupid but he's had some problems."

"Does anyone have any suggestions as to how Jeff might deal with his home situation?" Franklin challenged.

"Yeah, don't go home," an attendee named Syl volunteered and drew smirks.

"How about, for starters, go to meetings and get a sponsor," Franklin suggested.

"I just thought I heard you volunteer for the sponsor gig," Jeff/Slim joked.

"We can talk about that after the meeting. Any other suggestions for Jeff?"

"How about not hanging out with people who use it? I suppose that's going to be tough since your brother and mother are both users," another attendee was heard from.

The meeting continued in that vein as the meeting goers bandied about prospective solutions to Jeff's dilemma; some humorous, some serious and some ridiculous. The hour that the jail allotted to the meeting was fully used for the first time in Franklin's tenure, and when it expired, there were hugs, shaking hands and some indecipherable combination of the two bestowed upon Jeff.

Franklin, Jeff, and Josh went down to the elevator together. Jeff went through the checkout process while Franklin and Josh looked on. Jeff was given back the clothes that he was wearing when he was arrested, and there were, of course, forms to sign and then he was sent through the entrance doors with this admonition from Sergeant First Line of Defense, "They say in our training classes for guards that the purpose of incarceration is punishment, deterrence and rehabilitation. I sincerely hope that you have been rehabilitated and won't show up here again." The Sargeant then shook Jeff's hand and said, "Now get the fuck out of here," with a smile.

As soon as they were outside of the jail walls, Jeff knelt down and kissed the ground, which was wet and white from melted rock salt. "Every day for the last three years, I have wanted to do this, and I don't give a fuck if it's moist and salty," then Jeff laughed uproariously.

As Franklin expected, on the short drive to Jeff's apartment, Jeff kept up a steady patter. At one point, Jeff remarked as he rolled down the window, "I just want to breathe fresh air and not jail air. It stinks in there."

At this point, Josh, who had not uttered three words since the meeting, chimed in and, in partial repetition of what Franklin had said, groaned, "Yeah, it smells like desperation." Jeff looked askance toward the back seat where Josh was located and said simply, "I don't know about that but it definitely smells shitty." Franklin smiled and thought that the kid wasn't as dumb as he looked. That was a fairly clever comment.

When they arrived at the projects, and Jeff directed them to the exterior door, which serviced three apartments each on the first and second floors, they stepped inside to the odors of stale cigarette smoke and various cooking smells. They traipsed up the concrete stairs, occasionally encountering a stray cigarette and candy wrapper, until they arrived at Jeff's apartment. He knocked once, and the door swung open.

"My baby is home!" a woman looking to be once – attractive and in her forties enthused. She embraced Jeff and seemingly didn't want to let him go. "Mum," was the only word uttered by Jeff.

As Franklin stood beside Josh, he noticed two boys looking to be in their late teens. He exchanged glances with the two and when Jeff and his mother disengaged, Jeff provided introductions, "This is my mother, Barbara, and these two are Brad and Kip. They are boyfriends and Brad here is my brother."

The two teenage boys giggled at their presentation as boyfriends, Franklin assumed, when Jeff issued a clarification, "They ARE boyfriends. They're gay."

Franklin tried to maintain a matter-of-fact reaction, but Josh's mouth fell agape. Franklin stammered, "That's nice," and immediately felt embarrassed. As if in an attempt to assuage their uneasiness, Barbara announced, "I have a whole case of your favorite, Pabst Blue Ribbon in the fridge. Why don't we all have a beer to celebrate your homecoming?"

"Mom, I thought I told you that I'm on the wagon. I want to stay clean. I think getting fucked up was one of the reasons that I ended up in jail."

"Yeah, you mentioned it on one of your brother and mine's visits, but what would it hurt to do a little celebrating? After all, you just got out of jail."

"Mom, that's not the way it works. In fact, Franklin here is going to be my sponsor, and he's going to try to keep me unpissed-a-fied. Aren't you, Franklin?"

"Yes, if you want me to be," Franklin replied while his mind was considering the seemingly insoluble situation in which he was leaving Jeff. He decided on a plan of action.

"Do you have a cell phone, Jeff?"

"Are you forgetting where I just was, Franklin?" Jeff answered with a wry smile. "I just bopped down to the Walmart last Saturday and bought one."

"Sorry, stupid question. It just so happens that I have a prepaid cell phone in my car. I bought it about a year ago before I had a contract for my iPhone. I want you to have it if it still works."

"He can just use mine," Mom volunteered.

"But what if he's out and you're not around? No, I just want him to have a phone."

"Suit yourself."

"Jake, you stay here. I'll be right back." Franklin and Jeff then made their way to the car, and Franklin asked, "You know why I wanted you to have a phone, don't you?"

"So I could call you?" Jeff answered quizzically.

"Yeah, if I'm going to be your sponsor, I want you to call at least once a day, and especially when you are tempted."

Then Franklin digressed, "I didn't know that your little brother was gay."

"I keep hoping that he'll grow out of it."

"I don't think it works that way."

When they arrived at the car, and Franklin was certain that the cell phone worked, they retraced their steps and reentered the apartment. Not surprisingly, he found Mom, Jeff's little brother and his boyfriend all with cans of beer. Thankfully, Josh went without, or at least hid his can appropriately.

"We ought to get back because this young man," and Franklin pointed to Jake, "has got school tomorrow."

After perfunctory goodbyes, during which he learned that Jeff's brother was named Brad and his boyfriend Bob, Franklin shook hands with everyone. Jake very obviously avoided shaking hands with Jeff's younger brother and his boyfriend. Franklin opened the apartment door and admonished Jeff, "Remember what I told you." Jeff nodded his head.

On their way to Franklin's car, Franklin asked if Jake had learned anything from "this evening's festivities?" Jake responded, "Yeah, I don't want to end up like them." Franklin was tempted to have him elaborate but thought better of it.

They rode mostly in silence, except that Jake wondered aloud, "What did you think of Jeff's brother being gay?"

"Not much, it didn't faze me one way or another," Franklin lied.

"It's odd that I met a gay guy tonight after the names those assholes at school called me."

"The longer you live, the more coincidences you will find in life," Franklin said, all the while thinking what an understatement he was sharing with Jake.

CHAPTER 17—SAM AND RHONDA DISCUSS PHILOSOPHY

When he awakened, still fatigued, little did Sam expect that the theme of the day would be set by his very limited knowledge of Sartre, but it was. It all started when he told Becca before he left for the office that he still felt tired. She expressed her concern and suggested that he make an appointment with his PCP. He had opined previously to Becca that what used to be called family doctors were, in fact, glorified nurses, and he flippantly reiterated that belief to her now. She didn't think that it was funny.

When he got to the office, Rhonda informed him that Stewart Sonnenberg had called the office and identified himself as a professor at Duquesne.

"He's also the ex-boyfriend of my soon-to-be ex-wife."

"Ah, that's why the name sounded familiar."

"I wonder what that son of a bitch wants with me. He already took my wife."

"Now, now, you have Becca. I think that she's a damn sight better than what's her name."

"That's good, Rhonda. I don't want her name spoken around here," he joked. "And I might call Sonnenburg back someday, but it would have to be a day that couldn't get any worse."

"Sam, let me ask you something. It's a weird question, I realize, but have you ever seriously considered death?"

"You mean mine or somebody else's? Because my attitude would be somewhat different depending upon whose ox was being gored," Sam chuckled. "Why do you ask? I realize that winter in Pittsburgh can be depressing, but God..."

"Apocalypse now was on last night. There was nothing else that I wanted to watch, and it was one of my dad's favorite movies. God rest his soul. So I decided to watch it again, and it got me to thinking about my own mortality."

At the risk of sounding like Franklin, Sartre said, "Life has no meaning the moment you lose the illusion of being eternal."

"What do you mean at the risk of sounding like Franklin?"

"Well, when he first walked into our lives, he was the only homeless person that I was aware of that had a repertoire of French philosophy quotes, don't you remember?"

"Yeah, now that you mention it, I do," Rhonda hesitated and then questioned Sam, "Do you believe that life loses its meaning when you realize that you are not eternal?"

"I think when you realize, I mean really realize and internalize that you are going to die, it makes you wonder about what the purpose of life really is."

"What do you think it is?"

"I'm going to give you another quote from Sartre, 'Everything has been figured out except how to live.' I think what he meant was no one has figured out a good solution to the question what do you do to give life its meaning…"

Then, he returned Rhonda's volley, "What do you think the meaning of life is?"

Rhonda shot back with a smile, "Haven't you noticed that I have a dirty forehead every Ash Wednesday?"

"Yeah, but there are a lot of people who believe in one religion or another who still wonder about life's purpose."

"I guess I do too, but I keep coming back to what I have been taught since I was little, 'he that believes and is baptized shall be saved,' and we should live a Christ-like life."

"I wish that I could be so sure. I am an agnostic."

"I have known some people who doubted Thomas and have become believers."

"I think that whether you're a believer or not is pretty much baked in. In other words, I think that there are people who are predisposed to believe in religion, and those that aren't."

"Well, now, Mr. Attorney, do you think that you have a purpose?"

"I suppose I do." Sam then elaborated jocularly, "I believe in truth, justice and the American way."

"Well Sam, you do help people to be treated fairly."

"If you mean getting them money."

"What's wrong with that?"

"I guess nothing. I guess maybe I have the best of two worlds; I can believe that what I'm doing obtains justice for my clients, and I make a handsome living. At least that's what I tell myself most days."

"I guess you don't believe in heaven or hell either."

"I am an agnostic when it comes to the afterlife. Although I'm willing to concede that there are some Goddamn odd things that I have witnessed."

"You mean that shit with Franklin?"

"Yeah, and some things that happened in my cases before him."

"You will have to tell me about them sometime."

The phone rang on Rhonda's desk, and after picking it up, Rhonda announced, "It's the professor again."

"Tell him that I'm in conference."

Rhonda carried out the directive, and Franklin responded to Rhonda's quizzical look with, "Maybe he'll get the message."

CHAPTER 18– NICOLE AND THE STONEWALL JACKSON DEMONSTRATIONS

On the night of the West Virginia rally, she drove her roommate for approximately one and a half hours to Clarksburg. Her roommate, Aleki Reinhart, a huge young man of partially Samoan descent, asked to be reminded of the significance of Stonewall Jackson in the American Civil War.

"Why is he so near and dear to the hillbillies?"

Nicole laughed, "You, of all people, ought to know the answer to that question. You're from West Virginia. He was born there in Clarksburg, and he led the Confederate cavalry before he died part way through the Civil War. His family is all from Clarksburg. What were you doing at the meeting in our apartment where the statue was being discussed?"

"I wasn't paying much attention. I was only there because they needed someplace to hold their meeting, and I am interested in asking if this girl could use our apartment for their get-together." Alecki followed up, "How do you know any of this? My knowledge of the Civil War is very sketchy."

"I had a boyfriend last year who was a Civil War nut. In fact, we went to Gettysburg a few times. He talked about the Civil War constantly, and I couldn't help but learn a few things. Actually, it was somewhat interesting."

"I never heard about him before. Why haven't you mentioned him? Did it end badly?"

"He wanted to get married, and I didn't, at least not in the near future. I guess you could say we got divorced before we even got married."

She could see that Aleki didn't know quite what to say, so he simply nodded his head.

"And now I have Steve."

It was night when they got to Clarksburg, and they could see the Tiki torches, which had become de rigueur at these times of events, near the courthouse, which sat on a hill. Nicole parked the car, and they joined the handful of people walking up the hill toward the courthouse.

As they were walking, a young bearded man of about their age caught up with them, and initiated a conversation. "What brings you guys out on such a cold winter night? Protecting our heritage?"

"I'm actually a reporter," Nicole clarified as she was fishing around in her coat pocket for the press credential that Tim had given her.

"You ain't from Fox because I don't see no cameraman."

"No, I'm covering this for the Greene County Gazette."

"Ain't never heard of that, where is Greene County?"

"It's just across the Pennsylvania border."

"Did anyone ever tell you that you look like a young Meg Ryan?"

"Occasionally. People our age pretty much don't know who she is."

"I saw her in an old movie, something about email."

They continued to trudge up the hill when the assumed defender of heritage observed Aleki, "God damn, you are one big dude."

"He's on the Pitt football team," Nicole allowed, "he's here for protection of little old me."

When they got to the top of the hill, where the courthouse sat, there was a substantial police presence, prompting the defender of heritage to remark, "By the looks of some of these guys, they must have brought out every single retired cop in the state."

They had somehow or other divided themselves with pro-statue advocates on one side of the street and the anti-Stonewall protesters on the other. Both sides were sporting signs, some obscene, with the decided edge going to the antis. The antis were armed with a bullhorn, and the pro-statue crowd had somehow rigged up a microphone with a lectern. What ensued was a loud cacophony of shouting, some amplified by artificial means and some not.

Since she and Aleki had followed the defender of heritage to the statue-protecting side of the street. They ended up beside a handsome young red-haired man waving a Confederate flag. He was busy chanting, "We stand with Stonewall," when Nicole caught him staring directly at her. He said something that was indecipherable over the din of the crowd.

She pointed to her press badge, and he said something else that she couldn't catch.

The pro-statue speakers, as expected, leaned heavily on the theme of heritage. A few had blown-up pictures of Stonewall Jackson's headstone affixed to their signs. A man dressed in a suit and tie somehow commandeered the podium, and the crowd noise abated somewhat. He identified himself as a County Commissioner and pledged that he and his fellow commissioners would seriously consider both sides of the issue. He then proceeded to walk up the steps to the courthouse, and the temporary decrease in the decibel level proved to be indeed temporary.

What followed was what Nicole would later describe in her article for the Greene Gazette as "the launching of verbal missiles by both sides of the street, and ultimately, when the mutual volleys of obscenities petered out, in dispersal of the crowds, supervised and encouraged by the police."

When the noise level made shouting at least audible, the defender of heritage nodded at the red haired young man waving the Confederate flag and called out, "Hey, Bobby."

The red-haired young man responded with a nod and a smile and, looking at Nicole, sneered, "I see that you're hanging around with a better class of people than you did in high school." Then, stepping directly in front of Nicole, he offered his free hand and bellowed, "I am Bobby Wright, and who might you be."

The defender of heritage intervened and told Bobby that Nicole was a reporter. Bobby's face lit up, and he asked Nicole, "So, what are you reporting for?" to which she responded a newspaper - The Greene County Gazette.

"Oh, I know Greene County. You're right across the border in Pennsylvania." Nicole nodded her assent. "If you are ever looking for a story, I think you would find our group interesting. And then we could go out for a cup of coffee or a drink together," he leered.

He pressed into Nicole's hand a business card which had his name and number and was emblazoned with the legend Protectors of Our Ancestral Faith and Birthright. Shortly thereafter, Nicole, Alecki and the defender of heritage began to walk down the hill. Nicole pulled the card that Bobby Wright had given her out of her coat pocket and, pointing to it, asked the defender of heritage whether he belonged to the organization

Protectors of Our Ancestral Faith and Birthright and added apologetically, "We have been together all night, and I don't even know your name."

"It's Brandon, Brandon Smithkey. And no, I don't belong to the Protectors."

"Why not? It seems like you guys would be on the same side on the statue issue."

Nicole could see that Brandon was formulating his answer very carefully. "Well, we both believe in recognizing and celebrating our history, but the Protectors go quite a bit further, shall we say."

"What do you mean?"

There was no hesitation when Brandon put his index finger above his lip, as if it were a mustache, and raised his right arm in a classic Nazi salute.

Aleki, who had been mostly silent since their arrival, finally spoke after seeing Brandon's Hitler impersonation: "I despise those fascist fuckin' groups."

Brandon nodded his head in agreement and, after Nicole and Aleki had introduced themselves, exhorted them to look him up if they were ever in Clarksburg again. He gave them his number, which they both recorded on their cell phones.

"And," Brandon added, "I would appreciate you texting me a copy of any article that you publish regarding tonight."

When they reached the car and were on their way back to Pennsylvania, Nicole announced that this was her first gig as a real reporter. Little did she know that it would be the start of something that was more than one isolated gig.

CHAPTER 19– FRANKLIN AND JEFF GO TO A MEETING

In the ten days since he had dropped him off at his home, Jeff had called him precisely once, and that was to report cheerfully that he was doing just fine. When questioned as to whether he was going to any meetings, Jeff responded that he had no way of going to meetings but that he had a job at a local hot dog place, and he would soon be able to afford a junker.

Franklin could smell an excuse not to attend meetings like manure on a dairy farm, and so he was headed to Jeff's apartment to pick him up and take him to a seven o'clock meeting. He had so internalized the concept that he must "pass it on" to maintain his sobriety that there was little doubt that he would take Jeff to a meeting, even if he had to drag him there.

He had been reading a modern French philosopher, Pascal Bruckner, who argued, "We have a lot of power in our lives but not the power to be happy. Happiness is more like a moment of grace." He had been graced with happiness more than occasionally since he had become sober and believed that the continuing grace of happiness was dependent upon him helping a fellow traveler. At least, he thought so today.

Jeff had called him when he was on his way and said he would meet Franklin outside of the apartment building. When Franklin assured him that he would be happy to come up to the apartment because of the weather, Jeff replied tersely that the apartment was a mess. Franklin told him that he would call when he was in the parking lot so as to minimize his standing outside in the cold.

When Jeff got in the car, he was wearing a light jacket, which was inappropriate for the weather, and paint-spattered blue jeans. He didn't look like he had shaved since he came home.

"Staying sober?"

"Yeah, but it hasn't been easy with those two around."

"I bet it hasn't, but you have stayed away from the pills and booze?"

Jeff nodded his head. Franklin wasn't sure he believed him. They drove wordlessly for a few minutes when Jeff spoke, "I am most worried about my brother. Not that I don't give a shit about my mother, because

I do, but my mother uses my brother to score her pills, and he takes some himself and drinks on top of it. I wish I could get my brother into rehab someplace, but I don't think that he would go."

"I could have somebody who is a few years clean and sober and near his age talk to him if it wouldn't be a wasted effort."

"Is that guy who you would have talked to him gay because I think that would be best?

"Well, gay people do face their own unique problems, I guess, and the guy I'm thinking of is gay. In fact, there are a number of gay meetings that your brother could attend."

"I will tell him. He might even find a new boyfriend at a meeting."

"How did your mother react when she found out that your brother was gay?"

"At first, she was very upset, and saying that it must have been his father's genes because she always thought he was queer, but when she discovered that he could get percs at his school, she seemed not to give a shit whether he was gay or not. She doesn't really mention it anymore."

"He is still in school, am I correct?"

"Yeah, he is. Still goes to school occasionally," Jeff snickered, "but most of the time he spends playing computer games, mostly with his boyfriend, and occasionally with me. My mom says that a teacher told her that if he went to school more often, he could get into a college. He said he was some kind of fuckin' math genius."

"What do you do when you're not playing computer games?"

"Nothing much. I sleep and write. And I just started a job this week at the Brighton Weiner Shop."

"I didn't know you wrote. What do you write about?"

"Life in its fucked up glory in general, and what it's like being caged like an animal."

"I'd like to read some of your stuff."

"I don't think I'm ready for that yet."

"Well, when you are."

They pulled into the parking lot of the church where the meeting was held, and, as was usual on meeting night, there were a number of people milling about and enjoying their last cigarette before the start of the meeting.

"Hi, Jeff," remarked an attractive young woman, "what brings you here? I haven't seen you since high school."

"Hello, Mara. I haven't been around much. What brings you here?"

"Horse," Mara quipped, and Franklin immediately caught her meaning and it wasn't the mode of transportation.

The meeting was pretty much unremarkable for an AA/NA meeting, but Franklin could tell that Jeff was paying uneven attention. The speaker related an incident in which he found himself disembarking from a plane in Las Vegas. He had no recollection of how he got on the plane; he was in a blackout. Jeff laughed where appropriate.

As the meeting broke up, Mara said that she hoped to see Jeff next week. Jeff nodded.

On the way back to Jeff's apartment, Franklin wondered aloud why so many of his calls to Jeff had gone unanswered in the last week. Jeff just shrugged.

"We are going to do better next week with the telephone calls, aren't we, Jeff?"

"If you say so, Franklin," was Jeff's non-reassuring response.

As Jeff was getting out of the car, Franklin reminded him, "And don't forget to see if Brad might want someone to talk to him." Again, simply a nod.

Franklin wondered if he would ever see Jeff again.

CHAPTER 20–SAM AND THE PROFESSOR

It was a typical January day in Pittsburgh, cold, flurrying and gray, when Sam's cell phone rang and interrupted funk brought on by what everyone in Pittsburgh thought that day suffered from: seasonal affective disorder. He looked at the phone and saw that the caller was a Dr. Sonnenberg. He sighed; so the son of a bitch had gotten his cell phone number, probably from his soon-to-be ex-wife. He had called his office three or four times, and he had given Rhonda various excuses as to why he couldn't take the call. He would have to bite the bullet.

"Hello, Stew. Sorry that I didn't get back to you sooner. What can I do for you? I wasn't expecting you to call my cell phone."

"I asked your ex for your number."

"As I understand it, she's your ex too."

"Yes, I think we both share that status now. No hard feelings, I hope."

"Of course not," he said with feigned equanimity. Why would he have hard feelings about the asshole who wrecked his marriage? He couldn't help but think about his son's entirely appropriate nickname for Stew, Pavlov's dog, because his son said that Stew always salivated when his ex showed him any affection.

"I thought not; we are all adults here."

"Well, I would love to compare notes with you since we both apparently loved the same woman, but maybe some other time."

"Let me get right to the point then: as you know, I am a professor of psychology at Duquesne University."

"Yes, I am well aware of your status as an academician." How could he not be? That is how her affair with Stew started: he was one of her professors, and she sought advice from him when she opened her own counseling practice.

"I have been offered a position as an advisor to the psychologists who work at the Allegheny County Jail. It's a part-time job setting policies and working with the warden in a management capacity."

"Congratulations, I wish you well," Sam lied.

"Thank you. I know that you were a public defender and that you spent a good deal of time at the jail so I thought I would solicit your opinion on whether I should take the position."

"If you don't mind a little controversy occasionally, and depending on what it pays, I would see no reason that you wouldn't want the job. It's not like you'll be raped by the inmates."

Obviously unamused, Stew replied, "No, I, of course not. Well, thank you for your input. I should ask you to come up here to give a lecture to my class on psychology and the law."

"Yes, you should." *No harm in asking,* he thought, *but I will help you out and speak to your class when hell freezes over.*

When he had hung up, he walked out of his office to get a cup of coffee and told Rhonda that she wouldn't have to dodge the professor's calls anymore because he had spoken with him.

"What did he want?"

"Just some advice."

"From you, the man whose marriage he ruined?"

"Yeah, but as he said, we are all adults here."

CHAPTER 21–NICOLE AND TIM DISCUSS HER NEXT ASSIGNMENT

When she stopped into the offices of The Greene Gazette a few days after the Stonewall Jackson rally Tim emerged from the near-constant cloud of cigarette smoke that enveloped him and enthused, "Well, if it isn't the next Martha Gellhorn. To what do we owe the pleasure of your company?"

"I just stopped by my mother's house to check on my brothers. I don't have any classes tomorrow. Who is the Martha Gellhorn that you're comparing me to."

"She was well before your time, but she's often referred to as the twentieth century's most influential war correspondent. She covered the Spanish Civil War, Adolph Hitler's rise to power and the Vietnam War. She covered civil wars in Central America in the 1980s when she was in her seventies. If you couldn't tell, I have a great deal of respect for her."

"I would have to do a hell of a lot more to be compared to her. All I did was attend a Tear Down the Stonewall Statue rally. It wasn't an active war zone," she demurred with a smile.

"Yeah, but it could have become one according to your description. By the way, I am running your description of the rally in the next edition. Would you like me to post it on our website, too?"

"I would be honored."

"I particularly liked the sentence, 'What ensued was the launching of verbal missiles by both sides of the street, and ultimately, when the mutual volleys of obscenities petered out, in the dispersal of the crowds, supervised and encouraged by the police.' Sounds like it could have developed into a war zone or at least a skirmish."

"That reminds me, have you ever heard of the Protectors of our Ancestral Faith and Birthright? I ran into a member of that group at the Stonewall rally."

"No, I haven't but I assume that it is a neo-Confederate group."

"We ran into someone at the rally who described it as a neo-Nazi group."

Nicole could see Tim's face redden as he took a long drag off his cigarette.

"Those Nazi groups are making a comeback, the bastards. My old man would be turning over in his grave."

"Was he a World War Two vet?" She assumed that since Tim was almost seventy, there was a good chance that his dad was involved somehow in the Second World War.

"Yeah, he was in the Navy. He went in '44. The war was almost over, and he got to see many of the islands recaptured by the Japanese."

Nicole could practically feel Tim studying her. Then, as if he read her mind, he posed this question: "You're not thinking about doing a story about this group, are you?"

"Well, the thought had crossed my mind. This guy that I met gave me his card and invited me to one of their meetings. I thought that it might be disgustingly interesting to see what makes these guys tick."

"I can tell you what makes those guys tick in a single word: hatred. Hatred of people who don't look like them, worship like them, make love like them or believe what they believe. That's all you need to know. I don't want you getting involved with them on any basis."

She laughed and replied coquettishly, "Yes, Daddy."

They spent the rest of her time in the office discussing the post on the website and her plans for future Sam-centered articles. As always, her clothes bore the unmistakable odor of cigarettes when she left the office. She rather liked it.

CHAPTER 22–FRANKLIN AND JEFF AT THE HOT DOG SHOPPE

After Franklin had made his weekly trip to the Coalton Jail to run the AA/NA meeting, he traveled into downtown Coalton to pick up Jeff at his new job at the Brighton Weiner Shop and take him to a meeting. He knew that it was a popular place since it was the only fast food in Coalton, but he never expected this degree of wiener worship. The place was packed. He saw Jeff behind the frenetic counter, slapping hot dogs into buns, and he held up two fingers, which he took to mean either two minutes or twenty minutes. He opted for the latter and decided to join the line awaiting wieners.

When Franklin got to the counter, he ordered two hotdogs and a large Coke, which was served in a plastic cup emblazoned with a uniformed wiener in a military outfit and the legend "We Support our Troops."

As he was trying to find a table, a rotund, florid–faced man looking to be in his 40s entered the restaurant and shouted, "Well, hello, Jeff." Jeff, from his position behind the counter, shouted back, it seemed to Franklin reluctantly, "Hi, Jim."

When he was almost done with his second hot dog, which he had to admit was tasty, Jeff stood over him, apparently done with his wiener slinging for the day.

"Ready to go to the meeting?"

"Yeah, but I would like to stop at home first and change. I smell like hot dogs."

Franklin glanced at his watch and concluded that they could still make the meeting on time and nodded his head. As they were getting in Franklin's car, he asked if he had spoken with Brad regarding Franklin's offer to have a gay, sober person speak to him about rehab.

"Yeah, I have spoken with him but I don't think he's ready."

"He wouldn't be the first person that preferred to stay high all the time. I hope he hits bottom soon."

They had just pulled into the project's parking lot when Jeff said, "I think it's a little more complicated than that. I'll tell you when I come back out."

So Franklin waited for Jeff to come out and wondered how his homeless compatriots were doing. How many of them were left he wondered.

When Jeff made his appearance, smelling like cologne, which he assumed was for the young woman that he had met after the first meeting that he and Jeff attended together, he questioned Jeff, "So, what's the story with your brother?"

Jeff began, "You know that fat fuck that hollered hello to me in the restaurant?"

Franklin hardly thought that Brighton Weiner qualified as a restaurant but he nodded his head.

"That is none other than Jim Straka, the owner of Straka's Pharmacy here in town and one of the biggest shitheads that you would ever want to meet."

"What's he got to do with your brother?"

"He does my mother," Jeff let out a wry laugh at his double entendre.

"Okay, but what does that have to do with your brother."

"For years, my brother had connections that got my mother some of her pills; she has a really bad habit. Then, that asshole Straka came along, and he became her supplier. He had an endless supply of Blueberries. Of course, I assume that she had to put out for him. Kinda a little tit for a tat."

"So…" Franklin felt badly that anyone would view their mother in that light and make a joke about their mother's breasts, but, he supposed, where entire families were users, he suspected that that was relatively mild.

"The other day when I was at work, Straka and my mother had it out, according to Brad. They came out of my mom's bedroom, screaming at each other. He slapped her and pulled her hair and said she couldn't rely on him anymore for her percs."

"So, Mom told Brad that he would need to help her get her Oxy."

"So, that shouldn't have any effect on Brad at least meeting with someone."

Jeff threw him a look of disbelief and asked, "You were an alcoholic, right?"

"I am an alcoholic, just a recovering alcoholic."

"Brad's situation is like if I told you that you had to make deliveries of vodka every day. I think Brad would have been willing to at least talk with your gay friend if he didn't have to be one of my mom's suppliers."

Franklin could see Jeff's point. "Okay, Jeff, but the offer to have someone talk to Brad remains open, and it always will. Did you ask him at least?"

"Yes, but he just sort of laughed."

The meeting was, to his mind, relatively ordinary: man gets drunk and high, man has an epiphany, and man gets clean and sober. There was one extraordinary feature to the typical narrative, though, the speaker was doing cocaine with his friend in the restroom of a bar in Pittsburgh and they both were drinking heavily. His friend recognized that he was in no condition to drive them home to Colaton so the speaker became a passenger in his own car and his friend drove.

The speaker's next conscious recollection was coming out of anesthesia in a hospital, minus his right leg. Several days later, he was told that his friend had driven his car in which he was a passenger over an embankment and sustained mortal injuries. Corralling the determination of an addict/alcoholic, he used for another couple of years until he had parked his car in his parent's garage and passed out with the car still running. His parents hauled him off to rehab, and he had been clean and sober now for seven years. Oh yes, and his lawsuit against his friend's estate netted him a handsome amount.

It appeared to Franklin that Jeff was touched by the speaker's story, and Jeff spent several minutes once the meeting was over engaged in conversation with the speaker, which pleased Franklin. On their drive back to Jeff's apartment, he learned that the speaker had given Jeff his contact information.

He dropped Jeff off at his apartment and drove home feeling ever more optimistic about the possibility that Jeff might remain clean and sober.

CHAPTER 22–SAM AND HIS BOYS DISCUSS EVIL

When they sat down for dinner that night to Becca's outstanding lasagna, Sam's youngest, Sean, who was 11 years old, said that he had read an online article on human trafficking. Becca wondered aloud whether that topic was fit for dinner conversation, but Sam, who had repeatedly impressed upon the boys that they could ask him anything, probed:

"And what did you learn, Sean?"

"I learned that there are incredibly evil people in this world."

"That is sad but accurate," Sam acknowledged.

"Did you know that there are people in India and other countries who cut the arms and legs off of kids and have them beg where the tourists are hoping the tourists will feel sorry for them and put money in their cups? Of course, the adults who cut off their arms or legs get to keep the money."

Marcus, Sam's thirteen year old, chimed in, "I didn't know that. I thought that human trafficking was only about selling young girls for sex."

Becca raised her eyebrows and Sam could tell that she was concerned about where this conversation would lead. Sam wasn't sure either but honestly instructed, "They are both forms of human trafficking, and there are many more. Any time a person forces somebody to give him or her something like their person against their will, I guess you could say it is human trafficking."

"Their person?" Marcus was baffled.

"Something intimately connected to their body," Becca said.

"Yep, that's a good way to put it. Like their body, their organs, their sexuality or the fruits of their labors," Sam expounded.

"There sure are some evil people out there." Marcus' statement brought a temporary halt to the conversation, and silence prevailed for a short time.

"I wonder what makes people evil," Sean mused.

"Well, there are a lot of theories out there. Some say that environment contributes, some say upbringing, some say that anti-social behavior is just baked in." Sam explained.

"'Baked in,' what does that mean?" Sean questioned.

"Basically, what it means is that it's difficult for some people not to do anti-social things."

"It would seem that if you believe that, that absolves people from doing evil things," Becca commented.

"It just means that some people are genetically predisposed to do bad things. For example, we know now that sociopaths-"

Sean interrupted Sam with the question, "What is a sociopath?"

Becca said, "It means a person without a conscience."

"Maybe born that way," Sam completed his sentence.

"You represented a whole lot of criminals when you were a public defender, didn't you, Dad?" Marcus questioned.

"Yes, I did. At least those accused of a crime."

"Did you think that those people were genetically predisposed?"

"Most of the people that I represented were mixed up with drugs, and we do know that some people are predisposed to becoming addicted."

"So you think that people aren't responsible for their own actions?" Becca was somewhat incredulous.

"Maybe they are not entirely responsible for their own actions, Becca."

"That smacks of predestination," Becca countered.

"What the hell is that?" Sam could see that Sean was engrossed in their discussion.

"Becca, why don't you take this one since you brought it up," Sam demurred.

"It means that God chooses who will go to heaven when we are born. So... We do not have free will. Everything is chosen for us by God. How's my theology, sweetie?"

Sam chuckled. and said, "Goddamn good!" Sam knew that his sons weren't used to hearing that expression from him, so when the titters of laughter had subsided, he attempted to summarize their dinner conversation: "So… There are many, many factors that go into making up our personalities some of which we have no control over. But, I would say that there is nearly universal agreement that Hitler and Stalin were truly evil people because they had no regard for human life."

"Dad, then you must agree that there are people who deserve to fry," Marcus guessed.

"No, I don't. I don't think that it's ever okay to take a life."

"What about war?" Sean countered.

"That is self-defense. The opposing army is trying to kill you. I should amend my previous statement: I don't think that execution by the state is ever appropriate."

The remainder of the dinner conversation was centered around the Pirates' chances of having a winning team this year. All except Sean didn't see much hope, and Sam called Sean an eternal optimist.

By 9 o'clock, Sam could hardly keep his eyes open.

CHAPTER 23—NICOLE AND BOBBY

As Nicole was fighting a frigid wind on her way to the diner, which was a block from the Greene Gazette, she reviewed why she was going to have greasy spoon meatloaf and mashed potatoes.

She hadn't given much thought to the young man who introduced himself at the Stonewall Rally as Bobby Wright, Protector of Our Ancestral Faith and Birthright, until he emailed her address at the Gazette. Thereafter, she had the following conversation with Tim, "I just got an email from the guy who belongs to the Protectors of Our Ancestral Faith and Birthright. He must have read my online article."

"I hope you're not thinking of having any contact with that Nazi."

"I thought it might be interesting to interview him, you know, and do an article on his organization. Right-wing groups like his have made a resurgence."

"Don't I know. In fact, I think the Internet is partially to blame for making it easier for birds of a fascist feather to flock together. The Nazis don't need any more free publicity."

"So you wouldn't publish an article written by me about how horrid they are?"

They engaged in their verbal duel for several minutes more until Tim finally temporized, "I'll tell you what, I will consider publishing an article about that fuckin' group, and I said consider if you agree to my conditions."

"And they are?"

"Well, first of all, you need to meet him at Chelsea's place just down the street so I can be there if you get into trouble."

Nicole smiled at the thought of a seventy year old man as her defender. What was Tim going to do, blow cigarette smoke in his face until he succumbed to smoke inhalation? She smiled inwardly and, appearing to concede that condition, requested his further stipulations, "And you must make it clear that you are interviewing him for an article, and he is not to consider this a date or whatever your generation calls dates, and you are not to give him any personal information. In fact, if he didn't already know your name, I would have preferred you use a nom de plume."

"How about Samuel Clemens?" Nicole winked at Tim.

Tim was unamused and made her promise that she would tell him when she was to meet with the 'fascist' and he assured her that he would be seated a few booths down from her, whether she liked it or not.

She had stopped in the office of the Gazette on the day she was supposed to meet Bobby Wright and was now almost to the restaurant. Phil said he would be along shortly and occupy a booth in close proximity to hers, as promised.

When she got to Chelsea's place at 4 o'clock there was practically no one there. The matronly older woman, who apparently served as the hostess and the sole waitress at this hour, confirmed the obvious, "You can sit anywhere you want, sweetie."

Nicole found a booth about halfway back in the restaurant and informed the hostess/waitress that she was waiting for another guest and that they might not be ordering dinner for a while. The hostess/waitress shrugged and joked, "Suit yourself, but my boss has told me that on account of the line of potential customers out the door, I'm to make life miserable for whoever stays beyond an hour. What'll you have to drink?" Nicole smiled; she liked this lady.

After she had ordered her diet Pepsi, and before it was delivered, she sat her tape recorder on the table and reminded herself of her interviewer's commitment not to betray her emotions, which she thought might be sorely tested by her interviewee. Then, in walked Bobby Wright.

"Mean night out there," he observed.

"Yes, it is. I didn't have far to travel, but you did. We could have rescheduled if you wanted to. You have my email address on the paper."

"Yeah, but I was on my way to a meeting in your neck of the woods anyway. In Coalton."

"If you don't mind my asking, is it a meeting of your group?"

"Yeah, we are based in West Virginia, but we're opening a chapter in Pennsylvania, Coalton specifically. There's a guard at the Coalton County jail who has recruited enough of his friends who are philosophically in line with us, so we are going to meet with them tonight. I've never been to Coalton; I never heard of it until the guy contacted me."

Nicole restrained herself: she almost mentioned that her brother had received something of an education at the Coalton jail. She thought that she would open with a softball question, "If you can, in a couple of sentences, could you summarize what the goals of your organization are and how you wish to achieve them."

She switched on her tape recorder and obtained his consent to be recorded.

"We want to return this country to its origins as a white, Christian, God-fearing country. There, I did it in one sentence."

"What if you are none of those things? What will you do?"

"We will tolerate you as long as you know your place."

"Sounds like you would like slavery reinstituted."

"Listen, we would have no problem with the Negroes going back to Africa and the Jews and Arabs going back to wherever they came from, but the power structure in the US will be exclusively with white Christian men."

"Do you consider women to be an inferior sex?"

"Not inferior, but we celebrate the differences in the sexes. We believe that the highest calling for a woman is to raise children, not work."

She was about to pose her next question about how they planned to do away with constitutionally guaranteed rights when Tim walked in and engaged in friendly banter with the hostess/waitress, whom he obviously knew.

She was just about to pose a follow – up question, namely, what about people who must have two wage earners to make ends meet, when Bobby held up his hand as if to silence her.

"I want to hear this conversation. It'll be interesting, I heard the word drug addict."

Nicole then caught a snippet of the conversation between the waitress and Tim, "So we want to get him into rehab for his drug problem, but because it's a long wait list for people who don't have insurance…"

Bobby made a motion with his hands as if he were playing the drums and predicted, "This is where all she asks the old guy for money."

Nicole then caught the waitress mid-sentence, "…So we set up a GoFundMe page, and since you have known our son since he was a boy, I thought you might want to help."

She heard Tim respond, "Of course I would. How do I do that?" What followed was the waitress' explanation of how to make a contribution online.

"That's another communist idea: Spending our tax dollars on rehabs and Narcan. Hell, most of those addicted bastards aren't worth saving anyway."

Nicole abandoned her pretense of objectivity, "Many of those 'bastards', as you call them, have become addicted to prescription pain medication. And we know that some people are genetically predisposed to addictive behaviors."

"There is no room in our world for addicts, and the sooner they kill themselves off, the better we would be as a society."

Nicole abruptly excused herself, claiming to go to the ladies' room. Actually, she had to get away from Bobby. As the ladies' room door closed behind her, she couldn't help but think what kind of monster essentially denied the humanity of certain people. She wondered if he would apply the "better off without them" standard to any psychologically disturbed person.

What about people with a physical handicap? Wasn't he espousing essentially Hitler's attempt to create a master race? The thought almost made her physically ill. Although the thought of abandoning the interview caused her some hesitation, she exited the ladies' room with a clear intention of getting away from Bobby immediately.

She feigned illness and held out, as a promise that she fully intended not to keep, that they might meet again sometime. Little could she imagine the circumstances of their future meeting.

She heard Bobby say something like, "I was hoping to get to know you better," in what she interpreted as a very suggestive manner, continued past Tim's booth and his quizzical look, and went straight out the door and into the wind and darkness.

Of course, as she expected, she soon heard Tim yelling out her name on the sidewalk behind her. As he breathlessly approached her and made a comment which she could barely decipher about his 50-year smoking habit, she confessed, "I'm sorry, but I couldn't stand one more moment with that vile human."

Tim chuckled between his gasps for air and said, "Why are you sorry?"

"Because it's not going to be much of a story when I only spent five minutes with the dude."

"I wasn't going to run the story if you had spent an hour with him. It runs totally contrary to my principles. And before you say I promised to run your article, I didn't promise, I said I would consider it."

They walked the rest of the way to the Gazette office in silence and with the snow falling.

CHAPTER 24—FRANKLIN PROPOSES TO KIM

On Friday night, Jeff was to come to the apartment and have dinner with him and Kim, Franklin prodded Kim only half-jokingly, "So, Kim, when are we going to make a baby."

"Don't you think that we ought to get married first?" Kim replied with obvious irritation.

"Haven't we played this scene before?" Franklin muttered.

"Yes, we have, and it didn't turn out so good the last time."

Franklin dropped to one knee and, with exaggerated emotion, asked Kim for her hand in marriage. She laughed and deliberately, Franklin thought, avoided the question.

As he was driving to pick up Jeff at the bus station, where there were a few buses from Coalton every day, he was left to contemplate the first time Kim became pregnant. The miscarriage, or more precisely, the stillbirth, began his more intense odyssey into the bottle. But, he was convinced, no he knew, that the outcome of Kim's pregnancy would be different this time if it came to pass. And, he projected, he was certain that he could land a job as a drug and alcohol counselor after graduation; after all, he possessed unique qualifications, having been homeless and all.

He was rolling these pleasant thoughts around in his mind when Jeff got off the bus. He had a winter coat pulled over his white T-shirt, the most notable element of which was a smiling hot dog snuggled in a bun.

"You didn't have time to change from your work clothes? Am I going to have to look at that smiling weiner on your shirt all through dinner?" Franklin teased. He didn't get the reaction he expected from Jeff.

"No, you would think that my mother could do the fuckin' laundry since I am the only person bringing clean money into the house, but she's too busy taking pills and drinking. I asked her to wash a couple of shirts for me before I went to work and she never got around to it."

"Things are still bad there, huh?"

"Yes, between my mom and my brother…" Jeff shook his head.

"So your brother Brad is still supplying your mum with pills?"

"Yeah."

"What does Brad do all day? He's supposed to be in school, isn't he?"

"Mostly, he sits around getting high with his boyfriend, that and scoring pills for hisself, his boyfriend and my mother."

"It must be really tough to stay sober and clean in that environment."

"No shit, it is."

"Are you staying clean and sober?"

"Yeah, but it's one day at a time."

"Well, it is for all of us."

They pulled into the parking lot for Franklin's apartment, and Franklin offered, "I can loan you some clothes if you want; you smell like hot dogs. They may be a little small on you…"

"I would welcome that. I don't want to smell like hot dogs any less than you don't want me to."

When they had entered the apartment and Franklin had introduced Jeff to Kim, Franklin took him into their bedroom and was looking through his shirts and pants for something suitable for Jeff's build when Jeff divulged, "I haven't had a shower in days."

"Why not?"

"The bathroom is filthy and hasn't been cleaned since I got out of jail. And with three zombies…"

"The bathroom is down the hall. There are washcloths and towels in the cabinet underneath the sink. There is soap and shampoo in the shower. "Having so instructed Jeff, Franklin rejoined Kim in the dining room, where they would continue to sit until Jeff was showered and dressed.

"I am awfully proud of you, Franklin. You have overcome much," Kim declared.

Franklin was inwardly ecstatic at Kim's compliment, but he replied, as matter-of-factly as possible but with a smile, "Why because I am now living a fairly normal life instead of being a homeless and hopeless drunk?"

Kim returned his smile, got up from her chair and, sitting on Franklin's lap, elaborated, "No, silly! Because I know how difficult it must have been to remake yourself, and now you're giving back, and that young man in our bathroom is proof."

"Well, against all odds, and the odds are tremendous against him because he's living with two, maybe three people who are active drinkers and users, he's maintaining his sobriety. At least he says he is."

"I am very, very proud of you for the way you have given back. It makes me want to marry you again."

"Then why don't you?"

"Are you proposing to me again," Kim said warily.

It didn't take Franklin long to give his stock answer, which Kim had brushed aside multiple times, "Yes, I am."

Kim stood absolutely still for a long moment and then cautiously responded, "Yes, Franklin, let's give it another try."

Franklin's reaction was immediate and ecstatic; he pumped his fist, said "yes" excitedly and wrapped Kim in his arms. Of course, Franklin was keen on attacking all of the wedding details immediately, but Kim would have none of it. Instead, she maintained that they ought to just enjoy the moment, and Franklin reluctantly complied. Then they spent some time reminiscing about their first wedding until a clean Jeff appeared in the dining room.

"I hope you don't mind, but I used one of your disposable razors," Jeff confessed to Franklin.

"No, not at all. In fact, you must be good luck to me. I just proposed to Kim, and she accepted."

"You mean Kim is your ex-wife and your soon-to-be wife. I am confused because you sometimes talk about your ex-wife and sometimes talk about your wife. She's one and the same?"

"Yes, we divorced years ago, and now she has agreed to marry me again."

"You are in a good mood then," Jeff was looking for confirmation.

"I guess you could say that." Franklin knew that Jeff wanted something besides Franklin's forgiveness for his purloining Franklin's razor.

"I was hoping that you'd let me crash here until Sunday night. I have to be at work Monday."

Franklin glanced at Kim, and she gave a practically imperceptible positive shake of her head. Franklin specified, "As long as you don't use any alcohol or drugs, it's okay. But as your sponsor, I am entitled to know why."

"You know that guy who you saw in the restaurant the other day and who I told you owned a pharmacy in town, Jim Straka?"

"Yeah, the man who supplied your mother with Percocet for certain 'favors' shall we say."

"That's the asshole. My brother almost kicked his ass yesterday but somehow kept his cool."

"And…" Franklin knew there must be more to the story.

"My mother asked Brad to stop by the drugstore and tell Jim that she was sorry. She wanted her supplier back; she didn't say that, but we both knew that was why. I assume that he's going to take her back."

"I can see why you would want to be out of that environment. I wouldn't want to be there," Franklin sympathized and then added, "but until you find a place of your own, you will have to go back there eventually."

"Don't I know. But I hope in a week's time, this whole thing blows over and Mom gets him back or forgets about him. I just don't want to get dragged into this and risk violating my parole."

"Why would you get 'dragged in'?" an obviously concerned Kim asked.

"No offense intended, but you obviously don't know my mother when she runs out of bananas. You will do anything just to shut her up."

"Bananas," Kim was confused.

"It's just another street name for Percocet," Franklin advised.

"I will be praying for you." Kim betrayed her Catholic upbringing.

"Thank you, Kim, and congratulations on your engagement, if that's what it's called."

"That's as good a description as any, I suppose," Franklin confirmed.

"You know, I have never been to a wedding," Jeff said.

"Well, you'll be invited to ours then," Kim promised, "you might be one of the few people there," she added with a smile.

"You have never been to a wedding?" Franklin was incredulous.

"There aren't a lot of formal weddings in the projects."

"No, I guess not," Kim acknowledged.

The dinner conversation then shifted to Franklin and Kim, both reminiscing and regaling Jeff with stories of their first wedding. Jeff was relegated to their living room couch when Franklin and Kim went to bed. They engaged in pillow talk about Jeff. Kim worried aloud whether Jeff would avoid jail, let alone remain clean and sober. Franklin expressed his optimism at Jeff's chances of achieving both but his uncertainty regarding Jeff's brother.

"I have had this sense that something might happen to Brad which will involve us all to a certain extent."

"What do you mean sense, like a dream?"

"No, not a dream." Descartes said about dreams, "When I consider this carefully, I find not a single property which with certainty separates the waking state from the dream. How can you be certain that your whole life is not a dream."

"Oh, Franklin, there you go with the French philosopher crap again," she said with a smirk, "what does that mean?"

"It means that you can't be absolutely certain that life isn't completely a dream. But whether it is or not, I can't shake what you might call this premonition about Brad."

"Do you often have premonitions about people that you hardly know?"

"No," if you disregard the medical malpractice case that Sam handled, he thought.

"Then, I wouldn't lose any sleep over it." Kim's eyes twinkled. Franklin knew that Kim was amused by her own cleverness.

"No, I suppose I shouldn't." But he did that night, and that was just the start of it.

CHAPTER 25-SAM'S TEST BEGINS

Sam looked down on the street below from his window on the fourth floor. It was a typical January day, cold and gray and flurrying. He felt like shit and was baffled by its cause. All in all, it was a dreadful day, and it was only 10:30.

The words of an old Simon and Garfunkel song were an appropriate description, "Gazing from my window to the streets below, on a freshly fallen, silent shroud of snow." That's when his personal sound of silence was shattered by his cell phone ringing. Goddamn, it was Stuart Sonnenberg, the psychology professor. He wanted to ignore the call, but he reasoned his day couldn't get any worse.

"Hello, Professor," he hoped he had disguised the sarcastic edge to his voice. Maybe he didn't.

"Well, hello there, Sam. I'll cut straight to the chase because I always like to plan out my semester. Have you given any further thought to whether you can deliver a lecture on psychology and the law?"

"Stu, you only asked me a little while ago. I haven't had much time to think about it." Marcus had told him about how his ex-detested Stu's impatience. Well, she was rid of him now, and she had visited him upon Sam. Sam smiled wryly, and Stu was persistent.

"How about the third week in February?"

"That's fine." Sam was hoping for a quick exit from the conversation. But Stu apparently was in a chatty mood and asked, "What do you know about the Coalton County Jail?"

"I was in it a few times when I worked as a PD, but that's been years."Sam wasn't the least bit interested in Stu's motivation for asking the question. Not only didn't he care, but he felt as tired as he was after pulling an all-nighter, which he hadn't done since law school.

"Well, there's this woman named Annette Paulson, who is the jail psychologist. Do you know her?"

"No, I don't. As I said, it's been years since I had any contact with anybody in the Coalton County Jail. Stu, can we make this quick? I have a client waiting," he lied.

"I had a Zoom call with several of the jail psychologists from other counties, and she was very strange is all."

Sam's curiosity, having been piqued despite his fatigue, asked Stu why.

"She wasn't very sympathetic to the plight of her clientele, shall we say. It was obvious that she considered them the scum of the earth. She referred to them as her collection of zombies and petty thieves."

"Yeah, she doesn't sound like she gives rehabilitation much of a chance. Maybe she's burned out. I've seen it when you're fed a constant diet of antisocials."

"Maybe, but you would think that she would be more empathetic. I will let you get to your client, and I'll see you in February. I'll call you with the precise date."

As he hung up the phone, he began to feel sick to his stomach, And his heart began to flutter. He wandered over to the couch which was in his office but couldn't get comfortable; it was, after all, only three quarters of his body length. He shut the door to his office and stretched out on the floor. He thought that maybe if he closed his eyes, this feeling that his body was approaching catastrophe would pass. It didn't.

He would eventually call for Rhonda, and when she finally heard him through the office door and saw him lying on the floor, she called for an ambulance. His thoughts were jumbled until several hours later, but he did remember telling Rhonda to place his waste paper basket next to him so he could throw up in it. He croaked, "I don't want to ruin my new carpeting."

CHAPTER 26-NICOLE AND JOSH DISCUSS HIS TRIP TO THE JAIL

A few weeks passed between Franklin's visit to the Coalton County Jail with Jake before Nicole caught up with him. They were all sitting down to a Sunday dinner prepared by Phyllis (her father had been seeing Phyllis for several months now) and since she had set it up and therefore felt entitled to ask, inquired about his visit with Franklin to the Coalton County Jail.

"How did you like jail?" she asked lightheartedly.

"I suppose that if the reason that you had me go with Franklin was so I wouldn't end up there, it worked. I can say I wouldn't want to go there."

"That was the purpose, and I'm glad that you feel that way. Nobody wants their brother to be in jail." Nicole was content to leave it at that when Josh volunteered:

"Yeah, I don't want to end up like Jeff."

"Who is Jeff?"

"Oh, just some dude that Franklin drove home from the jail. He was released from jail that day, and he lives in what Franklin called the projects with his brother and mother."

"I wish him well," Nicole said.

Her father, who hadn't been paying rapt attention to Jake and Nicole's conversation, mostly because he was engaged and playing footsie with Phyllis, recognized an opportunity to extract gratitude from Jake. He gloated, "It makes you a lot more grateful for what you've got, doesn't it?"

With that, Jake put his arm around Josh's neck and, rubbing Josh's head with his knuckles, joked, "Yeah, and I've got a gay brother too."

"Do you mean the guy that Franklin took to his home lives with a little brother who is gay?" Her father was bewildered.

Nicole could see where this was going with her father, and she didn't like it. She interjected, "Gay people are people just like you and I. Any one of us could have been born gay."

"Is that what I am sending you to college for? So you can be fed that bullshit by your professors, little girl?"

"I am putting myself through school with my mother's settlement money, and it's true; homosexuality is not a choice. Some people have brown eyes and some have blue. That's true of your sexuality as well."

"I don't know what you're saying about it being like the color of your eyes. All I know is that my mother and my father didn't raise me to be no fag."

She could see that there was little percentage in arguing with Tyler, so she allowed, with a wry smile, "Father, you are incorrigible."

Her father's response led her to believe that she had been successful in defusing the situation when he asked, "What's that mean, little girl?"

"Basically, it means that you can't teach an old dog new tricks."

When her father responded with "grrrrr…" everyone at the table smiled except Josh, who giggled.

The remainder of the dinner was uneventful except for Jake's discovery of a piece of plastic in Phyllis's Apple cobbler.

When Jake went to his room after dinner (the boys no longer shared a room since Nicole went to college), Nicole waited until it wouldn't be obvious that she wanted to talk to Jake alone, knocked on the door of his bedroom, and entered.

"How are you, really?" she asked.

"I'm doing okay. I just wish I had more friends."

"I am thinking, why don't we plan on having you stay at my apartment some weekend? There is always lots going on on the weekends."

"I would love that. When?"

"I think February. How are you getting along with your father? I hope he wasn't too rough on you after your, shall we say, attempted sale?"

"Nah, he was okay. He screamed a little, but he didn't hit. Not like he did you right after mom died."

Nicole knew he was referring to a slap that their father had meted out when she had alluded to his possible responsibility for their mother's death shortly after the funeral. She didn't think that Jake knew anything about that. When she asked how he knew, he responded, "Both my brother and I knew. You could hear the slap all over the house, and then you started crying and slammed your bedroom door."

She was surprised that the slap had apparently had such a lasting effect upon her brother but, in an effort to diminish its continuing fallout, said quietly but convincingly, "That's water under the bridge now."

"And I hope that you're not adopting his intolerant attitude."

"What do you mean?"

"Well, judging people unfairly because they are different. For example, his comment about gay people."

"Nah, as mom used to say, 'it's a free country.'"

"It certainly is, despite the best efforts of some people."

"Do you know very many gay people at college?"

"Yeah, they are some of my best friends. In fact, there is an organization on campus called the Rainbow Alliance dedicated in part to eliminating prejudice against gay, lesbian and transgender people."

"That's good, I guess."

"Do some of your classmates still call you fag?"

"Yeah, they do. They troll and flame me online."

"As I told you, if you want, I will find you somebody that you can talk to."

"I will keep that in mind, but I don't think I need it now."

Their conversation then meandered to far less consequential topics, like how he liked Phyllis, drawing a "she's all right, but she isn't mom" as a response. Nicole and her brother then concluded what she would later call her "bonding session" with Jake and announced that she had to get back to Pittsburgh because she had class in the morning.

As she was driving, the thought occurred to her that she should email her thanks to Franklin for taking Jake to the Coalton County Jail and tell him that it appeared that their time together was of benefit. Her father, she felt certain, had not properly thanked Franklin. She barely remembered Franklin from her mother's trial and the one night during the trial that he had spent at their house, but her recollection was positive. She should call Sam and get his email address.

CHAPTER 27-JEFF CALLS FRANKLIN ABOUT BRAD

The reminiscences of their first wedding at irregular intervals went on well into the night after Jeff had left their apartment. Neither one of them mentioned what was one of the most significant events in their past life together: The cause of Kim's father prevailing upon Kim to postpone their wedding.

It was several months before their wedding date, and he had accompanied Kim to a work picnic with Kim's employer, which, at the time, was a law firm where Kim was a secretary. While Franklin made every effort to confine his heavy drinking to times when he was alone or infrequently when Kim was around, he had made an exception for the picnic. Or maybe he hadn't made a conscious decision to overindulge, he thought in retrospect; perhaps the lure of the mojitos was too formidable to resist; it didn't matter now. In any case, he had serviced copiers at the law firm and had become convinced that a young man of about his age was running an illegal gambling operation out of the office. Not that it was any of his business. At that point in his life, Franklin tilted at impossible windmills that bore little relationship to his life.

He recalls his nearly constant haranguing of the young man whenever he quite literally stumbled into him. Finally, the young man squared off with Franklin, and only Kim's tearful intervention averted physical harm. He had only a vague recollection of the incident, and soon thereafter, he had no recall at all. However, Kim most certainly did then and now. Thankfully, she didn't make reference to it that night: The night after she had accepted his proposal of marriage a second time. But it had followed them like a malignant specter throughout their time together.

Apparently, after the near–fisticuffs, he had somehow convinced Kim that he was fit to drive. When going through a tunnel, apparently, he had almost scraped the side of the tunnel several times. Of course, Kim was petrified.

He made it to her apartment, he was told, and promptly passed out on her couch. Thereafter, while he was unconscious, Kim's telephone conversation with her father ensued.

Franklin was, of course, uncertain of what was said during that conversation precisely, but he presumed the words "drunk," "fight," and "alcoholic" figured prominently. When he came to, he was informed of Kim and her father's joint decision that the wedding was to be postponed a couple of months while Kim, and presumably her father, monitored his intake of alcohol. The wedding invitations had already gone out weeks before, and Kim had even had her bridal shower. This was excruciatingly embarrassing to him, but he continued to drink, albeit more surreptitiously. Apparently, he hid it well enough to gain Papa's blessing.

As he lay there with Kim, he was convinced that their life together would be much different than the last time now that he had abandoned the demon rum. He was brimming with gratitude to all of those who had brought him to this point in his life. As these thoughts were playing through his mind as a prelude to sleep, his cell phone, which he had neglected to turn off as was his custom, played "Rolling on a River," which was his ringtone from his earliest days of sobriety. It was Jeff.

"Franklin, you said I could call you any time, and I'm sorry, but I need to talk to someone now."

Franklin could hear the near-panic tenor of his voice and knew from the time that he must be home. And, living as he is with two drug and alcohol-addled people, it was a fair guess as to what the genesis of Jeff's obvious discomfort was.

"Yes, that's what I told you. And I hope someday you'll do the same for another person who is trying to get clean and sober. It's your mom and little brother, isn't it?"

"No shit, Sherlock. How'd you guess."

Franklin thought that he was successful in masking his irritation over the lateness of the call, and now he had to deal with Jeff's sarcasm. "What's the problem?"

"Ever since Jimbo Straka cut off my mother, they have been on edge and bitching at one another. Mom thinks Brad's responsible for feeding her habit because she says he's young and healthy. I am afraid of what Brad might do."

"What do you think he might do?"

"I'll tell you one thing: he ain't going to pray and trust that God will provide."

"Is there someplace else you can go?"

"Not at this hour. Besides, I have work tomorrow."

"I don't know what to tell you, Jeff, except…" Jeff interrupted Franklin and exclaimed, "Oh shit, Brad's out here." Then Franklin heard muffled sounds, and finally, Jeff terminated the conversation, saying, "I'll get back to you."

Franklin then placed the cell phone on his nightstand, and Kim gently inquired, "That was Jeff, wasn't it?"

"Yeah, it was, and I am sure that the last chapter in the saga of Jeff and Brad is far from being written if it ever will be."

"I hope that it has a happy ending. Good night, love. I will remember this day forever."

"Good night, sweetie." Franklin knew that he risked disappointing Kim by not echoing her sentiment about her remembrance of the day, but he had a niggling feeling that they were just at the start of life-altering events. He briefly considered and then rejected any effort to convey to her his jumbled feelings about the future events of which they would be a part because he didn't know if he could translate the feelings into words.

He only knew that he, and to a much lesser extent Kim, would be players in a storyline that included them, Sam, Jeff and Brad. As if to further torture him, he couldn't shake the image of Sam walking very slowly from his car with something in his hand toward some type of facility. Perhaps an old folks home. He was up for quite a while trying to divine the meaning, if any, of Sam's intrusion into what should have been a day of unrivaled happiness.

CHAPTER 28-SAM AND INFORMED CONSENT

On the night before his triple bypass surgery, he watched the Steelers play in their wild-card game with Becca. His soon-to-be ex-wife brought his two sons to watch with him for part of the game; thankfully, she dropped the boys off at his room and went to the cafeteria until she picked them up midway through the fourth quarter. Then, his soon-to-be ex bent over and gave him a peck on the cheek and wished him good luck. Becca watched this with great interest. The Steelers lost.

After a dinner of veal parmesan, which Becca ordered delivered from a local Italian eatery, the two made small talk until the head of the cardiology group stood in the doorway to his room and announced that he was there to explain the risks (and rewards) of bypass surgery. He suggested that they go down the hall to a patients' lounge, which was unoccupied. He was hoping that Becca would accompany him, but she excused herself to go to the hospital cafeteria for a coffee.

As they stepped out of the room, a young man, who looked to be no more than in early puberty, rushed up to the older man and apologized lavishly for being "tardy," a word he had not heard used since high school. He asked the more senior man if he could accompany him, to which the youngster received a nod of the head. The older man then introduced them to Sam as they were walking down the hall, "Sam, as you might know, I am Dr. Ableman, a cardiologist here at the hospital. This young man is Dr. Carpenter, my resident."

The teen physician then said, "Sam, nice to meet you." Sam could hardly suppress his irritation at the youngster for calling him by his first name before he told him that that would be acceptable. He never called his clients by their first name until he was told he could. It was always Mr. or Mrs. or Ms. when he first met them. In response to the introductions, Sam merely nodded.

Interestingly, Dr. Abelman had a horseshoe mustache, which gave him the visage of a motorcycle gang member rather than a heart doctor.

After they had settled into their seats, Dr. Abelman explained what he already knew that the triple bypass surgery which he was about to undergo was routine these days and that the chances that he would make a full recovery and be better than new were outstanding. His attention was diverted during this presentation by the Chutes and Ladders box that he saw sitting on a table. He had spent hours playing that game with the boys. Those were pleasant memories; he hoped he would have more pleasant memories of playing the game with his grandchildren. Oh well, he thought, it was out of his hands.

As if on cue, Ableman was telling him whose hands would be intimate with his heart: "And you will be operated on by one of the premier cardiothoracic surgeons in Pittsburgh, Dr. Sharma."

Feeling jocular, Sam kidded, "Unless he has won the Nobel Prize for medicine, I don't want him."

Ableman laughed, and the teen doctor's face registered confusion for a millisecond. Then, when it registered to him that his superior thought Sam's comment was funny, he giggled.

"Look, I have one question. When can I get back to the office?"

"We will discharge you a couple of days after the operation, and if the healing process goes well, you can return to work in about a week. I wouldn't drive for a couple of weeks, though."

Having thus answered Sam's most pressing concern, he pretty much went into what he called his client mode: It looks like you are intently paying attention but giving your mind free rein to wander. When the doctors were convinced that they had adequately informed consent, they wished Sam good luck and Dr. Ableman told him that if he didn't see him immediately after the surgery tomorrow because one of his partners might be covering, he would definitely see him in about a month for a follow-up.

He spent the rest of the evening watching Seinfeld reruns with Becca. She engaged him in what he recognized as intentional small talk designed to keep his mind off of the operation. She was partially successful and when she left, she left a pretty relaxed Sam. He acknowledged her "pleasant dreams" directive with a smile and a nod of the head.

He laid there in a bed for which he could never get the head elevation perfect for what seemed like hours after Becca had left. For some reason, his mind dredged up memories of summers spent at the railroad tracks.

A few blocks from his house, there were railroad tracks that transported material in and out of the steel mills, he presumed. The heyday of Pittsburgh as a steel town was pretty much at an end, so there was no significant traffic on the track. There was sufficient traffic for him and his friends beginning the summer of his twelfth year to flatten pennies on the tracks, though. They would place pennies on the tracks and recover flattened and thinner pieces of copper the following day. He smiled at the thought of the controversy which periodically occupied his gang of friends as to whether they could be arrested for defacing United States coinage.

When they were not riding their bikes, they walked the railroad tracks and the undeveloped property adjacent and discussed issues of importance to boys barely pubescent: namely, the mysteries of girls and the female body. Of course, they sometimes smoked cigarettes that they had stolen from their parents and occasionally shared a can of purloined beer. He could almost smell the tar and creosote made viscous by the hot summer sun.

The daily trips to the tracks were all over by the summer after they were fourteen, but not before he and his best friend, Frank Aldrin, had discussed the physical attributes, and sometimes the personalities, of all of the girls in their classes. Of course, the most mysterious parts of the female body were the subject of some speculation since there was no Internet, only Playboy.

Somehow, the summer of his and his friend's fifteenth year saw increasingly infrequent afternoons spent at the railroad tracks, and by the time he was sixteen, it became only a fond memory, but it helped him focus his mind on something besides going under the knife on this night before his arteries were tinkered with.

He slept well and when a lady came with a cart ("bring out yer dead") and wheeled him down at 5:30 AM in the morning to be prepped for surgery, he was anxious to get this done and thought that it would be a less than significant chapter in his life's story.

The prep nurse who shaved his chest asked him what kind of music he liked, and said she would find a station that played that preference while she pruned. He responded to classic rock, and the station that she picked played "Another One Bites the Dust" and "Don't Fear the Reaper." When the anesthesia was started, he was asked to count backward from 100. Sam got to 98.

CHAPTER 29-NICOLE VISITS HER MOTHER

On what would have been her mother's birthday, Nicole was driving to her mother's grave. It was the second such visit that she had made during January. Her mother's date of death happened to be a couple of weeks after her birthday.

She measured the passage of time by what she was fretting about in each successive year. This year, as she was driving to the grave site with a wry smile, it was the semi – conclusion of her first serious relationship. She labeled it a semi-conclusion because he wanted to get back together, a desire that he made abundantly clear in the numerous text messages that she received daily since their breakup.

She had met the first-year law student at a college bar. While this might have been de rigueur for members of her parents' generation, it was far more common for romantic attachments nowadays to be preceded by an Internet interaction. So, right off the bat, her relationship with Steve had been unusual. Not that that, in and of itself, was of great significance because it wasn't, but their disparate backgrounds were.

Steve's parents were divorced, nothing unusual there, and his father was the founder and president of a major Philadelphia law firm and his mother was a poet. Steve had inherited his mother's creativity and casual approach to life and his father's disciplined and infuriatingly more conventional approach. This duality caused Nicole to sometimes label him laughingly as schizophrenic.

But that was hardly the biggest problem in the relationship. Rather, it began when Nicole thought that she might be pregnant. She would never forget their discussion of this possibility and his flippant attitude about terminating the imagined pregnancy.

"Well, we'll schedule you for an abortion. No big deal. In fact, you might be able to take that abortion pill, I don't know. But whatever, we'll take care of that."

"You don't understand." She was incredulous at his insensitivity. "You make it sound like it's a mosquito that you can just crush on your arm."

"Isn't it? After all, it's just an aggregation of cells at this point. Sweetie, I'm sorry to make you go through the pain, but having a child now would have a major impact on our lives."

She was near tears: "Our lives. I daresay it would have the most effect on my life. Who do you think you're looking at? You are looking at an aggregation of cells named Nicole."

"Come on, you know what I mean."

"I support a woman's right to choose, but my father wanted my mother to get an abortion. My sister was so much older than me, and he told my mother that he didn't want to start over again raising a kid. She didn't abort me, and ta-da, what you see standing before you is the incarnation of my mother's choice."

Steve had then attempted to hug her, a show of affection which she accepted halfheartedly.

It turned out that she wasn't pregnant, but she feared what she saw as Steve's thoughtlessness might haunt the relationship from that point onward.

She had her boots on and intended to make her way across the snow – covered field to her mother's grave, but, she thought, she might not get out of the car. If there was some vestige of her mother's spirit which resided here, it would understand.

While she was settling this internal debate, a pickup truck pulled alongside her. It was the cemetery's caretaker who she had gotten to know over the years and she had assigned a nickname, "Digger," a name which always brought a smile to his black, craggy face.

"Well, if it isn't Digger. Weren't we discussing your retirement when I last saw you?"

"Yeah, we were. Come June, I am going to hang up the shovel. Are you here to see your mother?"

"It's the anniversary of her death."

"It seems like only yesterday I was digging a hole in your mother's grave with a garden spade. I think you told me that the paper published your obit, didn't you?" Digger was referring to an obituary which Nicole had composed and which Digger, at Nicole's request, had placed in an old peanut butter jar in which he had formerly kept nails and screws in the cemetery maintenance shed and buried at Nicole's mother's grave.

"Yes, and now I am a part-time reporter for the Gazette."

"You don't say. And what have you written about?"

"I covered the protest and counter-protest when Clarksburg, West Virginia, was thinking about pulling down the statue of Stonewall Jackson that stood in front of the courthouse."

"You mean Clarksburg had a statue of Stonewall Jackson outside its courthouse?"

"Yeah, and I guess it's going to remain there, at least in the near future. They decided that it would continue to stand guard. Old Stonewall was born in Clarksburg."

"I ain't never going to understand it. They used to call anybody that wanted to overthrow the government traitors and hang them, but I guess if you have a whole section of the country bein' traitors, you get statues."

Nicole smiled and said, "I guess I know where you stand on the issue."

Digger chuckled and challenged, "Who do you think you're looking at? Of course, a black man wouldn't want the defenders of slavery to get statues like they were some kind of heroes."

Nicole grinned. It was the second time today that "who do you think you're looking at?" had made an appearance in her thought lexicon.

"Of course not. I agree with you. No offense intended."

"None taken. Missy, are you going to get out of your nice warm car and visit mom?"

"No, mummy's spirit can come over here. It's too cold and snowy."

"And I am sure that it will. In fact, if I was a bettin' man, which I ain't, I would bet that it follows you wherever you go."

"Ah, Digger, you always make me feel better."

"Now, go on and get out of here, Missy, and be careful driving back to that college of yours."

She blew Digger a kiss and began her trek back to Pittsburgh. Along the way, she thought that she would check in with Sam as to whether he had given any thought to the subject matter for her next article. Her call went to voicemail, and she left a message.

CHAPTER 30-JEFF TELLS FRANKLIN ABOUT BRAD'S ARREST

On the morning after his late – night telephone call from Jeff, Franklin was preoccupied at work with thoughts of his do – over marriage to Kim. He could hardly concentrate on his work, not that it required a whole lot of concentration. He had come to think of his job as a copier repair guy as simply a way station on the way to what he saw as his life's work: a drug and alcohol counselor.

He could hardly wait to tell Kim the idea which was rolling around in his mind. It was Paris; with his love of French philosophy, it was entirely fitting, he thought, to go to Paris on their honeymoon. They had discussed getting married in the winter months, and while he was eating pizza at a downtown pizza joint, he looked up airfares to Paris. He thought that they could swing the cost because it would be the off – season, and what could be more romantic than Paris for a honeymoon?

When he got home and finally broached the idea of a Paris honeymoon with Kim after dinner, she bristled at the suggestion.

"I thought that we were saving money for a house. It devastated me when I had to sell our old house. But you didn't see that because you had taken up residence in some tent down by the river.

Sartre said, 'It's quite a job starting to love somebody. You have to have energy, generosity, and blindness. There is even a moment, in the very beginning, when you have to jump across a precipice: if you think about it, you don't do it.'"

"Don't you see, I don't think I could love anyone or anything when I was drunk? Now, I love you with all my heart, and it's like falling in love for the first time. I am jumping across a precipice, and Paris would give us a memory that will last until we die."

Kim started to move her lips as if to respond and then apparently thought better of it. She stood there, looking bewildered, and then temporized and said, almost under her breath, "Let me think about it." Then, in what he saw as an obvious attempt to defuse what was becoming a tense situation, she kidded, "Do you have to have a French philosopher's quote for every situation? I really prefer French kisses to French philosophers."

He recognized Kim's ruse but succumbed anyway and kissed her passionately. They spent the rest of the night watching Kim's favorite shows. After spending years of only periodically being exposed to television, he was still amazed by the number of stations that were available. When the last medical mystery had been solved, and he and Kim were just about to retire, the phone rang. It was Jeff.

"The asshole has finally done it. He got himself arrested."

Although Franklin was almost certain that he knew who Jeff was talking about, he asked anyway for the identity of the asshole.

"Brad, of course."

"Tell me what happened."

"He tried to break into Jim Straka's pharmacy. The police caught him coming out of the broken window of mom's boyfriend's place. He had a whole boatload of pills when they caught him. I guess our mother thought that despite their breakup, he should still be her pill man."

"How do you know he was getting them for her?"

"Because she told me so. When the police called her and told her that they had arrested him, she went hysterical. Then she told me that she bet that she had caused him to be pinched because she told my brother that she didn't know who would keep her in pills now that that fucker Straka wasn't doing her anymore."

"Where is he now?"

"In the Coalton County lockup, I think."

"It's late, but I will call my lawyer buddy in the morning. Are you okay?"

"If you're asking if I'm clean and sober, yes, I am."

"Where are you now? Are you staying in your mom's apartment?"

"I am in the apartment parking lot, and it's fuckin' cold. I will go back in in a minute."

"How's your mother?"

"Passed out. Too many pills and vodka. She had a good excuse to get wasted with my brother's arrest."

"Well, as I said, I will call my attorney friend in the morning. I want you to get to a meeting after work, and if you don't need me before then, I'll talk to you after work tomorrow and report to you what the lawyer says."

"I am worried about Brad more than mom. You know, about the gay thing. You hear stories about young gay men who are locked up…"

Franklin tried to be as reassuring as he could, but he could tell by Jeff's tone that he had minimal success. When he hung up after what he thought was his valiant effort to comfort Jeff, he couldn't shake the ominous feelings that first had crept into his consciousness recently and were now magnified since his conversation with Jeff. Curiously, he believed that he saw Brad blowing smoke in a prison cell. This is despite only having met Brad one time.

CHAPTER 31-SAM COMES TO

When he emerged from the anesthesia in a semi-conscious state, there was someone who he took to be a nurse sitting right beside his bed in the ICU. He was restrained, and he was in incredible pain.

He turned his head toward the nurse, who must have read his look of abject confusion and terror through his facial paralysis, because the nurse said, "I am not supposed to give you any more pain medication than is scheduled, but I'll give you a little more."

This little bit more must have done the trick because he descended into a torpid state punctuated only by bizarre dreams that he was in a dungeon – like medical facility of some sort. When he next opened his eyes he confirmed that he was in something of a restraining system, and he tried to shout out, but his mouth was not working. This couldn't be normal for re-awakening after anesthesia, could it? He tried to turn his head toward the nurse, who was still present, but the effort exhausted him and a troubled unconsciousness descended again.

When he next grasped what he believed to be reality, Becca was beside his bed and appeared to have been weeping. She was asking the nurse, who continued to be at his bedside, something indistinct. Could it be that his hearing had been affected? He really didn't care, the pain was too fierce.

Becca spoke, "My Love, you are going to be just fine." Then, turning to the nurse, Becca quietly questioned: "He can hear me, can't he?"

"No, I don't think he can."

Sam rolled his eyes at the nurse's infuriatingly negative assessment and was certain that Becca caught it. That was confirmed when Becca protested, "No, he can hear. I saw him roll his eyes."

Out of the corner of his eye he saw Becca extract a tissue from her purse and dab her eyes. This confirmed for him: Becca had been crying. Ordinarily, this would have engendered a strong emotional response in him but he felt nothing. It was as if all traces of humanity save his hearing and his sense of pain had been erased.

Becca whispered to the nurse in a volume sufficient for him to hear, "What should I tell him?"

The nurse, apparently relying upon his opinion that Sam could not comprehend anything that was said, responded in a conversational volume, "I don't know. You know him better than I, but I can outline for you what happened during his surgery."

The nurse continued, "Stroke is a recognized risk whenever the body is opened for any reason. A stroke, as I suspect you know, is a thrombosis, or blood clot, and it can travel to the brain, cutting off the blood supply to a portion of the brain. When that happens, it can mean that a portion of the brain which regulates certain functions is rendered inoperable."

"And what has been 'rendered inoperable' in Sam's case?" Becca continued to whisper, but he detected in her voice some irritation with the nurse, which he assumed was because of the nurse's obvious indifference to what Sam heard.

"We might not know for some time. It appears that the stroke affected the nerves on his right side. He seems to have lost the ability to use language. They were considering transferring him by helicopter to a hospital that specializes in brain surgery to stop the brain bleed but the bleeding stopped on its own."

He heard Becca sigh, and he was certain that he knew the reason, which was confirmed by Becca's insistence, delivered with obvious friendly intent but firmly: "I think he can hear every word we say."

"Oh, I get it now," the nurse continued in a whisper that he nevertheless heard, "I think, and I'm no doctor, but I have seen a number of stroke patients, but I think that he may need extensive rehabilitation, and you might have to look into a permanent placement."

Becca murmured, "No, that would kill him." Then, directing her comment to Sam, she said, "He's a fighter, aren't you, Sam?" Try as he might, he could not nod his head nor make a sound, anything approximating yes.

Becca was tearing up again.

Then he saw a white – coated figure that seemed to him to be floating make his appearance in the room. Becca sobbed something that he couldn't understand and then disappeared. He attempted to activate his left arm and leg and shake off his restraints but his right side was useless.

The white – coated man, who he assumed was a doctor, solemnly disclosed in a British accent, "Sorry about the restraints, old boy, but you tried to get up at least two times and disconnected some of our life — giving contraptions."

The limey doc (that's what his father called the British) then proceeded to do whatever doctors do in a man of his half-dead condition. At the same time, pain relief continued to be his overwhelming preoccupation. His thoughts, at least those which he could identify as coherent thoughts, centered on the question, What would become of him?

He thought of his maternal grandmother who had had a stroke and was paralyzed on one side of her body. She awakened from a comatose state six months after the stroke event and could speak and make sense as well as before. Nearly every weekend for the three years that she was confined to a "home" until her death, he accompanied his parents and brother to visit her. He always thought that he would rather be dead than in a piss and shit – smelling environment like her "home". Now, the nurse was suggesting he may need to be placed in such a facility. Maybe, he thought, he could pull a trigger with his finger if he could get either of his hands to work.

The latest installment of pain medication began to have its effect as the Limey doctor was examining him for what he felt was certain to become the doctor's assessment of when he would die. He imagined there would be a pool amongst the hospital staff on the precise date and time when he would expire. As he was drifting another toward a painkiller — induced oblivion, his parting thought on this operative day one was of the catacombs which he and Becca had toured on their trip to Paris. In a scene that he would remember for the rest of his life, he was in a hospital bed in a cave – like a room in the catacombs right next to a room filled with skulls.

CHAPTER 32-NICOLE AND TIM DISCUSS HUMAN EQUALITY

When Nicole called Tim Black and informed The Greene Gazette owner and editor that her article might be a little late, she heard him laugh and complain, "You goddamn reporters are always late. What's your excuse?"

Nicole giggled and replied, "It's not like you're paying me like I was a reporter for the Washington Post." She and Tim obviously liked playing the game wherein she was a real reporter, and Tim was the owner and editor of a real newspaper, and not a small, community–based, weekly publication that resembled more a newsletter than a newspaper.

"Why are you unable to meet the deadline?"

"Well, we had discussed me doing a regular column based upon my mother's attorney Sam's cases, but when I tried to call him today, his secretary said that he had had heart bypass surgery this week. Is that a good enough reason for not making the deadline?"

"I suppose that it will have to be. I hope Sam is all right, but heart bypass surgery is routine now. I have several friends that have had it."

"Yeah, that's basically what his secretary Rhonda said, and she told me that he would be back in the office in two weeks."

"For what it's worth, I wish him well."

"Since you are so interested in me making the deadline, how about I try again to do some investigative reporting on that white nationalist group? The guy gave me his card and said I could call him anytime. You know, the guy that I met at the diner."

"I thought he made you sick, and he would me too. And I absolutely forbid you to investigate those horrible and dangerous people under my auspices."

Nicole stifled a snicker and said, "Yes, sir, Mr. Bradlee."

The reference to the managing editor of the Washington Post during Watergate prompted Tim's immediate reply, "How in the hell do you know about him? They must be teaching you something in those journalism courses at Pitt."

"Yes, indeed they are, but I will need to take a psych course to learn about these hate groups."

"To some degree, it's a natural human trait."

"You mean hatred is a natural human trait? I can't be that bleak about human nature."

"Well, it's only natural for human beings to think they're somehow special, or in a special class or group and somehow they are above other people. Didn't your father, or maybe a boyfriend, tell you that you were special?"

Nicole thought for a moment. Although her father didn't say those precise words, whatever his faults, he did imply that she was special, and her boyfriend, Steve, was certainly forever telling her that she was special.

"Yes," Nicole conceded.

"It made you feel good when you were called special, didn't it? By the way, I think that you're very special."

Nicole blushed, and mumbled, "Of course it did, and thank you."

"You are very welcome, young lady, and I'm not just BSing you. But the natural inclination of people is to look for something that makes them special. That quest for the speciality is the genesis of a lot of religious intolerance, racism, sexism, ageism and, dare I say, patriotism."

"I see your point about religious intolerance and the other isms, but patriotism?"

"Yes, patriotism. It's rooted in the feeling that you are somehow special because of where you happened to be born. What's that Country and Western song that they trot out during Fourth of July fireworks every year: 'I'm proud to be an American, where at least I know I'm free' as if you did something to deserve your freedom."

Nicole grimaced at the truth of what Phil was saying. Perhaps he was right. It's only natural to want to feel yourself better than other members of the herd. However, she needed some clarification.

"You aren't saying that these pseudo-Nazi groups are natural, are you?"

"Of course not, they represent the most evil of humanity's need to be special. Thank God that in most people the desire to feel special is tempered by some sense of morality. But remember it was less than fifty years ago that large swaths of people in southern states believed that black people were something less than fully human, and it was less than a hundred years ago when Japanese – Americans were sent to internment camps."

And he continued, "Young men were recruited in World War II by some of the most racist depictions of the Japanese. And eugenics, which was, and sometimes still is, a pseudo-scientific method to support racism, was popular in the twenties and thirties and even resulted in an immigration bill passed by Congress in 1924. The bill was particularly aimed at restricting the immigration of Jews and Italians."

Nicole appreciated Phil's sense of history, as well as his journalist's take on complex issues. In fact, she was beginning to view Phil almost like the father or grandfather that she wished she had, and she told him so.

She could hear the touch of surprise and emotion in his voice when he corrected her, "not grandfather, I'm not that Goddamn old." Then, she heard laughter.

Phil concluded the conversation with the flippant admonition, "And I hope that this will be the only time that you miss a deadline. Tell your attorney buddy that I wish him well, mostly because I want you to get a freaking story from him."

She would summon up this conversation with Phil often in the next few months as serving as her bedrock understanding of people's motivations, and Sam would be intimately connected with her stories, some of which she wrote about and some that she had just experienced.

CHAPTER 33-FRANKLIN LEARNS ABOUT BRAD'S HANGING

It was late in the afternoon of the same day of his early morning call from Jeff regarding Brad's arrest when he got another call from Jeff. After Jeff's emotionality of this morning, he hoped that this call would be nothing more than a routine discussion of the logistics of getting him to a meeting, but it turned out to be more, much more.

Luckily, he was in his car between jobs, so he could talk freely. Without a greeting, Jeff launched in, "They just found Brad hanging by a sheet in his cell."

"Oh my God, is he dead?"

"No, but he is just barely living. He's still breathing. At least, that is what my mother was told. He's being life-flighted to a hospital in Pittsburgh."

Franklin pulled over and coaxed Jeff to "Tell me everything you know."

"Mom was pretty fucked when she called me at the Winter Wonderland. But, from what I could gather, Brad called her from the jail and said something that made her think that he was jonesing for a cigarette because he apparently wanted her to bring him a carton when she was able to visit him. After that call, mom undoubtedly returned to Lala land, but she says she got a call from the jail a couple of hours later that Brad had been found hanging from a sheet in his cell, and that he was unconscious and they would be life – flighting him to Pittsburgh."

"Do you know what hospital in Pittsburgh?"

"No, I asked Mom, but she couldn't remember whether they told her or not. And when I tried to call the jail and find out, they gave me the runaround."

Franklin thought that, undoubtedly, the jail staff were huddling with their attorneys and trying to come up with the most innocent face that they could possibly put on this tragedy. As if Jeff were reading his mind, he blurted, "I doubt we'll ever know what exactly happened unless Brad recovers. I don't know whether you know this, and we never discussed it, but there are some pretty nasty – ass guards in that shithole."

Thinking of Darius, his AA sponsor, who just happened to be a Pittsburgh detective, Franklin was tentative in his claim: "I may know just the person who could do a little investigation for us."

"Who?"

"Let's just say he's a member of the law enforcement community. Maybe I'll introduce you to him someday. Are you okay?"

"Well, what do you think? My baby brother just hung himself in jail. If you mean, will I get fucked up? I doubt it. I think I will go to a meeting instead."

"Good boy."

Once he hung up with Jeff, he immediately punched Darius' number on his phone. Darius picked up after a few rings.

"Darius, remember I told you about Jeff, that young guy who I met in the Coalton County Jail and am sponsoring now?"

"Yeah, vaguely."

"His eighteen year old brother just hung himself in the Coalton County Jail, and from what I can understand, is near death."

"That's awful. What was he in for and how did it happen?" Franklin explained how he had just been arrested for attempting to rob a local pharmacy to supply his mother with Ox. "Was this guy a pillhead too?"

"Yep, the three of them lived in the projects and all three, mom and her two sons, are all users. I shouldn't say all. Jeff, the guy I am sponsoring, has a few years of sobriety inside and I think he's been sober and clean for a couple of months now since he got out."

"And you want me to see what I can find out about this kid."

"If you wouldn't mind. His name is Brad Moran."

"Anything more I should know?"

"Well, he is gay."

"Is he a white boy?"

"Yes, why do you ask?."

"Because if he were black and gay, they might have lynched him. There is a very, very rough element in that jail. I understand that there may even be a few closet Nazis among the guards."

"Look, if you feel uncomfortable making some inquiries…" Franklin thought that Darius might be hesitant because he was black.

"Hell no, I'm not reluctant at all. I'll find out what I can."

Immediately after he hung up with Darius, he tried Sam's cell phone again. He had left a message for Sam that morning, as he had promised Jeff, but when Sam didn't pick up, he left a message. Now, he left a second message for Sam, telling him that they needed to talk pretty much immediately. He must be in court, Franklin thought and quickly dismissed any of his more ominous thoughts.

CHAPTER 34-SAM LEARNS ABOUT BRAD

On his fifth postoperative day, he fell out of the chair that a nurse had placed him in and it was his introduction to what he came to think of as a caveman- like pictogram chart.

The day was also his first foray into the world of non-recumbent existence and it began well enough. Becca had found a dusty CD player, in which she had placed an equally dusty CD of the Rolling Stones, and it was playing constantly. A nurse had told her, within his earshot, that it was potentially beneficial for him to hear his favorite music. He imagined the Stones, a bunch of octogenarians, strutting around on stage and became depressed at the thought that he could no longer strut, even if he ever wanted to. Hell, he would be happy if he could even stand up and walk, which he had begun to doubt he ever would.

Of course, he still couldn't talk, but he had begun to eat puréed food because the medical powers that be thought that he would have enough mouth control to handle damn – near liquefied food. He had moved up the food ladder to mashed potatoes now, which his nurse covering the lunchtime shift apparently thought was a reason at least for him to smile. He had to put up with her constant harassing for him to smile. He didn't, partially because he saw nothing to smile about and partially because he didn't have the muscle control to accomplish even the slightest of grins.

After lunch came his tumble.. The whole process began when two nurses propped him up in a chair with pillows behind him. He was told that it would be good for his circulation or something if he sat up. Immediately after the chair-installing the nurses left the room and he began to list to one side. He continued his impression of a partially capsized boat for about fifteen minutes, and when he tried to right himself, he fell off the chair and onto the floor. Since he couldn't speak, it took him what seemed like forever whimpering until, at last, a passing nurse sensed that he was fully capsized, and the two chair nurses became bed nurses and re-bedded him.

Later that day came the pictogram chart. It had pictures of various everyday objects, and the theory was that he could communicate in some fashion by pointing to an object. Most prominent, of course, was a toilet. It also contained an alphabet, and it was explained to him that he might wish to spell out words and thus communicate in that fashion.

Although the letters of the alphabet were large by healthy person standards, since he had severely limited use of his one hand and no use of his other, he found it nearly impossible to point to a specific letter and spell out a word. He ultimately became too frustrated with this process and, in a surprising show of manual dexterity, was able to throw the chart across the room.

Rhonda visited shortly thereafter. He hated for people to see him in what he assumed was an extremely debilitated state. He had not looked in a mirror, and taking a selfie was completely out of the question.

"Hi, boss!"

He made a valiant effort to smile, and it must have taken because Rhonda compassionately said, "You have still got that killer smile."

Rhonda must have consulted with Becca and/or the nursing staff because she recounted all of his recent accomplishments, from his chair-sitting adventure to mashed potatoes. Only then did she mention what he was most interested in, how things were going at the office.

"Since I absolutely know that you're going to be back in the saddle before you know it, I have just been telling people that you are out for a few weeks, and, if pressed, I will tell them that you had heart bypass surgery, and are expected to make a full recovery. I don't mention the stroke."

As near as he could, Sam nodded his head. Rhonda understood.

Rhonda next recounted all of the building's gossip although he had only been out of the office for a few days and had heard much of it and didn't care about most of it. Then came a discussion of putrid petunia, Rhonda's name of the week for an attorney who referred personal injury cases to him.

His mind wandered and was refocused when Rhonda reported, "And she wanted your take on a commercial that she would be running featuring a cartoon version of joy for justice, as if she were anything but a cartoon to begin with."

She must have seen the flicker of interest in Sam's face because she continued, "she also mentioned the Coalton County Jail hanging and wondered if you would be interested if she could sign up the client's mother. She had represented the mother in a rear – end accident case, in fact, and I think that her boy is in this hospital now. Poor kid, they think that he will be a near – vegetable for the rest of his life."

"Oh, and Franklin and Nicole both called the office because they couldn't reach you on your cell phone, and I told them the whole story. I didn't think that you would object, and I thought you might like visits from the two of them."

Of course, he had no idea what the Coalton County Jail hanging was all about, and his recent pictogram experience had convinced him that he couldn't communicate by spelling the words out. He had an idea, though. He motioned to the chair on which the pictogram resided. He must have been fairly accurate in his motion, as Rhonda confirmed with him that he wanted the pictogram.

Rhonda laid it on the mattress beside him, and he made a valiant effort to point to the question mark. After Rhonda had made half a dozen guesses, which included that he was pointing at the toilet and a sweater, he gave up, and Rhonda got the message. He must have looked exhausted from the effort with the pictogram because shortly thereafter, Rhonda took her leave, but not before promising that she would be back tomorrow or the next day.

Luckily, he didn't have to rely on any aborted pictogram effort to be introduced to one of what would turn out to be a major event in his life. After a short, and he was sure medication – induced nap, a nurse brought in his dinner, which featured mashed potatoes and pudding. She had been tasked with his relearning to use eating utensils. The 6 o'clock news was on a local channel as he was attempting to find his mouth with a load of mashed potatoes.

The anchor intoned, "An attempted suicide by hanging at the Coalton County Jail has left a teenaged boy fighting for his life." This teaser was followed by several commercials, including a Joy for Justice ad, which thankfully did not feature Joy as a cartoon character. When the commercial break was over, the anchor provided scant details other than that the boy's name was Brad Moran and he had been jailed for attempted robbery of a pharmacy. Then, his old rival and nemesis, Dr. Stewart Sonnenberg, who was identified as a professor of psychology at Duquesne and a special advisor to the Allegheny County Jail, provided several soundbites as an expert in the field. No mention was made that he had acquired his "expertise" only days earlier.

He professorially opined that typically, jail suicides are committed by those jailed for the first time, had a substance abuse problem and/or had been assaulted by another detainee. *Christ,* he thought, *I could have told them that.* He supposed that he would be excused from lecturing to Stew's class, given the state that he was in. Little could he have imagined that not only would he be lecturing to Stew's class before the end of the year, but the lecture would have a great deal more meaning to him than he could currently imagine.

CHAPTER 35-TIM INSTRUCTS NICOLE ON THE WALL OF SILENCE

When Nicole next contacted her editor Tim, she had been to see Sam in the hospital and had discussed with her brother his link to the young man who had hung himself in the Coalton County jail. She explained why it wouldn't be a legally–oriented article in light of Sam's condition, which she described in detail, and secured Tim's approval of an article that focused on one of the town's councilmen, who was also the owner of the town's largest dealership. Their conversation then drifted to the Coalton County jail hanging.

"You know, my brother met the kid who hung himself."

"Oh yeah, how?"

"Long story. Basically, I thought that my brother needed to learn about the trouble he could get into with drugs, so I talked to Sam and he knew of a friend of his who ran an NA/AA meeting at the Coalton County Jail. He took a guy who had been just released from jail home from the meeting with my brother in the car, and they, the person who ran the meeting, my brother, and the fellow he was giving a ride to, all went up to this fellow's apartment in the projects, and he met the fellow's younger brother. That was the guy who hung himself."

"I heard from the news report that he had just been arrested for trying to steal Oxy tabs from a local pharmacy."

"That's what they say. You know, the kid was gay."

"Uh oh. The Coalton County Jail is not where you want to be as a gay young man."

"You don't think that the jail administration or guards had anything to do with it, do you?"

"No, but I daresay that some wouldn't be extremely supportive or sympathetic to him if they knew he was gay. Did they know he was gay?"

"I don't know if they did or not, and I didn't know that guards were supposed to be supportive in any event."

"They are in the more enlightened model. It's like the age-old question of whether the police should be primarily a paramilitary organization or more service-oriented."

"What do you mean?"

"I mean that there has always been, and frankly always will be, I think, this tension between guards' duties as being exclusively to maintain order or partly to assist in the rehabilitative process through being supportive of prisoners."

"But that doesn't mean that the guards or administration were involved in the hanging, does it?"

"It's been known to happen. Not so much actively involved these days, but there was a time… These days, it is more likely that, if they were involved at all, it would be what the law calls deliberate indifference. I learned that much from covering civil rights cases."

"What's that?"

She could hear Tim chuckling on the other end of the line. "No one really knows. But it's somewhere between negligence and intending the result. But this is all hypothetical. I doubt we will ever really know what happened to that young man."

"Why not?"

"Have you ever heard of the blue wall of silence?"

"Vaguely."

"Basically, it means that the police won't rat on one another, and if they do, they will be ostracized or worse. The same wall applies to prison guards."

"Sam told me that he has handled jail hanging cases."

"Maybe he'll handle this one, that is, if he recovers sufficiently and doesn't retire."

"Maybe he will."

She had her doubts, though.

CHAPTER 36-DARIUS SHARES INFORMATION WITH FRANKLIN

"Well, what did you find out?" Franklin was talking to Darius after an AA meeting. Darius had told him that he needed to go to the Coalton County Jail and interview an inmate regarding his knowledge of a burglary that occurred in Pittsburgh. While he was there, he had promised Franklin that he would "snoop around" and see if he could get any information on the jail hanging.

"I didn't find out much. I talked to a few guards, but they were suspicious of me. You know, I have two strikes against me." Franklin knew that he was referencing the fact that he was both a Pittsburgh detective and black.

Darius added, "By the way, they knew he was gay."

"How? He didn't announce it, did he?"

"No, some guard's son went to high school with him, and the son knew."

"And he spread the word around?"

"Apparently, because this guy that I talked to, Walter Schmidt, knew."

"Who was the guard whose son knew?"

"He wouldn't give me his name. Asked if I was on official business, and when I answered no, he said he preferred not to ID him."

"Did you get the feeling from this Schmidt guy that they were hiding anything?"

"He certainly wasn't what I would call forthcoming. He and the other guards that I talked to said it was a by-the-book admission."

"Meaning?"

"Suicide questionnaire didn't indicate any particular problem. He had a cellmate, who was apparently asleep when he attempted to hang himself, and he was visited by a couple of 'inmate rovers'."

"What the hell is 'inmate rovers'?"

"That's exactly what I asked. Apparently, they are veteran inmates who keep an eye out for any problems among new admitees, including any potential suicidal ideation. You have seen prison movies, I'm sure:

think trustees. It's apparently a fairly unique program at this jail. Schmidt talked about it with great pride."

"Well, apparently, it didn't work with this kid."

Darius took a sip of coffee from his Styrofoam cup and asked, "Did this kid make any phone calls before he did the deed?"

"The brother says he called the mother, but I don't think she was of much help. Apparently, she was the impetus behind the robbery; he was trying to get mom her pill fix."

"It probably would be worthwhile to talk to her further."

Then, Franklin's demeanor changed by degrees when he began to tell Darius about his plans to remarry Kim.

"And I think we're going to Paris for our honeymoon."

"I guess congratulations are in order," Darius allowed.

"Yeah, they are. And I want you and Sam to be co-best men."

Darius chuckled, and asked, "Is it going to be that big a wedding that you need co-best men?"

"No, I just thought that it would be an honor to have you two guys, who started me on my path to a new life as co-best men."

Franklin could see in Darius' face that he was touched, and he hoped against hope that Sam would be recovered enough by the wedding that he could stand beside Darius.

CHAPTER 37-SAM IN REHAB CENTER

On his last night in the hospital, somehow or other, his favorite nurse, Erica, had wrangled crab cakes for him for dinner. They were delicious, and he could easily chew them, even if he needed help to spoon them into his mouth. Erica on the assist.

It was late when the ambulance arrived to take him to the rehab center. It was also cold as hell, so the ambulance guys strapped him in with what felt like a blanket cocoon. He had to chuckle at the thought; maybe after a stint in the rehab hospital, he would emerge from his chrysalis a beautiful, rejuvenated monarch. He smiled, at least he thought he did; you never know how your facial muscles are going to move from moment to moment.

The ambulance passed by a strip mall that he and his friends used to walk to when he was twelve. They used to get cheeseburgers at the McDonald's, which happened to be the first place he kissed his high school sweetheart. He wondered what she would think of him now, wrapped up as he was like a pathetic enchilada. No use dwelling on that.

After what seemed like an interminable ride, finally, the ambulance stopped and the ambulance personnel unloaded their enchilada: him. Because he had arrived so late, he was wheeled down a bright hallway, unwrapped in a dark room and deposited on a garden-variety hospital bed. A curtain separated the room, and he assumed that on the other side of that curtain, there was a similarly situated son of a bitch. His eyes, which were darting about and trying to assess his surroundings, soon closed and gave way to trance-like slumber.

He was awakened by the sound of his roommate apparently talking to someone. In short order, he thought he was able to ascertain that his roommate was talking to his wife on a cell phone. The roommate was talking quite matter-of-factly to his wife about committing suicide. Apparently, from what he could glean from the conversation, his roommate was a pilot and was concerned about functioning in that capacity without a leg, which had been amputated. The wife, which he could hear very distinctly because his roomie had his cell phone on speaker, was equally matter-of-fact in her contention that an artificial leg should allow him to continue to fly. The conversation concluded, predictably enough, matter-of-factly, with neither his roommate nor his wife betraying any emotion.

Then, two burly aides yanked him out of his cocoon and quite literally dragged him (because he couldn't walk yet) to the bathroom. One of the aides remarked that, "This guy doesn't belong here. He's not ready yet for rehab, if he ever will be." They were then joined at the bathroom door by a woman who identified herself as an occupational therapist, who said that she would be assisting him and getting ready for the day. "And what a day it would be," she added, "physical therapy, occupational therapy and speech therapy were all on the agenda."

She then squirted toothpaste onto a toothbrush and told him to brush his teeth using his left hand; his right hand was practically useless, after all. He grasped the toothbrush and promptly, attempted to insert it into his forehead, and not because he couldn't control his hand, but because he thought somehow it belonged there. He would look back on this attempt to brush his forehead with great amusement.

After being put back in bed by the orderlies like a two-year-old and listening to another phone conversation between roomie and his wife (roomie reported to his wife that he had a roommate named Sam who couldn't talk and therefore could not provide him with the social interaction that he so desperately needed), an aide eventually deposited him in a wheelchair, and proclaimed, more to himself than to Sam, that he would be going to physical therapy first then occupational therapy and finally speech therapy. Thankfully, the aide was now not the one who said he shouldn't be here, implying that he was a lost cause.

They stood him up on parallel bars, and he was able to put 1 foot in front of another for maybe two steps with the assistance of the physical therapist in PT. In OT they had him attempting to pick up blocks with his left hand and drop them in a receptacle. He was unsuccessful ninety percent of the time. In speech therapy, they had him try to mimic the speech therapist's mouth movements and thereby make recognizable sounds. He only was capable of grunting like a caveman.

That night, Becca brought the boys out to see him. They put him in a wheelchair and wheeled him all over the facility. He was taciturn. He was tired and depressed. When they wheeled him back into the room, a rerun of Cheers was just coming on. He was capable of humming part of the theme song and even singing a creditable, "taking a break from all your worries sure would help a lot". Becca and the kids were shocked and then cheered enthusiastically. He even heard the roommate saying "atta boy" from the other side of the curtain. Maybe, just maybe, he thought, he could return to some semblance of his prior life.

CHAPTER 38-NICOLE AND STEVE VISIT SAM

She had convinced her on-again, off-again boyfriend, Steve, to accompany her, meaning drive her to visit Sam in rehab. While in Steve's Lexus convertible, which his parents had bought him, they were discussing the prospects for Steve's summer employment.

"My dad wants me to work for his firm in Philadelphia, but I can't see that. First of all, I want to be a trial lawyer, and my dad's firm only deals with corporate law, securities and tax shit."

"So, there won't be a Steve in Philadelphia," she teased.

"I want to feel like I'm helping humanity in some sense and not merely the rich assholes that my dad's firm caters to."

"Then why don't you become a poverty lawyer or a public defender? There are probably precious few of those that drive Lexuses," she goaded. She enjoyed getting a rise out of him because of his privileged background, but he didn't bite. For a few minutes, they rode in silence.

"Maybe you could make your career representing plaintiffs who have been injured or had their rights trampled on, like Sam does."

"I have thought of that, but I don't want to be seen as an ambulance chaser. And the advertising… DISGUSTING!"

"Then maybe the law isn't for you. Perhaps social work or the ministry…" she said with a grin.

"I couldn't wait to see my parents' reaction to me saying that after seven years of school, I want to be a social worker."

Her retort, "I have little doubt that social workers help make as many people's lives better, and quite possibly more people's lives better, than lawyers," prompted him to concede.

"You may be right."

"Maybe Sam could hire you as a summer clerk."

"From what you have told me about Sam's condition, he will be lucky if he works again."

That was a monstrously depressing thought, but she acknowledged that it might, in fact, be true. In her young life, she had experienced her mother's death and now the wrecked life of maybe the adult who she most respected.

"But", Steve added, "whether he recovers or not, he is what I would call an ambulance chaser, which I don't want to be."

Nicole bristled at the thought of Steve attaching such a pejorative label to Sam, but she said nothing. She hoped her expression would adequately convey her disgust with the statement. However, he was singing or more precisely saying, along to a rap "song" which was playing on the radio. When she last asked him how he could listen to that shit, he said that it allowed him to keep up with the "street slang;" besides, he insisted, he liked it.

As they pulled into the parking lot of the rehab facility, the sun had caused the recent snowfall to turn to slush, and Jeff suggested that he could pull out of the parking space and "deposit" her by the front door. She played the coquet and demurred, "No, but you could lay down your coat for me so I wouldn't have to wade through this slush." They both laughed.

When they reached Sam's room, Sam was sitting in his wheelchair, and smiled. "Sam, this is my friend Steve, Steve Black." In the first words that she had heard Sam utter since he had his stroke, Sam haltingly made a fairly good approximation of the word "pleasure" and shook Steve's hand. Steve then excused himself to use the room's bathroom, and Sam made a gesture forming his thumb and index finger into a circle, which she interpreted as a sign that Sam approved of her escort.

Acting on that interpretation of Sam's meaning, she conceded, "Yes, if you like tall, blonde, blue-eyed men with chiseled faces, I guess he's okay," she then added, "you know he's a first-year law student."

That prompted an obviously deliberate formation of an o on Sam's lips, and a second later, the verbalized, "Oh!" Then Steve came out of the bathroom, gave a cursory greeting to Sam's roommate, and joined Nicole and Sam.

"I am honored to meet the guy who got such a fantastic settlement for Nicole here and her family."

Sam made a bowing motion with his upper body.

"I was saying to Steve that if you ever need a summer law clerk…" Nicole could tell by the look on Steve's face that he wanted her to abandon finishing that sentence, but not before Sam caught the gist of it and laboriously responded, "Welcome aboard, Steve."

Steve just laughed dismissively, Nicole thought.

With Nicole pushing the wheelchair, they left Sam's room and engaged in small talk with Sam. It was very small talk as they toured the building. They saw the cafeteria where somehow Sam made them understand that he ate while he was a "remedial eater," meaning that he and his fellow remedial eaters had to be constantly monitored because the muscles and/or nerves in their mouths made them constant choking risks. Sam promptly announced that he had graduated from the remedial eaters. Of course, it took Sam quite a bit of effort and quite a bit of patience on Nicole and Steve's part to decipher what Sam said, but he made himself understood eventually. Nicole commented, "You have come a long way, Sam, and you should be proud. You will be back in the saddle again before you know it." Sam twisted around in his wheelchair and gave Nicole an appreciative look. Then Sam's face assumed a serious countenance, and he struggled to launch a single word several times.

"Dictaphone," he said.

"Did you say Dictaphone?" Nicole asked.

Sam nodded his head affirmatively.

"Rhonda brought it," Sam croaked.

"You'll be dictating in no time, I'm sure."

They came upon a room with chairs scattered about and a platform upon which a life-sized dummy rested. A placard on an easel with step-by-step instructions disclosed the dummy's purpose, which was obviously to be a teaching tool for a class in CPR. Nicole and Steve exchanged witticisms directed at the dummy. Sam grinned. Then Steve, a sometimes smoker, put a cigarette between the dummy's lips (who they had named Donald after a recent president), and they all howled. Their tour of the facility was complete, and Nicole wheeled Sam back into his room.

"Well, Sam, I will be back, but I am unsure when. You might be out of here before I can get out to see you again." Nicole bent down and kissed him on the cheek. He formed an O with his left thumb and forefinger, which she again assumed meant okay.

"Sam, you better be careful of using that okay sign because the white power movement has appropriated it. I recently attended a rally in West

Virginia when the county commissioners were considering tearing down a statue of Stonewall Jackson, and I saw many of the white power people using it."

Sam looked puzzled, and Steve mumbled, "I didn't know that."

"We were on the outs that day. Here's something else you didn't know," she revealed. "I briefly sat down with one of those white heritage guys after that. You know, to interview him for the paper. I ended up walking out, though, he was just too disgusting."

"And," she went on, "I learned from him that Coalton County Jail might have several guards who are in this white supremacist organization."

"That's where the kid who hung himself was jailed," Steve observed, directing his comment mostly to Sam.

Then, Nicole confirmed with Sam that he had handled a couple of jail-hanging cases himself, and Sam nodded. She thought she read his face as betraying a lack of enthusiasm, but she wasn't certain given his condition.

"Maybe you can help him out once you get out of here and back on your feet."Sam grimaced, and she was uncertain as to whether that was related to the first part of her statement about helping, or the second part about getting back on his feet or both. She didn't press.

On their ride back to Pittsburgh, Steve mentioned that he wouldn't mind being a summer clerk for Sam if there was a viable case on the Coalton County Jail hanging, and Sam was hired to represent the kid.

"I thought you didn't want to work for an ambulance chaser."

"Yeah, but that case would be interesting. In my senior year in college, I took a 400-level sociology course entitled Crime and Punishment in America, and I became interested in the constant tension between punishment and rehabilitation. Besides, the way we treat prisoners in some jails is downright inhuman."

"And what would your father think about you clerking for an ambulance chaser who was involved in prisoner rights cases?"

"Probably, he would think it's just a phase I'm going through. When he was in law school one summer, he hitchhiked and rode the rails all across the United States. In fact, that's how he met my mom. But that's another story."

She was going to ask him to tell the story but decided to leave that for another day.

CHAPTER 39-FRANKLIN AND JEFF VISIT BRAD

It was a blustery March day when Franklin drove into Coalton to pick up Jeff at his new apartment. He had promised Jeff that he would take him to the Meadows, the warehouse for the seriously disabled where his brother was housed. He pulled into the parking lot of an apartment building that undoubtedly was built in the 1930s and reminded himself that he ought to gush over Jeff's apartment, it being the first apartment that was his and his alone post–Coalton County Jail and all.

As he ascended the stairs to Jeff's apartment a question occurred to him. After the requisite gushing was accomplished he posed the question to Jeff, "Hey Jeff, did you ever tell anyone, especially any guard, that your brother was gay?"

"No, but my brother used to visit me, and once or twice, he brought his boyfriend along. Why do you ask?"

"Well, my sponsor, the Pittsburgh detective, asked one guard that question, and he said that he knew. I just wondered how widespread the knowledge was of his sexual preference."

"Do you think that he might have been harassed, and that's why he tried to commit suicide?"

"Maybe, but maybe we will never know." The statement was accurate, but he couldn't shake his visceral feeling that somehow Sam would be involved in investigating Brad's suicide attempt and his precognition that they would find out that a cigarette was an inciting event.

When they got into the car and began the trip to the Meadows, Jeff made the offhand remark that his mother tried to hire an attorney to look into his brother's attempted suicide.

"Oh, who did your mother consult with?"

Jeff laughed. "She didn't really meet with anyone. Apparently, she was so fucked up when the lawyer came to her door that she ended up leaving after five minutes of banging on my mother's door and getting no response. Her neighbors told me about it when I went to visit mom a few days later, said they recognized the woman attorney from television ads."

"Oh, who was it?"

"That Jen for Justice woman."

"I think Sam has some relationship with that woman."

"You mean the two of them are fucking?"

It was Franklin's turn to laugh. "My mother would say, 'get your mind out of the gutter.' No, I think that she refers him cases."

They made small talk on the rest of the trip: their jobs, the people that they had in common, and interesting occurrences at AA meetings. Franklin smiled and then chuckled as Jeff told a story about a recent meeting that he had attended in which an attractive young woman shared in a discussion that she was horny and the many young men who ostensibly volunteered to assist her with staying sober after the meeting.

As they approached the home, Franklin asked Jeff if he had any update on Brad's condition. "No, I only saw Brad twice while he was in the hospital, and both times he was comatose. My mom called a few times since he has been here, and all she could get out of them was that he was stable, whatever the hell that means."

Franklin only nodded. He was certainly not a doctor, but he thought what it meant was that Brad would need to be cared for the rest of his natural life.

Jeff asked a question that had bothered Franklin for a long time, ever since he heard about Brad's attempted hanging. "They say they always give the new guys in Coalton County Jail a roommate. I know that was standard procedure when I was locked up. If that was still the procedure, why didn't the son of a bitch roommate stop him or at least yell for a guard."

"Good question. "Franklin then posed a question to Jeff: "Have you ever spoken with a doctor regarding what you can expect in terms of recovery?"

"Yeah, I asked the neuro-man about what was wrong with Brad. He gave me some mumbo jumbo that I didn't understand. I think he called what happened to Brad a toxic event."

"You mean an anoxic event. That just means that his brain was deprived of oxygen."

"Yeah, I guess that was it."

When they got to the receptionist's desk, she politely asked who they were visiting. Jeff responded that they were visiting his brother Brad Moran, and the receptionist then shifted into officious mode and said that she would have to see their driver's licenses and have them sign in, "Because we have been asked by the police to have every visitor to Mr. Moran produce identification and sign in."

"Why, because he's up and walking around?" Jeff asked hopefully.

"No, I'm afraid he isn't."

"Then why in the fuck the production, excuse my French?" a perturbed Jeff demanded.

"It's my understanding that he is still technically in police custody."

Franklin intervened, "Let's just do what the nice woman told us to do. As Montesquieu said, 'Liberty is the right of doing whatever the laws permit.'" He noticed the bemused look on both the receptionist's and Jeff's faces, but Jeff reluctantly produced his driver's license. Franklin did, too.

When they got to Brad's room, which he shared with two other poor souls, the smell of human effluvia assaulted his nose. When Jeff pointed to his brother, who came with all sorts of attachments, he noticed that the floor around Brad was littered with medical packaging debris. Brad hardly looked human.

While Jeff tried to rouse some recognition of his presence from his brother, Franklin stood at the foot of the bed and imagined he saw a jailed Brad rooting in a backpack and extracting something, maybe a cigarette. It was such a strong illusion that it caused him to lurch backwards ever so slightly. When he refocused on the hospital bed and Brad, he saw Jeff bending over him, nearly in tears.

"It's all my mother's fault," he declared in a choked-up whisper, "she raised a couple of dopers, and she made life for Brad so miserable that he had to steal for her habit."

Franklin threw his arm around Jeff and was just about to offer an AA bromide, "We will not regret the past nor wish to shut the door on it," when a nurse walked into the room. A rather rotund middle-aged woman with a friendly face asked, "And what relationship are you two fine gentlemen to Bradley here?"

Franklin looked at Jeff to provide the answer, which he did, saying that he was his brother and Franklin was a friend of his, and then he asked, "Will my brother ever wake up? From his coma, I mean?"

"I'm afraid that only God knows the answer to that question. But in all my years of nursing, and there are many more years than I care to admit, I have seen some really strange things."

"Have you ever seen anyone as bad as my brother recover?"

"I have seen stroke patients who were basically in the same condition as your brother and who went on to lead productive lives."

Franklin thought that he hoped Sam would ultimately fit the nurse's category of productive lives regained, and if his feeling was correct, he would. He didn't have any such hunch about Brad, though.

"Look," the nurse went on, "your brother has had a brain injury. There is no question of that. But the brain is an amazing organ. We only use a small percentage of our brains. Sometimes, the brain may be rewired and pick up functions that a damaged part used to do. There is even a case of a baby born without a brain who was able to communicate and say mama and dada."

The nurse's pronouncement caused what Franklin saw as a contemplative look from Jeff, which all but evaporated when Jeff said, "I promised his boyfriend Kip that I would let him speak to Brad."

"I guess hearing the familiar voice of his boyfriend might be of some benefit," Franklin offered.

"Yes, you never can tell what they can hear and make some sense out of," the nurse concurred.

While Jeff placed the call to Kip, the nurse introduced herself to Franklin. Her name was Carrie, and she asked him why Brad was in jail in the first place.

"He broke into a local pharmacy and stole a bunch of Oxy pills."

"Oh, I should have guessed that it had something to do with drugs. It almost always does. Forgive me for asking, but boyfriend? Is Brad gay?"

"Yes, he is."

Their conversation was interrupted by a pitiful wailing originating from the speaker of Jeff's phone. Jeff then turned the speaker off, attempted to comfort Kip, and eventually hung up.

Directing her question to Jeff, Nurse Carrie asked, "Being a mother myself, where is your mother and in all of this?"

"Oh, she's around. In fact, her habit is the one that got my little brother here," his voice dripping with derision.

"Does your mother know that he's gay?"

"Yeah, but how do you know?"

"I heard you say Brad's 'boyfriend.'"

"I guess I did."

"How old was Brad when he 'came out?'"

"I guess he was around fifteen or so. I was still in jail when he told me."

"And what was your mother's reaction?"

"She had no reaction, really. She accepted it like Brad's blue eyes."

"Then she's a good mother with a drug problem, and I hope she gets help. She'll need help, especially when she has to deal with this," and she pointed at Brad and then muttered something about her rounds and left the room.

Franklin and Jeff stayed for a little while longer. Now that they were alone with Brad, Franklin felt uncomfortable as hell, and he could tell that Jeff did, too. When Jeff mercifully said, "I guess we'll be going," and kissed his brother on the forehead, they bounded out of the building, but not before they ran into Nurse Carrie in the hallway, who reminded Jeff to treat his mother respectfully and with compassion.

On the drive back to Jeff's apartment, they mostly discussed sports and Jeff's newly acquired knowledge regarding the wonders of the brain that gave him hope for Brad's recovery. Franklin smiled and nodded.

"Jeff, did your mother mention anything about cigarettes in the telephone conversation that she had with Brad before he hung himself?"

"Only what I told you before is that Brad wanted her to bring cigarettes when she came to visit."

Franklin nodded and wondered whether his feelings about that cigarette were a clue to the mystery of why Brad attempted suicide or some fanciful and illusory attempt to assist Sam as he had done in Nicole's mother's case.

CHAPTER 40-BECCA BAKES CAKES

When Becca came with the two boys to pick him up on the day of his discharge from rehab, she brought half a dozen little cakes that she had baked for members of the staff who were particularly helpful to his rehabilitation. It had been a month since he had come to the facility, a mute, non-ambulatory, non-self–feeding, toothbrush in his forehead mess, and he would be leaving as a close approximation of a disabled human, but a human nonetheless.

The first stop was the speech therapy room. While he was being wheeled there to bestow Becca's cake upon his speech therapist, Marcus commented that Sam's speech was much improved, but he wasn't sure if he wanted Sam's continuing silence because of Sam's constant dad jokes. His whole family was duly amused at all of Marcus' remarks.

Sam then haltingly related how it wasn't the first time he had had speech therapy. "I had it in the first grade as well because they said I couldn't pronounce my er sound correctly. My only memory of why I was sent to speech therapy was that the speech therapist was awfully cute." Whereupon, Becca giggled, punched Sam's arm and declared, "Always the eye for the women." The two boys looked embarrassed beneath their smiles.

When he presented the cake to the young woman therapist, who couldn't have been more than twenty-five years old, and he was wheeled out of the speech therapy room, he reflected on what seemed to him to be the bizarre incongruity between his hesitant, stammering speech when engaged in regular conversation, and his decidedly more fluid speech when he was dictating into his Dictaphone. But that wasn't the only weird thing that made no sense to him about his post-stroke condition.

For the last couple of weeks now, he has been communicating with his friends and coworkers by text or email. He was much slower with this medium now since he only had one functioning hand. He was gradually able to recognize the positioning of the letters on the keyboard like before, but he found himself baffled at times when distinguishing between the b and the d.

The next stop on the cake walk was occupational therapy, or therapy, in his instance, directed at hand dexterity. He was admitted with very little use of his right hand, and he was right-handed, with, pre-stroke, a minimally dexterous left hand. He had made acceptable progress in accomplishing the "tasks of daily living," as the therapist liked to call them, with his left hand; namely, holding a fork or spoon in his left hand and bringing it to his mouth, dropping marbles in a receptacle with his left hand and holding a pen in his left hand. His writing though was as large and tentative as a first grader. They said he might regain partial use of his right hand, but from what he read on the Internet, he would never again be able to take notes with his right hand. Thank God for cell phones because he hoped that he could type on his cell phone quickly enough that it would at least approximate taking notes on what another person was saying.

His occupational therapist was an attractive older woman of about his age who had presided over that first trip to the bathroom in which he had stuck his toothbrush on his forehead. During a couple of their early sessions, she wheeled him into the bathroom, helped him to sit on the toilet, and assisted him in getting back into his wheelchair. In other words, she was intimately involved in his most intimate functions, and he had a certain fondness for her that he hoped was reciprocated.

When Sam confirmed that this was his last day and that his soon–to–be wife had made her a cake, she was obviously on the edge of becoming emotional. She wished him luck and, turning to Becca and the boys, extracted a promise from them that they would take good care of him. Before he was wheeled out of the occupational therapy room by Marcus, he offered encouragement to a new admittee who was considerably older than him: "Don't worry, you will master dropping marbles in an empty plastic ice cream container with your left hand before you know it, and if you don't, there's not a great deal of demand for marble droppers out there anyway." He was proud of himself for getting out what was a fairly complex sentence for him and waited for atta boy. It never came.

Then, it was on to physical therapy. Becca presented the cake to his physical therapist, a doctoral candidate in physical therapy who was completing her internship. She had taken him from his first very tentative steps between the parallel bars, through the brace-making for his permanent drop foot, to his current state, which was walking about fifty steps with a quad cane and his brace. He would sorely miss his morning runs, but he supposed he was lucky to be alive.

When he was safely in the car with Becca driving and the boys in the backseat, they drove toward the exit and he caught a glimpse of the windows in the cafeteria. About a month ago, he was sitting in his wheelchair there, a speechless, nonambulatory, barely functioning shell who was struggling to get a spoon from the bowl of gruel into his mouth. He ultimately had to be fed. The snow was piling up in the parking lot that day, and he watched the cars as they spun out. The winter of his discontent, he thought and chuckled.

Becca asked him why he was laughing to which he replied, "Oh, nothing."

"We were afraid that we were going to lose you for a while there, but you'll come back stronger than ever."

He grinned in response to Becca's hopeful prediction, but he feared, no, he knew, that his life from here on would be forever characterized as pre-and post-stroke.

CHAPTER 41-STEVE HAS A DECISION TO MAKE

It was early on the third day of spring break when Nicole, in the midst of wondering whether she could and should go back to sleep, heard her cell phone buzzing from the nightstand. She briefly toyed with the idea of peremptorily silencing the damn thing, but she had to look at the screen to see who was calling her at this hour. It was Steve.

"Why in God's name are you calling me so early in the morning?" Steve was in Philadelphia for spring break.

"My dad has a staff meeting of all the people who are working on this particular project, and I am one of the people. He has it scheduled for eight, and I thought that I would call you before he drives me to the office."

"So, what's on your mind besides missing me?"

"You will never believe what happened to me yesterday."

"Do tell."

"I was bored to tears with all of this corporate tax shit, so I went out in the stairwell and had a cigarette."

"I thought that you only had a cigarette occasionally."

"Well, this was one of those occasions. But there are smoke detectors in the stairwells and apparently they are very sensitive. One of them went off, and, long story short, the building was evacuated."

Nicole couldn't help but howl with laughter. "Did your father find out about, how shall I put this, your incendiary nature?"

"I had to admit it to him. Besides, there were many people that saw me hightail it out of the stairwell, and I'm sure they would have tattled on me."

"What did your father say?"

"Well, besides saying he was disappointed in me because smoking is a filthy habit, he said that if I were a 'real' employee, I would be written up and compensation exacted. He didn't say what the compensation would be, but I would guess that it would involve being locked in a room with the tax code and forced to come up with ways to circumvent tax obligations."

"Are you sure that you want to work there for your father's firm this summer?"

"No, I'm not sure. I've been thinking that for 99.9999% of people who walk this earth, after they die, at best, their kids and maybe their grandkids remember them. Who wants to be remembered as a corporate tax specialist?"

"I think you have a decision to make."

"Yeah, I do. If I decide to stay in Pittsburgh for the summer, where would I stay? My lease is up at the end of May."

Nicole was certain that he wanted her to say that he could move in with her, but she deferred that decision and responded, "If you want to stay in Pittsburgh for the summer, I am sure something will work out."

An awkward silence followed before she agreed to pick him up at the airport when his flight from Philadelphia arrived the next week. She wished that she had her mother to talk to regarding what she perceived as a monumental decision: Whether to permit Steve to move in with her.

CHAPTER 42-FRANKLIN AND JEFF VISIT BARBARA AND DISCUSS BASEBALL

"So your mother is looking for closure," Franklin acknowledged to Jeff, "and I guess you are too."

"Yes, I am, but I think in my mother's case the guilt is eating her up. She blames herself for what happened to Brad, and she's not altogether wrong about that."

"Have you seen her recently?"

"Last week but I call her every day. Some days she sounds really fucked up, and some days almost normal for her. I called her this morning to tell her that we would be coming over, and she didn't sound bad."

Franklin had been recruited by Jeff to speak to his mother and her, as well as Jeff's quest, for closure and justice. He couldn't help but smile when he thought of those two words in tandem; every disaster in which humans played a role covered on the local and national news had victims' families looking for closure and justice. They were currently on their way to Jeff's mother's apartment on what Franklin hoped wasn't a quixotic journey. Jeff's mother was apparently seriously considering hiring an attorney to at least investigate whether a suit could be brought, and Jeff had informed him that she was enamored by one of the myriad television advertisers. He was hoping to convince her to give Sam a shot, that is, if he felt up to taking it on and thought that it would be worth investigating.

"By the way, has your mother ever been out to visit Brad?"

"No. How would she get there? I understand that she asked that piece of shit Straka to take her, but he told her no because he said the police had questions since it was his drugstore that Brad broke into."

When they arrived at Jeff's mother's apartment, he searched his memory for her name (it was Barbara). Once Jeff used his key to enter it, they encountered a neatly ordered living room that reeked of cigarette smoke. From the bedroom, an obviously dyed blonde, slightly overweight, attractive middle-aged woman with an excess of makeup emerged. Without speaking, she threw her arms around Jeff.

"Jeffy, Jeffy, Jeffy, what are we going to do about our little boy?"

Jeff and his mother embraced, and then Jeff, gesturing toward Franklin, murmured diffidently, "You may remember my sponsor, Franklin."

Barbara gushed, "Of course I do. You're keeping my son on the straight and narrow."

"Well, he's doing it himself," Franklin gently corrected, "sobriety is an inside job."

They then confronted the real agenda for the meeting: How should Barbara go about investigating Brad's attempted suicide? It seems Barbara had called one of the local station's hotlines, and they had advised her that the surest way to get accurate information was to file a suit.

"And I was thinking of hiring that attorney couple who advertises on television all the time. They look like they get along so well together, and when he kisses her hand at the end…"

"Mom," Jeff could not disguise his exasperation, "that's just marketing bullshit. I bet they hate one another. And that's part of the reason that I brought Franklin here. He knows an attorney who has handled these types of cases before."

Franklin seized the moment, "Yeah, I have a very dear friend who has handled three or four jail hanging cases, successfully I think. He's just getting back to the office now after surgery, and I can't guarantee that he would even be interested in Brad's case, but I will be happy to see if he is. His name is Sam Wright."

"Will I have to pay him anything?"

"Not unless he gets you money. As one of the television commercials says, 'we take no reward, unless their ox gets gored', or something like that."

"As long as it won't cost me anything, your friend would be fine if he's interested."

"Good. I think he'll be out in the next couple of weeks if he is interested. I will let Jeff know."

"By the way, Mom, don't you think you should let Jeff's dad know about Brad, I mean?"

"I tried to call him once on his cell phone, but the call went straight to voicemail, and I guess it's somebody else's phone number."

"Why don't you just call your dad yourself, Jeff? Surely you know your way around a computer well enough that you should be able to find him," Franklin proposed.

"Different fathers," was Jeff's terse response, and then, Franklin thought intentionally. Jeff redirected the conversation by complimenting his mother's housekeeping acumen, "It's sure a lot neater than it was when I was living here. And you look great, Mom."

During the rest of their visit, Jeff and his mother's conversation vacillated between family reminiscences and what Franklin could tell were attempts to pry from his mother information regarding the state of his mother's relationship with Straka. Mom successfully parried these efforts. When the conversation became too incendiary, Franklin told Jeff that he would meet him in the car and left the two of them to verbally duke it out.

When Jeff appeared in the doorway of the complex and made the short walk to Franklin's car, Franklin started the car, and they rode wordlessly for a few minutes.

"Aren't you going to ask what my mother and I got into it over?"

"All I figured if you wanted me to know, you would tell me."

"Basically, it was over Straka and I wanted her to get clean and sober, and that's not going to happen as long as he's around."

"Your mother is a good person who has a disease."

"Yeah, she is. She sure loves her two boys, and now, one of them is a vegetable."

"I'm curious about one thing: when I first met you, you said that she blamed his father for being gay. Yet, when we were talking to the nurse at your brother's home, you said that your mother had accepted him being gay as she would his blue eyes."

"Well, both are true."

"And in the couple of months I have known you, I had no idea that you and Brad had different fathers. I know Brad's father is around someplace because your mother called his cell phone, but what happened to your father?"

"He's dead. Killed himself driving drunk. But he was a good dad while he lasted."

"I'm sorry."

"He died when I was twelve. He used to take me practically every weekend, and during the summer months, he would take me to my minor league and then Little League games. Hell, he was even my coach for a couple of years in the minor leagues. That's what they used to call the baseball league for six through ten-year-olds."

"He sounds like he was a good father."

Then, Jeff appeared to ask a question out of left field, "Have you ever seen a movie called The Pride of St. Louis?"

"Yeah, I think so. It was on a Saturday afternoon matinee movie on television. It's an ancient movie. Wasn't it about the pitcher for the St. Louis Cardinals named Dizzy Dean? Anybody that knows baseball history knows that Dizzy Dean was a Hall of Fame pitcher during the 30s and 40s."

"I can tell that you're wondering why I brought up Dizzy Dean. Well, you were curious when we first met about my writing, and I'm going to read you something that I wrote about my dad, Dizzy Dean, and baseball."

With that curtain-raising preface, Jeff pulled out his cell phone and began reading, "I always wanted to be a pitcher, maybe like Dizzy Dean, only I would be more careful with my rifle. As a seven-year-old, my father coached a team and let me relieve the pitcher on occasion when he had to relieve himself behind the backstop. I wanted to start though. Dizzy Dean would never have made it if he had to be relieved all the time. One day, while playing catch with my father, I threw the ball in a new way. It was my first fastball. I only threw changeups before. My father agreed to let me start. I can remember the power of standing on the mound with a shiny new Wilson in my hand. Three walks, a double and a home run later returned me to my former status of first baseman indefinitely. My pitching dream followed me through six more years of dugouts. Finally, I got another chance. The coach let me start against the best team in the league. I was a secret weapon. For three innings, I held them hitless and struck out eight. But in the fourth, my arm fell off in the dust beside the mound. I had to spit the ball over the plate. I have good control of my mouth but no speed. They scored six runs before the manager brought in a guy who still had his right arm from the bullpen. There is probably some kind of occupational hazard among pitchers, they are always losing appendages. Dizzy Dean lost his leg, and I lost the speed of my right arm and a dream."

Franklin smiled and acknowledged, "Very creative." From that moment on, his relationship with Jeff, and to some degree Barbara, morphed in practically imperceptible degrees from helpful supporter to something much more.

CHAPTER 43-SAM AND RHONDA MEET BARBARA

In the month since he was discharged from rehab, he had gone from spending a substantial portion of his time while he was in the office in a wheelchair to essentially being able to walk into the building, take the elevator up and into his office, and negotiate any place in the office on his own two feet; of course, his drop foot was in a brace and it trailed significantly behind his good leg. Since he only had his left hand, his right hand and arm dangled uselessly, and he still had to have Rhonda get his coffee; further, he suspected that he would always be unable to carry an open coffee cup. But he had mastered getting a diet Pepsi and carrying it back to his office.

He still had Becca drop him off at his office in the morning and pick him up in the evening, and he feared that he would never drive again. Consequently, when his physiatrist suggested he enroll in a hospital–sponsored course to re-train handicapped drivers, he was overjoyed. If he couldn't run, walk any more than a block, and even then on flat, unobstructed surfaces, at least the mechanized form of transportation might still be available.

But he hadn't taken a single lesson yet, so he had to recruit Rhonda to transport him to Barbara Moran's apartment in Coalton. He had promised Franklin that he would at least talk to her and had hoped that Franklin could drive him to her place. Unfortunately, Franklin had to deal with a photocopier emergency, whatever that was, on this their scheduled appointment day with Barbara Moran. His paralegal was on vacation, and he hadn't completed the interviews for the hiring of a young lawyer associate when he became stroke-stricken. (He liked the alliteration of that description.) Consequently, he had Rhonda drive him.

It was a bright April day when Rhonda brought the car around to the sidewalk in front of his office, where he was waiting. Rhonda questioned whether she should bring his wheelchair, but he nixed that, saying he could walk. On their drive, he brought Rhonda up to speed on the particulars of the case.

"Oh, that poor kid," Rhonda moaned, "had he ever been in trouble before?"

"No, I don't think so."

"And he was stealing the pills for his mother?"

"Yes, that's the story his brother tells."

"So… Barbara and the pharmacist were screwing and she was getting her pills from him; he broke it off and cut off her supply, so her son burglarized his pharmacy and stole some pills, leading to his arrest."

"That's more or less it in a nutshell. Her son then hung himself in jail and is now a vegetable."

"Wow! You sure do get some interesting cases, boss."

"I doubt whether this is the case. The burden of proving a civil rights case against a government is extremely high."

"Why is it a civil rights case?"

"Because it would be a suit against a municipality alleging that protected rights were violated, the right to be free from cruel and unusual punishment, and the right of prisoners to have access to proper medical and psychiatric treatment.."

"Sounds complicated."

"It is. That's why these cases are so difficult."

"I didn't know that prisoners even had rights."

"That's another reason that these cases are so difficult. You have to convince a jury not only that they have rights but that they deserve to be compensated for a violation of those rights."

When Rhonda dropped him off in front of the building, the moment before she joined him to enter the complex, he thought of the many times he had been in similar government-subsidized buildings to interview witnesses for his job as a public defender. These were rough places where drug and alcohol abuse was rampant.

After Rhonda had parked the car, and they entered the building, he immediately encountered a situation unique to a one-handed, handicapped person: there was only a hand railing on the right side of the stairs, and he was forced to mount the steps backward.

When his laborious ascent was complete, and Rhonda knocked on the door, the woman who stood at the door's threshold, and who he assumed was Barbara, appeared to focus her gaze on his quad cane. Damn, he thought, wait until she hears my halting speech.

Then Barbara, who looked as if she was a real beauty in her younger years, offered them coffee, and he introduced himself and Rhonda as his legal assistant. Rhonda liked to be introduced by that title now that the word secretary had fallen into disuse, and he embraced that moniker as more descriptive than secretary. Rhonda was much more to him than just a typist.

They settled in on a couch that smelled of stale cigarette smoke, and he caught a whiff of a vaguely chemical odor; could it have been a peroxide for her hair?

He asked the typical preliminary questions and was somewhat impressed that he got through them with no stumble. When he asked if her son had ever been in trouble with the law before, he mispronounced the law as lawn, quickly corrected himself, and smiled at his mistake. He thought he saw Barbara's eyebrows raise ever so slightly. "No, he was a good boy," was her response.

He established that Brad was a high school senior and then stammered an apology for asking this question: "I understand from Jeff that Brad was gay. Because it might have something to do with his attempted hanging in the jail, was he gay? And was his sexual preference widely known?"

"Brad did nothing to hide it. What you saw with Brad is what you got. I love that about him."

"So, some of his classmates knew. Can we assume that some of their parents knew, too?"

"Yeah, I guess so."

"What I am trying to get at," he prodded haltingly, "is whether you think that any of the people who he came in contact with, guards or otherwise, knew he was gay?"

"I wouldn't be surprised."

Sam then excused himself to go to the bathroom and struggled to get up off the couch. Finally, using his quad cane for leverage, he was able to rise without Rhonda's proffered assistance. While he was in the bathroom, he heard Barbara quite distinctly, "Do you think he's up for this?"

"He's one of the best lawyers in this town. He'll be alright." When he emerged, Sam explored Barbara's relationship with Straka, and the reason why Brad is burglarizing pills from his pharmacy.

"Lemmee set the record straight on this. Did I occasionally get pills from Jim? Yes, I did when I ran low on a prescription. I have neuralgia, you know, and I have a doctor prescribed OxyContin for me. As far as what Brad was doing breaking into the drugstore, I have no idea. He wasn't doing it for me."

"How would you describe your relationship with Jim Straka."

"We're just old friends, is all. Jim's married, you know. I have known him since high school."

"Did Brad have a problem with pills?"

"Half the kids in the projects do. What do you think?"

After a desultory conclusion to his interview, Sam explained what he perceived as the only way to get answers regarding what happened to Brad was to file a lawsuit "because only by filing a lawsuit, and putting the jail personnel under oath will we stand any chance of uncovering any liability that the jail may have for what happened to Brad. But", Sam cautioned, "there may not be any liability. We need to prove that the jail was deliberately indifferent to the possibility that Brad was suicidal, and that is damn near impossible to prove."

"But, you will take the case?"

"Yes, but I want you to understand that I am going to withdraw or quit as your attorney unless there is a real possibility that we will win or settle the lawsuit."

He then concluded the interview with the mundane issues of what a contingent fee agreement is, the necessity of appointing her as guardian for purposes of the lawsuit and a brief description of how he thought the lawsuit might progress. Then, almost as an afterthought, he asked in an embarrassingly halting fashion, at least that's what he thought, "Did Brad ever mention cigarettes to you when he called?"

"Yeah, but just that he was dying for one. Oh my God, that's an awful thought." She teared up. "Why do you ask?"

"It's not important."

Barbara signed the contingent fee agreement, and he and Rhonda left the apartment. Thankfully, he was able to go down the steps while forward-facing because the banister was on his left side.

When they were in the car and out of the parking lot, Rhonda challenged, "Sam, I have a few questions about what went on in there. Sort of a post-game interview of you."

Sam responded, "Fire away," but it came out sounding more like fur away. Rhonda got it.

"First of all, she seemed pretty normal to me. Do you think she could be telling the truth, and she only takes what is prescribed to her?"

"Addicts can act normally for a little while, and I've seen it in my days as a public defender. And Franklin told me that her other son, whom he knows quite well, says she's an Oxy abuser. In fact, that's the reason I asked her about her relationship with the pharmacy owner, Straka, who, according to the info that Franklin got from her other son, was supplying her with pills in exchange for sex."

"Then why did Brad break in if she was getting her pills in exchange for certain services."

"Apparently, they had some sort of falling out and he cut her off. I take it that they have kissed and made up."

"One last question: Why in the hell did you ask about cigarettes?"

"Because Franklin told me that he had one of his premonitions that Brad's suicide attempt was related to cigarettes or smoking. He couldn't be more specific than that."

"His visions sure helped you on Nicole's mother's case."

Sam smiled and remarked, "That's why I asked the question."

CHAPTER 44-NICOLE AND STEVE DISCUSS HIS SUMMER PLANS

Nicole was seriously flummoxed by what she was going to write this week for her bi-weekly piece that ran in both the print and online versions of The Greene Gazette. She had profiled all of the county and municipal political figures, at least those that were the least bit interesting, and had even gone so far as to have played food critic at the diner down the block from The Greene Gazette's office. She had contemplated doing a semi-regular piece on Sam's interesting cases, but poor Sam had his own problems now, although he appeared to be recovering. Still, she didn't want to bother him now.

So she decided to call Phil and see what he would suggest. "Phil, who should I write about for my column? I was thinking about interviewing a cop about his or her most interesting experiences."

"How about a prison guard? They have one of the most thankless jobs that I can imagine. They get a lot of bad press. And there was the thing at the Coalton County Jail, which could very well end up being placed at the guard's feet."

"Good idea! Who do you know? You are the guy with the local connections."

"I know, or knew of a few of them. Let me get back to you on that. You envision it as a puff piece?"

"Yes not investigative although if I happen to trip over something... Why do you say the Coalton County Jail thing? Do you think that the guards had something to do with that?"

"The keepers are always implicated when something bad happens to the kept."

"Do you know any prison guards at the Coalton County Jail?"

"No, only the Greene County Jail."

"How am I ever going to win the Pulitzer Prize when my editor doesn't send me where the action is?" she smiled, then announced, " My boyfriend is buzzing in, so I will get that name from you later."

"I will get back to you in a few," Phil assured her, and with that, Nicole connected with Steve.

"What's up?" she asked tentatively; they were moving into their "off again" phase rapidly.

"Guess what? I think Sam just offered me a job as his summer clerk."

"Oh yeah, and why didn't you tell me you had been in contact with Sam."

"It just happened. I was sitting here thinking that in two weeks, I would be working at my father's firm. I thought about how awful that would be, so I picked up the phone and called Sam's office. He was in. He remembered me from our visit to the rehab, asked me about my grades, and when I told him that I would be looking for a summer clerkship, he onboarded me."

"WTF, on-boarded? Is that a new expression? Did he 'reach out' to you? That is another expression that I hate."

"I asked him if he was going to be involved in the Coalton County Jail hanging case, and he told me that he had been retained."

Although she knew to be near certainty about what the answer to her next question was going to be, she posed it anyway, "And where are you going to live while you are advocating for prisoners' rights?"

"Well, I thought I might move in with you."

"I already have a roommate."

"Yes, but you don't have a bedmate."

She smiled and said, "That's true." He and she could rely on his rich daddy if it didn't work out.

CHAPTER 45-FRANKLIN TALKS TO PROF. SONNENBERG

Franklin was almost asleep in the lecture hall when he heard Professor Sonnenberg say that he had been made the Allegheny County Jail psychologist. That got his attention. He mentioned various psychological issues of the prison populace. Prison suicides were among the most vexing. He explained that the leading cause of deaths in jails and prisons was prisoners taking their own lives.

He noted that, unsurprisingly, a significant percentage of those incarcerated are people from marginalized communities and are confronted with issues of poverty, substance abuse and mental illness, as well as unemployment and homelessness. With respect to mental illness and behavioral health issues, typically, there is a paucity of mental health treatment services designed to prevent, detect or respond to mental health crises. Some sixty-three percent of the jail population have experienced drug dependence or abuse, and forty-four percent reported having had symptoms of a mental health disorder in the prior year.

Then he said," The serious mental health needs of the typical prison populace are not met with correspondingly serious psychological and psychiatric treatment. One study found that only one-quarter of New York City corrections staff reported completing suicide prevention training, and a recent investigation of an Indiana jail found that many suicide attempts occurred openly, including among people on suicide watch or those being monitored by video. The latest available data suggests that sixty-two percent of jailed inmates were not receiving mental health care."

"Finally, there are the conditions inside most jails that are not conducive to the maintenance of mental health by even the most healthy minds. Bright lights, threats of bodily harm, enforced confinement, unsanitary conditions and loud and unpredictable noise are all part of the typical jail experience."

He continued to expand on what he termed "the sorry state of incarceration in America" and spouted numerous studies and statistics that he contended proved his point. He mentioned the three goals of imprisonment, which are punishment, rehabilitation, and deterrence, and contended that only the punishment goal might be effectively reached. Professor Sonnenberg cited numerous studies that proved that deterrence and rehabilitation were essentially only paid lip service in most jails.

As the professor was reaching the concluding remarks of his lecture, he mentioned, almost offhandedly, that he intended to bring a guest lecturer who had been a public defender. This attorney could speak to the environmental factors that he thought contributed to crime, but he cautioned that he was uncertain that the proposed guest lecturer could make it to health problems. Franklin knew in an instant that he was talking about Sam.

When the lecture was over, and as students were filling out, he joined the queue of ass–kissers who hoped that their apparent interest in the professor's remarks would translate into A's, and when he got to the front, asked, "Professor, were you talking about Sam Wright as the person who you wanted to be a guest lecturer?"

"Yes, I was. How do you know Sam?"

"I worked for Sam for a while." Franklin smiled inwardly: he had served as Sam's "pack mule," carrying boxes of evidence during the malpractice trial on behalf of Nicole's mother.

"I guess you know him from the public defender's office. I know from the crime shows that criminal defense attorneys frequently have psychologists testify," Franklin added.

"Let's just say we have a mutual ex-friend."

"Professor, I have a question. You said that you have been recently hired as the jail psychologist. Have you ever heard of jails hiring inmates, trusted inmates, to be suicide prevention workers or rovers? They would, I guess, tip off the jail staff if they thought an inmate posed a suicide risk among new admittees."

"I think I have heard of it, but you have got to be careful giving any inmates any authority over other inmates."

"To paraphrase Rousseau, you mean that no prisoner should have any natural authority over his fellow prisoners."

"Precisely."

"I would think that would be unwise too", Franklin agreed, nodded to the professor, and yielded to the next ass-kisser. As he exited the building, he noticed several students standing outside and puffing on vape cigarettes.

CHAPTER 46-STEVE BEGINS AS SAM'S SUMMER LAW CLERK

During his first week in the office, Steve assisted Rhonda with obtaining the proper waiver from Brad's father, which involved Sam listening in on the phone call in which Steve patiently explained to the dad, who had abandoned his son, why there wasn't any money in it for him. He also aided Sam in preparing the complaint in the federal lawsuit that Sam filed on behalf of Brad, although Sam did most of the dictation of the complaint. The phenomenon which still persisted of his more closely approximating his natural enunciation and speed of his speech when he dictated, but his stumbling over his words and searching for appropriate verbiage in conversation constantly troubled him.

Although his right side was essentially useless and he couldn't write, in this computer age with the prevalence of a dictation feature on practically every device, he thought he could make a creditable effort at practicing law the way he used to. He still had his doubts though.

On Friday of Steve's first week as his summer clerk, Sam decided that he should at least meet Brad, although he questioned the usefulness of the meeting because the reports he had obtained were that Brad remained in a vegetative state. Still, he should meet with his client, and he had heard that even in what appeared to be an unresponsive condition, people often retained some awareness.

He recruited Jeff to drive him, and he could tell by Steve's reaction that he was thrilled at the thought of meeting his first client and in such a significant case to boot. In contrast, Sam dreaded the meeting, as it would most certainly bring back memories of his recent confinement in a rehabilitation hospital. The trip started out badly.

As Steve was picking him up on the sidewalk, which ran in front of the office building, Sam couldn't get his bad leg, brace and all, into the car. Steve put the car into park, and when he attempted to get the recalcitrant leg into the car. Sam's shoe came off. Steve was the picture of nonchalant as he put the shoe back on Sam's foot and loaded his right leg into the car.

Sam was able to stifle his embarrassment and even joked that he bet Steve didn't anticipate that his summer clerking job would entail valet duties. Steve seemed graciously over–amused.

Steve began the conversation, "How do you think the practice of law has changed between now and when you first started?"

"Well, for one thing, there was a lot less advertising then. It seems like now, success is measured by how many clients you can get and how much money you can make by clever advertising. Don't get me wrong, when I started, money was still a measure of success, but in my field at least, skill in the courtroom was also important."

"In my dad's firm, it's all about money. It's about how the wealth gets redistributed from one rich corporation or man to another."

"Everybody is entitled to representation in this country." Sam bellowed emphatically. "Would your statement explain why you didn't go back to Philadelphia to clerk for your dad's firm?"

"As I told Nicole, I don't want my legacy to be helping redistribute wealth between the already wealthy. Besides, we are only remembered for a millisecond in the universe's time. I doubt whether two thousand years from now most people will know who Abraham Lincoln and Mohamed Ali were, let alone which attorney negotiated even the most brilliant merger."

Sam smiled and said, "Aren't you a little young to be concerned about your legacy? What you say, though, is very true, but with the vast majority of us, it's going to take much less than two thousand years to be forgotten. When I first started to practice, there was very little doubt as to who the best plaintiff's attorney was. He has been dead for twenty years, and I bet if you said his name now among young attorneys, ninety percent of them would not know who he was."

"What's his name?"

Sam chuckled, "You are part of the Google generation." Sam had difficulty with the word Google. It took him three times before he got it correct, "Look him up and let me know what you find. Clue: he wrote a book on trial advocacy, which I think is still in print."

"But," Sam went on, "his name is somewhat irrelevant. It's what he told me that is important. He told me that everyone wants immortality. Some want an immortal legacy for themselves. In other words, to have their name emblazoned on buildings, monuments or firms when they're gone. As you say, that type of immortality will fade to nothingness within a couple of thousand years. Some, with a religious bent, think they will live on in heaven or some such equable celestial place."

"Which one are you?"

Sam chuckled and confided, "I am neither. I suppose I am what you might call a seeker of the truth regarding immortality. All I know is that I'm mostly happy to be among the living, especially after what I have been through."

When they got to The Meadows, and Sam had produced his attorney identification card at the front desk and told the receptionist that he was Brad's attorney, an attendant ushered them down the hall and into Brad's room. They found it littered with medical package wrapping on a floor which hadn't seen a mop in days. They found Brad with his eyes open and appearing to move. Sam was getting a real-life demonstration of what was meant by the medical term "doll's eyes," he realized. They were shortly joined at Brad's bedside by a nurse who identified herself as Carrie.

"And you are…" Carrie was looking at his quad cane and his lifeless and dangling right arm.

"I am Sam Wright, and this is my summer law clerk, Steve Black. We are Brad's attorneys."

"Black and Wright catchy name. You guys ought to advertise on television with that name."

"Unfortunately, that seems to be what it is all about these days—advertising." It took Sam three times to get out the word, unfortunately.

"You guys just missed the doctor who examined Brad here by a couple of days," Carrie said as she pointed to Brad, "He said he was the jail doctor."

"Really, did he give his name?"

"Yeah, but I don't remember it. He was here with an entourage."

"Oh," is all Sam said, preferring to keep his more cynical evaluation unspoken.

"If you don't mind my asking, and I don't mean to be undiplomatic, how long ago did you have a stroke?"

"It's only been four months now."

"I wish you well. As you can see, Brad is not matching your recovery, and I suspect from his brain MRI that he will require pretty much round-the-clock care for the rest of his life."

They spent several awkward minutes doing nothing but staring at their client and patient from the foot of the bed until Sam announced, "I think we'll be heading back to the office now. You'll be seeing more of us in the future." Sam, who was constantly evaluating his speech, was impressed that he got this sentence out with a garble.

"So long the firm of Black and Wright. Ah, oh, I just put the young guy's name before the mature attorney's name. But I don't suppose that you would mind being his age again. I will tell you that I wouldn't."

"I wouldn't either," Sam confirmed with a smile.

As they were driving back to the office, Steve asked Sam what his thoughts were regarding the visit. "It was pretty much as I expected. The kid's life is pretty much over. Only an organ container is left. He might as well be dead, and I think there are some people who would be happy if he died tomorrow."

"You mean the anti-gay, anti-prisoner rights people?"

"Yes, definitely those brainless assholes. But consider this: if Brad were to die, his case would be worth a lot less than if he required round-the-clock care for the rest of his life."

"So?" Sam could read the curiosity on Steve's face.

"There might be jail personnel who would be very happy if we abandoned the suit, which would be more likely if Brad just died, to say nothing about the insurance company people."

"I am sure they would, but why do YOU think that? Do you think that the jail is legally responsible?"

"Where there's smoke, there's fire, now proving it is another issue."

Sam sensed Steve's bewilderment with his obtuse statement. It required a more robust explanation.

"I have a friend, Franklin. Perhaps Nicole has told you about him, who helped me with Nicole's mother's medical malpractice case. He called me this morning and told me that he thought Brad's case had something to do with smoking."

"Forgive me, but I just don't get it. Is this guy a psychic or something?"

"Yes, in a manner of speaking, he is. He wouldn't mind if I told this story," Sam continued with obvious affection, "Shit, he is willing to tell it to total strangers."

Sam then proceeded to tell him Franklin's history, from the homeless guy bedded down in Sam's office building, through opening the box of Sam's personal items and having inexplicable flashes that helped him with Nicole's mother's case, through the halfway house after hospitalization for damn near killing himself with drink, to Franklin's current status as a photocopy repair man who is studying to be a drug and alcohol counselor. Sam's enunciation deteriorated the longer that he spoke, but in spite of that, he had Steve's rapt attention.

"That's quite a tale."

"He's quite a guy." Sam's voice needed a rest, so they spent the rest of the ride to the office in silence.

CHAPTER 47-NICOLE MEETS A GREENE COUNTY JAIL GUARD

As she was walking to Mac's Diner to meet Jerry Lamont, the Greene County jail guard that Phil had set up for her to interview, she reflected upon Steve's morning question: What did she know about a guy named Franklin? She told him the story of Franklin, which Steve said pretty much tracked what Sam had told him.

She then disclosed that Franklin had had much to do with the settlement and her mother's case. When asked why, she told him about Franklin sketching a dog named Fox during settlement negotiations, and since her mother had an affinity for foxes, she told her father he needed to settle the case for the amount offered.

"Why this sudden interest in Franklin?"

"Because, apparently, he has a sixth, seventh or eighth sense about these things, and he led Sam to believe there was something to Brad's case, although Sam said proving it was another matter."

"I would pay attention to Franklin based on his track record," she affirmed.

When she arrived at Mac's, Jerry was already there, consuming a huge pile of pancakes. He looked pretty much as you would expect a prison guard in the movies would look: A large man with an obviously shaved head and huge hands who were currently engaged in shoveling pancakes into his mouth. When she introduced herself, she was immediately struck by his pleasant, baritone voice:

"So this is the Nicole who is going to make me famous all around these parts."

Nicole was instantly smitten by his voice initially and, thereafter, by his obvious humanity. In response to her question about how she would describe the duties and responsibilities of a prison guard, he replied: "If you watch enough prison movies, especially older ones, you get the impression that we are all stereotypical quasi-sadists that look like me." He chuckled and questioned, "Isn't that what you thought when you saw me?"

Embarrassed, Nicole nodded her head.

"Well, that points up the tension between the old view of prison guards as a paramilitary type organization and the more modern view of us as primarily ensuring the health and safety of inmates, as well as assisting inmates on their journey to rehabilitation. In fact, many guards have college degrees. My degree is in psychology."

"Come on now," she teased, "it doesn't hurt to look like you do, does it?"

"No," he confirmed affably, "it doesn't. We deal with some rough characters, and size can be intimidating. But we do have female guards. In fact, there are studies that say that the presence of female guards helps to reduce the culture of domination and competition that is present in all prisons."

"Jails and prisons are dangerous places, and I assume that they could use a little less domination, couldn't they?"

"Yes, they are more dangerous than many environments, but that also can mean that the work is exciting. You always have to be alert. And the physical plant, as some would call it, of jails and prisons often leaves much to be desired."

"I know an attorney, Sam Wright, who gets a lot of letters from prisoners, he says, and he read one to me. Among other complaints, it said that in the winter, it was frigid."

"Yes, that might be true of a lot of jails. Poor heating and air conditioning. Politicians hate to spend money on prisons and jails. Hell, some secretly, and not so secretly, believe that making prisons as miserable as possible will deter crime, but it doesn't. I know of very, very few people who commit crimes and think they will be caught."

"Besides being exciting, what is rewarding about being a jail guard?"

"Hmmm... No two days are the same. I have had many experiences where I have felt that I made a difference in a prisoner's life. I think that a good jail guard is a counselor in addition to ensuring the health and safety of inmates. We also have training in security, defense, and counseling. Constant, continuing training in all of those fields. I have even heard of some psychologists, counselors and social workers who started out as prison guards."

"I understand security and defense, but I think my readers would be interested in what type of counseling training you get."

"Obviously, jail is not someplace that anyone wants to be, so we receive training in the manifestations of anxiety and stress and how to defuse potentially dangerous situations. And, of course, depression and the identification of potential suicides."

When queried about his single greatest inmate success story in which he believed he had a hand, he responded with a story about a prisoner with multiple arrests who became a successful carpenter and had his own company now, which employed a half dozen carpenters.

"You see, as The Rolling Stones said, 'just as every cop is a criminal and all the sinner's saints, there was a little good and bad in all of us."

"Yes, I suppose so. Well, on that note, I will leave you to further attack your humongous stack of pancakes."

"I have one question to ask of you. You said that your attorney friend got a letter from an inmate. What else did the inmate say in his letter? It's always good to get intelligence on the other side."

"He said, as I told you, that the place was frigid in the winter, that the food was bad, implied that the guards were vicious. He called them Nazis."

"I hope it wasn't from our jail, but, like I said, nobody wants to be in jail and prisoners bitch."

"No, it wasn't your jail. It came from an inmate in the Coalton County Jail."

"No surprise there."

"What do you mean ?"

"Let me just say that there is a faction there that proves, 'every cop is a criminal'."

"And what does that mean?"

"You are a bright woman. You figure it out. And when you do, you didn't hear it from me. What's the term, off the record?"

"Yes, of course," Nicole assured him, "we are off the record."

"I wouldn't be surprised to learn that the guards had something to do with that most recent suicide attempt of the eighteen-year-old kid."

"What do they have to do with it? Do you know?"

"That's all I'm going to say," and with that, he resumed his pancake siege.

CHAPTER 48- FRANKLIN AND KIM MEET AN OLD FRIEND OF FRANKLIN AND VISIT THEIR SON'S GRAVE

It was a warm April day, and he and Kim had just disembarked from the brunch cruise on the Gateway Clipper, the riverboat on which he had first proposed to Kim many years ago. It was, for him at least and he hoped it was for her, a regenerative experience after the dark time period of their separation. As they walked through the pedestrian tunnel, which led to the street level, he caught sight of a man and a woman standing by the side of the tunnel, clearly sporting non-brunch clothing. The woman held a sign that read, "We live in a tent by the river. Homeless but not Hopeless." It was Jane.

Fortyish, braless, cut-off shorts Jane, who had loaned him her cell phone when he was a co-inhabitant with her in the river homeless encampment. He had called Kim on Jane's cell phone that day three and a half years ago and spoken with Kim for the first time in a couple of years. She made it clear that she wanted no part of him, causing him to drink constantly for three days and end up hospitalized. Sam paid for him to go to the halfway house after he got out of the hospital. He and Kim began communicating regularly, and he thought the rest was history.

He approached Jane, stood several feet from her, and murmured, "Jane?"

"That's my name, kind sir. I don't know how you know it, but would you care to help out poor, homeless Jane?"

"You don't know who I am?" Franklin prodded.

Jane squinted, and a smile seemed to emerge slowly. "Why Franklin, is that you, cleaned up and lookin' pros-pers like?"

"Yes, it's me."

"Besides, when you came to pick up your stuff, the last time I saw you—you were bein' carried out of your tent by the ambulance people. I called them, ya know. I guess you might say that I saved your life."

"Jane, I guess you could. And I think about you and thank you every day."

"I want you to think about that when you drop a donation in my hat. Who's this lovely lady standin' beside you?"

"She's my wife, Kim."

"You had an ex-wife that you wanted to talk to when you borrowed my phone a while back. So, since cleaning herself up, you found somebody new, did you?"

"She's the one and the same person."

Franklin could see the confusion on her face, but she quickly refocused and, again extolling her life–saving actions with the comatose version of himself long ago, thrust out her hat to receive his expected donation. He obliged, dropping a twenty dollar bill into it.

"It's been good to see you all sober and upright. We will be here off and on all summer, taking collections, so please stop by again. Aaron and I would love to see you again." Jane winked.

After saying goodbye to Jane, he and Kim walked to his car, whereupon Franklin suggested that they visit the grave of their son Ian.

"It's funny, but I have been thinking a lot about the day I was told that Ian had died while still in my womb, and they had to get him out. I think it was the worst day of my life." Kim stared out of the window for a good long time and then added, "I guess it must have been a bad day for you, too. It wasn't long until you started your self-destructive drinking."

"Yep." Franklin wanted to say a lot more about his experiences as an inebriated itinerant, but he wanted their day to end on the high note he had planned. He had hoped that his terseness would foreclose further discussion of that period of his life, but it didn't.

"You know, seeing that woman today… What was her name again?"

"Jane."

"I was wondering if you had any, you know, romantic relationships while we were apart and, how shall I say this, you were living off the land?"

"The only thing that I was interested in was where my next drink was coming from." Then, in an effort to deflect further inquiry into that subject, he remarked cheerfully, "So, I was wondering, should we take our honeymoon in Paris right after we get married, or should we postpone it to the springtime, you know, April in Paris…"

"Oh, I don't know, and really I haven't thought about it."

"You know what Victor Hugo said, 'He who contemplates the depths of Paris is seized with vertigo. Nothing is more fantastic. Nothing is more tragic. Nothing is more sublime.'"

"Then I guess it's good that I haven't contemplated our honeymoon in Paris. I don't want any of those things. I just want us to live a quiet, happy life."

They arrived at the gravesite in the old part of the cemetery. When Ian was buried, Franklin discovered that his grandparents had bought a couple of plots in the ancient part of the cemetery, which had been unused for some reason. He had inherited them in effect.

As they approached the small marble headstone, Franklin asked Kim what happened to the engagement ring that he had given her years ago before their marriage.

"Oh Franklin, I hocked it. When you left, money got real tight, and I was trying to keep the house from being foreclosed on."

Franklin took her hand, led her within a foot of Ian's tombstone, took out a diamond ring, which he had recently purchased and which was nearly a replica of the pawned ring, and slipped it on her finger. They both cried.

CHAPTER 49-SAM ATTENDS A PRETRIAL CONFERENCE WITH JUDGE HARRIS

The case of Barbara Moran, as guardian of Bradley Moran versus Coalton County, had been assigned to Judge Harris in federal court for the Western District of Pennsylvania, and Sam and Steve were headed to the federal courthouse for the initial status conference on a rainy April day.

"Judge Harris," Steve asked Sam in the car, "what's he like?"

"I am sure that you Googled him. What do you know about him, Steve?"

"Not much, other than he was appointed by Bush Two, and that he was known as a moderate Republican."

"I have many stories that I can tell you about him, but all you need to know now is that he's a fair man and, like most federal judges, is a strict constructionist when it comes to holding a government liable on a civil rights claim."

"A strict constructionist. What does that mean?"

Sam had a fairly complex answer to Steve's question at the ready, but to preserve his voice and so his facial muscles didn't become tired, which tended to happen when he talked too much, he answered flippantly but accurately, "It means you have to prove your case."

Unfazed, Steve posed another question, "So what's going to happen here today?"

"Dates, dates for motions, dates for when discovery closes. Discovery is where you get to conduct witness depositions and get answers to interrogatories, and they have to produce documents."

"I know what discovery is, Sam," Steve, betraying irritation, observed, "I have gone to a year of law school and I am sixth in my class."

Sam ignored the interruption and pressed on, "And, of course, a trial date."

When Steve parked the car and they passed through security, which was in itself quite a task with Sam's quad cane and leg brace, and arrived at Judge Harris' courtroom, Sam could tell that Steve was somewhat awestruck to be sitting at the counsel table in a federal courtroom. He laid his hand on Steve's arm gently. He was going to say, "We are in the font of justice, or if you prefer the church or synagogue of justice," but he tripped over the word synagogue. He was interrupted as he was struggling to get the word out by the arrival of opposing counsel.

Opposing counsel, who he didn't know, was a rotund, totally bald young man who looked to be in his thirties. When he took his seat at the defense counsel's table, he gave a slight nod in the direction of Sam and Steve. He didn't introduce himself.

When the clerk came out and called the three of them into chambers, Judge Harris revealed the name of opposing counsel by shuffling through a few papers and saying, "You must be Mr. Lanning Fume because I know Mr. Wright here." Lanning Fume acknowledged that that was his name and blustered, "I am here representing Coalton County and this meritless suit."

Sam noticed that the judge raised his eyebrows when Fume declared the lawsuit, and by extension, Sam, to be a blight on the cathedral of justice and, directing a question to Sam, asked, "Who's this young fellow with you, Sam?" After Sam introduced Steve, the judge observed, "It's a horrible tragedy that occurred to this young man, but is there any reason to believe that anyone associated with the jail was deliberately indifferent?"

Fume launched into a diatribe, essentially reiterating that the claims embodied in the suit were meritless and vile until the judge raised his hand and Fume wisely shut up.

"I think we should hear from Mr. Wright about his theories of the case. Don't you agree, Mr. Fume?"

Fume nodded and Sam spoke, his voice tentative, "People don't just attempt suicide, typically, there is an inciting event," only it came out of Sam's mouth sounding more exciting than inciting.

"We want to explore in discovery if there is anything rooted in jail policy that might have caused this poor kid to try to take his own life, and/or any actions taken by the jail personnel or at the direction of jail personnel which might have contributed to the attempted suicide. We don't even know the particulars of the mechanism of his attempt."

"That's simple," Fume interposed, "he fashioned a noose out of his shirt, attached it to a horizontal bar, tied the noose to the bar and voila, you have a suicide-producing mechanism. You will get the pictures of the cell, the bar he tied his shirt to and pictures of what remained of the shirt on the bar after they cut him down. And I might add that it's not deliberate indifference to permit a prisoner to be clothed in a shirt, and jails typically have bars on a cell to keep that bad guy in."

Sam thought that Fume was being a little too flip about a young man who would likely be severely impaired for the rest of his life and told Fume so, to which Fume replied with a shrug of his massive shoulders and muttered, "No offense intended."

Judge Harris redirected the discussion, "Well, we are not going to resolve this case on its merits now. What do you think is a reasonable time frame within which we can try this case, assuming that it's not dismissed or settled?"

Sam was pretty much clear until the end of the year and, of course, Fume was vague about his schedule until Judge Harris betrayed his impatience, and then Fume "guessed" he could be ready for trial by the end of the year. A trial date was tentatively set for October 27, and then, working backward, dates for discovery, depositions, disclosure of experts' reports and motions were scheduled.

"We will have a final status conference two weeks before the trial date, at which we will discuss settlement", the Judge advised.

As they all were filing out of the Judge's conference room, Judge Harris asked Sam if he could speak with him in private. "And you, young man," the judge declared, "you have one of the best mentors that I can think of. You can wait in the courtroom while I talk to your boss; we have old men things to discuss."

When they were alone, Judge Harris began: "Sam, I shall be forever in your debt for the way you defused that episode of near fisticuffs at the bar association convention." Sam immediately knew what he was referring to: twenty years ago, and before the Judge was appointed to the federal bench, the Judge became involved in a shoving match with another inebriated attorney at two o'clock in the morning, and Sam broke it up.

"So I want you to take my comment with the deference that I would give an esteemed member of the trial bar, but do you think you are ready to try this case? You know, there's no dishonor in hanging it up, at least temporarily, with the career you have had and what you have been through."

Sam opened his mouth as if to say something, but no sound issued forth for seconds. *I am just proving to the judge that I am irreparably damaged goods,* he thought. When he was finally able to form words, albeit haltingly, he responded, "I can still think, Your Honor, although I am slower at translating thoughts into words. I believe I would like to give it a try, but if I don't think I can do it, I will get someone who can well in advance of trial."

Harris said, 'You know I will cut you all the slack I can.' What are the chances that this case can be settled? It seems as though Fume is an asshole cowboy, and I'm guessing that if this kid has got to be cared for for the rest of his life, it's going to cost millions. On the surface, I wouldn't think that the prospects of settlement aren't real good."

Sam nodded his head.

"Well, Sam, I'll let you go. I can't imagine what you're going through with this stroke shit, but I know that whatever it is, you will do it with aplomb."

If he only knew, Sam was thinking as he exited the judges' chambers and slowly made his way into the courtroom, but Steve was nowhere to be found. He had difficulty opening the courtroom door with just one working hand, but when he got out and into the hallway, he saw Steve speaking with a reporter that he knew from the Pittsburgh Informer.

As he approached the pair, the reporter, Harry, whose last name he couldn't remember, exploded, "I didn't know that the Moran kid was gay. Steve here just told me. It's not mentioned in your Complaint."

Sam looked at Steve disapprovingly and then stammered, "I didn't know that sexual orientation was required in a legal pleading."

"It's not but it's an interesting angle. Do you think that the kid might have been mistreated because he was gay?"

"That's what we will find out in discovery, I hope, but until then, I would appreciate it if you didn't disclose that fact."

"Why in God's name would you want to keep that quiet? I would think that that would make him seem even more sympathetic."

"More sympathetic among a certain portion of the population, but you know there are crazies out there who would like nothing better than to hang all LGBTQIA people. His mom lives in Coalton, and I don't want her to be unnecessarily harassed." Sam was impressed that he got all of the letters which had become descriptive of alternative sexual orientations out without hesitation and in correct order.

"Yeah, but it's bound to be revealed, and I might as well be the one to reveal it. Tell you what, I won't say where it came from. I will just say, 'Sources tell me' or some such bullshit."

Sam only nodded and was silent until they left the building and were partway to the car when Steve asked, "You're not pissed at me for letting the cat out of the bag, are you?"

Sam shook his head and didn't say another word during the ride back to the office. His voice and facial muscles were exhausted from the pretrial conference, and he was depressed over the Judge's private comments. Perhaps the judge was right, and he should just hang it up.

CHAPTER 50- NICOLE TAKES STEVE TO MEET HER FAMILY

"I am afraid that Sam thinks I'm a fuckin' asshole who can't keep his mouth zipped," Steve lamented to Nicole as they rode in the Lexus convertible, which, Nicole often teased him, was supplied by "daddy". They were headed to Nicole's house for her father and two brothers to form their initial in-person appraisal of the man in her life.

She frankly wasn't looking forward to it; her father's reaction was unpredictable. When he became aware of Steve's presence in her life (and her apartment), his reaction ranged from happiness at the thought that she might be marrying a man from a wealthy family to disgust with what he termed the moneyed, hoity-toity snobs. She wondered what she and he would get as far as her father's reaction today.

"What did the asshole do?"

"Well, we went to the first status conference in the Moran case, you know, the jail hanging case, and I was talking to a reporter and told him that the kid was gay."

"And what did Sam say?"

"Well, at first, he wasn't pleased, but I think he was ultimately okay with it."

"And here I thought the concern on your face was because you were meeting my family," she taunted.

"I think that I can take care of them."

"By the way, you know that jail guard that I interviewed on that fluff piece."

"Yeah."

"He implied that there was more to that jail hanging thing than met the eye."

"Hmm… Did he tell you what?"

"No, he wouldn't say."

When they pulled into the driveway of Nicole's girlhood home, Josh must have spied the car from inside the house because he came running down the stairs of the porch and exclaiming something that was unintelligible. However, it contained the word "badass". She assumed that it was in reference to the car.

He was followed closely by Jake, who joined Josh in expressions of wonderment over Steve's car. Following her introductions of her brothers, Steve responded to their questions about the car, which necessitated a review with them of the esoterica about the car. She tolerated their discussion with a smile, but she had little interest. Then her father came down the porch stairs, holding Phyllis's hand.

"It looks like my daughter has got herself a boyfriend with a really boss car."

Steve smiled and said, "And you must be Nicole's father, Tyler. Who is that beauty whose hand you're holding?"

Nicole interjected, "That's Phyllis, my father's girlfriend."

"And soon-to-be wife," her father revealed.

Nicole struggled to contain her astonishment at her father's announcement and stammered, "I guess congratulations are in order."

"You're fuckin' right they are," but when he picked up on Phyllis's frown, he corrected himself and mumbled: "Phyllis doesn't like me to use that word being a devout Christian and all."

"Phyllis," Nicole snickered, "I don't envy you. You have decades of my dad using that word frequently to overcome."

Her father took the comment surprisingly affably, and Phyllis called them into the house for her homemade lasagna.

After saying grace at Phyllis's insistence, dinner conversation was desultory until her father switched to what she saw as the money questions. And they were, almost literally, "So Nicole tells me that your dad is a big-time lawyer in Philly."

"Yeah, he is the president and founder of a large Philadelphia firm. He mostly practices corporate law."

"Are you his only son?" Nicole figured that the question was based on her father's somewhat outdated concept that sons inherited the business.

"Yes, but I have one sister, Robin."

"Older? Younger?"

"She's three years older than me."

"Is she a lady lawyer?"

"No, she and her husband have four kids, and she lives what you might call an alternative lifestyle. They all live in a couple of converted school buses in Maine."

"How do they support themselves? That's a lot of kids."

"She has a bachelor's in education and home-schools the kids, which, as you might imagine, is a full–time job. He's what he calls an arborist. So, he's both a tree hugger and tree trimmer."

That must have struck her father as uproariously funny because he nearly spit out the lasagna noodles as he laughed. "That's fuckin' hilarious," he gasped. Then, responding to Phyllis's glare, he offered, "sorry, honey."

"Why aren't you working for your dad in Philadelphia then?"

Steve winked at her and teased, "Because I wanted to spend the summer with your daughter." He then disclosed, "And, Sam is working on a case which I find to be very interesting."

"You mean the kid who hung himself in the Coalton County Jail. You know Jake here met the kid very briefly."

"Yeah, I know, Nicole told me."

"Sam did right by this family. He made the son of a bitch half–blind doctor who misread my poor wife's x-ray pay. Of course, I understand that Sam is not himself these days. What a pity!" Nicole noted that Phyllis had no visible reaction to her father using "son of a bitch" so on the profanity spectrum it must have been rated as acceptable. Nicole giggled imperceptibly.

"That's the reason he needs me."

Her father grinned and said, "I like that piss-and-vinegar attitude." No visible reaction to the urine synonym from Phyllis.

Nicole recognized that Steve had secured the approval of her father and tuned out for most of the remainder of the dinner time conversation. But she regained awareness of the subjects of the discussion when she heard the words, "gay boy who hung himself."

"Jake, you met his boyfriend, didn't you?" Her father asked.

"Yeah, but it was so brief that I don't even remember his name or what he looks like."

Phyllis then solemnly intoned, "We are all God's children, including faggots. Condemn the sin and not the sinner. Steve I hope you can help your boss to get God's justice for the young man."

Steve glanced at Nicole with a mixture of well–disguised shock and amusement.

Phyllis continued, "And we know that all things work together for good to them that love God, to them who are the called according to his purpose.'Romans, chapter 8, verse 28. His will be done."

Shortly after Phyllis's entreaty to God, a cake was served for dessert, and later, when Nicole calculated a polite lapse of time post-dessert, Nicole and Steve made their exit.

"My father really likes you."

"Yes, he seems to."

"And what did you think of my family, Steve?" Nicole wondered aloud.

"Interesting."

CHAPTER 51-SAM CONSULTS WITH PROF. SONNENBERG

Sam had just received the first tranche of documents from Coalton County and had called his soon–to–be ex–wife's ex–paramour, Stewart Sonnenberg, to assist him in evaluating the suicide risk assessment checklist in use in the Coalton County Jail. Who better than the recently appointed jail psychologist at the Allegheny County jail to assist him, despite the fact that he didn't like Stew, because, for the longest time, unbeknownst to him, they had shared the same woman's favors? Stew had insisted on meeting him at his office rather than having a phone conversation, which he was reluctant to do because he would be exposing the full extent of his disability. He only hoped that his communication skills were passable around him.

When Stewart's figure darkened the door to his office he immediately commented on the folded wheelchair in the corner of his office, "I heard that you're getting around quite well now. Why the wheelchair?"

"Good morning, Professor. I don't use it much, only when I have to go more than a couple of blocks, and I have to have someone push it since I only have one functioning hand. I didn't know that the state of my recovery was common knowledge."

"Our ex keeps me updated. We still talk, you know."

"I bet you do. Did you get a chance to review the checklist?"

"Yes, I did. It's the Federal Bureau of Prisons assessment checklist. It records that there are no medical, psychiatric, psychological or behavioral issues. Moreover, there is negative intentionality and a lack of a plan. Of course, you will want to depose the guard who completed the form."

"That's the plan. The checklist was not reviewed by the jail psychologist because it was after hours for her. He hung himself before she could get a chance to review it," Sam explained.

"Then, it would be doubly important to depose the guard who completed the checklist."

Sam nodded and divulged that his plan was to depose that guard and the prisoner who shared Brad's cell with him first.

"You mean that there was someone in his cell when he hung himself?"

"Yep. Odd, isn't it? You would think that the cellmate would have taken some action while he was making preparations to hang himself or at least alerted jail staff that he was making the preparations. There's another strange thing. I didn't think to take pictures of Brad when I visited him at the home, but his brother, who was there a couple of days after the incident, did."

"What was strange about them?"

"Well, I had a doctor who I have regularly consulted with on cases, and he said that there was bruising on the face that was inconsistent with a ligature around the neck."

"Oh yeah. What did he think caused the bruising?"

"He wasn't sure, of course. But it was consistent with the poor kid being punched and beaten about the head."

"Might they have bruised his face when they were getting him down?"

"I guess it's possible. By the way, have you ever heard of inmate rovers or suicide prevention workers?"

"One of my students asked me about them. I told him that I had heard something about that. I ended up looking at the literature on prison suicides and found that there was a now largely discredited practice of paying trusted inmates a couple of bucks a day, enough to keep them in cigarettes, to be, in effect, another set of eyes and ears among the newest prisoners. They would obtain some training in recognizing suicidal tendencies in new admitees."

"Why is the practice now largely discredited?"

"Basically, because you have to be very careful when you give inmates apparent authority over fellow inmates. You know, give some people an inch, and they'll take a mile, especially folks who have demonstrated some anti-social behavior before. Why do you ask about inmate rovers?"

"I have some information that some inmate rovers visited my client before he attempted suicide."

"Are you going to depose them?"

"I will if they're not scattered to the wind. It's my understanding that these rovers are prisoners that are near the end of their sentences."

Although Sam suspected he knew who the student was, he wanted confirmation, "Who asked you about it in your class? Was his name Franklin?"

Stuart laughed. "I was going to say it was Benjamin, but yeah, it was Franklin. Does he work for you?"

"Long story. But yes, in a manner of speaking, he does. In fact, I have him serving the subpoena on my client's cellmate who was recently released on bail."

"My friend, you sure have yourself an interesting case."

"Glad you think so because I suspect that I'll be calling on you to write a report and serve as an expert in the case," to which he silently added, despite the fact that I don't like you.

Stew smiled and declared, "I'll cut you a break on my fee."

"That's the least you could do."

CHAPTER 52-SAM DEPOSES THE UNCOOPERATIVE CELLMATE, BUT FRANKLIN GETS A CLUE

Franklin had consulted with Darius, Franklin's AA sponsor and a Pittsburgh police detective, to determine the current whereabouts of Jimmy Davis, who was Brad's cellmate when he attempted to hang himself. The Pittsburgh Police Detective didn't disappoint: he secured Jimmy's address from his bail bondsman. Franklin had volunteered to serve Jimmy with a subpoena and notice of deposition since he knew Jimmy from a prior stint that Jimmy had served in the Coalton County Jail. He had attended a few of Franklin's AA meetings.

When Franklin appeared at the door of Jimmy's friend's residence, where he was currently residing, Jimmy studied him through the glass door for a few moments while he repeated Jimmy's name a few times. Finally, Jimmy opened the door and barked, "You're the AA guy from the jail. What the fuck do you want?"

Franklin responded that he had some papers to deliver. Jimmy looked suspicious but opened the door. Franklin handed him the subpoena and notice, turned on his heel, and made a rapid retreat toward his car. Since he had served Jimmy, Franklin asked if he could also attend the deposition on behalf of Jeff and Barbara if he could arrange a day off work. Sam said, of course, and the deposition date, June 3, found Franklin in Sam's office immediately prior to the deposition.

"Do you think this guy is going to appear? I have my doubts. After all, it is a subpoena in a civil, not a criminal, case, and we would have to jump through many hoops to compel his attendance."

Franklin shrugged his shoulders and sighed, "It depends, I suppose, on who he asked for advice on whether he had to show or not."

Their conversation was temporarily interrupted by the opening of the elevator doors and Rhonda's businesslike inquiry as to the business that he had on this floor.

"Lanning Fume for the Moran case deposition," came the response.

Franklin could hear Rhonda directing Fume to the conference room when he saw a neatly dressed young man with shoulder-length brown hair get off the elevator. It was Jimmy.

When everyone was seated in the conference room, including the videographer and court reporter, and the introductions were made and preliminary instructions given, Sam began by asking the witness to identify himself. Franklin knew that they were in for an interesting time when the deponent answered, "James Davis and I don't know nothin' about the hangin' and I want to assert my fifth amendment rights against self-incrimination."

He could tell that Sam was temporarily stymied and sputtered, "But this is… this is a civil case. You're not… you're not being accused of any crime. Although you can plead the Fifth Amendment in a civil case, in this instance, it doesn't make a lot of sense." Clearly, that is what he intended to say, but the word "sense" came out of Sam's mouth as stents.

"I don't know what you might accuse me of, but I ain't gonna answer any questions that I think might be misconstrued as a potential crime."

"I can assure you, Jimmy, you don't mind if I call you Jimmy, do you?"

"I don't care what you call me, but I ain't going to answer any questions that I figure might get me into criminal trouble."

Sam, clearly flustered, spoke overly loudly and began his assurance rapidly and nearly inarticulately before slowing down. "I can guarantee you, Jimmy, I won't ask you any question which, if you answer it, could be even vaguely interpreted as sustaining a criminal charge against you."

Jimmy nodded his head in acknowledgment, and added in a less combative tone, "I just don't wanna be accused of aidin' and abettin'."

Sam countered, "Unless you fashioned the noose, you wouldn't be."

Fume then moved to have Sam's comment stricken from the record, and Sam smiled, and conceded that he would withdraw the remark if Mr.Fume found it to be so offensive.

"Now, I understand that you were Bradley Moran's cellmate on the day of his suicide attempt by hanging?"

"Yeah, but I was asleep through most of it."

"Most of it?"

"Yeah, it was around lights out time, which is always noisy. I was tryin' to get some shuteye when I heard a commotion and guards yellin' about cuttin' him down and whatnot."

"Do you remember overhearing any conversation that Bradley might have had with anyone that night?"

Franklin saw Jimmy's countenance transform from wary to downright mistrustful, and after a long pause, he insisted, "As I said, it's always real noisy before lights out, but I thought I heard the words 'Sledge Hammer', or something along those lines. I don't know nothing else, so it ain't no use askin' me any more questions."

But Sam was undeterred, as Franklin knew he would be, and the deposition went on for another twenty minutes, with Jimmy answering each question Sam put to him with a variation of I don't know or I don't recall. *At least he kept his invocation of the fifth amendment to a minimum for the rest of the deposition,* Franklin thought.

When the deposition was finally concluded, and they were filing out of the conference room, he overheard Sam saying that he would like to speak with Fume in his office. Sam must've gotten a signal of assent from Fume because the two were just about to disappear into his office and Franklin to summon the elevator when Sam called out to him.

"Would you mind running down to the liquor store and buying some wine for my wife? I promised her…"

"No, not at all," Franklin assured Sam.

"Are you sure, because…"

"Because I'm in recovery? Hell, Sam I'm not that fragile. And you certainly can't walk that far with your gimp leg."

Franklin took note of Sam's grimace at the word "gimp", but gave Franklin the money for a bottle of Whispering Angel Rose.

Franklin then walked the block and a half to the liquor store that he once frequented. The same rotund, florid–faced cashier was on duty, but directly in front of him in the check–out queue was Jimmy.

"Jimmy, I didn't expect to see you here since you attended one of my AA meetings while you were in jail."

"Yeah, and what are you doing in a liquor store, buying communion wine for your church?"

"I'm buying wine for Sam's wife."

"Sure you are."

"Weren't you in jail when I saw you about a year ago on a DUI charge?"

"Yeah, I spent some time, my license was revoked and I was sentenced to community service, which was a fuckin' joke."

Franklin bit, "Why?"

"Because one day we were to pick up trash on the side of the road. We were driven to a road in the country and told that our project was to clean up the berm. Someone must have bought a shitload of porno mags and tore them up because pages of beaver for the length of about a football field was all you saw. We spent about fifteen minutes picking up the porno, but he gave us credit for four hours."

Franklin smiled and said, "Camus said, 'Basically, at the very bottom of life, which seduces us all, there is only absurdity and more absurdity.' That sounds absurd."

"Like I said, it was a fuckin' joke."

Jimmy bought his fifth of whiskey, and Franklin his bottle of wine. When Franklin exited the store, he found Jimmy waiting for him outside.

"You know, tell that lawyer friend of yours that the info I gave him will put him on the right track."

"What information?"

"You just tell them what I said." Then he opened the whiskey bottle, took a long hit and said, "Cheers." Franklin never saw him again.

CHAPTER 53-SAM DEPOSES GUARD SCHMIDT

Curiously, as he sat at his office desk two days after Jimmy's deposition, he was more focused on his review of the quality of his speech during the deposition instead of its content. He had done a creditable job, he thought, hardly tripping over his tongue at all, but his speech was still slower. He might have to live with that.

He was thinking that he was ambivalent when it came to cultivating thankfulness for merely being alive, when Rhonda buzzed him. "Mr. Fume and his client are here for the deposition." He detected a note of derision and her voice; she didn't like Fume. Consistent with her manufacture of humorous variations on the names of people she didn't like, she alternately referred to him as fumigate and fuming.

He had scheduled the deposition of Walter Schmidt, the guard who Darius, the Pittsburgh Police Detective that Franklin said was his AA sponsor, had informally interviewed regarding Brad's hanging. His intent was to obtain as much information as he could regarding who might have seen Brad that night.

He began the deposition of the fortyish, relatively nondescript looking guard by obtaining information regarding his background. If he were called as a witness at trial, background information would clearly influence whether the jury found him to be credible or not.

Walter Schmidt had a two year degree from a community college and had been employed for ten years as a guard at the Coalton County Jail. When asked a simple and routine question about the duties of a guard at the jail,he launched into a lengthy answer, mentioning his responsibilities regarding the physical plant, prisoner safety, rehabilitation and maintaining order. When he inquired as to whether Corrections Officer Schmidt had received any commendations or honors from his work at the jail, he expounded proudly:

"Chronologically, I received a commendation for discovering and confiscating a prisoner who was making a liquor–like liquid in his toilet. I got a commendation when I administered what I was told was life–saving aid to a prisoner who another prisoner had stabbed. That same year, I was recognized for my, I guess you would call it courage, in breaking up a fight between two prisoners, and I was named correction officer of the year in 2019."

"And," Schmidt went on, "I have been told that I will receive another commendation for my quick action on behalf of your client here, Bradley Moran."

"We may be getting a little ahead of ourselves, but I understand that you cut Brad down. Correct?"

"Yeah, I did."

"How were you first notified that Brad had hung himself? "

"I don't really remember who specifically told me. There was such hullabaloo on the floor, I think I was responding to that."

"Was there anyone in Brad's cell when you arrived?"

"Only his cellmate."

"Jimmy Davis?"

"Yeah."

"Anyone else in or around Brad's cell?"

"Only Jimmy in the cell, and it seemed like everybody who was a prisoner on the floor was gawking at one time or another."

"Your counsel has provided all of the names of anyone who was on the floor that night. What did you see when you arrived at the cell?"

"I saw that evidently, Brad had fashioned a noose out of his shirt. His face was red, and he had lost control of his bowels and bladder. Apparently, he had attempted to free himself because he had fingernail marks on his throat. His tongue was out, and it was nearly severed by the force of his jaws clenching. He was foaming at the mouth and had small broken blood vessels around the eyes."

"Anything else?"

"His hands were clenched into fists, which I learned from my first hanging suicide is what happens when the brain starts to die."

Schmidt then began to detail his resuscitative efforts and describe what occurred until Brad's body was taken out of the jail. Sam was particularly interested in any facial trauma that Schmidt might have noticed.

"Now you have said that he had fingernail marks around his neck. Did you notice any other facial trauma?"

"Yeah, I did. There appeared to be bruising around the jaw, and both eyes had been blackened. There was also bruising on the cheeks."

"Did what you described as bruising around the jaws and cheeks, as well as the black eyes, appear to you to be a result of the trauma of hanging?"

Sam expected an objection on the record, and he got it. Fume registered an objection because "the witness is not qualified to render a medical opinion."

Sam pressed on. "Objection noted. You may answer the question."

"I can't speak to the jaws and cheeks. It may or may not have been the result of the hanging. But I would have to say the black eyes didn't seem to me to be at all related."

"Are you familiar with a prisoner who goes by the nickname Sledgehammer?"

Schmidt chuckled and responded, "Yeah, I am familiar."

"What is his full name?"

"Jacques Lindstrom. He's a Canuck. He was released months ago. Huge guy. He used to play semi-pro hockey."

"Was he anywhere in the vicinity when you discovered that Brad had hung himself?"

"I don't really know. Like I said, it was pandemonium in there, and I was most concerned about Brad."

"Why was he in jail?"

"Assault and battery. But, since then, he has served his sentence and was released. I wouldn't want to meet him in a dark alley, that's for sure."

"Are you familiar with a program where certain prisoners were variously designated as inmate rovers, pod runners or suicide prevention workers?"

"Yeah, I was. We mostly referred to them as inmate rovers. Their function was basically to be on the lookout for new admittees who might be prone to self–harm. They were supposed to be trusted inmates who received special training in identifying potential suicides, and they were paid, I think, three or four bucks a day."

"Do you know who were the inmate rovers in January of this year?"

"I couldn't tell you. They changed all the time."

"Was Jacques Lindstrom a pod runner?"

"I couldn't tell you."

"Who would be the person or persons that I would ask about the pod runner program?"

"Dr. Rodriguez, the jail's psychiatrist, set it up, but he's been gone for a couple of years now. Annette Paulson, the jail psychologist, is in charge of the program currently I suppose. Lieutenant Kevin Hodgson picks the prisoners who participate."

"Was Bradley's alleged homosexuality ever discussed with you?"

"Yes."

"When?"

"Well, it was after he was admitted, but before he made his suicide attempt. Another guard told me that he was gay. Allegedly."

"Who told you, and what did he say?"

"Another corrections officer told me, Todd Shanahan. He said that his son, who was in high school with Brad, told him that Brad didn't try to hide his homosexuality."

"What else did he say?"

"Not much."

"Did he tell any other corrections officer?"

"I assume that he did because it would certainly be relevant, but you'd have to ask him."

"Why would it be relevant?"

Sam saw Schmidt's smirk as Schmidt derisively explained, "Prison is not the best place for a gay youngster. I'm surprised that you didn't know that."

When Sam asked whether Schmidt had had any other significant contact with Brad that he recalled, Schmidt responded that he had not. After a few more insignificant questions, the deposition was concluded.

As they were walking out of the conference room, Sam said to Fume, "Well, I guess we need to talk to Sledgehammer."

He was surprised by Fume's quick response, "Since he was in fact an inmate rover on the night in question he had been technically in our employ as well as being in our custody. I anticipated that you would want to depose him, and we are looking for him. But, we learned that he may have returned to Canada."

While Sam's only visible response was to nod his head, his pulse raced at what he saw as Fume's admission that Sledgehammer had been employed by the jail as a rover. So he wouldn't need to fight that battle. And his cellmate Jimmy, in his only piece of useful information, said he heard Sledgehammer's name on the night that Brad hung himself. Further, Franklin mentioned that cellmate Jimmy had told him in a post-deposition conversation that the information that he gave Sam would put him on the right track. Was Sledgehammer that information?

CHAPTER 54-NICOLE VOLUNTEERS TO COVER THE GAY PRIDE PARADE

When Nicole called Tim to discuss her next article for The Gazette, the conversation quickly devolved into a catch-up session.

"How's your boyfriend slash roommate working out?"

"I took him to meet my father and the boys recently. My father was enamored of him."

"How's he like his job with your attorney buddy?"

"He likes it. Except he almost got into trouble with his big mouth over the Coalton County Jail hanging case."

"Oh yeah? What did he do?"

"When Sam wasn't looking or hearing, he told a Pittsburgh newspaper reporter that the kid who hung himself was gay. Sam was temporarily pissed."

"I can see why."

"Steve couldn't and I'm not sure I can."

"I can. Suppose that's for one reason or another that case doesn't work out. He might have subjected the kid's family and friends to ridicule and possibly worse for nothing."

"That's basically what Sam said. I know a bunch of gay people at Pitt, and they are mostly treated with the respect due to every other human. But I know there are some people that would judge a person depending on their sexual orientation."

"You are goddamn right there are. My father, who was in the Navy during World War Two, told me that if you were suspected of being gay, they would toss you overboard without a second thought. I don't know whether that's true, but that attitude is still rampant in some circles."

"That attitude is downright medieval."

"But it's out there, and with so-called respectable groups. For example the Catholic Church. They prohibit same-sex marriages, gay men from entering the priesthood and if you are a practicing homosexual from communing, until recently. It hasn't been that long ago, maybe twenty years, that we had a senator in Pennsylvania who said that homosexuality would lead to beastiality. And I don't need to tell you that a lot of right-wing politicians decry gays, trans people and bisexuality."

Nicole nodded in agreement, although she knew that Tim couldn't see it and Tim wasn't done with his tirade, "Years ago, Justice Douglas wrote an opinion basically saying that the bedroom is sacrosanct. There are a lot of people who don't believe that. But it's not the guys with American flags flying from their pickup trucks or the ultra-religious right that we really need to be concerned about. It's the crazies who find their ungodly place on the Internet. They're the ones who want to stamp out homosexuality and are prone to violence."

That gave her an idea, "Why don't I do my next piece about next week's Gay Pride Parade in Pittsburgh?"

Phil was enthusiastic, "That's a capital idea! There are not a lot of local folks who will be there, let alone who are aware of it. Mildly controversial. I like it."

"I only hope that the weather is good, but I intend to be there, hell or high water."

CHAPTER 55-FRANKLIN, KIM AND JEFF CLEAN HOUSE

It was a gorgeous, early June day when Franklin took Kim out for a drive. He had no particular agenda, but knowing how much Kim liked shopping for antiques, or more precisely, looking at antiques they could rarely afford, he decided to take her to a local antique mall. He was looking at a fifty dollar letter purportedly signed by Gen. George Patton and writing in glowing terms about a mother's gallant son who had been killed in action when he got a call which registered as being from Jeff. He let it go to voicemail as he continued to consider what was, for him, a major investment in World War Two memorabilia.

He had not come to a firm decision when Kim corralled him and interrupted his Patton musing by suggesting they have lunch. As he was finishing his BLT, he decided to play his message from Jeff.

"Hey Franklin, it's Jeff, but then I guess you know that. Can you call me? I need some advice. My mother is fucked up."

He glanced across the table at Kim and announced, "I have to call Jeff. It sounded important."

When he got safely out of earshot of the other luncheonette patrons, he dialed Jeff and asked presumptively: "Do you think your mom needs hospitalization?"

"No, I have seen her this way before and if I stay with her and don't let her get any more pills or booze, I think she will be alright. I told her that I was going to drop in, and she freaked. I suspect that she had tried to hide her stash before I got there."

"Excellent. What do you want me to do?"

"If you're available, I could use some help in searching her apartment for her stashes."

Franklin recognized this as a ruse: He needed company for fear he might use or drink. "It may take me half an hour to get there, but I will be over. You'll get two helpers for the price of one; Kim is with me."

After disclosing to Kim what their mission would be and getting in the car, Kim asked, with what he perceived as a note of peevishness, "Isn't there a French philosopher's quotation that covers having a nice spring day with your husband interrupted?"

"No, not that I can think of, but there is a quote from the Big Book of Alcoholics Anonymous that I think covers this situation."

"And what is that?"

"Helping others is the foundation stone of recovery. A kind act occasionally isn't enough. We must act the good Samaritan every day, if need be. It may mean the loss of many nights' sleep, great interference with your pleasures, interruptions to your agenda."

Franklin smiled at the thought that that quotation seemed to satisfy Kim, and they spent the rest of the ride listening to the radio and occasionally commenting on a song.

When they arrived at Jeff's mother's apartment, they found Barbara looking spaced out, with a trash can beside her, which Franklin assumed was for her to vomit into. The apartment was a mess and had dirty dishes, beer cans and clothes strewn about. Jeff provided this explanation for the condition of his mother:

"That asshole Straka went on a two-week cruise with his wife to Europe. One thing I'll say for him, he usually tries to regulate mom's Percocet intake by giving her only a few days' worth. But he gave her a couple of weeks' worth because he was going on the fuckin' cruise and she must have been popping them like M&Ms."

While Franklin searched the apartment for pills, booze and any other mind-altering substances, Kim and Jeff tidied up the apartment and took out the garbage. As befitting someone who saw no need to hide their pills and booze, he found pills in the bathroom medicine cabinet and a few in a bottle by the commode. He poured the pills into the commode and, thinking that his job in the bathroom was complete at least, started to walk out toward the kitchen.

Something stopped him, though, and he thought of his hiding places for booze when Kim and he had a house. He then took the lid off the commode tank, and there, floating freely, were three pill bottles, each containing a couple of Percocet. He smiled. He had hidden vodka bottles in the toilet tank.

There were a couple of half–empty cheap liquor bottles in the kitchen and about half a case of beer. All were poured down the toilet. Jeff and

Kim weren't yet done with their cleanup, and he joined them. Barbara was beginning to come around and was moaning and crying.

"Since tomorrow is Sunday," Jeff advised, "I will sleep over tonight and spend all day tomorrow with Mom. I have to go to work on Monday, but I think that I can get our Jehovah's Witness neighbor to watch her during the day on Monday."

"It would be nice if we could get her into some sort of recovery facility," Franklin mused.

When the apartment passed Kim's muster, and as they were ready to go, Jeff said, almost offhandedly, "There is a guy that goes to my Monday night meeting who said he knows somebody who may have some information about Brad's case. He is supposed to let me know Monday if the guy will talk to me. I'll let you know what he says and you can pass it on to my brother's attorney if I think it's worthwhile."

Franklin replied that it sounded interesting.

"Yeah, but it's not going to make my brother the way he was."

CHAPTER 56-SAM DEPOSES LT. HODGSON AND GUARD SHANAHAN

The day he was supposed to depose Todd Shanahan, the guard whose son told him that Brad was gay and Lieutenant Hodgson, who was in charge of the Rover program, Sam couldn't pull up his zipper in the office bathroom. Unfortunately, he needed two working hands to accomplish that with this particular zipper. So he went back to his office in hopes that when he was seated he could accomplish this most personal task. He couldn't. Try as he might, this was a particularly intransigent zipper, which Becca had to help him "zoom up" at home before he came into the office. Despite his embarrassment, he buzzed Rhonda for assistance.

"Boss, my boyfriend would be upset with me if he knew that I was helping another man with his trouser zipper," Rhonda laughed. Sam's face reddened.

After Rhonda had ushered Fume and Lieutenant Kevin Hodgson into the conference room, and the court reporter and videographer were seated, Sam entered the room. Kevin Hodgson was a sturdily built man with a full head of salt and pepper hair and a mustache to match. He supposed that women would find him good looking or at least distinguished. When he started the deposition he learned that the Lieutenant was forty-eight.

He was a Marine Corps veteran of ten years, but curiously, he spent most of his time in the Corps as a cook or food service specialist and rose to the rank of Master Sergeant. Upon his discharge, he returned to his home in Coalton County, where he eventually married, had two children, and became divorced. His children were of school age. He had worked at the jail for fifteen years. He had accumulated a few accolades over the years for his work.

"Tell me what you know about the Inmate Rover Program, also known as the suicide prevention worker program."

"As I understand it, the Inmate Rovers began when the jail psychiatrist Dr. Rodriguez proposed it at a meeting with the Warden and

Annette Paulson, the jail psychologist. The meeting was several years ago. I am told that the program was aimed at new admittees, who are the most likely to attempt suicide. As you may know, jail suicides are one of our biggest problems."

"Were you at that meeting?"

"No, but I was told about the meeting by Annette Paulson."

"When did the meeting take place?"

"It's been at least seven or eight years ago."

"Did the program start shortly after the meeting to your understanding?"

"Yes, it did. Within weeks after I became aware of the meeting, there was an educational meeting to introduce the concept and explain the program."

"I know that Dr. Annette Paulson is the current jail psychologist, but I understand that Dr. Rodriguez has left his position as jail psychiatrist. How long ago did he leave?"

"It's gotta be about four or five years ago."

"And who was the warden at that time?"

"Scott Solomon, but he's long gone too. He left about the time Dr. Rodriguez did."

"How were these 'trustees' or Inmate Rovers chosen?"

"For the first several years of the program, I would in effect nominate them, and Dr. Rodriguez would administer some psychological testing. If they passed the 'test', he would give them a couple of hours of training on what to look for. When Dr. Rodriguez left and for a little while, Dr. Paulson would administer a psychological test on the candidates who I would pick."

"Is that still the process?"

"Well, no. There has been no psychological testing for a couple of years now."

"Why not?"

"We just decided that it wasn't necessary. In all the time Rodriguez was giving the tests, there were only two or three inmates that he rejected for the rover program. Dr. Paulson and I just decided that I knew the prisoners well enough to be able to choose."

"You said that Dr. Rodriguez gave them a couple of hours of training. I assume the training was mostly about how to spot likely suicides?"

"You would have to ask him about that. I never went to one of his 'classes'."

"But you have received training on spotting potential suicides, haven't you?"

"Every year, we need to attend a class on suicide prevention."

"How long is the class?"

"Two hours. It's a two-hour movie."

"What training did the Rovers receive after Dr. Rodriguez left, if you know?"

"Dr. Paulson was in charge of the training, but it's my understanding that she showed them the same movie as the guards saw."

"We are going to switch gears now. Are you familiar with a prisoner, I believe he's an ex-prisoner now, by the name of Jacques Lindstrom. It's my understanding that his nickname was Sledgehammer."

"You are right, he's an ex-prisoner, and yes, I am familiar with him."

"Now, how were… Let me first ask you, was it you that picked Mr. Lindstrom as a Rover?"

"Yes, I pretty much have exclusive authority over who I pick as Rovers. Of course, Dr. Paulson would have the right to veto any selection, but she never has."

"Why did you pick Mr. Lindstrom as a Rover?"

"Because he was respected as an ex-hockey jock; he was a big guy, he was in for what I considered to be a relatively minor offense and I liked the guy and thought that he would have a way with new prisoners."

"Did he have a way with new prisoners?"

"In my estimation, he did, yes."

"Were you aware that his nickname, Sledgehammer, was heard by another prisoner within the time period when Brad hung himself?"

"No, but so what? Prisoners are always yelling something."

"Have you ever conducted an investigation regarding Brad's attempted hanging?"

"Yes, but I didn't learn much. Only he knows why he tried to hang himself, and he can't talk. At least that's what I understand."

"Are your investigative findings contained in your report?" Sam had obtained through discovery a report authored by the Lieutenant. It didn't contain anything of interest.

"Yes, and that's all I know. As I said, we don't know much, and your client is not talking."

"Have you ever discussed Brad's hanging with Mr. Lindstrom?"

"No, why would I?"

"How about previous to Brad's attempted suicide by hanging? Had you ever discussed any aspect of Brad's incarceration with Mr. Lindstrom?"

"I don't believe so."

"Prior to Brad's attempted suicide, had you had any conversation with Guard Shannahan?"

"Yeah, he told me that his son told him that Brad was gay. We briefly discussed the results of his suicide assessment questionnaire. It was a brief conversation."

"Did you relay the information that Brad was gay to any person after your discussion with Guard Shannahan?"

"No."

"It's my understanding that Mr. Lindstrom has been discharged. Do you know where he is now?"

"Yeah, he was discharged a couple of months ago. I understand that he went back to Canada."

Sam asked many more questions in an effort to flesh out the rover program and then brought the deposition to a conclusion. He was suffering from a mild anxiety attack because of his grim concentration on his word choice during the deposition as well as his infernal consciousness of the muscle movements necessary for the formation of words. He closed his eyes and put his feet up on the desk before Rhonda buzzed him and told him that Todd Shanahan was in the conference room for his deposition.

"Oh, and Steve asked me to remind you that you said he could sit in on this deposition."

"I did, and am reminded, and tell Steve to meet me in the conference room."

When he entered the conference room, he saw Fume seated next to a white-haired, blue-eyed, bearded man in his late forties, which he assumed was Todd Shanahan. Steve sat across the table from Fume, and Hodgson sat directly across the table from Shanahan and next to Steve. Sam looked askance at Hodgson and flippantly asked Fume, "Didn't the Lieutenant have enough of me this morning?

Fume's response, "You wouldn't mind if the Lieutenant sat in on Officer Shanahan's deposition, do you?" to which Sam replied with a shrug of his shoulder, the one that he had control over and a negative nod of his head.

He then began with a request from Fume. "Mr. Fume, before we begin, I am going to ask for any and all documents pertaining to the Rover Program since its inception."

Fume nodded and said, "Put it in a request for production, and we will respond appropriately."

He then began the deposition with the standard questions regarding his background and discovered that Shanahan was a Coalton County resident, was married for a little over twenty years, had an associate's degree in psychology, and had been employed for fifteen years at the Coalton County Jail.

He then inquired about any honors or commendations and got an entire laundry list. He didn't betray his amusement, but he thought that commendations were so frequent that these guards must get a commendation every time they took a shit.

Shanahan was, of course, aware of the Rover Program and Lieutenant Hodgkin's involvement with it. When he asked if he knew that Jacques Lindstrom was a Rover at the time that Brad attempted suicide by hanging in January, he responded that he did.

"And did you have any contact with Brad when he was admitted to the Coalton County Jail?

"Yes, as a matter of fact, I was responsible for his initial processing."

"And what does that initial processing entail?"

"Placing the new admittees personal belongings in a receptacle for safekeeping, a body cavity search, the issuance of inmate clothing, fingerprinting, paperwork and administration of the suicide questionnaire."

Of course, Sam had had the questionnaire and Brad's responses reviewed by Stewart, who had found nothing unusual about them, but he asked Shanahan whether he found any "red flags" in Brad's answers. He snapped, "Well, no one likes to be arrested and thrown in jail; needless to say, it's a very stressful event. But if you're asking whether there was any indication of suicidal tendency that required immediate action, I would say no."

"Now, we have learned that you told some people that Brad was allegedly gay, correct?"

"True."

"Was Lieutenant Hodgson one of those people?"

"Yes, I thought he ought to know."

Shanahan then clarified, "Because gay people, particularly young gay people, are at much greater risk in the prison environment."

"And what did Lieutenant Hodgson say?"

"Nothing much. I told him that my son told me about your client a couple of weeks ago; he said there was a guy in his class who was gay. Didn't try to hide it. And I told Lieutenant Hodgson that the kid that he told me about was Brad and he had just been arrested and was here."

"You have related what you told Lieutenant Hodgson and I suppose I should have asked you first what you told him. Now I am asking what he said to you when you told him about Brad."

Shanahan's brow furrowed, and he looked directly at Lieutenant Hodgson. For the briefest of moments, their eyes locked. Then Shanahan, in what Sam interpreted as a very slightly timorous voice, asked the court reporter if he could read back the question. He did, and Shanahan, in a timbre slightly louder and more emphatic than the rest of his answers, declared, "You would have to ask him that question. I really don't remember much about what he said to me."

"Did you have any other conversation either with Lieutenant Hodgson or any other person, or overhear a conversation regarding Brad before Brad attempted suicide?"

"I don't think so.."

Sam, sensing that Shanahan's response might be less than complete, pressed, "You don't remember anything that your superior told you when you told him that an eighteen year old admittee to the jail was gay? I suspect that that doesn't happen every day."

Fume interceded, "Was that a question or an observation? If you could consider the first part of the question a question, I am going to object because it has been asked and answered. You may answer it again if you wish, Officer Shanahan."

"I don't remember distinctly what he said to me."

"Do you remember anything about what he said to you?"

Sam got the reaction from Fume that he expected, "How many more times are you going to ask him this question? It's been asked and answered. I am going to object, but I will allow him to answer it one last time and then I will direct him not to answer the question."

"Well, Officer Shanahan, do you remember anything about your conversation with a Lieutenant?"

"Only what I told you previously. That whole night is a blur."

"Have you discussed Brad's suicide attempt with any person, whether employed by the Jail or otherwise, since you became aware of his attempt?"

"I did discuss it with my wife and my son, but I only told them that we had an attempted suicide by hanging at the jail, and I told my son that it was his classmate, Brad Moran. They were saddened by the news of his attempt. We discussed, my wife and son and I, his devastating injuries. Other than that, there was just idle talk around the jail that I heard and pretty much disregarded."

"Anything specific?"

"No, just idle talk, and I don't even remember what it was. They know better than to make tasteless and vicious comments about gays around me."

"May I ask why?"

"Because I have gay friends and relatives if you must know."

After a few more perfunctory questions about the Rover program, to which Shanahan added little to Sam's knowledge, Sam concluded the deposition. As all the participants in the deposition filed out of the conference room, and as Sam passed the desk of Rhonda, she whispered, "You look like you have been FUMigated." Sam smiled; she was obviously attempting to lighten his mood.

Steve followed Sam into his office, and Sam asked him what he thought of his first real deposition. "Shanahan is probably hiding something, but it seems his heart is in the right place. Maybe it will come clean."

Sam, who was physically and psychologically exhausted, could only muster a nod and a halfhearted smile.

CHAPTER 57-NICOLE COVERS THE GAY PRIDE PARADE

The morning of the Gay Pride Parade held the promise of being a fantastic day, weatherwise, if somewhat hot and sticky. Since Steve had been out drinking until 2 o'clock in the morning with his summer school–attending law student buddies, Nicole was forced to roust him out of bed. She had been up since 8 o'clock, watching a special that CNN was running on the history of the gay rights movement.

She plied him with French toast, his favorite breakfast food, and he seemed to rally.

"We want to get there early enough so that we get a good spot on the sidewalk. I want to be close enough to gather in some of the candy that's thrown," she said with a grin.

A French toast muffled grunt was all she got in reply.

"I was just watching a program about the gay rights movement. The historical treatment of gays in this country has been disgusting."

This time, she got a more cogent response from Steve, "We don't celebrate differences in this country. We demonize them. And color, religion and sexuality are all differences. I sometimes think that a lot of human beings would really want a society where we all were the same, like those fifties and sixties sci-fi movies where everyone looks and acts the same."

"You sound like my editor, which reminds me, Tim gave me a press credential when I was working on that West Virginia piece. I can hang it around my neck. It might help us to get closer to the action."

"Tim is obviously a brilliant man, and his press credential might let you get more candy."

When they had both donned their summer outfits of shorts and a T-shirt and while they were driving the short distance to downtown Pittsburgh, Steve observed that he doubted that many readers of the Greene Gazette had ever attended any celebration in which gays were welcome, let alone a gay pride parade.

"That's why I am here, to enlighten and educate." That brought a snarky chuckle from Steve.

The parade had drawn quite a crowd. There was a lot of candy tossed to children and adults; Nicole gave most of the candy that she and Steve were able to snag to three delightful elementary school-aged kids standing beside them on the sidewalk. Most of it, she noted, was tossed by clowns dressed in drag in colorful tutus. There were a dozen or more obviously opulent floats that bore the logos of many Pittsburgh–based and a few national companies. Many organizations had their banners carried by presumably gay members and employees.

Steve specifically commented on the many major law firms in the city represented in the parade, as well as the County Bar Association. He related a story told by his father, "My Dad said that in the mid-90s, his firm realized that they needed to approach the gay community for business. Those were in the days when law firms had brochures, and my dad's firm produced a brochure directed at addressing the legal issues confronting gays. He said, 'Leave it to capitalism and greed to make that which was once thought to be disgusting a revenue source to be pandered to.'

Several politicians, including a United States Senator, were walking in the parade, waving to the crowd. She couldn't help but think that the Stonewall Riots, which she had learned about in the television program this morning and which sparked the gay rights movement, were a little over fifty years ago. How many politicians, let alone United States senators, would have openly supported gay rights then? In some ways, she thought, the country had become more enlightened in fifty years but had regressed in other ways.

She first saw him in the distance: He looked to be an unkempt and confused teenager with a sign dangling from his neck, standing and talking to someone. He then rejoined the parade, but she suspected that he was not a credentialed parade participant. As he came into clearer view, she could see that the homemade but obviously artistically drawn sign said, "Remember Brad–Justice for Brad." Her pulse quickened.

The acne–faced young man with a sparse beard growth was passing out photocopied papers that read, *Bradley Moran suffered injuries which made him a vegetable when he hanged himself in the Coalton County Jail. Was he mistreated in jail, and was that the reason that he hanged himself? Brad was gay, and was that the reason that he was mistreated and hanged himself?"*

Nicole told Steve, "I've got to talk to this guy," and she ran down the street. "Hey Justice Guy, can I talk to you for a minute?"

She could tell he was looking at her press badge and deciding what he should do. He asked the obvious question, "Am I going to be quoted in a newspaper? Who do you work for?"

"I think I am going to write a story about this parade for the Greene County Gazette, and I'm interested in your sign. What do you know about Brad? I am somewhat familiar with what happened to him."

"How?"

"My boyfriend works for the attorney who represents Brad in his case against the jail."

She could tell by the look on his face that he was deciding whether he should talk to her or clam up. He apparently had decided on the former: "I'm Kip. I am Brad's boyfriend."

"My name is Nicole, a reporter for the Greene Gazette. And I am sympathetic to the cause."

"If your boyfriend works for the lawyer who represents Brad, you know all about him. What can I tell you?"

"For starters, you can tell me why you think that Brad was mistreated."

"All the kids at school think that him being gay had something to do with his hanging, and a couple of them have parents that work at the jail. Maybe they know something."

"In what way was he mistreated?"

"I can't really say; it's just the talk around the school."

"Okay then, what can you tell me about your and Brad's relationship?"

"Well, first of all, Brad was devoted to his mother." He then went on to explain what she already knew from our conversations with Steve, that basically, Brad was motivated to break into the drugstore to satisfy his mother's addiction.

"And I spent a lot of time with Brad and his mother; Brad was not an addict. He might sometimes take a few pills, but in no way was he a space cadet."

He talked about Brad's kindness to him when his own mother was debilitated with "cancer".

"That's when I guess you could say we fell in love."

Kip then sat down on the curb, chin in hands, and tried to suppress his tears.

"That's why when those fuckers at school refer to Brad as 'my vegetable boyfriend' or say, 'Is he a carrot today?' I just want to kill the fuckers. They don't know how kind Brad is."

He then went on to describe their first date together, which was a movie and ice cream, the first time making out in the car and other intimate details of their relationship. Then Kip, holding back the tears that had periodically erupted throughout their curb-side chat, was adamant, "You said your boyfriend works for the lawyer who represents Brad. Tell him that I know Brad, and he wouldn't have attempted suicide unless he had given up hope."

Nicole assured him that she would relay that message to Steve and watched Kip as he made his way back into the parade.

She rejoined Steve on the sidewalk, and Steve asked her who the kid was that she had been talking to. When she told him it was Brad's boyfriend, Kip, and that all the kids in their high school think that Brad's sexuality had something to do with his suicide attempt, Steve responded:

"That may be, but Sam says we would need to prove either a jail employee participated in some action that made Brad's suicide a foreseeable risk or prove that the jail or its employees were deliberately indifferent to the risk of his attempted suicide. We don't have proof of either. Did he say that he had proof, or was this just idle talk among his classmates?"

"I guess that it would fit the category of idle talk. He wanted me to tell you that he knew Brad and that Brad would not have tried to commit suicide unless he felt hopeless."

"Hmmm… Did you learn anything else?"

"Just about how typical their relationship was to any teenage romance. I guess that love really is love." And when she wrote the article for the Greene Gazette, "Love is love" was her concluding sentence.

CHAPTER 58-FRANKLIN AND KIM DISCUSS SUICIDE

"Kim, you are a Catholic. Even if you're not a practicing Catholic, you must know the rules, don't you?"

Franklin and Kim were watching a movie on Netflix together, and some question of Catholic dogma was broached by a character. It reminded him that he had been thinking about Brad's suicide attempt and its religious implications off and on. Jeff had told him that he and Brad were lapsed Catholics and that Jeff's mother, Barbara, had been obsessing about whether he was consigned to hell or not because of the attempted suicide.

"You mean the no fish on Friday deal?"

Franklin smiled, "No, a little more philosophical than that. I've been thinking about Brad's attempted suicide."

"What about it?"

"Is suicide still considered to be a mortal sin for which there cannot be forgiveness?"

"How do you know about mortal sins?"

"I overheard a conversation about them in the student cafeteria. Duquesne is a Catholic school, you know."

"I am well aware of that." Kim smiled.

"Well, is it an unforgivable sin or not?"

"It used to be, but I think the church now recognizes that if it's the result of a psychiatric problem or fear of suffering or torture, the severity of the sin is lessened."

"What the hell does lessening the severity of the sin mean?"

"I think that the Catholic church now leaves it in God's hands as to whether some psychological problem or fear of suffering or torture makes you eligible for eternal salvation."

Franklin thought for a moment and then offered, "According to Albert Camus, 'There is but one serious philosophical problem and that is suicide. Judging whether life is or is not worth living amounts to answering the fundamental question of philosophy.' of course, Camus meant it was in each person's hands."

She frowned, in part because he knew that she found his constant quoting of French philosophers to be irritating as hell, but conceded, "I suppose you and Camus are right about it being the most fundamental question."

Franklin effectively concluded the conversation by getting off the couch to score a bag of potato chips. As he was walking into the kitchen, he thought that the mitigating factors for suicide as a sin, namely, psychiatric problems, fear of suffering or fear of torture, were probably always present. He theorized that all three of these mitigating factors might apply to Brad. Of course, he was much closer to Camus' position on the issue, but if Jeff ever raised his mother's concern again, he could give Jeff something to allay her fear of Brad's eternal damnation.

CHAPTER 59-SAM MEETS BRIAN (CALL ME B)

He took a limousine to meet Brian Lowe, who, Jeff told him, preferred you to call him B. Lowe. B had come to him through a circuitous route. Franklin told Sam that Jeff, whom he was sponsoring, had met a guy at one of his AA meetings who said he knew a guy who might know something about Brad's attempted hanging. Franklin and Jeff then approached the AA guy, and he offered to introduce them to the purported witness, B. Lowe. They, Franklin and Jeff and "the AA guy" went to where B, who had been recently from the Coalton County lockup, was staying. They found his story to be credible.

So, he was going to meet Jeff and together, they would attend a prearranged meeting with B. But first, he had to endure his limousine driver spouting all sorts of conspiracy theories, including that multimillionaire Jews, in league with Hillary Clinton, were having tracking devices implanted in the arms of anyone who got a flu shot. Thankfully, he wouldn't have to put up with the driver on the way home. Jeff had offered to drive him back to his office.

The driver pulled up to a multi-story, totally nondescript red brick apartment building with balconies that could accommodate two lawn chairs and maybe a little round table on which you could place drinks. He saw a tall, very slim, good–looking fellow who appeared to be waiting for someone. He approached the limousine, and as Sam awkwardly emerged with his cane, offered his hand and introduced himself. It was Jeff.

He proceeded with Jeff into the building and knocked on the nondescript door, which had a marijuana leaf decal under the peephole. After half a dozen knocks, a fortyish-looking balding man with what was left of his hair tied back in a ponytail opened the door. His well-lined face was a testament to a life that had seen its share of excitement, most of it, Sam suspected, of a legally questionable sort. He was dressed in cutoff shorts and a Megadeth wife beater.

"I remember you. You are Jeff, Brad's brother, and," pointing at Sam, "you must be his mouthpiece."

Jeff affirmed their identities, and Brian Lowe introduced himself, "But my friends all call me B."

The apartment's living room contained two battered chairs and a round, small metal table of the sort that would typically be a balcony appointment. B explained the paucity of furnishings by saying that he was temporarily staying in his friend's apartment, which his friend had vacated because he had rented another apartment. His friend's lease on this apartment was up in two weeks, so, he explained, he would need to find someplace else to crash.

He pointed to the two chairs and announced, "You guys sit in the chairs and I'll sit on the floor. How did you become a gimp?" B asked, pointing to Sam. Sam responded that he had suffered a stroke, to which B mused, "That's probably good that you are representing Brad. You will get a lot of sympathy from the jury because you're a gimp, and hopefully that will carry over to your vegetable client."

Sam was stoical during B's projection of the jury's response to having a gimp represent a vegetable and did not betray his disgust. Instead, he smiled and declared, "So, it's my understanding that you were a witness to Brad's being assaulted, correct?"

"That's right, I saw the whole thing, that fucker Sledgehammer beat the shit out of Brad while another prisoner held him by his arms."

"Who was the guy that held him?"

"I only heard him referred to by his nickname, which was Flake. I assumed that it had something to do with what he was in for. My guess is that he was a coke dealer."

"What caused you to be in Brad's cell that night?"

"I wasn't in Brad's cell, but you gotta understand that it was quiet time. Meaning that cell doors would still be open, and the guys could mill about as long as they were sort of quiet. I was milling outside of Brad's cell."

"What did you see and hear?"

"Well, what drew me to Brad's cell was sort of a commotion that was outside his cage. I walked over there, and I saw Sledgehammer yelling, 'You better be careful gump or you'll get fucked up like this every day'."

Sam knew that "gump" was prison slang for gay. He asked B what happened next.

"Then, I saw this guy Flake grab Brad, and Sledgehammer hit him in the fuckin' face a few times. And it weren't no love tap."

"Did you see where he struck him on his face?"

"I saw punches to his jaw and eye area and that's when I high-tailed it out of there before the son of a bitch came for me."

"What do you mean, 'came for you'? Why would he come for you?" Sam sensed there was a story there.

B cackled, then explained, "Let's just say that Sledgehammer and I had a history."

B attempted to clarify, "We had a fight over chalk, and he attacked me."

Sam was bewildered by what B meant by chalk.

"It means moonshine: hooch made by prison chemists like me."

"So you got into a physical altercation over alcohol. Were you hurt?"

"I ended up in the infirmary over it."

"Was any guard aware that Sledgehammer was involved in causing your injuries?"

"I told the doctor who stitched me up. Look, you can still see the scar on my cheek. I used to have such a fuckin' angel face. The asshole guards did an investigation and said that I started the fight, and Sledgehammer was just protectin' hisself. What a fuckin' kangaroo court."

Sam realized that, if the case ever went to trial, opposing counsel would imply, no outright scream, that B's testimony against Sledgehammer was due to his personal animus towards Sledgehammer. Then, Sam decided to explore another subject of what he was certain would be an additional area of attack on B's credibility.

"B, I pulled your criminal record and you have quite a few convictions that bear upon your honesty and credibility."

"Oh yeah. Well, I ain't lying now, and I ain't never been convicted of lying per se."

"I know, but you have a number of convictions, albeit minor convictions, of crimes that involve dishonesty. For example, you have three convictions involving stolen credit cards and a bad check conviction. Opposing counsel will use these in his cross-examination of you."

"Is that lying? No."

"I see your point," Sam temporized. He saw no need to correct B's obvious misstatement of the law. " But they are crimes involving dishonesty. And what you were in jail for last time, defrauding an elderly couple on a home remodeling contract. That's a crime involving dishonesty."

"Yeah, but I wasn't the mastermind behind that. It was my buddy. I was going to do the work. I pled guilty because my shitty public defender told me to."

Sam spent another fifteen minutes or so fleshing out B's story of Sledgehammer's assault on Brad, and try as he might, Sam was unable to find any inconsistencies in B's account. He expressed his concern again about B weathering a withering cross-examination regarding the altercation with Sledgehammer and his personal animosity towards Sledgehammer.

"I'm an old courtroom veteran, I can handle it," was B's retort.

"Opposing counsel will undoubtedly want to depose you, but I will prepare for the deposition in my office."

Sam then confirmed B's cell phone number and told him that he needed to inform him of whatever his current address was. Sam then shook hands with B, and Jeff and B went through an elaborate mutual smacking and grabbing of hands, which Sam assumed was their equivalent of shaking hands.

They got into Jeff's car for the trip back to Sam's office. Sam's mouth was tired from concentrating on forming words, so he was glad when Jeff prattled on about the Pirates' chances of making the playoffs, his baseball career, and his recollections of his father's coaching of his teams. Jeff then became somber, and it was revealed to Sam that his father had died in an automobile accident. That prompted an extended period of silence.

When they were almost to Sam's office, Jeff asked the million-dollar question, "Did you believe B?"

Sam replied, "Yes, but I am not sure that a jury will."

CHAPTER 60-NICOLE MEETS BRAD AND GEORGIA

When Nicole mentioned off-handedly that she might be interested in writing an article or maybe a series of articles about Brad, Steve said that he and Sam were attending opposing counsel's deposition of Brad on Wednesday. He was driving Sam to Brad's facility, and he asked if she wanted to come.

"I'm not sure that you could attend the deposition but you would get to see Brad because we are meeting with him privately before the deposition."

"I thought that, for all intents and purposes, Brad was in a vegetative state. What does the attorney for the jail hope to get out of him?"

"Not much, except I have been told that if you ask him what his name is he can give a pretty good approximation of Brad Moran. But I think opposing counsel really wants to get a look at him so he knows what the jury might see."

She surely must meet the person who would be the subject of her articles she thought, and agreed to accompany them. Wednesday came and she found herself in Sam's car. Steve had driven them to Sam's office in his Lexus convertible and secured Sam's car from the parking lot of his building.

When Steve brought the car around the front of the building and picked up Sam, who was waiting on the sidewalk, Sam smiled and asked, "To what do we owe the honor of the attractive young woman sitting in the backseat?"

"Oh, her," Steve teased, "she wants to do an article or a series of articles or a friggin' book about Brad and I told her that she could see Brad before our deposition."

"Well, Ms. Lois Lane, I can think of a lot worse things you could write about than poor Brad," Sam said.

"I guess that makes me Superman, eh Sam," Steve cackled.

"Hardly," she said with feigned disgust.

When they got to The Meadows, Sam merely nodded to the receptionist and she directed him, "Go on back, Mr. Wright." They found Brad sitting in a wheelchair with some sort of contraption around his neck, which, she assumed, was to keep his head from flopping around. Then the nurse, who Sam called Carrie, cheerfully said, "Here's Brad. Are you ready for your deposition, Brad? "

A faint smile graced Brad's face as Sam enthused, "Brad, the last time I saw you, you were um… asleep."

"Why do they want to take Brad's deposition anyway?" Nicole could see the look of puzzlement on Carrie's face.

"Opposing counsel just wants to see Brad here and gauge how sympathetic he will be to a jury. I suspect that the deposition will only last a few minutes if that."

"Well, they could get him to answer one question: Name, name, name Brad." Carrie prompted. He responded with something like an approximation of Brad Moran.

"Will he improve much more?" Sam whispered to Carrie, she assumed so Brad wouldn't hear.

Carrie replied in a normal volume, "His doctor doesn't think so. Oh, the family might be able to take him out for a few hours eventually, but nothing more. He can't understand anything other than one-word directives, so you don't have to whisper."

"You have some experience and knowledge, Carrie, and we will have an expert project his lifetime medical costs at trial, which will be considerable, but how much longer do you think he may be with us?"

"I prefer not to predict what God is going to do. I know who you guys are, the firm of Grey and Wright, but who is the beautiful young lady with you?"

Sam reported, "That's Nicole. She is the girlfriend of Mr. Grey here, and an ex-client of mine. She won't be attending the deposition; she will wait here. She is thinking about writing an article about Brad."

From across the room, standing by the bed of Brad's only "roommate," came a half-shout, "She would be welcome to keep me company for a little while, and to make it worth her while I would buy her breakfast."

"That's Georgia Imhoff," Carrie advised, "and if I were you, Nicole, I would take her up on the offer. I hear she buys one helluva breakfast."

Nicole smiled and, directing her comment across the room to the person identified to her as Georgia Imhoff, bellowed, "It sounds like the deposition is only going to take a few minutes, so I can't have breakfast, but I'm happy to keep you company until my men get back."

While "her men" and Carrie exited the room with Brad in a wheelchair, Nicole walked the few steps over to the roommate's bed and saw an emaciated-looking man of indeterminate age, eyes closed, laying in bed. Standing beside him and holding his hand was an attractive middle-aged woman whose dark hair was flecked with white.

After introductions, Nicole asked if this was Georgia's son.

Her answer was a faltering, "Yes, it is, his name is Daniel. And what is your relationship with that poor young man? I understand that he hung himself."

"I am the girlfriend, I guess you could say, of the law student who works for the attorney. The attorney is an older man who has a quad cane. If you don't mind my asking, what is your son here for?"

"That's a long story, but the condensed version is this: Daniel here was born with cerebral palsy. Severe cerebral palsy. We, his father and I knew it from shortly after his birth. He has to be fed, is incontinent and can speak only a few words, but when he smiled, it would light up my world."

"Does his father visit him as well?"

"His father, my ex-husband, has a second family now with his new wife, but he has been here a couple of times."

"Has he been here for long?"

"Only for four months. I cared for him and our home until then, with the exception of his hospitalizations, but most of them were for a couple of days and at most a week."

"What happened?"

"He suffered a stroke; they don't know why. He is comatose now, and they say not to get our hopes up that he will ever recover and be like he used to be."

"It's good that he has a mother that is as dedicated as you. He must feel your presence. Do you come to visit him often?"

"I am here every day from morning until night." Her voice began to catch. "He's my baby, and I am his mother. Isn't that what mothers are supposed to do, take care of their babies."

Nicole said, almost in a whisper, "My mother died about three years ago now, and I can hear her voice as you say that."

"She must have been a good mother then."

"She was the best, present company excluded of course. In fact, you two would have been in a competition for best mother."

"Thank you, Nicole," Georgia whimpered.

"Mom wrote poetry, and this was the last poem that she wrote to me before she died, and something tells me that she would want you to have it because I think it describes you and Daniel..."

Nicole always kept a copy of that poem in her purse, and when she had extracted it, she handed the poem to Georgia. Georgia read it aloud:

We are as doves in summer sky,

Through laughter and tears, we fly,

Free, but following the other's flight,

Fearful but trusting the other's sight.

Our wings are stretched around white clouds of love,

With security below and independence about,

Doves in summer sky,

Sometimes wanting safer stands or to pass the other by,

But never leaving, we fly.

Then Georgia embraced her, and Nicole and Georgia spent the rest of the time before Nicole's "men" came back, holding hands and gazing down at Daniel.

When Carrie wheeled Brad back into the room, followed closely by Steve and Sam, Nicole, still holding Georgia's hand, asked them how the deposition went.

Sam growled, "It was just as I thought, primarily to allow Fume to assess the sympathy which he thinks Brad would engender in a jury. Brad gave him a fairly credible answer when Fume asked him his name. He had to ask him what his name was three times, though."

Directing her question to Nicole, Georgia asked, "In all the time I have been in here with Daniel, I have never seen Brad's mother visit him. I hope she's not ill or, God forbid, deceased."

Nicole wondered what she should divulge to this woman who was a total stranger half an hour ago. She decided to be deliberately vague, "Oh, she doesn't have a car or any way of getting here from Coalton, and I guess that's why you haven't seen her. Brad's attempted hanging put her in a tailspin I am told."

"I drive, and I wouldn't mind some company on occasion. Is there any way of telling her about my offer?"

"I would think we can get word to her."

Georgia wrote her cell phone number on a piece of paper and gave it to Nicole.

When the three of them were in the car and headed back to Sam's office, Steve asked her, "So what's the deal with that woman you were talking to; was she Brad's roommate's mother?"

"Yes, and she has basically dedicated her life to caring for her son." Then Nicole explained that her son was diagnosed with severe cerebral palsy at birth and suffered a stroke months ago.

"And she is at the Meadows every day from morning until night. She says it's what mothers do. She hadn't seen Brad's mother make an appearance, so she volunteered to pick Brad's mother up in Coalton occasionally and take her to the Meadows. She wrote down her number."

Sam asked her for the number, and told her that he would see that Brad's mother got it.

CHAPTER 61-FRANKLIN'S CHANCE ELEVATOR MEETING

Franklin called Sam on his Tuesday lunch break to recount the conversation which he and Officer Todd Shanahan had at his regular Monday night AA/NA meeting at the Coalton County Jail. Thankfully, Sam picked up. Franklin then launched into his narrative:

Acknowledging that it was pure coincidence that caused Franklin and Shanahan to be on the same elevator last night, Franklin told the as yet unknown guard sharing an elevator with him that he had observed an inmate knitting at his meeting that night.

Franklin explained that after getting a nod from the guard, who later introduced himself as Shanahan, he told the guard, "He was a big guy, and I had never seen that before. He said that recently, you guys had permitted knitting with plastic needles, of course. He said that a guard had told him that it was a gentle pursuit and allowable because prisoners had a lot of time on their hands."

Franklin reported that Shanahan told him, "That guard was me who told him, and the big guy was an inmate named Miller"

"I didn't know that, but it makes sense," Sam sounded truly surprised and interested, "but I am glad that the jail only permits knitting with plastic needles."

Franklin got to the point. "And then, in a fit of dark humor, I said, 'I'm just glad he wasn't knitting a noose.' Well, if looks could kill, Shanahan's scowl would have been the last thing I ever saw. Then, after giving me his obviously pissed-off look, he says, 'You probably don't want to kid about that around here.'"

"Well, one thing led to another. We got off the elevator and continued to talk, and he told me that he had recently been called in for a deposition on a jail-hanging case. That's when I made the connection to you, but I just played along like I didn't know shit about it."

"Go on."

"We talk a little longer, and he says, 'You know, I don't know why anybody gives a damn about who's zooming who, even if they are of the same sex, and I sure as fuck don't think that a kid should almost lose his life over stealing a smoke. I hear they roughed him up pretty good."

"Did he say who roughed him up?"

"No, he didn't. And when I asked him whether anyone had okayed roughing him up, he just stared at me as if I knew something that I shouldn't. And then, without a word, he walked away."

Franklin heard Sam whistle and then theorize, "I think he knew something more than he let on during our deposition."

"I guess that Jeff and B must have told you all about this fellow Sledgehammer?" Sam said.

"Yes, and what did I tell you? It did have something to do with cigarettes," an exultant Franklin gushed.

"Indeed, you did. You have been given a gift from someone or something."

"De Chardin said, 'We are not human beings having a spiritual experience. We are spiritual beings having a human experience.'"

There was an uncomfortable silence from the other end of the phone as if Sam was considering what his reaction should be. Then, Sam launched a totally different topic because he knew that he was discomfited but accepting of Franklin's "gift": "I deposed Dr. Julio Rodriguez via Zoom yesterday, and he had some interesting things to say about inmate rovers."

"Oh yeah, like what."

"Like about how critical it was that safeguards be established to assure that the program didn't go off the rails."

"Like, what was going to keep it on the rails?"

"Rodriguez said that it was important that he psychiatrically screen all inmates suggested as candidates for rovers, and he stressed that inmate rovers who were walking around observing other inmates in their cells should be stable."

"That is interesting."

"And… he said that the primary purpose of having inmate rovers was to have another set of eyes and ears to assist in assessing suicidality."

"What was their training regarding recognizing suicidality?"

"Now, or when Rodriguez was there?"

"Both."

"When Rodriguez was there, he personally held a two-hour class on suicide recognition and prevention for the rovers. Now, it's an hour movie, and they may serve popcorn for all I know."

"How were the rovers selected at the time Brad was in?"

"The jail psychologist has basically transferred the responsibility to Lieutenant Hodgson. He said that he knew the inmates best. So, I suspect that whoever were the biggest ass kissers got the job."

"Jeff told me about your meeting with B. Does that make your case?" Franklin was curious.

"Although it's an awfully thin reed, I think it does give us a case that won't be dismissed and a jury will render a verdict. You see, as with all civil rights cases against a government, you have got to prove that the government was deliberately indifferent to the rights of the person who is making the claim."

"So the mere fact that Brad tried to hang himself is insufficient?"

"No, otherwise, there would be more lawsuits than the courts could possibly handle. Jail hangings are an everyday occurrence. No, you have to have some connection to the jail administration or employees. Sledgehammer gives us that nexus because he was technically an employee of the jail. But even that may not be sufficient, we need to prove that the jail administration was deliberately indifferent in his selection and training."

"How do you do that?" Franklin's head was swimming.

"We prove that by the fact that the jail psychologist and Lieutenant Hodgson should have known having rovers was a disaster waiting to happen, particularly when they were not given psychological tests or adequate training."

"But, if what I hear is correct, you need to have a jury believe first that this dude Sledgehammer beat the shit out of Brad, causing Brad to hang himself, and this dude B is the only one that can say that. Do you think the jury will believe B?"

"That's going to be the million-dollar question, Franklin."

"Oh, I have some news on the Barbara front". Franklin thought that in mind as well end the conversation on an upbeat note.

"What's that?"

"I think that she has been clean and sober for a couple of days."

"How did you accomplish that miracle?"

"I didn't. Jeff did. We went to Barbara's apartment and threw away all of her pills and booze. Then, Jeff contacted two or three doctors in town who were writing scripts for Barbara's pills, and somehow or other, they quit writing scripts. She has no car to get out of town to replenish her supply, and she was forced to go cold turkey."

"That's great, but do you think her abstinence will hold?"

"Well," Franklin proclaimed, "I am somewhat optimistic. Of course, as Voltaire said, 'Optimism is the madness of insisting that all is well when we are miserable.'"

CHAPTER 62-A BERET TOPPED B IS DEPOSED

Rhonda buzzed him and told him that there was a Mr. B to see him. It was the day that Fume had scheduled Brian Lowe's deposition, and he was here early for his prep prior to being deposed.

As he opened the door, he was confronted by the countenance of B, clad in a starched white shirt, red beret and, incongruously, a pair of cut-off blue jean shorts, which were definitely too short. He didn't know quite what to say, so he settled on "nice beret".

"I figured I would look good for the deposition, so I borrowed one of my buddy's white shirts and got it pressed at a dry cleaners down the street."

"You make a dashing figure in your shorts and beret." Sam struggled to disguise any note of amusement that he might reveal. Apparently, it worked.

"I have worn a beret off and on for years and I figured it fit the occasion. And I know that I will be sitting at a table, so they'll not see my shorts on camera."

"So you have been deposed before?"

"Yeah, once before when my ex-friend who ran the home remodeling scam was sued. That fucker ended up getting me convicted of theft by deception, but then you already know about that."

"I'm glad that you showed up. I thought you might not."

"Why? I might have been in a little bit of trouble with the law, but I am an honorable man. Besides, I want to see that son of a bitch, Sledgehammer get his. Do you think they might charge him, if they can find him that is?"

"I am afraid that is out of my hands, but they might, and they certainly should." Sam didn't want to dampen B's motivation.

"Can't we sue the jail for him assaulting me? I'm a little light right now."

Sam effectively parried the question by giving B a densely ambiguous answer.

While he was trying to decipher what Sam had said, they went over what B saw and heard the night that Brad hung himself two or three times, and B did not indicate that he would vary his story. They also reviewed the odyssey of B's criminal activity because it was certain to be highlighted by Fume in the deposition and, more importantly, at trial. B didn't broach the subject of suing Sledgehammer anymore that day.

Then his intercom lit up and Rhonda announced that Fume was here for the deposition and he had made a quick bathroom stop. That gave Rhonda license to quip because Fume was out of earshot that the Fume was off the rose. Then when he assumed that she heard his laughter through his office door, she added, "Get ready for some gloom and Fume."

The deposition began pretty much as he expected it would but for B's slight embellishment on the story that he had told Sam. When Fume asked him what he heard Sledgehammer say to Brad that night, he answered emphatically, "You better be careful, Gump, because I have permission to fuck you up like this every day." He then went on to describe how Flake grabbed Brad by the arms, and Sledgehammer beat him about the head, and, he added as he did during his initial meeting with Sam, "and it wasn't no love taps." He repeated that he heard that threatening language from Sledgehammer consistently, and through many iterations of what was essentially the same question.

Fume must have gotten some information that Sam didn't have concerning B. Sam was incredulous when Fume asked B why he was discharged from his employment in a New York brokerage firm, and B related that his brother, who was employed as a broker by the firm, got him a job running errands. But B testified, "It only lasted a couple of weeks, and then I was fired. I wanted to return to Pennsylvania anyway. Besides, I couldn't take all the dishonesty." B then winked. Sam suppressed a snicker, and he could tell that Fume did too.

Then, Fume's inquiry turned to B's criminal history, as extensive but nonviolent as it was. He went through every arrest and conviction, eliciting multiple excuses from B as to why many arrests were invalid and the result of being framed. He admitted to some of the convictions, just enough to maintain some believability.

When Fume asked, melodramatically, how he expected a jury to believe him with all of these arrests and convictions, Fume got the expected objection from Sam. But before he could direct B not to answer the question, B insisted that "There weren't nary a one of them that involved lying when I was sworn to tell the truth."

Then, Fume got into the history between B and Sledgehammer, "It's my understanding, Mr. Brian Lowe, that you and Jacques Lindstrom, also known as Sledgehammer, had an altercation before the date of Mr. Moran's attempted hanging."

"Yeah, you could say that. He damn near broke my jaw."

"What prompted your physical altercation with Sledgehammer?"

"Let's just say it was over ownership of a liquid libation."

"Your testimony here today couldn't possibly be colored by your dislike of Mr. Lindstrom, now could it?"

"No, because we kissed and made up," B said sarcastically, "besides, I'm a hockey fan, and I always wanted to be checked by a semi-professional asshole."

Fume's follow-up questioning prompted B to go into a detailed description of how hooch was made in a toilet, a not uninteresting but irrelevant oration to which Fume paid rapt attention. Sam couldn't help but imagine Fume brewing a batch in the toilet. He let out a snicker, and Fume looked at him quizzically.

Shortly thereafter, the deposition was concluded, and Sam confronted the question every deponent in his career had posed: how'd I do?

"You did fine, B. But I was interested in what you said Sledgehammer told Brad before he beat him up. You said, let me find my notes, 'You better be careful, Gump, because I have permission to fuck you up like this every day.' Did Sledgehammer say he had permission to fuck him up like this every day?"

"Is it important to get the words right?"

"It might be. There is an implication in that language that you used that a guard might have told Sledgehammer or someone with authority that he or she gave him permission to rough up Brad."

"Yeah, I wouldn't be surprised."

"But was that the precise language that Sledgehammer used?"

"What does you the best?"

"It's not what does me the most good, it's what the truth is."

"That's what he said," B insisted with a wink.

Sam thought to himself, that's what you get when your star witness is an inveterate con man.

Sam sent him on his way with instructions to let him know if he changed his cell phone number or address. Then, although he was loathe to do so, he had Rhonda get his ex's old lover and the current psychologist for the Allegheny County Jail, Stuart Sonnenberg, on the phone. Regrettably, he was the perfect expert witness in this case.

"Hello, Professor, how's the world been treating you?"

"Existence is a cruel prank. Otherwise, I'm good. How's your recovery coming?"

"Well, they tell me that you can improve from a stroke, sometimes dramatically, within the first three years. I suspect that my right side is going to be useless for the rest of my life, but my speech has improved, and I think that I think as well as I ever did."

"I suppose you are calling to get my expert's report on the Moran matter. I have a draft of it here. I can read you the highlights."

"First, let me tell you about my Zoom deposition with Dr. Rodriguez. You will remember he was the Coalton County Jail's psychiatrist who left their employ years ago."

"I remember."

"Well, he testified that initially, he had insisted upon psychiatric testing for inmate rovers, which he would administer, as well as him training them. But, eventually, he was not consulted for psychiatric testing, nor did he conduct the training for the inmates. And he discovered that the jail psychologist, in effect, assigned the designation of inmate rovers to a guard Lieutenant."

"Why did he allow himself to be cut out of the loop?"

"He really didn't say. Maybe he didn't want to rock the boat and lose the handsome consulting payments from the county." Sam got some satisfaction out of this subtle dig, but it apparently went over Sonnenberg's head.

"That dovetails nicely with my ultimate opinion. I say, 'Imbuing sentenced inmates with some apparent authority as 'inmate suicide prevention workers' without psychiatric evaluation of those inmates is reckless and, in my opinion, evidences indifference.'"

"Go on."

"My opinion continues: 'Almost by definition some, if not many individuals who are incarcerated have evidenced some antisocial behaviors, and giving them authority as suicide prevention workers without somehow vetting those individuals makes abuse of another inmate, as occurred with Mr. Moran, a relative certainty over time.'"

As much as he hated to admit it, Stewart's was an intelligent and succinct summary of their position, and he told him so.

"Why thank you," Stewart gushed, "I am flattered. I never doubted your taste. You did, after all, choose Jenny." Stewart's reference to Jenny was to Sam's ex-wife and Stewart's ex-girlfriend. Sam wished he hadn't brought up how they shared the same woman for a little while; in fact, he hoped he never had to deal with Stewart again.

"Don't forget, I want you to present a lecture to my psych class in the fall," Stewart reminded me.

Fat chance, Sam thought, but he replied, "Sure," no use risking pissing off his expert until after trial.

CHAPTER 63-TIM TELLS A STORY ABOUT GOLD STARS

"Tim, you don't say much about your kids. I know your wife has been dead now for a few years, but I don't know much more about your family." Nicole was questioning her editor and Greene Gazette owner during her regular weekly call to discuss her upcoming column.

"I have one child, Jerry, who is almost forty years old and is an attorney in Minnesota, and I have a daughter, Marsha, who is involved with what they call 'the biz' in California, and she is a production manager for TV shows in LA. I don't see them much, and no, no grandchildren. Why the interest?"

"I would like to hear more about them. I'm interested because I met a woman in the home where Brad is whose son had a severe case of cerebral palsy and had basically spent almost twenty years doing nothing but caring for him. It got me thinking about what it must be like to feel that responsible for your child's life."

"Being a parent is an awesome responsibility, especially if you do it right," Tim offered.

"Can you believe Steve says that Brad's mother hasn't been to see him while he was in the hospital or the home."

"Don't be too hard on her."

"Yeah, but there's Brad's roommate's mother who has basically given up her life for her child, and then there's Brad's mother…"

"Let me tell you a story: My father was in the Navy in the Second World War. He went in in '44. By the way, his mother, my grandmother, wouldn't see him off when he boarded the train. Said she couldn't bear to see her son go off to war. That's one illustration of a mother's love. Well anyway, those were the days when there were star banners on houses when you had people in the service. A blue star meant you had one son in the service. Two, two sons etc. There were a few houses with as many as four stars on banners at that time, my father said."

"It must've been something to see the nation united in those days," Nicole sighed.

"According to my Dad, it was. My Father told the story of how a guy named Skeets Paukey, who was a friend of his, was reportedly killed on some island in the South Pacific. He was a Marine. And you displayed a gold star on your banner if you had someone that was killed while they were in the service."

"I have the feeling that this is going to have a very tragic ending."

"Skeet's mother was told about her son several days before the Gold Star for the banner was delivered. The day she got the Gold Star for the banner, she learned that he wasn't dead at all but that he was on a hospital ship headed home. My dad said that was not unusual in the war: That a mistake was made in reporting somebody dead. Well, she and her husband waited every day for a letter or some communication from him. They finally got word that he was in a hospital in Norfolk, Virginia."

"So it's not so tragic. At least he was alive."

"That's not the point of the story... if you stick with the ramblings of a seventy year old owner of a small-town newspaper, you might learn something." She pictured him smiling on the other end of the line.

"I'm with you."

"When they got to the hospital to see poor Skeets, he couldn't communicate. In fact, he was barely alive. The entire left side of his body had been blown away, and he was effectively in a vegetative state. The doctors said that Skeets would never recover, but with proper care, he might live for years."

"How awful."

"Well, they spent several days visiting Skeets and then came back to Pittsburgh. Two days after they got back, Skeets's father found Skeet's mother with her wrists slashed in the bathtub."

"Did she die?"

"No, she recovered. But my dad said she was in and out of institutions for the rest of her life. You see my point: Sometimes death is easier to deal with than what I might call a living death. There is no finality. People know how to react when somebody dies. Hell, they send flowers and cards and say what a wonderful person he or she was. What do you say to a person whose loved one is, for all intents and purposes, dead but is still breathing?"

Nicole had to concede, "I see your point."

"So, don't be so hard on Brad's mother."

CHAPTER 64-BARBARA'S DEPOSITION

Sam had only spoken with Brad's mother, Barbara, a couple of times on the phone and only met her once, so despite her assurances during his last conversation with her that she would appear for her deposition, he was uncertain. He had asked her to meet him at his office for a deposition prep lunch prior to her deposition. And, true to her word, at around noon on the day of her deposition, she appeared with a woman who he recognized from his visit to Brad in The Meadows before Brad's deposition.

After Barbara reintroduced Sam to Georgia Imhoff, she timidly asked, "You wouldn't mind if she sits with me for a while, would you?"

Sam could tell that she was nervous as hell, and he replied, "Of course not. But when we get into the meat of your testimony, for reasons that have to do with attorney-client privilege, I would ask that Barbara wait in the lobby."

"Have you had a chance to visit Brad at the Meadows?" Sam had told her that she should.

"Yes, I have. Two times. And I want to thank you for providing me with the name and number of this marvelous woman here." Barbara beamed at Georgia.

Barbara's enthusiasm led Sam to notice how similar the two women were. They were both obviously attractive women in their fifties. While Barbara was blonde (probably dyed) and Georgia had salt and pepper hair, both women were dressed in pantsuits and had similar facial features. Both appeared pallid; he surmised that Barbara's washed-out face was due to her dissolute lifestyle, and, he supposed, Georgia's was a result of the round-the-clock care that she had provided her son for many years.

"Well, ladies, help yourself to sandwiches," Sam urged

"Sam, when did you have your… event? I assume a stroke," Georgia asked. "I hope you don't consider me as being too forward."

"Is it that obvious," Sam teased. "I had a stroke in January. I've only been back to work for a few months."

"You're doing tremendously well."

"I speak more slowly than I ever have, and I mangle words and have some difficulty with word-finding skills, but I suppose, all in all, I'm lucky to be here at all."

"Since we're on the subject of recovery, tell your attorney what you told me in the car." Georgia smiled affectionately at Barbara.

Barbara enthused, "Thanks to Jeff and Georgia here, who called me every day since we met. I haven't had a drink or a pill or any drug stronger than Tylenol in two weeks."

"Congratulations Barbara. I suspect that must be very hard."

"Sam, I need to ask you this: Will my pill popping come up in the deposition?"

"We can broach that subject when we get down to serious deposition preparation."

As they made small talk while picking at their sandwiches, Sam could tell that Barbara was troubled. He assumed that it was because she fretted about whether she was going to get drug abuse questions, but it wasn't.

"Sam, if we get any money, what happens to it? Brad ain't in any condition to spend it."

"Excellent question. Let's see if I can answer it without getting in the weeds too much. If we should get a verdict, there will be what is called a lien, a payback, for the medical care and the home. That can be complicated if the projection is that he will spend the rest of his life in a facility, but if the jury verdict is sufficient, he might be able to be placed in a first-class facility. And, you may be able, if the verdict is sufficient, to be able to purchase a house with handicapped features so you can bring him home, maybe permanently."

"Who decides what I can do?"

"Well, since you are the Guardian, you can decide. But everything you do will need to be approved by a court as necessary for his care. Typically, courts are very liberal with respect to that."

"I might be asking a question that you would prefer not to think about, Barbara, but you should know the answer. Sam, let's say that Brad dies before his money runs out if he gets a lot. Then what happens?"

"Then, Barbara inherits the money. And, if she's gone, Jeff would inherit."

"I don't even want to think about that," proving the truth of Georgia's utterance.

The rest of the luncheon was filled up with meaningless jabber, at least that's what Sam would label it as. When he gently requested that Georgia wait in the lobby and warned her that the deposition might take as much as three hours, she decided to "snoop" around downtown.

After running through what were his standard deposition instructions and warnings, he began by asking Barbara how often she had visited Brad and whether she had any thoughts on his condition. It brought the not-unexpected tearful response:

"What they did to my little boy... all because he was gay? I was brought up Catholic, but I don't have it in my heart to forgive. I wish whoever did this a horrible death."

Sam slid the box of tissue across the desk to Barbara and murmured, almost in a whisper, "We don't know that Brad was attacked because he was gay."

"You told me on the phone what B said that hammer guy threatened, and I know my son, and he wouldn't have hurt himself unless he figured he was in for a life of hell."

Sam thought, *If the jury believes B, especially what he testified to in his deposition, that would be a reasonable conclusion,* IF,,,,

"I know that this is going to be difficult for you. I have two sons of my own, and if anything like what happened to Brad happened to them, well... I wouldn't know what I would do. But, as far as Brad's sexuality goes, I think you should be very open and honest in your answers in the deposition, not only because it's the right thing to do but I think it will be one of our themes at trial."

"Brad wasn't ashamed of it, and he would want me to be honest about it."

"Which brings me to this question, which I'm sure will be difficult for you as well. I understand that you had some sort of relationship with Jim Straka, the owner of the drugstore that Brad is accused of robbing."

"Yes, I know him. I have known him for years."

"Were you romantically involved with him?"

"Do I have to answer that question? You know, he has a wife. I ain't gonna be the cause of the breakup of his marriage."

"If he asks you whether you two were romantically or sexually involved, I will object to the question. But, let me tell you why he would ask that: Jeff, your other son, has said that Brad might have been robbing Straka's Pharmacy of oxycodone to, in effect, feed your habit. He may have heard that rumor."

"How am I supposed to know what was in his mind."

"That's your answer then," Sam was emphatic in his reassurance.

"And, I am assuming that any medical professional has told neither you nor Brad that you are oxycodone-dependent, have you?"

"No, we haven't."

"Well, if opposing counsel, his name is Fume, asks you if you or Brad are addicted to oxycodone or any other chemical substance, I am going to object, saying that calls for a medical opinion and you're not qualified to give a medical opinion. Understand?"

"Yes, I do."

Sam then reviewed with her some of the more mundane questions that he was sure Fume would pose: Where Brad attended school; what sort of activities did he engage in; what were his grades like; had he ever been in trouble with the law or because of truancy; what occupation he aspired to when he got out of school.

Sam learned some interesting things from that review. First of all, despite the fact that he had to repeat 10th grade due to excessive truancy, Brad was something of a math savant, and had gotten A's in trigonometry class for the first semester of 12th grade. In addition to truancy, he had been in trouble with the local police force several times for defacing property with graffiti and underage drinking. Barbara attributed these run-ins to "hanging with the wrong group of friends." He was hoping to put his math skills to work as an engineer and had often talked about enrolling in the local community college after graduation from high school.

When the deposition was convened, it went pretty much as Sam expected. Fume asked the anticipated background questions, and Sam thought he saw a flicker of surprise in Fume when Barbara related his obvious aptitude for math. When Fume asked if there were any particular reasons that Brad might have chosen to target Straka Pharmacy, Barbara replied, "It's the largest drugstore in town, and Brad knew that I got my prescription pills there."

Fume looked interested in her answer and followed up:

"What is your condition that requires prescription pills, and what are those pills?"

"Spinal stenosis and regional pain syndrome, for which I am prescribed Percocet and muscle relaxants. But, I have quit using the Percocets and now take over-the-counter pain relievers."

"Have you ever been treated for addiction to oxycodone?"

"No."

After several questions relating to her physician and his duration of treatment, Fume's interrogation refocused on Brad.

"Do you have any idea why Brad would steal Percocet from the pharmacy?"

Sam cautioned, "I don't want you to speculate."

"It would only be a guess, and Sam here has told me he doesn't want me to guess, and the jail and their goons have seen to it that my little boy ain't talking."

Fume then tried a different approach: "Let me ask you this; did your son ever take Percocet or any other prescription medication?"

"Yeah, I expect that he did. You know how teenagers are. Maybe you don't know, but in the projects we do."

"Do you think he stole the pills to sell them?"

"Again, I don't want you to speculate," Sam sat forward in his chair.

"He ain't never sold drugs."

"Then why did he steal thousands of dollars worth of Percocet from Straka's Pharmacy?"

"Asked and answered, and I direct the witness not to answer."

Barbara started to bawl, and between sobs, whimpered something incomprehensible followed by, "He ain't going to say because you fuckers obliviated him."

Sam recessed the deposition to allow Barbara to collect herself, and when the two of them were safely behind the closed door of Sam's office, he told her that she was doing a "bang up" job under difficult circumstances.

Drying her eyes, she asked how much longer he thought the deposition would last.

"Not much longer, I don't think. He has yet to explore with you Brad's sexual preference, but I think that will be relatively quick."

"Why is that even important?"

"Because, based upon B's testimony, in which he implied that some employee of the jail either approved of Brad's being beaten because of his sexual orientation or at least didn't try to reign Sledgehammer in."

"What if there is someone on the jury who doesn't like gays?"

"We get to interview jurors, and hopefully, we find that out."

He could tell that Barbara was becoming thoroughly confused, so he made an effort to simplify his theory of the case even more: "We need to prove that the jail was deliberately indifferent to how Brad was treated. Since Sledgehammer was technically an employee of the jail, because he was paid a couple of bucks to be a rover, we make that case barely if B is believed. It's a much stronger case if a guard or a member of the administration is implicated."

"Oh, okay." But, he knew that her only grasp of a "theory" of the case was that her boy went into jail as an eighteen year old kid and was carried out on a stretcher with the intellectual functioning of a baby. Boiled down to its true essence with the legal bullshit extracted, he could hardly fault her for this view, and he hoped a few jurors might simplify it that way too.

When reconvened, the rest of the deposition was quick. As anticipated, Fume posed questions designed to get at Brad's sexual orientation, which Barbara answered without the slightest hesitation or embarrassment. In fact, when Fume inquired about Brad's friends, Barbara responded:

"Kip Anderson was very close to him. I guess I shouldn't say was... I should say he is Brad's boyfriend. Brad and he were talking about attending the prom together."

Fume could hardly reign in his astonishment at Barbara's nonchalance, and Sam, who had heard this revelation for the first time himself, thought that the kid must have had brass balls to have even considered doing this in rural Coalton County.

Then Fume shuffled through his notes, which was a sure sign that a deposition was about to be over. Sam positioned his cane to hoist himself out of the chair when Fume said, "I almost forgot. Did you have any conversations with your son while he was in jail? I assume that it had to have been by phone."

"Yeah, he called me from jail. I can't say I remember much about the call. I was so goddamn upset."

"Do you remember anything?"

"Only if you remember. I don't want you to speculate." Sam was still poised to exit his chair; after all, he knew from his prep session that the conversation purely centered around Brad's desperation for a cigarette.

"He said something like he would kill, or die, one of the two for a cigarette. I could tell, being his mother that he was nearly crying. And then he said something about a nice guard saying that he had cigarettes in his car and would give him a pack when he got off and warning him that gays needed to be careful in here. Said that there were guards that would look the other way. Sam moved forward in his chair.

"Did he tell you what he meant by that?"

"No, he didn't."

"Did he tell you what the name of the guard was who told him that?"

"No."

"Did he tell you what he meant by 'look the other way'?"

"No, he didn't, but it didn't sound good."

Shortly thereafter, the deposition was reluctantly ended by Fume. As Sam and Barbara were making their way back to the office for what Sam had come to think of as "post-game analysis", he saw Georgia sitting in the reception area and motioned for her to join them in his office.

"Barbara, what made you think about the guard warning him that gays better be careful?" Sam was interested since the deposition was the first time that he had heard that.

Barbara smiled uncomfortably. Her explanation was convoluted: "Well, Georgia said she would prefer that I didn't smoke in her car, but if I had to have one, she would let me. I didn't smoke in her car all the way to your office, so I have gone most of the day without a cigarette. I was thinking about Georgia's offer to have a cigarette in her car, and I was hoping that it was near the end of the deposition. Then he asked his question about Brad's telephone call from jail."

Georgia sighed, "You can smoke on the way home. I will turn the AC off, and you can open a window."

"Anyway," Barbara pressed ahead with her story, "I was thinking about having a cigarette in the car, and it reminded me that Brad had told me what a guard said about him having cigarettes in the car and about what the guard had told him about being careful if you were gay because there were guards that would look the other way. Is that important?"

"It might be."

He was certain that the guard who told Brad to be careful was Todd Shanahan, the guy whose deposition the Lieutenant had sat in on and who said he had relatives who were gay. While he had suspected that Shanahan knew more than he disclosed in this deposition, putting together what Franklin had told him about the elevator conversation and now what Barbara had testified to, he was convinced of it.

CHAPTER 65-NICOLE AND STEVE MOVE INTO THEIR OWN APARTMENT

It was mid-September when she and Steve finally got their respective acts together and moved out of "her apartment" and into "their apartment". She had recruited her oldest brother, Jake, to assist them, not because they had a lot of stuff, but because she didn't want to see him attending community college for a semester and dropping out, as she suspected most of his male classmates would. She hoped that helping her move might generate in him some excitement over the prospect of living independently at college, and that would provide additional impetus to improve his grades at school. At least that was her plan, overly grandiose though it might be.

"Hey Steve, I thought I told you to be careful with my ceramic fox. It's a family heirloom." It was originally Nicole's grandmother's, and had value much greater than monetary.

"It is firmly ensconced in my armpit, so as the British would say, 'bugger off'."

"Steve, I understand that you're working for Sam part – time while you go to law school," her brother Jake mentioned as he picked up a box.

"Yep, and I hope to get some real courtroom experience when Sam tries the Brad Moran case."

"Hey, sis, did you know that I wrote a paper on Brad for civics class?"

"No, I didn't. What was it about?"

"It was about how I met him, and how he was arrested for stealing pills and him trying to off himself. But mostly, it was about equal protection of the laws; that was our assignment."

"That's a heavy subject, that's law school shit. What did you say about equal protection?" Steve was obviously intrigued.

"I did a little Internet research and came to the conclusion that despite gay people being equal now under the law, there were still plenty of people that thought they weren't equal."

Nicole was obviously pleased with what she saw as his enlightened view, and she told her brother that she was proud of him. "I hope you got an A on the paper, Jake."

"I did! And it was in the running to be read to the school board. You know, they're requiring civics now for the first time in many years. Well, at the first meeting of the school year, the school board wanted a couple of papers to be read. Mine was in the running. It wasn't read to the school board, though."

"That's something to be proud of, Jake," Steve extolled, "I only wish that it was picked."

Jake's eyebrows raised. "I'm glad I wasn't picked. I don't need anybody thinking I'm gay. I get picked on enough as it is. Besides, Mrs. Brennan, our teacher, told me that the board didn't want to open that can of worms and said that there might be some parents who got pissed at the mention of gay rights."

Steve was sardonic in his comment, "Yeah, I guess equal protection of the laws only extends to white, male, straight Christians. We wouldn't want to upset any of the good citizens of the county."

Nicole wasn't certain that Jake would appreciate Steve's sarcasm and mistake it for an accurate statement of his feelings. She glanced at Jake, and when she was convinced by his smile and demeanor that indeed he had gotten it, said:

"You know Tim, my editor, says, and I'm paraphrasing now, that people are constantly looking for some reason that they or their group is better than others."

"Or they want to convert them and bring them more into conformity with what they feel, act or believe." Steve raised his voice slightly as if he were giving a speech. At least, that was Nicole's impression.

"You know, there are some people who believe that the concept of free will is totally bogus. That we are born with a certain psychological and physiological makeup which determines how we will act and what we will do," Nicole volunteered.

As Steve was wrapping the heirloom fox, he concurred, at least partially, "At least that's true with respect to sexual orientation. I don't think it's generally a choice that anybody has."

"I think it might be more than simply that we don't choose our sexual orientation. We, all of us, may be born with a makeup that dictates whether we are ambitious, which will lead to success, at least by the world's standards, or not, which will be labeled as lazy. So who are we to look down on any person?" Nicole said as she was wrapping her mother's Lladro figurines.

Nicole could tell that Jake was bewildered by their discussion. "What about people that commit crimes, murderers and serial killers."

"I agree that society ought to be protected from these people, and they should be locked up, but maybe we shouldn't pass moral judgment on them."

"I guess then any attempt at rehabilitation of criminals is a waste of time if it's preordained that they will return to a life of crime or straighten themselves out." Steve's smirk resulted in an unusually long period of silence while they continued to pack. She hated when confronted with his smug smile, but now was not the time to call him out on it. Instead, she changed the subject:

"How are you getting along with Mr. Coates these days?"

"Who is he?" Steve wondered aloud.

"He's the vice principal of Jake's school. He was vice principal when I was in school, too. You know, I told you about him. Shaved head, Mr. Tough Guy, ex-Marine. He was in charge of punishing Jake for his little foray into dealing in weed."

"We get along great now. He's trying to start a JROTC chapter, and I signed up for it. All we do is march around the school parking lot during lunch hour for one day a week. It's kinda badass."

"Oorah!" Steve barked. Nicole grinned.

CHAPTER 66-FRANKLIN REITERATES TO SAM TO FOLLOW THE SMOKE

"Well, how'd my boy do?" Franklin was calling Sam the day after Jeff's deposition.

"He did fine. Of course, I told him that unless he was certain that Brad was stealing the pills to feed his mother's habit, his best answer was, 'I don't know'. He wasn't absolutely certain, and so he answered that he didn't know."

"Refresh my recollection. Why is that so important? I would think that it would make Brad all the more sympathetic."

"I don't want them to think that Barbara, his mother, who is also his legal guardian, would blow the money on Perks. I tried a case once where a heroin addict who was in the Allegheny County Jail lost his leg due to the jail doctor's negligence. The jury agreed that he was negligent but didn't give him any money. They thought he would spend it on drugs."

"How is Brad's case going? You have a trial within a month, don't you?"

"Yeah. Did I tell you that the jail has located Sledgehammer? I'm supposed to take his deposition via Zoom tomorrow. I could have traveled to Vancouver at the Jail's expense, but that's an awfully long flight for me in my gimp state."

"I would have been happy to chaperone you if I could have gotten off work," Franklin snickered. Sam was aware of Franklin's fondness for travel.

"That reminds me, I would pay you handsomely to accompany me to trial. I will have Steve, but he is a callow youth. Besides, I could use any um…direction that you would care to give me."

Franklin knew he was referring to his sixth sense but that Sam couldn't bring himself to fully acknowledge it, because that would imply its legitimacy. Franklin teased, "Descartes said that we ought also to consider as false all that is doubtful, but that we ought not meanwhile to make use of doubt in the conduct of life."

"I love it when you put Descartes before the horse's ass," Sam countered.

"I told you with this case, you have to follow the smoke but don't ask me why."

Sam didn't, and they wound up the conversation with Franklin wishing Sam luck with his deposition of Sledgehammer tomorrow.

CHAPTER 67-SAM DEPOSES SLEDGEHAMMER

When the visual came through on Zoom for the deposition of Sledgehammer, the first thing Sam saw was this blonde, Adonis-like creature with shoulder-length hair and a Manitoba Moose sweater/jersey. He must not have realized he was on camera because he inserted a dental plate containing his two front teeth.

The first words out of his mouth, "I do", in response to the oath, revealed a deep voice with just a hint of a French accent. The image was complete: He looked and sounded like the man you would see passionately kissing the heroine on the cover of those supermarket romance novels.

He asked the typical background questions and discovered the following facts, or supposed facts: Sledgehammer, or Jacques Lindstrom, twenty-nine years old and had played professional hockey for the Manitoba Moose, a "farm" team of the Winnipeg Jets. He had been out of professional hockey for two years now when he was invited to try out as a mid-season replacement for the Wheeling Nailers. He didn't make the team, but he met a woman in a bar who was from Coalton, and in short order, they became romantically involved, placing him in her apartment in Coalton for a period of months.

"While you were in Coalton and living in your girlfriend's apartment, were you employed?"

"Yeah, I worked part-time for You Move Me, a moving company."

"I know from your arrest record that you were arrested in a Coalton bar, Sweeney's Place, for assault and battery in November. Why were you arrested?"

What followed was a tediously convoluted recitation of Sledgehammer's history with the assaulted, one Herb Spencer, who was once romantically involved with Sledgehammer's then-girlfriend, Jennifer Steinhousen. It mercifully concluded thusly, "He called Jenny a whore, and I had a little too much to drink and punched him. He started to fight back, and, well, I broke his jaw. I had a lawyer who advised me to take a deal for a year in jail, but I would be out in six months."

"Out of curiosity, are you still with Jennifer?"

"Nah, she didn't wait for me. For all I know, she's back with Herb."

Then he added, "And after I defended her honor as a woman. I guess chivalry doesn't impress her none."

"And I see that you had a couple of charges of assault in Canada that ended up being dismissed."

"Yeah, well, everybody wants to take a shot at the big hockey goon, but not many got the better of me. And, as you say, the charges were dismissed because I was only defending myself."

"We can agree, can't we, that you spent six months' time in the Coalton County jail because of the fight at Sweeney's Place?"

"Yes, that's why I'm here, isn't it?"

"Yes, it is. And during those six months, did you know a Brian Lowe, who went, I assume, by the nickname B?

"Yeah, I knew him, and he was aching to take a shot at me and prove his, how should I say in polite company, I guess the size of his… manhood."

"He says that you broke his jaw in a fight over pruno or hooch."

"Well, a man has a right to defend himself, and he came after me and threw the first punch. In fact, he threw the first two punches. So I decked him. Lieut. Hodgson investigated and cleared me; they said it was self-defense. It wasn't long after that before Lieutenant Hodgson made me a rover."

"Were you two fighting over alcohol?"

"I don't know nothin' about that."

"I want to take you back to January of this year, specifically an altercation if we can call it that, which you had with Brad Moran."

"Yeah, that was crazy. Maybe I should say he was crazy."

"Why don't you tell me about your physical encounter with Brad Moran in January?"

"Well, it was about 7:30 at night or so, and everyone had to be on their unit but were allowed to visit within the unit. As you know, I was a rover, so I was allowed and encouraged to move between units to see if anybody had any problem. I heard a commotion, screaming, in a pod or section, so I went to investigate."

"What was being screamed, and could you tell who was doing the screaming?"

"Yeah, so I went to investigate and it's a new guy, who I later found out was Brad, and he was screaming that he wanted his mother, let me out of here. I can't stand to be locked up, you know, the same shit that I had heard many times before and you would expect from a new guy."

"So, what happened next?"

"I went into the new guy's cell, and I saw him pacing around like a caged animal, red-faced, and I could swear he was like foaming at the mouth, there was spit going everywhere."

"Then?"

"I sit him down on his bunk, and I tell him that he needs to settle down, that it's going to be okay, and he seems to settle down."

"What led you to believe he was settling down?"

"He asked me for a cigarette, and I told him that I don't smoke, bein' as I am an athlete. He asked me what I played, and I told him professional hockey. He seemed to be calming down. So, I got up off the bunk and was leaving."

"And did you leave?"

"That's just the thing, I was practically out of his cell when I heard this commotion in back of me. It turns out that he got up from his bunk and looked like he was about to jump me, according to Flake."

"Who is Flake, and what was he doing in the cell?"

"He was sitting on the commode and watching us and laughing. He was from the cell next door, and he must have heard the screaming and come in. I never had many dealings with him. But Flake came up to Brad from behind and grabbed him as he was getting close to me. Well, then there was a tussle and eventually Flake and I got Brad settled down and in his bunk."

"Where was his cellmate during all this?"

"He was in the top bunk, and I didn't hear nothin' from him, so I didn't pay him no mind. He was laying there facing the wall. I don't think he wanted any parts of it."

"You say there was a tussle. Did either you or Flake strike Brad?"

"Oh, we probably both did, and he hit us, and then we finally got him calmed down and in his bunk and he was just staring into space. So we left, and that was what I thought."

"Did you talk to anyone about the incident afterward? Any guard or jail employee or other prisoner?"

"Only Flake, and it was along the lines of what did you think of that? It was maybe a couple of minute's conversation if that."

"Had you ever had any discussion or conversation about Brad, either before or after the incident that you just described, with Guard Todd Shanahan, Lieutenant Kevin Hodgson or any other guard or employee of the jail?"

"Not that I remember."

"Well, you would think that you would remember since Brad committed suicide later that night. When did you become aware that Brad committed suicide?"

"Later that night."

"And you still don't remember whether you had a conversation with any employee of the jail concerning Brad before or after that?"

"I told you, not that I remember. I might have had a conversation with the Lieutenant afterward, and if I did, I basically told him what I just told you."

The deposition went on for another half an hour, with Sam collecting essentially meaningless information and probably, Sam thought, boring the hell out of the jury that would see the video. When the deposition for use at trial was finally concluded, and Sledgehammer thought that Sam couldn't see him, he asked Fume how he did. He would have loved to hear Fume's response, but the screen went blank shortly after he asked his question.

Within seconds, Rhonda buzzed him, and advised that she had Fume on the line. The sum total of his telephone conversation with Fume was that Fume hoped that he could produce Sledgehammer live at trial, and was exploring that option with him. Sam's response was a verbal equivalent of a grunt.

He was stiff from sitting in one place for so long that he damn near fell but grabbing his cane, he navigated out of his office.

"How'd it go, boss?" He could sense that Rhonda was more curious than usual, undoubtedly fueled by the fact that he had just taken the deposition of a semi-pro hockey player in Canada, not an everyday occurrence.

"The case is going to hinge on whether the jury believes B or Sledgehammer. Sledgehammer is a tall, good-looking semi-pro hockey player with a French accent, and B is a balding, middle-aged petty criminal who has a rap sheet for dishonesty as long as your arm. Who do you think the jury is going to believe?"

"Wasn't B the guy who wore the red beret?"

"Yep, it covered up his balding head."

"Hah, a French connection for both of them." Rhonda laughed at her own observation.

CHAPTER 68-BECCA APPEARS AT NICOLE'S NEW APARTMENT

Nicole's Aunt Becca had made an unannounced visit to her and Steve's new apartment on the Saturday before the trial of Brad's case, ostensibly to help her set up the apartment. Actually, it became clear to Nicole that they should gauge their opinion on Sam's fitness for the rigors of the trial. After embracing Nicole, Becca turned her attention to Steve, who was lurking at the door to their bedroom.

"Steve, I hoped I would find you here. How's law school treating you? And how is clerking for my soon–to–be husband, Sam, going?"

"There's an old saying about law school: the first year they scare you to death, the second year they work you to death, and the third year they bore you to death. It's true."

Becca laughed, Nicole thought politely and then followed up, "And how's the job with Sam going?"

"I have learned a lot from him. He's a great guy. And I will learn even more when we start the trial on Monday."

"Yeah, I know. I love Sam dearly, but I am also concerned about him trying the case. You have spent more time with him in work situations than anybody except Rhonda, his secretary. Do you think that he's up to this?"

She could see that Steve was somewhat taken aback by the question. He was being asked to render what might be perceived as a pseudo-medical opinion. She also sensed that the unusually long pause discomfited him before Steve spoke, "Oh, he should be okay. In fact, he will be more than okay. After all, he has me to assist him." Steve flashed a gawky smile and continued, "and I understand he's going to have that fortuneteller guy assisting him as well."

"You mean Franklin," Becca gently corrected.

"Yeah, I don't know him very well, but Sam seems to think he has a sixth sense or something."

Becca looked amused and replied, "He was very helpful to my sister's and your girlfriend's mother's case, and I think he will be helpful on this one as well."

"I understand that he told Sam to follow the cigarette smoke or something, and it looks like smoking must have something to do with the case," Steve revealed.

"I shall leave my love in your and Franklin's capable hands then."

Becca then made some suggestions as to how the living room should be rearranged, which Nicole welcomed. After about half an hour, as Becca was preparing to leave, she expressed surprise that Steve wasn't in Sam's office today helping Sam prepare for trial.

"I'll be headed to the office at around noon. Sam wants me to pick up some Pad Thai for him for lunch."

"At that Thai place in the back of his office?" Becca asked.

"Yep."

"That's where we had our first 'date' almost four years ago now. Boy, how things can change in four years."

Nicole nodded; *indeed,* she thought, *they could.*

CHAPTER 69-FRANKLIN GIVES HIS INPUT ON JURY SELECTION AND GOES TO A MEETING

As Franklin was waiting in line to get through the magnetometer at the federal courthouse on the first day of the scheduled trial for Brad's case, Steve asked Franklin what had happened with their search for "Flake."

"You know, the guy who was sitting on the toilet and who Sledgehammer said held Brad so Sledgehammer could pummel him."

Franklin saw Sam's expression as he looked at Steve and thought, *So this is what staring daggers looks like.*

"I will tell you in private. You never know who might be listening when you discuss trial tactics. Remember that." Sam was obviously stressed; he typically would have been much gentler with his charge.

Steve, having been thus chastened, continued to shuffle along. Franklin surmised that the line to get through security was lengthy because there were potential jurors in the queue, both for Brad's and other cases. It seemed like every other person had to be searched because they set off the magnetometer.

"Who is going to sit with you at the counsel table?" Franklin wondered aloud to Sam.

Steve, anxious to prove he was an integral part of the team after Sam's rebuke, responded, "Brad's mother, Barbara, of course. She is Brad's Guardian, after all."

Franklin puzzled over why Jeff hadn't told him that his mother would be required to attend every day of trial, and then Franklin thought it risky business; if Barbara showed up for trial impaired in any way, well…

At that moment, a group of five mostly unshaven men looking to be in their early twenties sidled up to Steve, and, after one of them announced in a loud voice, "We are not looking to cut in line," began talking and chuckling with Steve. Steve then announced to Franklin and Sam, "These are some of my classmates. We are all second-year law students. I invited them to watch the jury selection and then trial."

"Then I should get a law professor's salary for however long the trial lasts." Sam quipped and added, with a touch of desperation in his voice, "I need to sit" as he was shifting his weight on his quad cane.

The mostly unshaven law students quickly fetched a chair from the marshals manning the magnetometer station, and Sam was mostly able to sit as he moved through the security line. Franklin was left to brood over how Sam could make it through an entire trial if he couldn't make it through security.

After they had cleared security, gotten on and off the elevator and were standing outside of the courtroom, Sam played mentor, "Steve, you wanted to know why I had never deposed 'Flake', the commode sitter in Sledgehammer's account of what occurred the night that Brad attempted suicide."

"Yeah, I think he might have had something helpful to say."

"Apparently, Fume tried to locate him and came up empty. I could have had the trial postponed while we hunted him down, but chances were strong that he would buttress Sledgehammer's tale. We wouldn't have needed two people to endorse that version of events versus only B, would we?"

"No," was Steve's timid reply.

"Let me bring you both up to speed on what happened the other day at the pretrial conference," Sam said while he settled into a chair outside of the courtroom. "First of all, the judge denied the motion for summary judgment. Obviously, that's why we're here today and picking a jury. Steve, you did a good job on the brief."

"Secondly, I have made the decision that we're going to tell the jury the nature of the crime for which Brad was arrested. I don't want them speculating that he might have committed murder or something heinous. Now let's go pick a jury."

Since the case was in federal court, it would be decided by a jury of six people.

Before the actual jury selection process was initiated, Judge Harris gave a thumbnail sketch of the issues in the case. He told them that prisoners in jail did not forfeit all of their rights. According to the Supreme Court of the United States, they were entitled to humane treatment despite their criminal offenses. That would include making reasonable efforts to recognize and eliminate efforts by prisoners to commit suicide to the extent possible. Suicide is recognized as one of the primary problems in a jail setting.

The Judge further instructed, "You will hear testimony that in order to minimize suicide attempts among the inmates at the Coalton County Jail, a system of inmate rovers, or suicide prevention workers, was established. These rovers were trusted inmates who were given training in recognizing and reporting potentially suicidal inmates. They were paid a nominal sum for their responsibilities."

"The plaintiff contends that there was insufficient screening and training of these rovers or suicide prevention workers and that these failures led to a rover/suicide prevention worker assaulting Bradley Moran and was a substantial factor in causing him to commit suicide."

"The defendant, Coalton County, denies that any assault was committed by a rover/suicide prevention worker or that any physical contact between the rover and Bradley Moran was of an incidental and self-defense nature. Coalton County further denies that the screening and training of these workers evidenced the deliberate indifference which the law requires."

"Now you will hear evidence from a witness for the plaintiff that the alleged assault by the rover/suicide prevention worker was due in part to the fact that Bradley Moran was a homosexual or gay. The plaintiff does not deny Bradley Moran's sexual orientation, and I instruct you that all persons of any religion, race, national origin, sex or sexual orientation stand on equal footing before the law."

"You will also hear evidence that Bradley Moran was arrested on charges of breaking and entering and theft of OxyContin pills. While this is largely irrelevant to this case, where the issue is whether the county was deliberately indifferent to the rights of a prisoner in its custody, the parties have stipulated to advise you of why Bradley Moran was arrested. Of course, since there was no adjudication of his guilt or innocence, he is entitled to a presumption of innocence."

Sam had told him previously that Judge Harris interrogated the potential jurors in his courtroom, but he asked the jurors questions that both counsels had prepared. Since the litigants were not required to attend for jury selection, Sam and Steve sat at the plaintiff's counsel table, and

Fume and his assistant at the defense counsel table. Steve had further related that the jury array, which was the technical term for the group of potential jurors, was from the entire western part of the state.

In comparison to having sat through the jury selection process in Nicole's mother's trial, the jury selection process in this case was much more complex. Questions regarding homosexuality and the nature of Brad's criminal conduct caused many jurors to be excused for what Sam called "cause" or because their answers revealed that they couldn't be objective. Of course, no one really knew whether a juror who said he or she could remain totally objective in light of Brad's sexual preference or criminal activity and could focus solely on the issue of whether the county was "deliberately indifferent" to the welfare of Brad was lying. Sam told Steve that body language and tone of voice could be indicators of a potential juror's less-than-honest response, and he knew that if he, Franklin, told Sam that he had a bad "feeling" about a juror, that would be given tremendous weight by Sam.

Once they had more than enough jurors who could not be challenged for cause, Sam, Steve and Franklin found a place in the courthouse hall where they could discuss their peremptory challenges or challenges that could be based on something as simple as you didn't like the looks of a juror.

Ultimately, he had less than comfortable feelings about five jurors whose answers, at least, indicated that they could and would be totally unbiased so that they couldn't be disqualified for cause. He told Sam about his qualms. There was one woman who Sam thought gave him bad "vibes," who was not on Franklin's list of five, and Sam ended up striking her and three of Franklin's choices. This left two jurors, whom Franklin thought were questionable, on the jury unless they were stricken by Fume. They weren't.

By the time jury selection was complete, it was 11:45 in the morning, and the judge recessed court until 1:30. After lunch. Franklin asked Sam if he would mind if he attended a half-hour noon AA meeting, which was in a church two blocks from the court. He was hoping to see some of the old residents from his halfway house there.

"That's right, it's been almost three and a half years since your halfway house gig. Of course, I don't mind. I hope you run into some more success stories like yourself," Sam said.

"I will always be grateful to you, Sam; you started me on my new life. As Rousseau said, 'Gratitude is a duty which ought to be paid.'"

"Go on, get out of here," Sam exclaimed with a smile, "we'll be in the cafeteria when you get back."

On the short walk to the church at which the noon meeting was held, he thought about how he had almost recovered his former life. He was going to remarry his wife, he had his old job back as a photocopier repair man, and, as an added bonus, he was well on his way to a college degree and, hopefully, a position as a drug and alcohol counselor.

When he arrived at the church, sure enough, he ran into half a dozen of his old halfway house buddies. There was much handshaking and backslapping before the start of the meeting, and when the preliminaries were dispensed with and the speaker was introduced, he looked awfully familiar. It didn't take Franklin long to realize that it was one of the jurors selected for Brad's case, but what was his name? He really wasn't paying attention to the introduction.

The guy went through what Franklin had come to know as the standard litany of a drunk: hiding bottles, blackouts, driving drunk and marital difficulties. Then, after an excruciatingly long pause, he embarked on relating a story that caused some in his audience to weep, " My son was ten years old when I got sober, that was eleven years ago now. He was a good boy, did well in high school, and went away to college. He got in with the wrong crowd."

He then related his son's struggle with addiction and his efforts to come up with a delicate but impossible balance between the tough love that is prescribed for dealing with an addict and the unconditional love that one feels for one's son. Finally, after a stint of homelessness, his son came home and began attending meetings with him.

"His mother and I thought he was on the right track. He was even talking about returning to college. We didn't want to leave him alone, but we went out, just the two of us to celebrate our anniversary, and when we came home, we found our little boy, Ty, dead in the bathroom. He had injected himself with heroin cut with fentanyl."

Try as he might, the speaker took several minutes before he had composed himself sufficiently to continue, but it was only to add this anguished sentence, "I blame myself because he inherited my Goddamn addiction gene."

After the meeting closed, and as he was standing in line to shake the speaker's hand according to tradition, he overheard the speaker telling one of the people three or four persons ahead of him in the queue that he was in town because he had been picked on a jury in federal court. Their brief conversation yielded the speaker's name: Danny.

As he moved up to be the next person in line to shake the speaker's hand, he heard Danny say, "Yeah, I was picked, and the case involves some claim by a kid who stole a lot of drugs from the pharmacy and, when he got to jail, tried to hang himself. When the judge asked me if I could be fair, I answered I could. I hope I can, but what happened to my boy makes me wonder if I can when a dealer is involved."

Franklin then stepped out of line and exited the church, avoiding the efforts of his halfway house buddies to engage him in conversation. He thought briefly about finding a way to inform Sam of Danny's conversation, which he had overheard, and quickly concluded that he could not without impliedly breaking Danny's anonymity. If he did reveal the conversation, Sam would want to know which juror was the source, and if he then disclosed that it was Danny (which he wouldn't because that would involve a breach of anonymity), it might lead to the Judge's further inquiry of Danny. No, he would have to keep this under his hat, and hope that the case Sam put on would be so compelling that it would vitiate any misgivings that Danny would have about giving Bradley damages.

He arrived at the courthouse and located Sam and Steve in the cafeteria. "How was your meeting?" Steve asked cheerfully.

Franklin responded with a shrug, "It was okay, I guess."

Sam had apparently been in contact with Barbara because she and a woman named Georgia met them in the cafeteria. Sam introduced Georgia as Brad's roommate's mother and further explained that she had become Barbara's close friend. Barbara looked suitably nervous. After all, she had never seen the inside of a courtroom before, but, as far as he could detect, she was not under the influence of any chemical. That's great, he thought, now, if she can only keep up the good work.

Before long, the unshaven mob, who identified themselves as Steve's cohorts, filed into the courtroom and took their seats beside him. The only explanation that he could come up with regarding their proximity to him was that they knew he was with Steve. One of the crew who was sitting closest to him nodded, and he returned the nod.

The judge's clerk opened the door to his chambers to the right of the judge's bench to check on the courtroom and whether all of the parties were present and seated, at least that is what he assumed. He glanced at one of the law students and noticed that he had slung a black backpack neatly over the chair in front of him.

Upon seeing the backpack, he felt that combination of awe and agitation that he had come to recognize as a precursor of one of his "spells." He closed his eyes and then saw in his mind's eye a black backpack resting against the bars of a jail cell.

CHAPTER 70-SAM OPENS TO THE JURY

As Sam was awaiting the Judge's appearance in the courtroom, he felt the all too familiar pre-opening address apprehension with his post-stroke condition as a multiplier. He wondered if Judge Harris's unspoken but undisguised concern about his fitness to try a case before a jury was justified. He had prepared an outline of his opening address that would be displayed on the TV monitors placed throughout the courtroom, one of which resided on his counsel table for easy reference if he should become confused. Moreover, he had become somewhat adept at note-taking on his phone with one hand, but he had never even contemplated trying a case where he could not take handwritten notes until now.

Judge Harris called the Court to order and proceeded to give his preliminary instructions, which he read very quickly from what developed from his twenty years on the federal bench. Sam only paid attention to about one-quarter of the instructions, and he suspected that even the most focused of the jury probably caught only one-half. Then, Sam was called upon to deliver his opening address to the jury.

It began well enough. He thanked the jury for doing their civic duty for what was a pittance. He reviewed the history of the jury system from England through the founding fathers to the present, a brief lecture-like exercise which he thought of as delivering his Civics lesson.

Then, pointing to Barbara, he told the jury, "As a result of the actions and inactions of the Coalton County Jail personnel, this mother's son has been rendered as near to vegetable-like condition as is possible on this side of death. And you will get a chance to see Brad. We will wheel him in here and you will see for yourself what the Coalton County Jail has wrought."

"Now, as the judge has told you, you do not forfeit all of your rights because you have been arrested. First of all, you are entitled to the presumption of innocence. But more importantly, the Supreme Court of our land has said that you can't be deliberately indifferent to the health, welfare and psychological condition of a prisoner. And we contend that the employees of Coalton County Jail demonstrated deliberate indifference toward the psychological condition of young Brad."

"You see, as you might expect, prisoner suicide is a massive problem nationwide. It just makes sense. Nobody wants to have their freedom curtailed. And our courts have said that jails and prisons cannot be deliberately indifferent to the problem. In other words, jails and prisons must recognize the problem of jail suicide and take reasonable steps to minimize it."

"So, the Coalton County Jail came up with a program where hand-picked inmates, prisoners who were supposed to be first trustworthy and second trained to recognize when a new prisoner was prone to suicide, were to circulate among new prisoners and report to the guards any prisoner who they thought might be suicidal. Remember: trusted and trained. These prisoners, the ones that were hand-picked because they were trusted and trained, were called rovers, or suicide prevention workers, and they were employees of the jail because although they were prisoners, they were paid by the jail."

"Well, ladies and gentlemen of the jury, you will hear testimony from a prisoner who actually witnessed another inmate, with the nickname Sledgehammer, who literally beat up Brad, an eighteen year old boy. You will hear him testify about what Sledgehammer said as he was assaulting Brad and the implication that he had permission to rough up Brad because Brad was gay. And that was a major factor in Brad's attempted suicide."

"Sledgehammer, whose real name is Jacques Lindstrom, was at that time a rover, also called a suicide prevention worker. Let that sink in: a suicide prevention worker nicknamed Sledgehammer was a substantial cause of Brad's attempted suicide. As the judge will tell you in his final instructions, Coalton County is responsible for the actions of its employees."

"Now, you will hear from a psychologist who will make the link for you from Sledgehammer's threat and the beating that he administered to Brad and his attempted suicide. He will also testify as to why the concept of having rovers was a terrible idea, particularly the way that rovers were chosen and trained at the Coalton County Jail."

"We will also present testimony from a life care planner and an economist who will tell you what it will cost to give Brad the round-the-clock care that he will require from now until his death. As you might imagine, that will be in the millions of dollars."

"And we will present a neurologist, a medical doctor who specializes in the brain and the nervous system, who will explain why poor Brad will live in a near-vegetative state for the rest of his life. You will get a chance today to meet Brad."

"We will concede that Brad was arrested for attempted theft of Percocet pills from a local drugstore. But, the eighteen year old boy should not have been consigned to a life in a home where he needs constant care for a youthful indiscretion."

Sam was about to wrap up his opening statement, and placed a hand on Barbara's shoulder, and was going to let it reside there for a few dramatic seconds. He intended to conclude with something like "no one can possibly give Barbara her son back like he was, but your verdict can make his wretched life better," but, as sometimes occurred as a result of his stroke, especially when his brain was called upon to retrieve names, it froze.

He looked confused, embarrassed, and then horrified as he sat down heavily at counsel's table without another word. He hoped against hope that the jury didn't see the progression of his emotions, which he feared was all too obvious.

CHAPTER 71-NICOLE MEETS KIP AND CATCHES SAM'S OPENING

Nicole glanced at her watch when she parked her car at the lot within a couple of blocks of the federal courthouse. It read 1:30. She hoped that she would be able to get to court in time to see opening statements. She passed by several buildings that had ghouls and goblins displayed. Yeah, it was the Halloween season.

When she was about a block from the Courthouse, she saw what could only be described as a waif-like person in the distance, appearing to hold a sign. When she got closer, she recognized Brad's boyfriend, Kip Anderson, holding a homemade placard that read, "It is sad what happened to Brad. Justice must be done for Brad Moran."

She approached Kip and ventured, "You don't remember me, do you? I am the reporter who interviewed you at the Gay Pride Parade."

His response was quick and certain, "Yes, I do. And I remember you said you have a boyfriend who was working for Brad's lawyer. Is that why you're here?"

"Yes, it is. But I want to see justice prevail for Brad, too. Have you been out here all day?"

"Yep. Except for bathroom breaks. I was told by some official-looking dude that I couldn't block the entrance to the federal courthouse, but I could walk the street as much as I liked. Freedom of speech, he said."

"Well, if you're here tomorrow, I will buy you a cup of coffee in the morning and maybe lunch if you'll let me."

"I sure will. What time do you think the court will let out?"

"I would think by late afternoon or early evening. Do you want me to let you know what went on in there?"

"Please."

She made it in time to see Sam give his opening address to the jury, and while she wasn't a lawyer, she was impressed. Sam hardly stumbled over words at all, and she thought the jury was riveted by every word he spoke. That is, until his abrupt termination, which she would describe later as his collapse into his seat at the counsel table.

Immediately after his collapse, the judge had an unmistakably concerned look on his face and asked, "Mr. Wright, do you have anything further?"

Sam responded in a barely audible voice, "No, Your Honor." Whereupon Fume, proving himself to be a decent human being, asked the Judge for a brief recess, which she was certain was intended to serve as a "cover" for Sam in part.

Sam then waved Steve off in his attempt to assist him with standing, and he peered into the courtroom's gallery and his eyes locked with Nicole's. She saw his eyebrows raise and in what she took to be an agitated surprise.

When she caught up with Sam, Steve, and Franklin in the hall, she could tell from their conversation that they were deliberately ignoring Sam's abrupt termination of his opening. Finally, Sam broached the subject himself, "How do you think the jury reacted to my brain freeze?"

Steve looked at Franklin because, she thought, Franklin was the person to issue reassurance. "I think they hardly noticed, and if they did notice, it would make them review what you said in your opening. In fact, it might be a positive."

"True are not, Franklin, thanks for the positivity bullshit."

Nicole wondered aloud, to no one in particular, what would happen in court next, and Steve announced, "Remember I told you about Dr. Gross, the neurologist who we were preparing on Saturday? Well, he's next. Then we're going to wheel in Brad and call it a day. Sam says we need to start strong and leave an indelible impression with the jury on the first day."

Sam excused himself to use the bathroom, and Nicole whispered, "Is he all right?"

Franklin and Steve looked at one another; neither one answered.

CHAPTER 72-FUME OPENS, AND BRAD IS WHEELED IN

Although he was no attorney, he thought that Fume's opening statement was cogent, well-presented, and, most of all, short. From what he could understand of the law, Fume repeated several times the phrase, "Does that sound like deliberate indifference?" which, Fume said, had to be proven by the guardian for Brad. He remembered, almost word for word, the several times Fume employed it. "The Coalton County Jail had a suicide questionnaire in use by a majority of jails nationwide that had to be completed by a jail guard for each new admittee and was completed for Brad. Does this sound like deliberate indifference?"

"The Coalton County Jail employed trusted inmates, paid a nominal amount, to keep an eye out for suicidal new admittees. They were called rovers or suicide prevention workers. Suicide prevention workers. Does that sound like deliberate indifference?"

He proceeded to claim that the case could be resolved quite easily by comparing the versions of what occurred immediately prior to the unfortunate attempted suicide of Brad. "One told by an inveterate, meaning serial, liar, who had a reason to despise the trusted suicide prevention worker, and the other told by the hand-picked suicide prevention worker."

He then went on to give brief summaries of the testimony of B and Sledgehammer, referring to Sledgehammer as Jacques. The jury was attentive. He concluded with an acknowledgment of the human tragedy of Brad's attempted suicide and resulting condition, but, "You must not be swayed by sympathy for Brad but must look objectively at every piece of evidence that is introduced in this case, and you will conclude that the Coalton County Jail cannot be held to be responsible."

In the courtroom lull that occurred after Fume's opening and before Sam called his first witness, the neurologist, Dr. Gross, Franklin tried to be as inconspicuous as possible in exiting the courtroom. However, the cadre of Steve's law student buddies gawked at him as he rose from his seat. The nearest one whispered, "Are you leaving?" Franklin replied that he was going to wait outside the courtroom for Brad.

After all, he knew what the neurologist was going to say, essentially that Brad's brain had been deprived of oxygen for so long that it was only a functioning mind in the most rudimentary sense. Besides, he wanted to meet Brad's brother, Jeff and his nurse from The Meadows, Carrie, when they appeared outside of the courtroom from the ambulance that would drop them off.

As he sat there awaiting Brad, he couldn't help but reflect upon Sam's apparent memory lapse during his opening. He hoped that it was not a harbinger of disaster. However, his concern went well beyond Sam's presentation skills and to the substance of the case.

According to Sam, he had been unsuccessful in ferreting out what Sam described as the "smoking gun," which he suspected would implicate the jail much more solidly than the weak and less than credible testimony of B. He smiled to himself at Sam's use of the words "smoking gun" since he had the sixth sense feeling that smoking, presumably cigarettes, was one of the keys to the case. Oh well, as Voltaire said, "Faith consists in believing what reason cannot."

When Jeff and Carrie appeared, Jeff pushing his brother in a wheelchair, Brad looked frightened and disoriented. After all, he had spent many months in the familiar surroundings of The Meadows. He was dressed in pajamas for the occasion, and a bag which collected his urine was hanging by a hook from his wheelchair. He was drooling, and Carrie wiped his mouth several times before he was wheeled into the courtroom.

Carrie remarked, "In my twenty-five years as a nurse, I have never wheeled a patient into a courtroom, and from the looks of Brad here, he doesn't want to be the first."

"I guess Sam wants the jury to see what the jail wrought, to put it in biblical terms," Franklin solemnly intoned.

After Steve announced "it's time" from the open courtroom door, the procession, with Brad in the center, entered and wheeled Brad to the counsel table, where his mother was seated and Sam was standing. Barbara appeared visibly unnerved by her son's arrival, and Franklin could tell she was trying to suppress tears. Sam announced, "Your honor, as we discussed in chambers, I intend to ask Brad here his name, and we will see if he responds. Obviously, he can't be sworn in as a witness."

Fume said, "No objection, Your Honor."

Although Franklin only saw the back of the wheelchair and Brad from his vantage in the gallery where he had returned, he could see that Brad's chin was resting on his chest. Carrie stood beside him and whispered, loud enough for him, and he assumed the jurors would hear, "Brad, honey, pick your head up." But he didn't.

At this point, Brad's mother got up from her seat at the counsel table and attempted to elevate Brad's head so that it was off his chest. She encountered either a willful noncompliance or some physical reason why his head couldn't be straightened, which caused her to begin to cry hysterically and to howl, "My baby, what have I done to you? It's all my fault." Both Sam and Fume leapt to their feet, but before they could say a word, Judge Harris motioned for them to approach the bench, then cautioned, "Mr. Wright, tell your client to sit down and get her under control."

Subsequently, Sam was able to easily guide Barbara back into her seat, but it took a couple of minutes to get her calm enough so that she was only occasionally sobbing audibly. During that period, Fume stood ramrod straight, that is, as much as his girth would allow. He and Fume then stood before the bench and had a minutes-long whispered conversation with the Judge. After they returned to their respective counsel tables, Judge Harris was emphatic:

"I instruct you to disregard any comment made by Ms. Moran upon seeing her son. As I am sure, every one of you can sympathize with Ms. Moran, but you are not to allow that sympathy to taint your verdict."

Further, the Judge emphasized, "You are not to speak about this case with any person, most especially any reporter or person associated with any news outlet or blogger, and you are expressly forbidden to discuss this matter on the Internet or via social media. Since it is relatively late in the day, the Court is adjourned until 9:30 tomorrow morning."

While Carrie wheeled Brad out of the courtroom, Franklin assisted Steve in carrying the evidence boxes into the hall. Franklin asked what he had missed while awaiting Brad, and Sam reported, "The neurologist was excellent and explained Brad's condition very well. He basically said what the jury saw is what Brad's existence will be until he dies. Not surprisingly, Fume didn't have any cross-examination, which is smart. That's not where his defense lies."

"What about when you and Fume had that whispered conference with the Judge in front of the bench?" Franklin was curious.

"We both got what we wanted, but for different reasons. The Judge told the jury to disregard Barbara's outburst. I didn't want the jury to be speculating about what part Barbara could have had in Brad's theft of pills because she is, after all, his guardian and she will have partial control of whatever money the jury awards. Let's hope that the jury takes what the Judge said to heart and doesn't pay attention to her blowup."

"And what did Fume get?"

"He didn't want the jury to think of Brad any more sympathetically. You know, the jury could speculate that Brad actually stole the pills for his dear old mother. Of course, you can't erase from the minds of jurors what was said, so who knows what they might think."

"However, I am concerned about what the jury might have thought about forgetting my own client's name."

While he had detected a look of confusion on a couple of the jurors' faces, it served no purpose to tell Sam that. "As I told you before, no harm, no foul. The worst that they might have thought, in my estimation, was that it might be a form of courtroom dramatics, where you place your hand on the client's shoulder. You know people expect a little courtroom drama since everybody watches lawyer shows on TV."

Sam looked unconvinced, and as he reviewed the events of the day on his drive home, Franklin was beset with his own sense of disquietude.

CHAPTER 73-SAM CONFRONTS MARCUS REGARDING ENDS

After Steve had dropped him off at the parking garage behind his office and he had hobbled his way to his car, Saul, the parking attendant supervisor, asked him how it went in court today. Rhonda, who saw Saul regularly when they left their respective places of business to have cigarettes, must have told him that he was in court.

"Okay, but I couldn't come up with my client's name in my opening address to the jury."

Saul smiled and adopted what Sam thought was Saul's best effort in a reassuring tone. "That's okay; we are reaching that age." Without a word, Sam simply got in his car and left.

When he got home, Becca met him at the top of the steps and asked, "Clarence, how was your day in court?" Becca always called him Clarence for Clarence Darrow when he was involved in any trial.

When he attempted to recount the events of the day, Becca cut him off and, in explanation, related, "Nicole told me all about your forgetting Barbara's name, and flopping into your seat at counsel table, and Barbara's outburst when Brad was rolled into the courtroom. But, she said that she thought you had a pretty good day overall. And I have some good news."

"Oh yeah, I could use some good news."

"Your divorce is final. Our divorce lawyer called me today. She didn't want to bother you because you were in trial, and she said that since it's a public record now, she could share the news with me."

Sam smiled, and he realized that it might have been the first time he smiled today.

Then Becca proclaimed, "Now, you can make an honest woman out of me."

Sam grinned for the second time and asked, "How's Marcus?" His oldest son, Marcus, had a bad case of the flu.

"He's getting better. I will send him back to your now ex-wife tomorrow when your visitation is over. Then, I could come to the trial if you want me."

"We will have to see about that. I don't know if you want to see how many times I step on my tongue, or worse yet, have a cat get my tongue; a big cat, a lion. Or like what happened today when I forgot my client's name."

"Honey, Nicole said that she didn't think the jury even noticed it, and if they did, it was meant to be a dramatic pause."

Then Becca, ever fascinated by what she believed to be Franklin's preternatural powers, asked Sam if Franklin had provided any mystical guidance.

"Not exactly, but he did say that he thought that cigarettes or smoke might be the key to this case. Follow this cigarette smoke," Sam grinned a third time, then went on to say, "or where there's smoke, there's fire."

"I really didn't want to tell you this, with you being in trial and all, but I found a vape cigarette, or vape pen, whatever you call it, in Marcus's backpack."

"Oh shit, I had hoped that we had avoided the inevitable experimentation with nicotine. In our time, it was cigarettes, now it's ENDS."

"What's an end?"

"It's an electronic nicotine delivery system; in fact, I used an early form about 10 years ago when I quit smoking. Now, vaping is a fad among teenagers. You can do it in a lot of places that you can't smoke, and I suppose it gives you a rush."

"I didn't know that you used to smoke. But I do know what vaping is, at least enough to know what a vape stick is, or whatever it's called."

"Yeah, back in the day, there were a lot of young public defenders that smoked. Well, I will talk to him. Oh, and by the way, not that I care, but what led you to look in his backpack?"

"He said that he thought his mother packed some medicine for him in there."

Sam talked to Marcus, and after asking how he was, he broached the subject of the vape pen.

"Becca found this in your backpack," Sam revealed and pulled out of his breast pocket the offending vape pen. "I am certain that you are aware of the health issues surrounding the ingestion of nicotine because I know that it's been covered in health class."

Marcus' emphatic reply, "It's not mine, it's a girl's, and what right does Becca have to go in my backpack?"

Sam had to consciously stifle grin number four, which was activated by his thought that Marcus was certainly a public defender's kid. "She went in your backpack because you told her that your mother had put medicine in there for you. So, this is not a case of illegal search and seizure."

"Oh yeah, I did. But I swear, it's not mine. There's a girl I hang out with, and she gave it to me for safekeeping. She said that her parents were always sniffing around in her stuff."

Upon further interrogation of Marcus, it became apparent to Sam that this "girl" was, in fact, his son's first reciprocal crush. He believed Marcus was being truthful about the vape pen, and when he left Marcus and went back to the living room, his smile was incandescent.

When Becca asked about the source of his ebullient mood, he responded in a fake whisper, "I think Marcus has his first real girlfriend." After explaining his conversation with Marcus to Becca, they spent the remainder of the evening searching for something to watch on TV. He was about to go to bed and hoped that his post-trial exhaustion would successfully compete against his post-trial anxiety when Franklin called.

"Sorry to bother you, Sam. I realize that it's late, especially considering the day you have had, but I have a question for you."

"Go ahead, shoot."

"When are you going to call Brad's mom, Barbara, to testify."

"I thought tomorrow, why?"

"Because her other son, Jeff, says that she was pretty freaked out today, and he might spend the night with her, I assume, to keep her from taking anything. He says that he thinks you should call her first thing because the longer you wait, the crazier she will get."

"Well, then I'll call her first thing in the morning. No problem."

"I'll leave you alone now, then. By the way, I forgot to tell you that I had one of my feelings or visions, whatever you want to call them today."

"You don't say. Out with it."

"I saw a black backpack propped up against jail cell bars."

"That's interesting because a black backpack figured prominently in an issue that I had with Marcus tonight."

"Marcus wasn't recently in jail, was he?" Sam could hear Franklin chuckling.

"No, and I'll tell you the full story at lunch tomorrow. Oh, and by the way, it doesn't look like cigarettes played any role in Brad's hanging other than him telling his mother that he was jonesing for one."

"Why?"

"Because when smoking came up in the deposition, Sledgehammer said he didn't smoke; he's an athlete. So, while he might have needed a nicotine hit, it wasn't involved at all in the assault, at least not that we can prove. Sledgehammer denies it, and B doesn't mention it."

"That's not what Shanahan told me. Remember when I ran into him in the elevator, and he told me that they beat the shit out of Brad over a cigarette."

"Yeah, I remember. Maybe we will never really know, and on that note, I will bid you goodnight. I really need some sleep."

Post-trial anxiety won out; he slept fitfully.

CHAPTER 75-NICOLE MEETS ALICE

Because Steve had to leave for trial earlier than her so he could transport Sam to court, Nicole had to drive herself, and she was running late. She parked in the nearest lot to the federal courthouse but still faced a couple of blocks walk. She had promised Kip a cup of coffee; oh well, she hedged, she would just buy him lunch at a Chinese place within shouting distance of the federal courthouse.

When she was about a block away, she saw Kip and a half-dozen other people across the street from the federal courthouse. All of them came replete with signs: most were of variation on the theme of justice for Brad, one sign read, "Nazis gassed them, now we have them hang themselves," and one was a list of five names with Brad's highlighted in red. After apologizing to Kip for her broken promise regarding coffee, she approached the woman carrying the sign with names carefully printed on it and inquired as to its meaning.

The woman, white-haired and wizened–faced, carefully assessed Nicole with her stare before answering, "These are the names of people who hung themselves in the Coalton County Jail. All of them were successful suicides except the one highlighted in red, whose case I understand is being tried today."

Nicole was tempted to tell her that she knew all about the case because of Sam and Steve but decided that the good reporter she hoped to be would rather listen to this interesting-looking woman's story without risking tainting it. So she asked, "What was the woman's interest in the case that was being tried?"

"The first name on this list, Donald Almade, was my son. Since his suicide three years ago, I have been appearing at the Coalton County Jail Oversight Board meetings with my sign and adding to it the names of jail suicides. The last name is in red because he's still technically alive, and that's the case that's being tried."

"Why was your son arrested?"

"It was a Goddamn parole violation. He was an addict, but he was starting to get his life back. He missed a meeting with his parole officer, and they picked him up for it. He couldn't stand being in jail again, so he made certain that he wasn't."

"Wherever he is, I am sure he appreciates you keeping his memory alive."

"Why are you here?"

Now that she had obtained the woman's story, Nicole felt comfortable explaining her various connections to Brad's case, and the woman wished her "Godspeed." Nicole smiled and marveled at the expression, acknowledging, "Sometimes old-fashioned ways of saying things are the best."

"I guess I consider myself old-fashioned. I have an old-fashioned name."

"I'm sorry, I should have introduced myself. I'm Nicole."

"Alice here. Glad to make your acquaintance, Nicole."

"Alice," Nicole gasped, "that was my mother's name."

CHAPTER 76-BARBARA TESTIFIES

Franklin met Jeff and his mother outside of the courtroom the morning of the second day of trial. He pulled Jeff aside so that their conversation wouldn't be overheard by Barbara and told him that Sam was going to call his mother as a witness first thing. Jeff gave him a thumbs up.

Franklin made this observation of Barbara to Jeff, "She looks nervous, understandably petrified in fact, but not hopped up." She was dressed in a conservative skirt and blouse and Franklin couldn't help but appreciate that she had killer legs.

"I did end up spending the night with her," Jeff assured Franklin, "and can tell you that she is not stoned, and it takes one to know one. Will I be called to testify today?"

Franklin shrugged and asserted that the answer to that question was above his pay grade.

When they entered the courtroom, Steve and Sam were already at the counsel table. Barbara took her place beside Sam, and he and Jeff had their pick of seats in the courtroom gallery. None of Steve's law school buddies had yet made their appearance.

He saw Barbara nod her head affirmatively, and he presumed that this was a reaction to Sam's informing her that she would be called to testify first. In short order, Nicole entered the courtroom and sat next to Franklin, and Judge Harris gaveled the court to order and observed:

"I see that there are a few people who are exercising their First Amendment rights to protest outside of the courthouse. I would direct you, as jurors, that you are not to discuss this case with them, and I would advise you to avoid the appearance of impropriety and merely smile at them and walk on by if they attempt to speak to you. Mr. Wright, you may call your first witness of the day."

Although Barbara was obviously frightened when Sam began his direct examination of her, she seemed to become more relaxed as the questioning progressed. Her responses to Sam's questioning gave the jury a fairly complete summary of Brad's life. She told the jury that Brad's father had left them when Brad was a toddler, how his older half-brother,

Jeff, had helped raise him, about her disability and the necessity that they relocate to subsidized housing; that when tested Brad registered as a near-genius IQ, and was a math whiz; and about Brad's minor run-ins with the law for underage drinking and truancy.

"But," she maintained, "Brad was, I mean is, a sweet child. He was always looking out for me."

"As the Judge in his opening remarks indicated, Brad self-identified as gay, correct?"

"Yes, he did."

"When did he tell you that he thought he was gay?"

"Probably three or four years ago. At first, I was upset, angry even, but then I came to accept it. He's still my little boy, gay or not."

Franklin had heard about Brad's boyfriend, Kip, and about how the two of them were planning on going to the prom together. He thought that that might be a little difficult for a middle-aged jury to accept, so he was thankful when Sam avoided asking a question that might lead to that disclosure. Instead, Sam asked a series of questions which allowed Barbara to brag about Brad's math acumen.

"Now, you received a phone call from Brad when he was first jailed, didn't you?"

"Yes, it woke me up."

"What did Brad say during that call?"

Barbara mentioned the cigarettes, the kind guard, and the guard's statement warning him to be careful and saying, "There were guards that would look the other way."

"What do you think that meant?"

"Objection," Fume growled, "Speculation. How is she to know what was in his mind?"

"Withdrawn."

Sam then asked a question which was designed to elicit Barbara's, and hopefully the jury's emotional response, Franklin thought. "Describe your feelings when you saw Brad wheeled into the courtroom yesterday?"

Barbara shifted in her seat on the witness stand and, looking straight at the jurors (her eyes were downcast through most of the direct examination), dolefully replied, "I imagined him singing the Thomas the Train theme song for a moment."

Sam, obviously somewhat puzzled by her response, nonetheless pressed on, "Thomas the Train is an animated children's show, isn't it?"

"Yes," Barbara confirmed.

He knew Sam well enough to detect the uneasiness in Sam's follow-up, "Why?"

Barbara shifted in her chair again but continued to look straight at the jury box. "Thomas the Train was Brad's favorite kids show from the time he was about two, and he loved the theme song. Sometimes, even though he is 18, he would occasionally sing, 'They're two, they're four, they're six, they're eight,' which is part of the theme song. That's the last thing I heard before I fell asleep that night he was arrested. He won't be singing Thomas the Train anymore."

Barbara dabbed her eyes, and Sam was barely audible as he muttered, "Your witness."

Fume stood up and, in a sympathetic voice, inquired, "If you require a recess, Ms. Moran, I am certain that the court would accommodate you."Barbara responded, "No, I'm all right."

Continuing in a compassionate vein, In hopes that the jury would be assured of his humanity, he continued with a non-question, "On behalf of Coalton County and the Coalton County Jail, let me extend my sincerest sympathy for your son's condition."To which Barbara stifled sniffles and mumbled, "Thank you."

Getting down to business, Fume asked: "Now, Mrs. Moran, you have been on disability for a number of years, haven't you?"

"I would say 10 years or more."

"And the reason that you have been placed on disability is that you suffer from spinal stenosis and regional pain syndrome, is it?"

"Yes."

"And as I understand it, the cause of regional pain syndrome is not fully understood, is it?"

Sam knocked over his cane and, in an effort to stand, finally barked from his chair, "Objection, the witness is not a medical professional."

The judge swiftly bellowed "sustained," but Franklin realized that regional pain syndrome would probably show up on more than one juror's Google search when the jury was dismissed for the night. Fume's next question would make that even more likely, "You regularly take Percocet for your regional pain syndrome, don't you?"

"Yes, I am prescribed it by a medical doctor, but…"

Fume cut her off with the question, "To your knowledge, did your son Brad ever take your Percocet pills?"

Sam rose from his seat at the counsel table and shouted, "Objection, Your Honor." The judge motioned for both Sam and Fume to approach the bench. When they both were positioned in front of the bench, Franklin estimated about half of the jurors were surreptitiously straining to hear what appeared to be a spirited discussion from the attorneys' hand gestures and half looking bored. Barbara looked terrified.

When the attorneys were apparently dismissed by the judge and returned to their prior positioning in the courtroom, Fume insisted, "You may answer the question, Mrs. Moran."

Barbara looked down and breathed, "I wouldn't be surprised. You can't stop kids from experimenting, but I wanted to finish my answer. It's been weeks since I have taken any prescription medication."

"Congratulations," Fume graciously volunteered and, in what Franklin recognized was certainly an attempt to curry favor with the jury, observed, "I know how difficult that must have been for you."

"Thank you", Barbara acknowledged.

Fume then switched gears and had Barbara again relate the phone call which she had received from Brad the night he was arrested, including Brad's request for cigarettes and the offer he received from a sympathetic guard to obtain for him cigarettes from the guard's car.

"Would you say that your son sounded upset?"

"Yes."

"Desperate even?"

"I guess you could say that."

"Now, your other son, Jeff, was arrested when he was also eighteen, correct?"

"Yes."

"He was charged and pled guilty to stealing a car, isn't that right?"

"Yes."

"And before that, he had been charged as a juvenile with truancy, underage drinking and possession of a controlled substance, correct?"

Steve helped Sam to his feet, and Sam registered his objection, "Relevance! In fact, this whole line of questioning about Jeff should be stricken from the record. It's clearly irrelevant." Fume replied, "Withdrawn," prompting the judge to rule, "Objection sustained."

Sam passed on any redirect, and he did call Jeff as his next witness. Franklin happened to know that Jeff had been prepared by Sam over the weekend and that his testimony, as Sam described it, would be "short and sweet," and it was.

Because Fume had, in effect, "Let the cat out of the bag" regarding Jeff's past criminal record Franklin surmised that that was the reason that Sam posed a series of questions regarding prior Jeff's convictions. Having established Jeff's residency at the Coalton County Jail for a period of years and the reason for it, Sam inquired of Jeff about his post-release activities and his relationship with Brad.

Of course, as Jeff explained, Brad was barely thirteen years old when Jeff went to jail. Jeff proudly insisted that in the months that he had been out, he had been, to quote him, " a model citizen." He was working full time, had his own apartment, and had purchased an old car. He reported that he was "clean and sober" now for nearly four years.

Brad had visited him on a more or less regular basis while he was in jail, and he described those visits as "delightful." As much as he could, he kept up with Brad's school accomplishments and social life, and he was proud of his brother despite his brother's occasional run-ins with the law. He acknowledged that Brad had arrests for underage drinking and truancy, but he anticipated that Brad would eventually go to college and use his gift for mathematics in some way.

Then, Sam showed him half a dozen photographs of Jeff and Brad together, and they were put up on the jury monitors. They seemed to depict a normal relationship between an older brother and his younger sibling, and he assumed Sam wanted to neutralize the impression that this was a family of abject losers. Upon being asked by Sam to comment on the last picture of him and his brother on a roller coaster, Jeff became misty-eyed and said they had made plans to go to an amusement park, just the two of them, in the summer, but never made it. Then, Sam said, with something approaching a flourish, "Your witness."

Fume rose and stood about six feet from Jeff, studied Jeff, and then began his cross-examination with the statement, "I suppose you, as well as your mother, are due congratulations for being clean and sober."

Even from his vantage point, he could see Sam tense up. Fume went on, "Now, you were approximately eighteen when you were arrested and convicted of stealing a car."

"Yes."

"Did you have a drug or alcohol problem at that time?"

Franklin could see Sam attempt to leverage himself into a standing position, and when he achieved it, he almost breathlessly, because of this physical struggle, said, "Objection, your Honor, what is the relevance of this?"

Ruling from the bench and within clear earshot of the jury, Judge Harrison snapped, "Mr. Moran injected his sobriety on direct examination, so I think it is a fair question on a cross. However, I would caution Mr. Fume not to dwell on the subject."

Fume replied demurely, "It's the only question I will have on that subject."

Franklin realized the thought that Fume wished to implant in the jurors' minds: That this was an entire family of dysfunctional, drug-addled people. He thought, you have made your point, get Jeff's affirmative answer and then move on.

Franklin was astounded by Jeff's answer, "Yes, I had a drug and alcohol problem when I stole the car, but thanks to that guy," and he pointed straight at Franklin, "who put me on the straight and narrow, with God's help I hope to live out my life sober."

Franklin lost his focus through the rest of the morning.

CHAPTER 77-SONNENBURG TRASHES THE ROVER PROGRAM

Sam bought lunch for Franklin, Barbara, Jeff and Steve in the cafeteria. Nicole stopped by briefly, but she said that she was taking Brad's boyfriend, Kip, to lunch at a Chinese place. She had a question for Sam, however, "What was that brouhaha in front of the bench during Barbara's testimony?"

"I screwed up, that's what it was about." Sam looked down at his cafeteria tray. He hoped that he didn't look the way he felt: like a crippled-up old man.

"I should have objected when Fume asked Barbara whether she regularly took Percocet pills for her regional pain syndrome. I did object when Fume asked in the subsequent question whether Brad had ever taken her pills. Still, the judge convinced me that since the jury had heard that Barbara took Percocet, that I was probably better off to have Barbara answer the question of whether Brad ever took the pills rather than have the jury think God knows what."

Sam could see that Nicole was processing his answer. He quickly added, "Barbara, your answer that you haven't had any pills in quite some time was outstanding. I couldn't have coached you on what to say better than that."

"Thanks, Sam. And what did you think about my other son here, Jeff?" She asked while resting her hand on Jeff's knee.

Sam smiled and carefully considered what his response should be. His grin widened when he considered the variation on the old TV ad, "The family that prays together stays together." This was the family that abstained together stays together. It gave him the germ of an idea for his closing, though.

"I thought he did wonderfully, too. You guys certainly neutralized the point that Fume was trying to make that you were a project–dwelling, drug-loving family unit." Sam tried to sound convincing despite his uncertainty as to whether Fume's efforts along these lines would bear fruit with the jury.

"We will need to have a chat about anonymity, Jeff," Franklin murmured to Jeff in a tone that Sam thought sounded obligatory. "What's on tap this afternoon?" he asked with more engagement.

"Stewart Sonnenberg, the Allegheny County Jail psychologist who will give his expert testimony." Sam hoped he could successfully camouflage the disdain with which he had for Stewart. He really should try to get over his anger at Stewart for screwing his ex-wife.

Franklin nodded disinterestedly. Sam spent the remainder of lunch reviewing his notes on Sonnenberg's testimony which he had dictated and Rhonda had typed.

Despite what he had told Sonnenberg about court convening promptly at 1:15 PM under Judge Harris' watch when the gavel banged, Sonnenberg was nowhere to be found. Sam was considering what he should do and was on the verge of panic when Sonnenberg pushed open the courtroom doors with a bang and announced, "Sorry, Judge, I got tied up in class."

Judge Harris thundered, "We wouldn't want to deprive your future Freuds of your answers to their after-class questions, now would we, Professor? That might cause students' grades to Freudian slip badly."

Because it was expected of him, Sam smiled along with Fume, who did Sam one-up on in the ass-kissing department and remarked, "Good one, Your Honor." In his surreptitious glance over at the jury, he could see no sign that they were amused. As Sonnenberg was mounting the witness stand, Sam couldn't help but notice the Freud affectation, which he hadn't quite put together in their prior meetings: The white goatee, receding hairline, round glasses and paunch. He wondered, as he often did, why his ex-wife fell for this guy.

He ran through the standard qualifying questions of any expert with nary a stumble. Sonnenberg was an undergrad at Pitt, Masters and doctorate at U Penn, and eventually a full professor at Duquesne, with several stops in between his doctorate and Duquesne. He was appointed the psychologist at Allegheny County Jail.

He had an extensive and impressive list of published works in his field. In fact, Sam happened to know that his ex-wife had all but written several articles when she was an undergrad for which he took credit. Of course, given the jury's minimal knowledge of the secrets of academia, Sam could tell that they were impressed with Sonnenberg's claimed extensive authorship of academic articles. They all were paying rapt attention.

Sam asked Sonnenberg a series of background questions designed to illustrate for the jury the widespread nature of jailhouse suicides and the seriousness with which they were viewed by the correctional community.

"In fact," Sonnenberg testified, "there is a significant portion of correctional academic writing which addresses jail suicides, especially amongst recent arrestees and gay inmates. It only makes sense, recent arrestees are certainly facing one of the most stressful events in their lives, and gay inmates face harassment of other inmates and potentially rape."

Sam posed a follow-up question, "How has the United States Federal Bureau of Prisons sought to address the problem of jail suicides?" Sam had difficulties getting the words Federal Bureau of Prisons out but finally did on his third try.

"The federal government is quite concerned about preventing suicides in a Federal jail or penitentiary setting. Obviously, they can't mandate that actions be taken by a state, but they have come up with guidelines which many states and localities have adopted."

"Such as…?"

"Well, such as a suicide assessment questionnaire and training guards to be cognizant of prisoners who present a significant risk of suicide."

"Were both questionnaires and the training of guards present during the relevant period when Brad attempted to take his own life?"

"The short answer is yes. Brad was, in fact, administered what we might call a standard suicide risk assessment questionnaire, and I have no qualms with that. It was the questionnaire suggested by the Department of Justice. I do find that guard training with respect to the recognition of potentially suicidal prisoners to be less than adequate at the time of Brad's arrest, though."

In response to Sam's question, "How so?" Sonnenberg went into detail about what he thought would be adequate training for guards, including monthly guard meetings to share experiences. He concluded with, "They were only required to watch a one-hour movie once a year with respect to identifying potential suicides."

"You reserve most of your criticism of the policies and procedures at the Coalton County Jail for how what were known as inmate rovers or suicide prevention workers were selected and trained, don't you?"

"Yes, I do."

"Why don't you explain to the jury what 'suicide prevention workers' or 'inmate rovers' were?"

"It was a program in a very limited number of jails nationwide where certain hand-picked inmates were supposed to be chosen and trained to identify potential suicidal inmates among those that were recently incarcerated. They were paid by the jail; in effect, although they were prisoners themselves, they doubled as employees of the jail. The payment was paltry, but enough to buy cigarettes, candy bars etc."

"How were these inmates who were employed as suicide prevention workers or inmate rovers to be selected?"

"At first, the selection process was that various prisoners would, in effect, be nominated by the upper echelon of guards, approved by the jail psychologist, administered a psychiatric screening test by the jail psychiatrist, and only then if they passed each stage of this process, could they be rovers or suicide prevention workers."

"You said, 'at first,' I take it that that wasn't the procedure on the date Brad attempted suicide, was it?"

"No, it wasn't. Dr. Rodriguez, who was the jail psychiatrist, set out this policy five years ago. It was followed until Dr. Rodriguez left the employ of the jail three years ago. Since Dr. Rodriguez left, eventually psychiatric testing for inmate rovers was discontinued, and then the jail psychologist's approval. It was ceded to a Lieutenant of the guards, and in effect, he was the sole decision-maker."

"When you say 'ceded,' what do you mean?"

"I reviewed the deposition of Lieutenant Kevin Hodgson. He testified in his deposition that Dr. Annette Paulson, the jail psychologist, said that since he knew the inmates better than her, he could make the decisions as to inmate rovers. So, there was no psychiatric testing, no jail psychiatrist approval, and the selection was left solely to Lieutenant Hodgson."

"And what type of training were the inmate rovers given?"

"The same training that the guards got. They watched a one-hour movie on identifying potential suicide risks for one hour, once a year."

"But, is your only criticism of the Inmate Rover Program that it had strayed from its original procedure and design by the time that Brad came to the Coalton County jail?"

"No, that is not my only criticism. I believe that the program was fundamentally flawed and should not have been implemented in any form."

"Why?"

"First of all, there is the issue of the discontinuance of psychiatric or psychological testing and vetting."

"What do you mean by that?"

"When Dr. Rodriguez was in charge of the Inmate Rover Program, he conducted psychiatric and psychological testing and observation to ensure, as much as possible, that inmates who were walking around and observing other inmates in their cells would be stable."

"And what happened when Dr. Rodriguez left?"

"When Dr. Rodriguez left three years ago, Dr. Annette Paulson conducted very limited evaluations of proposed inmate rovers for a little while. I don't get the impression that the evaluations were nearly as intensive as when Dr. Rodriguez was vetting proposed rovers. Still, we do know that whatever evaluation Dr. Paulson was making was ultimately discontinued."

"Who, then, was making the selection of who could be an Inmate Rover?"

"According to Lieutenant Hodgson, Dr. Paulson gave him sole authority to determine who would be an Inmate Rover, and basically, Inmate Rovers were selected by whomever Lieutenant Hodgson liked. Absolutely no psychiatric or psychological testing was done by Lieutenant Hodgson, nor was he qualified to do that testing."

"Why was it critical that psychiatric or psychological testing be done on prisoners who were proposed Inmate Rovers?"

"It just makes sense. You are dealing with a prisoner population who, almost by definition, evidenced some form of antisocial behavior. It is my opinion that imbuing sentenced inmates with any apparent authority is reckless per se. And the problem is compounded by giving them some authority as suicide prevention workers or rovers without somehow vetting these individuals by having a professional interview them and perform psychiatric or psychological testing on them. It is, well, incredibly reckless."

"Now, Dr. Sonnenberg, I will read you part of the deposition of Brian Lowe. Later on in the trial, Mr. Lowe will be called to testify but he provided this sworn deposition testimony." Then Sam read to him B's deposition testimony regarding what he heard and witnessed regarding the Sledgehammer's interaction with Brad the night of Brad's attempted suicide.

"Taking Mr. Lowe's deposition testimony to be accurate, do you have any comment?"

"Yes, as I testified previously, almost by definition, people who are incarcerated have evidenced some antisocial behaviors, and giving them authority as 'Suicide Prevention Workers' or Rovers makes physical abuse of another inmate, as occurred with Mr. Moran, a virtual certainty. This is doubly true when you consider that Inmate Rovers weren't vetted at all by a qualified professional."

Then Sam, who was wavering on his quad cane near the end of his direct examination, virtually collapsed into his seat at the counsel table and gasped, "Your witness."

Fume, noticing Sam's noisy crumble into his chair at the conclusion of his direct examination of Dr. Sonnenberg, stood for his cross-examination but first asked Sam, in a voice loud enough for the jurors to hear, "Mr. Wright, are you all right?"

To which Sam replied, "Yes, all's right with the world."

Fume smiled, as did a couple of jurors. Then, Fume began his cross-examination, "Now Doctor, isn't it true that the Federal Bureau of Corrections suicide questionnaire and assessment was completed for Mr. Moran?"

"Yes, it was."

"And isn't it true that guards and rovers received at least one hour of training and recognizing potential suicides by being required to attend a showing of a movie on jail suicides?"

"Yes, but I hardly think that attending an hour-long movie is sufficient."

"Have you seen the movie?"

"No, I haven't."

"Now, isn't your opinion as to the recklessness of the Coalton County Jail's employment of Rovers based entirely upon the veracity or believability of Mr. Lowe's testimony?"

"No, I think it is reckless as it is currently implemented."

"But, wouldn't you concede that your testimony that a rover, namely Mr. Lindstrom, caused Mr. Moran's attempted suicide is based upon the accuracy of Mr. Lowe's observations, as the same are recorded in his deposition testimony, which was read to you?"

"Well, absent some other version of events, I suppose that's true, But I am inditing having rovers period. As I said, you shouldn't give any inmates apparent authority over other inmates."

"Allow me to read from the deposition of Mr. Lindstrom."Then Fume read Sledgehammer's account of his encounter with Brad, albeit overly dramatically, Sam thought. Of course, he emphasized with the tone of his voice how Sledgehammer sat on Brad's bunk, Brad's extremely aggravated state and his attempts to calm him down, and how he was essentially jumped from behind by Brad.

"Now, Doctor, assuming Mr. Lindstrom's account of his sole encounter with Brad on the night of his attempted suicide is accurate, can it be said that the Coalton County Jail and Mr. Lindstrom were responsible for Brad's attempted suicide?"

"No, if you mean assuming that Mr. Lindstrom is telling the truth without more inculpatory facts, no it would not be my opinion that the jail was not legally responsible. It couldn't be said that a policy of the Coalton County jail caused Brad's attempt at suicide."

"So, it all boils down to whether Mr. Lowe, also known as B, or Mr. Lindstrom, also known as Sledgehammer, is telling the truth."

Sam leveraged himself into a standing position and exploded, "Objection, Your Honor. Was that a question?"

Fume smirked, "Withdrawn."

CHAPTER 78-NICOLE LEARNS MORE ABOUT ALICE'S SON

When Nicole left the courthouse with Steve after Prof.Sonnenberg's testimony, there was a light rain falling, and the last of what she came to think of as the half-dozen or so "protesters" had vanished. All that is, except Alice.

Nicole told Steve that she would meet him back at the apartment because he had to drive Sam back to the office, and, popping up her umbrella, approached Alice.

"Alice, my car is parked about a block from here if I could drop you downtown somewhere. Or if you are waiting for someone I would be happy to loan you my umbrella. I find the rain reinvigorating after spending the afternoon in the stale confines of the courtroom."

"No, that's all right. My daughter is supposed to pick me up. But would you mind telling me what went on in there today."

"I have no place that I need to be, so I will wait with you so you won't get drenched. I don't mind telling you what went on in there at all," Nicole replied brightly while holding the umbrella over both their heads. "Brad's mother and brother testified this morning and basically told the jury that he was a nice kid and something of a math whiz."

"And this afternoon?"

"This afternoon was a psychology professor from Duquesne who testified regarding what he thought the Coalton County Jail did wrong. But I think it's all going to boil down to whether they believe one prisoner or another."

"A psychology professor? I hope he found fault with the jail, at least. I don't have a lot of respect for psychologists, not since I met with the jail psychologist after my boy's suicide."

"You met with the jail psychologist after his suicide? How did that come about?"

"I think that it was set up by the County politicians who were worried that I might sue. One day, a couple of months after he was gone, I got a call from this psychologist, Annette Paulson, who said If I had any questions about my son and what happened, she would be happy to answer them. So we set up a meeting."

"Annette Paulson, I think her name was mentioned by the psychology professor today. When did Donald die?"

"2 and a half years ago."

"How did your meeting with Paulson go?"

"Not real well. She was sort of matter-of-fact and not sympathetic at all. She brought a Colonel or someone who was a big shot guard with her."

"What was his name, the big shot guard?"

"It ended with son, that's all I remember. Because I thought it was odd that both of their names ended in -son. And then, I forgot my phone in the place where we met, like a conference room, and I went back in to fetch it after our meeting was over, and the two sons were hugging each other."

"That's odd. I will have to mention that to my boyfriend, Steve."

A horn sounded because a car came to a complete stop in front of them.

"Gotta go. That's my daughter."

And just like that, Alice disappeared totally from Nicole's life, and she was left to contemplate another mother's tragedy.

CHAPTER 79-A LUNCHTIME DISCLOSURE OF A ROMANTIC RELATIONSHIP

Late the night of Professor Sonnenberg's testimony, Franklin got a call from Jeff.

"Well, mama went several weeks without pills, but she is fucked up now."

"On what?"

"I went out for coffee after a meeting with a young lady that I met, and we… you know, and when I got to my mother's place, I found her with half a bottle of vodka gone and she told me she had gotten some Percocet."

"Do you think she will be able to make it to court tomorrow?"

"That, I couldn't tell you."

When Franklin called Sam and he asked a similar question, Franklin provided a similar response.

"But," he added, "I am sure that Jeff will call me first thing in the morning with a status update, and I'll call you."

When the morning of the third day of trial arrived, he reluctantly reported to Sam the news that he had been told by Jeff that Barbara wouldn't make court this morning. Sam responded that at least she would be spared Fume's cross-examination of B, which Sam expected to be brutal.

After Sam informed the judge in open court that his client was ill and wouldn't be appearing, Sam began the tedious slog through the expert testimony of the life care planner and economist.

The life care planner estimated that, if Brad had a normal lifespan, it would take nine million dollars to care for him through the end of his life. *Fume had a long and detailed cross-examination, which the jury found boring as hell,* he thought.

Next at bat was an economist, who performed some economic mumbo-jumbo designed to "reduce" the nine million dollars projected by the life care planner to "present value." He and the jury were thankful when lunchtime rolled around.

Lunch was attended by the usual suspects absent Barbara and Brian Lowe, also known as B. It was his understanding that B would be called to testify as soon as what was projected by Sam to be the relatively short cross-examination of the economist.

Once introductions were made by Sam, Nicole was the first to make any non–perfunctory comment: "I ran into a protester yesterday named Alice whose son committed suicide in the Coalton County Jail. She wasn't there this morning when I came in."

"Was she the older woman with a sign with the names on it?" Steve wanted to know.

"Yeah, she was. I forgot to tell you last night, Steve, but she said that after her son's suicide, she had a meeting with the jail psychologist and a guard who she said was a Colonel and whose name ended in - son. She said that they weren't very sympathetic."

"Hmm…" Sam said. "That's got to be a reference to Paulson, the jail psychologist, and Hodgson, but he's not Colonel. He's a Lieutenant. She must have had her badges of rank confused."

"Not only that," Nicole continued, "but she saw them hugging each other."

"Fascinating," Sam mumbled, "but I have no idea how I can use that."

Franklin volunteered, "As Voltaire said, 'in love, one and one are one'; didn't you tell me that the jail psychologist had given up sole authority to name rovers to Lieutenant Hodgson?"

"Yeah," Sam replied, "That might explain the reason that he was chosen to run the Rover program, but how are two employees being romantically involved relevant, even if they were romantically involved? It is interesting, though."

The remainder of the lunch hour was consumed by Sam's preparation of B for his imminent testimony, which Franklin pretty much tuned out, instead discussing Barbara's absence and its cause with Jeff.

CHAPTER 80-B TESTIFIES

When he appeared outside the courtroom at lunchtime, Sam noted that B had a shirt that was two sizes too large for him, a tie that was three decades too wide for him and a red beret which was too bizarre for him. Sam's first words to B before going down in the elevator with him were: "You know, the beret has got to go when you are testifying. In fact, I would prefer that when you are sitting in the courtroom waiting to testify that you didn't let the jury see it." B shrugged, took the beret off and stuck it in the pocket of his wide-lapelled sports coat which had been all the rage forty years ago.

Although Sam had prepared B on the weekend, he was glad that they got to talk over lunch. He was growing to genuinely like B, although he realized that B was a minimally moral rogue. And he was convinced of B's veracity despite placing the odds of the jury believing him over Sledgehammer at about 80–20.

When court was gavelled to order after lunch, and when Fume completed his tortuously boring cross-examination of the economist, Sam called B to the stand. On his short walk from the courtroom gallery to the witness stand, B attempted to engage the jury by looking at each one of them individually and smiling broadly. He didn't seem the least bit nervous. In fact, Sam was of the impression that he was genuinely enjoying the opportunity to be the center of attention.

Once B was sworn in, and the Brian Lowe, but you can call me B crap was out of the way, Sam's initial question was, "Have you been a life-long resident of Coalton County?"

B's response was unexpected, "Lord, I was born a ramblin' man, tryin' to make a living and doin' the best I can. But, yes, I suppose that you could say the base of operations for my life has been Coalton County." Several members of the jury chuckled openly. Sam realized that they probably welcomed the injection of humor after sitting through the morning wearisome dreariness.

After Sam asked him how he made a living ("handyman") he inquired as to why he was present in the Coalton County Jail in January. Although Sam had coached him to be as brief as possible and attempted to redirect him multiple times during his narrative, he was undeterred and went into a long explanation of how he was charged under the Home Improvement Fraud Act. But, he continued, his partner really had defrauded the homeowner, but he was swept up in what he termed the "cargo net of his partner's lies."

"So, that is why you were incarcerated in the Coalton County Jail in January of this year?"

"Yes, and unjustly, I might add. I coulda used some of the attorneys who prove that people that are in jail are actually innocent."

"Now, I want to take you back to January of this year. Did you witness an altercation between Jacques Lindstrom, also known as Sledgehammer, and Brad Moran?"

"Yes."

"And how did you know Jacques Lindstrom and Brad Moran?"

"I had known Jacques Lindstrom for months, and I knew it was Brad Moran because, well, when something like what happened to him gets out, everyone is talking about it. It was his cell that I knew he hung hisself in."

"Can you describe what you heard and saw relative to the altercation?"

He then described how Flake grabbed Brad from behind and Sledgehammer struck him multiple times in the head. "And, it all happened so fast, but I heard Sledgehammer say, "You better be careful, Gump, because I have permission to fuck you up like this every day."

"What does the word Gump mean in prison parlance? In other words, what's the generally accepted definition of Gump when it is used in a jail setting?"

"In prison parlay, what was that word you used? Well, never mind, it means gay, homosexual, faggot."

"And did you know before that that Brad was gay?"

"Yeah, I did. Don't ask me how I knew because I couldn't tell you. Word travels fast when there's a new guy that comes in, especially when he is of that persuasion."

"Now, you have described what you heard and saw, what happened next?"

"Well, it seemed like Sledgehammer was done beating on Brad, and I didn't want no trouble with Sledgehammer thinkin' that I had seen what he had done, so I hightailed it out of there."

"And yet you're here today."

"Yeah, but I'm here today because the kid hung hisself over Sledgehammer, and that ain't right."

"Were you aware that Jacques Lindstrom, Sledgehammer, was a Rover, otherwise known as a Suicide Prevention Worker?"

"Yes, I was. And he must've been on official rover business with Brad because his black backpack was in Brad's cell."

Sam was astounded by B's unexpected reference to a black backpack. He hadn't mentioned anything about a black backpack before, but then he hadn't asked if Sledgehammer was a Rover before, he had just assumed that the B would have known that he was.

"Of what significance is the black backpack?"

"You see, the Rovers, and there were only three or four of them, were permitted to keep personal items like candy, cigarettes, packages of doughnuts or packaged pies in backpacks because, I guess, their job was to rove among the prisoners. I saw Rovers who would drop their backpacks off in a cell, and then, well, rove about and come back to the cell where they had dropped the backpack off for a cigarette, some candy, or some reading material."

While B was answering the question, Sam's concentration lagged somewhat because of B's surprise injection of the potential significance of a black backpack, although he was mystified by what the significance might be. Chalk one up for Franklin, though.

Sam's awareness was startled back into the courtroom when, after an unusually long silence between questions, Judge Harris kindly inquired, "Mr. Wright, are you done with this witness?"

Sam responded, "No, I am not, Your Honor, I have a few more questions. Have you ever seen Mr. Lindstrom be physical or assault anyone else?"

"Yeah, yours truly."

"What were their circumstances surrounding your assault by Mr. Lindstrom?"

"He hit me in the jaw, and I had to have medical attention. It was a dispute over, shall we say, ownership rights."

"Are you aware that Mr. Lindstrom has testified that he struck you in self-defense?"

"You told me that's what he said. But all I have to say is Lindstrom has got to be 6'3" tall, he is what's known in professional hockey as a goon. And look at me. I'm 5'6" and skinny, although I have developed this paunch in later years. I ain't stupid enough that I would have thrown the first punch against Sledgehammer."

He had endlessly agonized over where in his direct examination he should place the prior conviction questions. Like any good trial attorney, when you know that damaging questions are going to be the subject of inquiry by opposing counsel, he recognized that it's always better when a jury thinks that you are being honest with them, warts and all. He had decided to save them for the end of his direct examination because, he hoped, B's natural roguish charm might captivate the jury and minimize the impact of his numerous attempts at chicanery. So...

He went meticulously through each of B's convictions for the relatively minor crimes of dishonesty, including a couple of bad check charges, a couple of stolen credit card charges and three theft of services charges. He concluded his direct examination with this question, "Have you been promised anything of value for your testimony here today?"

"Well, you bought me lunch in the cafeteria, and the hamburger was cold and lousy."

Several jurors snickered, and like a veteran comedian, B waited for their titters to subside and then answered, "No, sir."

Fume began his cross-examination with more of a preview of what was to come then a question, "Mr. Lowe, you do realize that Mr. Lindstrom's deposition testimony is diametrically opposed to your version of events?"

"Whatever you said, if I get the gist of it, I realize that his version of what happened is different than mine and that he's a liar."

"It's interesting you should say that Mr. Lowe, but let's explore again some of the crimes involving dishonesty that your attorney previously brought to this jury's attention." Then, Fume went through B's transgressions one by one, and contrary to Sam's instructions that on cross-examination, you only should answer with a yes or no, several times B attempted to explain away his arrests. Sam feared that B's efforts were met with skepticism by the jury.

"Isn't it true that you harbor ill will toward Mr. Lindstrom because of the altercation you described with Mr. Lindstrom in your direct examination?"

"If what you mean is, did I enjoy him almost breaking my jaw; no I didn't, but not enough to lie."

Fume concluded his cross-examination with an argumentative statement barely disguised as a question, "And with all of these crimes involving dishonesty, you really expect the jury that your dislike of Mr. Lindstrom hasn't colored your testimony here today?"

In a prior life, Sam would have jumped up rabbit-like to make an objection, but now he had to secure his quad cane and gain his balance before he registered the objection. By the time he had gotten to his feet, after one unsuccessful attempt, B was already into his answer, "I know that you must think that there ain't no honor amongst thieves, but I am here to tell you that although I have done some dishonest things in my past, I ain't never pounded on a defenseless young kid like Sledgehammer done. And I hear that Sledgehammer is going to be testifying, maybe tomorrow, and I wouldn't put it past him to try to find me. It would have been easier for me and probably safer, too, if I had just kept my yap shut, but I would have had trouble sleeping at night. So, yeah, I do expect the jury to believe me, thief and all."

Sam couldn't help but smile, in contrast to Fume, who, after he announced that he had no more questions, returned to the counsel table tight-lipped and looking unsettled.

CHAPTER 81-NICOLE AND TIM TALK ABOUT MOTHERHOOD

"What did the judge say after B testified and you rested your case? You were up there in front of the bench for a little while after the jury was dismissed." Nicole was expressing her natural curiosity to Sam when he came out of the courtroom and met Nicole and his retinue in the hall.

"Fume made a motion for a nonsuit, which means that he made a motion that the judge should rule as a matter of law, without jury input, that there was no legal basis for the suit. The motion by Fume was denied, and the Judge basically said that if the jury believed B's story, and since Sledgehammer was technically an employee of the jail, he would let the jury decide whether Coalton County was deliberately indifferent."

"And I bet that Judge Harris appreciated B's biblical reference," Steve interjected.

"You mean the honor among thieves comment of B? What would make you think that?" Sam sighed. Nicole sensed that Sam was running on fumes at this point, and she smiled at her own successful wordplay, even if it wasn't verbalized. Of course, Steve thought she was smiling at him, and he smiled back with a twinkle in his eye before continuing, "I googled him like you told me to. He's a Methodist minister's kid."

Sam smiled and allowed, "Yes, he did appreciate the biblical reference. As a matter of fact, he cited the chapter and verse in Proverbs that it came from, and said that was the most effective part of B's testimony. He added that he had his doubts as to whether the jury would believe B and said he would be anxious to hear Sledgehammer's side of the story."

Then Sam directed a question to Franklin, "Have you had any word from Jeff regarding his mother? Am I going to have to sit without a client tomorrow?"

"I talked to Jeff this afternoon, and he thinks his mother will be attending the festivities tomorrow."

Sam nodded.

After Nicole had exited the courthouse, she went across the street to see Brad's boyfriend, Kip and asked him if he knew where Alice, the woman who carried the sign with her deceased son's name on it, was. She noted that the crowd had grown exponentially since the trial started. She assumed because all of the local stations were covering it.

"Oh, she said that her daughter didn't like driving into Pittsburgh, and she might not be back."

She decided to call Tim on the short drive back to her apartment.

"How's my star reporter?" asked the editor.

"Fine", she responded reflexively.

"I can tell when there's something on your mind. Out with it."

"Nothing serious, but I was just thinking that in the past six months, I have met three different women who all have had to confront tragedies involving their sons. There's Barbara, whose son Brad is the subject of this case. Phyllis, mother of the roommate of Brad, who for almost twenty years has taken care of her son with severe cerebral palsy, and Alice, who I just met a couple of days ago and whose son committed suicide in the Coalton County Jail."

"You know what a writer would do?"

"Write about them?"

"Feel their pain, and then write about them."

CHAPTER 82-SLEDGEHAMMER TESTIFIES

When Franklin entered the courtroom, he first looked to see if Barbara had been delivered as Jeff had promised. When he saw her beside Sam and looking slightly green around the gills, he knew all was right with his part of the world, at least because Franklin thought of himself as coordinating the comings and goings of the Moran family.

He noted that the entourage of Steve's law school buddies had multiplied over the course of the trial and now took up about a dozen seats. They were talking and giggling amongst themselves, and, unlike the first day of trial when they were exclusively Steve's male buddies, they were now composed of young men with various levels of beard growth and young jeans-clad women. He had to smile at the fantasy of running the concession stand at the back of the courtroom and these law students forming a long queue to purchase their popcorn, Dots and Cokes before the start of the show.

Then, strolling down the aisle and taking a seat in front of the law students, was a striking young man dressed in a lime green double-breasted suit and white shirt opened just enough to show his male décolletage. His fashionably long blonde hair was collected in a bun, and his chiseled face featured deep blue eyes. He stood well over six feet, and Steve's law student buddies fell temporarily silent as he was settling into a seat. It was, Franklin surmised, a Sledgehammer in the flesh.

When the gavel fell, and Jacques Lindstrom was called to the stand by Fume, he made his way down the aisle to the witness stand flashing a smile and his blue eyes all the way. Franklin could see that at least three jurors, two women and one man, smiled back.

Fume moved through the preliminaries in short order, including Sledgehammer's current residence, which was Manitoba, and then he had him explain why he had found himself in the Coalton County Jail. In response, he went through his history, including playing hockey for the Manitoba Moose, the invitation to try out with the Wheeling Nailers, and his meeting with a woman in a Coalton bar.

"And, I take it, one thing led to another and you ultimately moved in with the woman? And we don't want to use her name out of respect for her privacy." Fume was attempting to move this narrative along.

"Yeah, the Nailers didn't want me, but she did." One of the women jurors poked another woman juror; she whispered something to her, and both grinned.

"And you lived with this woman in Coalton for how long?"

"I would say six months."

Fume then had him relate his employment history during the last six months. (a mover For You Move Me) and the occurrence which ultimately landed him in the Coalton County Jail, "This guy who was in Sweeney's Bar called my girlfriend, whose name will remain unspoken, a whore. One thing led to another and we ended up fighting and I broke his jaw. It was like a barroom brawl."

He then explained that although he didn't believe he was the guilty party, his public defender advised him to plead guilty and not go to trial. He was sentenced to a year but told he would be out in six months. When Fume asked whether he was still involved with the unnamed girlfriend, he responded with a line that, to Franklin, appeared to be rehearsed, "Nah, she didn't wait for me. And after I defended her honor as a woman. I guess chivalry didn't impress her none." The poker and the poker jurors looked at each other and smiled.

"Now, there has been some testimony that you were chosen as a rover or suicide prevention worker. Were you?"

Sledgehammer then provided a fairly detailed description of the program, how he was selected for the program, how they were trained (basically, they attended a movie on jail suicides), and what their responsibilities were as Rovers.

"And you say that you were chosen to be our rover by Lieutenant Kevin Hodgson, correct? What did Lieutenant Hodgson tell you about why you were so chosen?"

"He told me I was picked because it seemed as if I was respected because I played professional hockey and because of my size. The Lieutenant and I had a lot of conversations about hockey. He was a fan."

"Now, I understand that you had something of a run in with a prisoner by the name of Brian Lowe, also known as B, correct?"

"Yes, I did."

"And when was that altercation?"

"Sometime in the fall of last year."

"What happened?"

"Well, I come to hear that B was makin' pruno in his toilet. Pruno is hooch, booze, and I just casually mentioned that that was what got me in here; some people, not me, could not handle their liquor. Well, one thing led to another and he took a swing at me. Not only that, but that swing connects. A man has a right to protect himself."

"Mr. Brian Lowe says you almost broke his jaw. Were you subject to any disciplinary action as a result of your fight with Mr. Lowe?"

"No, I wasn't. Lieutenant Hodgson conducted an investigation, and I was cleared of any wrongdoing. He made me a Rover soon after that."

"Let me take you back to January of this year. Did you have any contact with Brad Moran?"

"Not much." Then, Franklin noticed, he looked directly at the jury and, in what Franklin perceived to be an over-exaggeration of his French accent, explained that he heard a commotion, and went to investigate. He described how he saw Brad red-faced, obviously disturbed and yelling.

"Did you attempt to calm him down?"

"Yeah, I did. He said he wanted a cigarette, but I said I don't smoke. I thought I had him calmed, but when I was walking out of his cell, another guy who was visiting his cell for some reason, Flake, yelled at me to watch out. I turned around and Brad was coming at me with his fists in the air."

Sledgehammer explained that a tussle ensued involving himself, Flake and Brad. Franklin thought that Sledgehammer was coached to use the word "tussle;" the word didn't roll off of the French Canadian's tongue. Finally, he said, they got Brad into his bunk, and he and Flake left.

Franklin then became distracted when Barbara turned around and looked straight at him rather mournfully in the midst of Sledgehammer embellishing his narrative; nonetheless, Franklin had captured the gist of it. Then, when Fume asked him what his thoughts were when he found out that Brad had attempted suicide, there was a long pause, which refocused Franklin's attention. Sledgehammer looked like he was going to cry. Then he did.

Sledgehammer sputtered between gasps, "I ain't never been in jail before this time, and then this kid tries to do himself in. I know I didn't have anything to do with it, but I felt guilty and awfully bad for the kid."

Franklin was monitoring the jurors' faces during Sledgehammer's response to Fume's final question, and he thought he saw what was initially surprised transform quickly into sympathy, especially among the female jurors. And why not? It wasn't often you saw a man with Sledgehammer's countenance and build demonstrating his sensitive and emotional side. He thought the women might just eat it up, and an extended glance at the jury confirmed Franklin's supposition.

After hearing this, Fume announced to Sam in an overly formal, bordering on pompous way, saying, "You may inquire." Sam rose from his counsel table and walked over to the now-seated Fume and whispered something to him. Fume's reaction was a barely perceptible smile.

Sam began his cross-examination cautiously enough. He asked a few inconsequential questions about his background, then followed up with a question regarding his prior testimony and deposition, "I thought you had given a deposition for use at trial, which would be played to the jury. But, you have obviously come to Pittsburgh to testify live at trial. What brings you here?"

"Well, what literally brought me was a flight from Vancouver to Pittsburgh on the county's dime. Then, the county agreed to pay for three days at the William Penn, all meals included, and my flight back to Vancouver. That, and the woman whose privacy needs to be protected, wanted to see me again." Sledgehammer smiled broadly as he made this last statement, and Franklin caught a few jurors smirking.

The remainder of Sam's cross-examination was meandering and, as far as Franklin could tell, relatively ineffective. He did get Sledgehammer to concede that he might have struck him in the jaw several times, but Sledgehammer insisted that it was in self-defense. And, Sledgehammer reiterated, he ultimately got Brad calmed down and he didn't see anything approaching what could be considered serious bruising.

Sam was obviously thrown by the emotive conclusion to Sledgehammer's direct testimony, and there were many long pauses in his questioning while Franklin knew Sam was searching for a word. He knew that since Sam's stroke when he got upset, his language recall skills sometimes suffered.

Franklin's attention was waning when Sam asked this question, "Are Rovers permitted to keep personal items in a backpack or some other receptacle while they are roaming about?"

Sledgehammer paused and looked at Sam quizzically or suspiciously. Franklin couldn't tell which and nodded his head. Sam instructed him that he had to respond verbally, and Sledgehammer said, "Yes."

"And was your backpack or other receptacle located in Brad's cell at any time before Brad attempted to hang himself?"

"Yeah."

Franklin was conjuring up the vision of the black backpack when Sam asked:

"Was it a black backpack that you left in Brad's cell while you were circulating amongst the other prisoners?"

He could swear he saw the furrowing of Sledgehammer's eyebrows before he nodded his head. Upon a reminder from Sam that the court reporter had difficulty interpreting non-verbal responses, Sledgehammer leaned forward in his chair and mumbled, somewhat sheepishly, "Yes."

"No further questions."

CHAPTER 83-SLEDGEHAMMER'S EMOTIONALITY PROMPTS THE JUDGE TO COMMENT

Sam had to consciously remind himself that the trial wasn't over yet, although he had to battle that sentiment after what he thought must be the wholesale acceptance of Sledgehammer's story by the jury. Next up was the testimony of Fume's life care planner, who took issue, in mind-numbing fashion, with the conclusion reached by his life care planner to the tune of a couple of million dollars less for Brad's lifetime care.

Of course, the lifecare planners, both the plaintiff's and defendant's, had to concede that they could not project future medical costs with godlike precision, the major reason being that no one could predict with anything near certainty how long Brad, or indeed anyone, would live.

Sam's cross-examination was desultory, he would concede. But he didn't think that the jury was paying much attention anyway, partially due to the coma-inducing nature of the testimony and partly due to the nearness of the lunch hour.

When Judge Harris dismissed the jury to have lunch, he motioned both attorneys to the bench. "Mr. Fume," he asked, "who are you going to call to testify this afternoon?"

"Dr. Annette Paulson, Todd Shanahan, the guard who administered the suicide questionnaire, and Lieutenant Kevin Hodgson. And then I will rest."

"Very good," and then the judge asked, "How did you get Sledgehammer to cry like that? Was it authentic, or did you ask him to think about all the hockey teams that didn't want him?"

Fume winked and demurred, "Now, your honor, you wouldn't want me to disclose the secrets of an effective direct examination, now would you?"

Judge Harris chuckled and said, "See you, gentlemen, after lunch."

CHAPTER 84-THE LUNCHTIME PALL

Sledgehammer's testimony was bound to be the main subject of the lunch discussion, and, sure enough, Nicole's predictive skills were right on target. No sooner had they sat down in the cafeteria than Steve posed the question, "Nicole, you and Barbara are the only women here. Did you find Sledgehammer's crying jag to be at all sympathetic?"

Nicole had briefly considered that it was not authentic but manufactured, so that's how she answered Steve's question. "So then you considered that and all be an act and rejected that notion?"

"Yeah, but I guess that I'm an overly trusting person, and I erred on the side that it was authentic, but that doesn't mean I viewed the rest of his testimony as authentic," Nicole protested.

"Well, let's hope that the jurors are able to make that distinction," Sam said with a hint of dejection in his voice.

"I'm sure that they will be." Nicole wanted to buoy Sam's spirits and hoped she was more convincing than she actually felt.

Steve asked Sam what it was that he whispered to Fume right before he began his cross-examination, and Sam replied dispiritedly: "How did you teach a hockey goon to cry on cue?"

Steve's follow-up, "Did he say anything?"

"No," Sam said, and Franklin interjected, "But I think I saw the slightest hint of a shit-eating grin on his face."

Then Nicole, who had picked at her salad, announced, "I think I'll go hang with the protesters until court reconvenes." At least, she thought, the protesters wouldn't be so somber.

CHAPTER 85-THE LUNCHTIME PALL CONTINUES

When Nicole declared her intention to spend the remainder of her lunch with the protesters, Franklin wished he could follow. If his mood was gloomy after Sledgehammer's testimony, it was downright sepulchral now that he had picked up on Sam's doleful behavior.

In an effort to lighten up the conversation, Franklin chattered, "So, what did you think of Sledgehammer's admission that he had a black backpack in Brad's cell?"

Sam shrugged his shoulders and conceded that it was interesting, "But," he mumbled, "other than you being right, it doesn't mean shit."

"So, what's on tap for this afternoon?" Franklin attempted to keep the tenor of his voice this side of cheerful. Sam's response was apathetic and delivered haltingly, "Two guards, and then I assume we'll do closing arguments if there's enough time. Judge Harris is a real move 'em in and out guy."

Sam then excused himself, saying that he had better collect his thoughts if he needed to do a closing argument this afternoon, and moved across the cafeteria to an unoccupied table, leaving Franklin, Barbara, Steve and Jeff alone to finish their lunches.

They were cleaning up their trays when Franklin approached Sam. Sam, his right arm dangling and leaning on his quad cane, spoke more animatedly than he had all lunch hour, "I have an idea…"

CHAPTER 86-SHANAHAN

First up in the afternoon session was Dr. Annette Paulson. She was as matronly and nondescript a psychologist as Sam had ever encountered. Her dowdy dress was reflective of her voice which had a sing-song quality.

Of course, she described the Jail's concern with any prisoner as young as Brad, especially when that prisoner was a gay young man. She described the Jail's suicide prevention program, which largely consisted of a once-a-year movie which all of the guards and rovers were required to attend and impromptu lecturers, which she gave to all the staff.

She chronicled the " inmate rover" or "suicide prevention worker" component of the Jail's efforts to minimize prisoner suicides In essentially similar fashion as did the guards in their depositions and conceded that jail suicide was a major concern nationwide.

She related the history of the "inmate rover" scheme, minimizing the psychiatric screening which had been done by the jail psychiatrist, saying that jail guards were better equipped to select the rovers than psychiatric testing by someone who had not had the opportunity to be exposed to the prisoners daily. She affirmed that she had placed the responsibility for the selection of inmate rovers in what she described as the "extremely capable hands" of Lieutenant Kevin Hodgson.

Sam's cross-examination of Dr. Paulson was essentially an opportunity for him to remind the jury of Dr. Sonnenberg's opinions. He got Dr. Paulson to concede that the psychiatric testing done by the jail psychiatrist, which Dr. Paulson had discontinued, was at least worthwhile to some degree.

But Sam focused on Sonnenberg's other opinion, "Doctor, would you agree that it's dangerous to tell someone who, by definition, has engaged in anti-social behavior that he has special authority as a suicide prevention worker?"

Dr. Paulson thought for a moment and then cautiously offered, "Well, in a perfect world, that would be true, but the prison environment is anything but a perfect world. There would be a hierarchy of authority in any event. The strongest, brightest or most ruthless have a natural authority in jail. So, I don't think that giving the most trustworthy prisoners some greater authority, especially when it has to do with stopping suicides, is a bad thing. I respect Dr. Sonnenberg's opinion, but I don't agree."

Sam had to acknowledge that Dr. Paulson's testimony was, at best, a "wash;" in other words, it would not play a determinative role in the jury's thinking. And it only made the despair that he felt after Sledgehammer's testimony worse.

As promised, Fume called Todd Shanahan to the witness stand next. Sam knew that Shanahan would make an excellent witness to demonstrate how concerned the jail was about the psychiatric well-being of its charges, and he didn't disappoint. Of course, Shanahan testified that he had administered the suicide questionnaire and test to Brad and that Brad showed no signs of imminent suicidal ideation, but he would have had the jail psychologist review the results.

He confirmed that he had a particular concern about Brad because of his sexual preference and his age but that it was his opinion that Brad didn't need to be isolated from the rest of the prison population. Brad told him that he really needed a cigarette, and Shanahan promised him that he had a pack in his car, and when he got off shift, he would go to his car, get the pack, and deliver it to Brad. Unfortunately, he related, he didn't have the opportunity to give him the cigarettes that he so desired.

He admitted that he had a conversation with Lieutenant Hodgson, but insisted that it was only about what his son had told him about Brad's sexual orientation and nothing more.

When it was Sam's turn to cross-examine, he temporized by going through the questionnaire/test item by item. He was awaiting Franklin's reappearance in the courtroom. As he asked the question of Shanahan if he felt, "it was important that inmates who were walking around and observing other inmates should be stable." Franklin appeared through the back doors of the courtroom and nodded.

"I guess so, but my answer is only based on my experience."

"Isn't that especially true when Rovers are not given a psychiatric test to determine their stability?"

Fume objected and, at the Judge's urging, stated as the basis for his objection, "Mr. Shanahan has not been qualified as an expert, and I suggest that the question requires an expert opinion." The last few words of Fume's utterance trailed off as Brad was wheeled to Sam's counsel table.

When Carrie had secured Brad's wheelchair brakes, and Jeff had patted his brother on the shoulder and retreated to the gallery, Fume sputtered, "This," gesturing to Brad and his wheelchair, "is highly unusual and disruptive."

Judge Harris countered, "I agree that it's unusual, but that young man is a party to the suit and he has every right to be here. Mr. Wright, do you have any response to Mr. Fume's objection that the answer to your question would require expert testimony?"

Sam was quick in his reply, "I will withdraw the question." As he was addressing the judge, he looked Shanahan straight in the eyes. Sam thought that he caught a fleeting look of confusion, or was it uneasiness, on Shanahan's face.

Sam continued with his questioning, more to keep Shanahan on the witness stand more than anything else, "Officer Shanahan, isn't it true that when Dr. Rodriguez was the jail psychiatrist, he would subject the proposed Rovers to psychiatric testing?"

"Yes, that's true." Brad, who was trussed up with the ever-present neck brace, let out what sounded to Sam to be a frightened moan right after Shanahan's answer. Fume leapt to his feet, seemed to want to make a comment about Brad's moan, thought better of it, and sat back down.

Sam, who wanted to ask one last softball question before he asked the most critical question, got more from Shanahan than he expected to his question, "Eventually, it's true that Dr. Paulson gave Lieutenant Hodgson sole authority in the selection of Rovers?"

Shanahan responded, "Yeah, let's just say that the Lieutenant and the doctor were very close."

Hodgson, who was seated beside Fume at the counsel table, whispered furiously in Fume's ear, and Fume nodded his head expressionlessly.

Then, Sam, leaning forward on his cane, asked the question which he hoped would yield an honest answer from Shanahan and for which he had Brad carted into the courtroom to give Shanahan an opportunity to see just how pathetic Brad was. "Did you at any time prior to Brad's attempted suicide have any conversation with Lieutenant Hodgson or anyone else in authority or in the employ of the Coalton County Jail regarding Brad, or overhear any such conversation?"

"Yeah, but only standard stuff. I had a conversation with Lieutenant Hodgson about Brad, but it wasn't anything unusual. You know, we have a new guy coming in, he's young, things of that nature."

"So, other than the conversation or conversations that you had with Lieutenant Hodgson that was of a 'standard nature,' you don't recall any other conversations?"

"No, I don't." Immediately after his answer, he gazed over at Brad, who had a phlegm-induced coughing jag. Sam thought he saw pity register on Shanahan's face ever so briefly.

"Did you ever have a conversation with Sledgehammer, Mr. Lindstrom, regarding Brad prior to Brad's attempted suicide?"

"No."

Sam, seemingly admitting defeat, said, "No more questions," in a barely audible voice.

"No redirect, Your Honor," Fume nearly gushed.

As he was making his way down the one step of the witness stand and about to proceed up the aisle, he had to pass Brad. Brad, who had lost his two front teeth for some reason since the last time Sam saw him, followed Shanahan's progress with his eyes and when Shanahan was nearly by him, gave Shanahan a goofy grin.

Shanahan turned around and re-took the witness stand. Sam was bewildered, and Fume looked stunned. He looked down from the witness stand and spoke, "What were your last couple of questions to me?"

"If the court reporter could please read back my last two questions," Sam directed.

All six jurors, sensing that something dramatic might happen, leaned forward in their seats. The court reporter read the questions back in a sing-song manner, and Shanahan looked at Hodgson, looked away, and began, "I was with the Lieutenant when Sledgehammer approached the two of us and said, as best I can recall said, something like, 'I caught that young faggot taking a drag off my vape, and who the fuck knows where that mouth has been.'" Upon hearing Shanahan's rendition of

Sledgehammer's statement, Sam thought he heard an audible gasp from at least one juror.

"Did the Lieutenant or you have any reaction, verbal or otherwise, to Sledgehammer's, what should I call it, complaint?"

"We both laughed about it, but not Sledgehammer. It soon became clear to me, at least, that he was expecting us to take some action. So Kevin says, so what do you expect us to do about it? And Sledgehammer says, 'I think he ought to be taught that you don't fucking take other people's shit.'"

"So Kevin says, 'And I suppose you want to be the one to teach him that lesson.' Sledgehammer says yeah. Then Kevin laughs and says, 'Be careful you don't kill him,' and laughs again." Sam cast a sidelong glance at Hodgson and saw that the Lieutenant's arms were crossed and his expression was dour. He assumed that Hodgson knew what was coming.

"Then, Sledgehammer was walking away, and he turned around and asked, 'Can I tell him this is what he'll get every time he touches another person's stuff?' And Hodgson says, 'Yeah, I guess so. But I don't want him roughed up too bad.'"

Sam stood there for a long moment, and, mindful of the verity that you always end an examination on a high note, he sat down and, in what seemed to be more of a challenge than a courtesy, said, "Your witness, Mr. Fume."

Fume first asked the Judge if he could have Shanahan ruled as an adverse witness of whom he could ask leading questions. Judge Harris immediately agreed.

Of course, Fume, fully conscious of the trial lawyering admonition that you don't allow an adverse witness to repeat their story too many times, instead focused on the minutia of time and place in an effort to find some uncertainty or ambiguity in Shanahan's recollection.

And then, in his sole foray into specific language in his entire cross-examination, he asked, "Isn't it possible that Lieutenant Hodgson said to Sledgehammer, 'But I don't want him roughed up at all?'"

"I don't think so."

"Of course, Shanahan, isn't it true that your deposition, or sworn statement, was taken in this case?"

"Yes, it was."

"And weren't you asked multiple times in your deposition who you talked to or about Brad before his suicide attempt?"

"Yes."

"And weren't you sworn to tell the truth by the court reporter?"

"Yes."

"I believe the court reporter's words were, 'Do you swear to tell the truth, the whole truth and nothing but the truth until you answer to God on the last great day.' Correct?"

"Something like that."

"And yet, you never ever described the conversation between you, Lieutenant Hodgson, and Sledgehammer regarding Brad that you just testified to, correct?"

"Correct."

"Now, Officer Shanahan, weren't you disappointed that you were not made Lieutenant and Lieutenant Hodgson was?"

"Correct."

"Didn't you write a letter to the prison oversight board and make a vague reference to what you called, 'multiple incidents where Hodgson acted less than professionally.'"

"And that was two years before Brad Moran's attempted suicide, wasn't it?"

"That sounds right."

"And right after Lieutenant Hodgson was made a Lieutenant?"

"Correct."

Then, without another word and without warning, Fume sat down precipitously.

"Mr. Wright, I assume that you have recross."

Sam looked over at Brad, whose head was now resting on his chest despite the neck collar and whose mouth and eyes were wide open. "Yes, Your Honor, I do."

"I am sure that the jury would like to know why, when you were under oath in your deposition, you didn't mention anything about what you testified to when you retook the stand."

"It's because of him," Shanahan said, pointing to Brad. "I couldn't live with myself if I didn't tell the truth after seeing what a pathetic wretch he has become. And don't think I don't realize that I bear some responsibility. I could have, and should have, intervened and told Sledgehammer don't you dare touch him."

"By the way, were you aware before the conversation you just described of the fact that Sledgehammer was in possession of a vape pen?"

"No, I wasn't. It was my understanding that prisoners were not permitted to have them."

"Why?"

"Because marijuana, LSD and ketamine have been known to be added to vape cartridges."

Sam appeared to stare into space for several moments while he considered whether to interrogate Shanahan about his poison pen letter regarding Hodgson. He supposed that Fume would claim Shanahan had ill will toward Hodgson and that colored his testimony, if not tainted it entirely. Of course, further explanation of whatever the incidents referenced in Shanahan's letter might yield some truly damaging information about Hodgson, making him less believable or worse in the jury's eyes. But, since he had no idea what Shanahan would say, he couldn't entirely discount the possibility that Shanahan might have been referencing some stupid shit which might lead the jury to disregard his testimony entirely. He decided to leave it alone; better safe than sorry.

"No further questions."

As Sam shuffled back to counsel table, Judge Harris asked, "Do either of you have anything further to ask of this witness?" Both attorneys were silent. "Hearing none, we will take a fifteen minute break."

When the jury had left the courtroom, and as Shanahan began to walk from the witness stand and into the aisle beside the plaintiff's counsel table, all the while enduring the poisonous glares of both Fume and Hodgson, Sam offered him his hand. "You are a very honorable man," Sam enthused.

"I should have told the truth in my deposition. And you," Shanahan laid his hand on Brad's shoulder, "I am praying for you." With Shanahan's touch, Brad raised his head, and Sam was certain that he saw a flicker of recognition in his eyes.

Jeff asked Sam whether he wanted to keep Brad in the courtroom for Hodgson's testimony, prompting Sam to respond, "If he's not too disruptive, we might as well let Hodgson see him. It might prompt him to tell the truth." As Barbara, Nurse Carrie and Jeff were fussing over Brad, Sam excused himself to go to the restroom, but, in fact, he found a secluded portion of the hallway and just reviewed the afternoon's tangled events.

He reentered the courtroom at the same time as Judge Harris took the bench and nodded at Fume. When Fume called Lieutenant Hodgson to the stand, he could sense that the jurors expected a battle royale, and they didn't have to wait long.

Fume's first question, after asking Hodgson to identify himself, was, "Now you have heard Guard Shanahan describe conversations between yourself, a prisoner who went by the nickname Sledgehammer, and Officer Shanahan when he retook the stand after Mr. Moran was wheeled into the courtroom, haven't you?"

"Yes, I have."

Then, in what Sam recognized as a teaser, Fume asked whether Hodgson's recollection comported with Shanahan's. "Never happened," Hodgson replied emphatically and with obvious disgust.

"Well, we'll get to that in time, but now I want to ask you…" and he went on with his direct examination with questions regarding Hodgson's background, his history at the jail, the responsibilities of a Lieutenant, and finally, the jail procedures for dealing with the potential of suicide amongst the prison population.

"Now it is my understanding that there were trusted inmates at the Coaltn County Jail who were selected as 'Rovers' or 'Suicide Prevention Workers,' is that correct?"

"Yes, it is."

Then Fume asked a series of questions designed to flesh out the history of Rovers/Suicide Prevention Workers: their training, selection process and duties."To sum up, then," Fume asked a leading question to which Sam didn't object, "initially, years ago, Rovers were administered a psychological test by the jail psychiatrist, and after he left, the jail psychologist and ultimately the testing was discontinued and the selection of Rovers was exclusively your province, correct?"

"Dr. Paulson had ultimate authority to veto my selections, but she never has. I suppose she thought that I knew the inmates much better than she did, so she didn't interfere with my selections."

"Now, did you appoint Jacques Lindstrom, known as Sledgehammer, a Rover or Suicide Prevention Worker?"

"Yes, I did."

"Why?"

"He was an affable guy, a big guy who used to play professional hockey, well-liked by the inmates, concerned about their well-being. He wasn't incarcerated for a serious crime. In short, he was one of the best selections for a Rover that I ever made."

"Was he a Rover on the night of Brad's attempted suicide?"

"Yes, he was."

"Did you have any conversation with Sledgehammer about Brad before his attempted suicide?"

"No!" Immediately after Hodgson's answer, Brad began to make a mewling sound, soft but loud enough for everyone in the courtroom to hear. Fume, obviously bothered by the distraction, stared at Brad while Carrie fussed over his positioning in the wheelchair. Fume proceeded:

"Then, I take it that you didn't have any conversation with, of course, Shanahan and Sledgehammer before Brad's attempted suicide on the night of his attempted suicide."

"No, I did not."

"Would you have any idea as to why Officer Shanahan could have gotten the idea that you, Sledgehammer and he engaged in any conversation regarding Brad on the night that Brad attempted suicide?"

"Yes, I do. There has always been bad blood between us. You see, he always thought that he should have been made Lieutenant before me. He thought Dr. Paulson had something to do with my getting the promotion. He wrote that letter to the oversight board shortly after I was appointed Lieutenant which accused me of being unprofessional."

"By the way, any idea what he was making reference to?"

"None whatsoever."

"So, you are saying that he lied under oath about the meeting that you, Sledgehammer and he allegedly had immediately before Brad's attempted suicide?"

"I will let you attorneys figure that out, but I am saying that we didn't have any conversation, Shanahan, Sledgehammer and me, along the lines of what Officer Shanahan testified to before this young man here attempted suicide."

"Is there any way that Officer Shanahan could have misconstrued any conversation?"

"No, I don't think he could have misconstrued. But we did have a conversation, Officer Shanahan, Sledgehammer and me that day or sometime before where I might have said something similar to what Officer Shanahan attributed to me during his testimony, but it was not in reference to Brad."

"And what was that?"

"I was always telling Sledgehammer not to rough up someone or other so that I might have said it, but I don't want a prisoner roughed up at all. It was like a joke."

"Why were you concerned about Sledgehammer roughing someone up?"

"No, no, in my experience, he only fought with someone when they picked a fight with him. He was always a peacekeeper. But, it was a joke about his role as a goon in hockey."

"Sounds like you had a great deal of respect for Mr. Jacques 'Sledgehammer' Lindstrom."

"I sure did, and that's why I absolutely hate that he is being drawn into Brad's suicide attempt. I don't mind if Officer Shanahan shits on me, excuse my French, but I don't want Sledgehammer to be made out to be the guilty party. It ain't fair."

The courtroom was silent as Fume shuffled through his legal pad, apparently looking for more questions to pose to the Lieutenant. Sam assumed he found none because he sat down without another word. Sam sat silently contemplating whether he even wanted to ask a question on cross-examination and give the Lieutenant another opportunity to repeat his story. Finally, Judge Harris nudged him out of his stupor and asked, "Mr. Wright, any further questions?"

Sam stood up and turned around briefly to view the courtroom gallery. As he scanned the crowd, he saw Franklin, and their eyes locked briefly. Franklin brought his index and middle finger toward his mouth, then turned toward the witness stand where Hodgson was deliberately avoiding Brad's blank stare. He knew what Franklin was trying to convey, and his zeal to give form to the question that Franklin's gesture had suggested forced him to start his question multiple times. When he finally got it out, it was greeted by a bewildered look from Hodgson, "Were you aware that Sledgehammer frequently used a vape pen?"

When Hodgson finally collected himself to respond, he said, "Yes" in a quavering voice.

He thought long and hard as to whether to ask Hodgson if, as Shanahan testified, it was against jail regulations for a prisoner to possess a vape pen but thought the better course was to leave it alone and let Fume deal with it. He was certain Fume would elicit some bullshit answer from Hodgson, either denying that there was such a regulation or that Sledgehammer was such a valued Rover so much that the rules could be bent for him. Sam sat down at the counsel's table with a thud.

"Anything further?" the judge looked quizzically at both counsel tables.

Sam and Fume looked at each other; Sam thought Fume was trying to read his face, and Sam knew that he was hoping to divine some subtle indication from Fume as to whether he intended to question Hodgson further. Fume surprised Sam, "Nothing further, Your Honor and the defense rests."

"Mr. Wright, any rebuttal witnesses."

"None, Your Honor."

"Court is adjourned until nine AM tomorrow morning when we will have closing arguments. I will instruct the jury, and the jury will begin deliberations. Anything further?"

Both Sam and Fume answered simultaneously, "No, Your Honor."

Sam exited the courtroom and told his entourage to go on without him, and asked Steve to bring his car around the front of the courthouse. Franklin was obviously uncertain about his request to proceed alone down the elevator, but Sam assured him that he would be fine.

After a stop in the restroom, he was about to wait for the elevator when he decided to sit on the same isolated bench that he had occupied frequently throughout the trial for a little while. He was glad it was isolated because he began to weep. Upon a reflection later, he thought it might've been because he realized that not only was he alive, but he was trying a case, and that was truly a miracle given what he had been through. And, he thought, he had a chance to win.

CHAPTER 87-NICOLE MEETS BOBBY AGAIN

As Nicole made her way out of the courthouse after receiving word from Steve that he was going to Sam's office and help Sam with his closing argument, the first thing she encountered was a reporter from a local TV station and her cameraman. She was interviewing a protester with a sign. Because she had had enough of the trial and the tragedy of Brad that day, she hurried past the reporter and protesters.

When she thought she had sufficient space between her and the trial devotees, followers and placard carriers, she heard a voice shouting, "Nicole! Nicole!" She turned around and saw a neatly dressed young man with a Confederate flag baseball cap. It was Bobby Blackmore, one of the Protectors of Our Ancestral Faith and BIrthright, who she had met and walked out on at Chelsea's Place on a winter night months ago.

"What are you doing here? Covering the trial for your newspaper?"

"No, my boyfriend works for the attorney who represents the kid who tried to hang himself."

"Your boyfriend? You mean that huge brown guy?"

"No, he wasn't my boyfriend. He was just a roommate."

"I'm glad he wasn't your boyfriend. Is your boyfriend white, at least?"

She had to stifle a smile given his somewhat clever wordplay, disgusting though it was. She hoped her silence and accelerated walking pace would cause him to bid her goodbye. It didn't.

"So, aren't you interested in what brings me to Pittsburgh from Clarksburg?"

"Not really."

"Well, I will tell you anyway. I'm thinking of going to law school once I graduate, and a guy in the Protectors told me about this case, and it sounded like something I would be interested in. You know, I am opposed to faggotry. It's one of the things that will destroy this country. Remember I told you when you were in Clarksburg in the winter that I was going to start a chapter in Coalton."

"Mmm hmm..." She sped up again.

"Well, I did. And like I told you, there were Coalton Jail guards who were interested in the Protectors. One joined, and I found out about the case from him."

Her interest being captured, she slowed down and asked, "What did he say about the case?"

"Oh, he knew all about it. The case and like hanging. In fact, he was surprised that no one wanted to take his statement, or what's it called, deposition, I guess."

"Didn't he tell his supervisors or the jail's attorney that he had some information that was relevant?"

"No, he was happy to fly below the radar."

"What did he tell you about Brad's hanging?"

"He told me what he told me in confidence, I guess. But, who knows if you joined me for a drink what I might say? I am easy when I have something to drink, are you?"

She avoided his obviously suggestive question and replied, "We'll see. Maybe tomorrow." She felt certain there would not be a tomorrow, despite her curiosity about what the guard had told this neo—Nazi. It wasn't worth spending time with this loathsome creature.

"Speaking of tomorrow, what's on tap? See, I didn't even make it to the courtroom before court led out today."

"Tomorrow is the closing argument."

"At what time?"

Nicole briefly considered misinforming him but thought better of it. After all, he did have her email address at the paper, and she didn't want him blowing that site up with unwanted emails. She told him nine o'clock, and thankfully, her rapid walking clip had brought her to where her car was parked. She said goodbye to the creep, but not before he gave her a lascivious look and made some comments about drinks tomorrow.

CHAPTER 88-FRANKLIN'S SMOKE

When Franklin arrived home that night, he could hardly contain his enthusiasm as he told Kim, "Well, score one for the home team again."

"What do you mean?"

"It certainly looks like smoking has something to do with Sam's case, a smoking e-cigarette as it were, rather than a smoking gun." Franklin smiled at what he thought was mildly clever.

"Franklin, I will need a little better explanation than that if you want me to understand what the hell you're talking about."

Franklin then explained Shanahan's dramatic revision of his testimony, the black backpack and the e-cigarette." And so, just as I predicted, smoking might be one of the keys to Sam's case."

"I thought that you meant a real cigarette when you first told me you had a hunch months ago."

"Apparently, whoever or whatever implants these thoughts in my mind about Sam's cases doesn't keep up with current developments in technology."

"Who or what do you think is responsible for this? What shall I call it? Is miracle the right word?"

"You know what Voltaire said, 'If God did not exist, it would be necessary to invent him. "Kim, you are a good lapsed Catholic girl. Is it a miracle worthy of sainthood?" Franklin smirked.

"If God is not responsible, who do you think is?" Franklin could tell when Kim was getting mildly irritated.

"I guess it's some power greater than me." Franklin shrugged.

"It wouldn't take much!" Kim drew him close and hugged him,

CHAPTER 89-FUME'S CLOSING

As was his wont on closing days, he arrived at the courtroom half an hour early. He liked the quiet solitude, and it gave him the opportunity to appreciate the secular spiritual magnificence of any courtroom, especially those of the older Courthouses. Jury duty is, along with voting, Sam thought, an ordinary citizen's most consequential participation in the democratic scheme, and he felt a certain reverence for a place where it occurred.

Before long, Fume and his young associate appeared. Fume nodded, approached Sam and offered his hand, "Nice job, especially given your condition. You have my respect."

Sam smiled and said, "You have been a worthy opponent, nice job. I am still amazed that you got that big lug of a hockey player to weep on cue." Fume smiled in a manner that Sam would later describe as a perfect shit-eating grin.

Gradually, the courtroom filled up, probably because of the exposure that the trial had gotten on social and news media. Franklin came in, accompanied by Jeff and Barbara, and Franklin gave him a thumbs up. Nicole entered, accompanied by a young man with whom he was unfamiliar. She looked irritated.

Not long after, Judge Harris entered the courtroom and asked if they were ready to proceed with closing statements. Upon both Sam and Fume's affirmative responses, he instructed the clerk to bring in the jury. He then dismissed the alternates and called on Fume to close.

Sam always had difficulty maintaining his concentration during his opponents' closing statements because he was always rehearsing his own closing statement in his mind, and a mind, divided against itself, cannot concentrate on paraphrasing an old adage. He forced himself to focus intensely on Fume's explanation of deliberate indifference, which, after all, was the legal standard which the judge would tell the jury to apply. Fume gave a creditable formulation of the incredibly amorphous legal concept, "As the judge will tell you in his instructions, you must find deliberate indifference on the part of Coalton County and, this and is the second prong of the test, that that deliberate indifference was a proximate cause of Brad's attempted suicide. Deliberate indifference is a legal term for a failure to provide a prisoner with his human rights. It is the intentional disregard of substantial safety to a prisoner."

"Now, the County does not dispute that it is necessary for a jail to recognize a problem with prisoners attempting to take their own lives. That's why Coalton County had a suicide questionnaire which was filled out for each and every new prisoner admitted to the jail and why they had inmate rovers, otherwise known as suicide prevention workers, who were tasked with identification, to the extent possible, of prisoners that were prone to suicide. Guards and suicide prevention workers received special training in identifying suicide-prone inmates. Does this sound like deliberate indifference to you?"

"Deliberate indifference is not negligence, it is a much higher standard. It implies knowledge of the risk and deliberate indifference to that risk. Deliberate. Deliberate implies only a shade below intentional. You cannot find that the program for suicide prevention at Coalton County Jail was deliberately indifferent to the risk of suicide when there were so many safeguards in place for identifying suicidal inmates. It just doesn't make sense."

"So, how does the plaintiff go about proving deliberate indifference? Well, by presenting testimony from a fellow who likes to be called B and who, he claims, saw Jacques Lindstrom assault this poor woman's son," at which point he pointed to Barbara, "and told him that he had free reign to, in his words, 'fuck him up' every day."

"The only problem with the plaintiff's assertion that this constitutes deliberate indifference is you have to believe B. I won't go through B's long criminal history of dishonesty, which establishes that he can't be trusted to tell the truth, but you remember it, I'm sure. Are you going to base a decision with such far-reaching consequences on the word of B?"

"This leaves you with the testimony of Guard Shanahan. I want you to remember that Officer Shanahan gave sworn testimony previously, in what is called the discovery phase of this lawsuit, in which he denied having any knowledge which would bear on Brad's suicide. He swore that, under oath. Now, all of a sudden, he tells you that because he couldn't sleep at night knowing that Lieutenant Hodgson actually gave permission to Jacques Lindstrom to rough up Brad because Jacques said that he had taken a hit off of his vape pen. He has to tell the truth."

"Well, there are two problems with Guard Shanahan's testimony. I'm sure that you remember that he was off the witness stand and then came back and spilled his guts about what he knew. You have a perfect right to ask yourself why he lied two times under oath, in his deposition, and in his courtroom testimony before he dramatically had a change of heart."

"And, if you are willing to accept his testimony despite the fact that he lied not once, but twice under oath, you must ask yourself this: what does Guard Shanahan have to gain from what he claims is a change of heart? We know that he was so upset about Lieutenant Hodgson being made a Lieutenant over him that he wrote a letter to the hiring board accusing Lieutenant Hodgson of not one, not two, but three incidents of unprofessional behavior. What that is, you don't know. Lieutenant Hodgson says he has no idea what was being referred to."

"There was obviously bad blood between Lieutenant Hodgson and Officer Shanahan. What does Guard Shanahan have to gain if you render a verdict against Coalton County? Well, it means that Lieutenant Hodgson's testimony was not believed, and who knows if it wasn't believed what problems there would be for Lieutenant Hodgson. I am sure that the powers that be wouldn't be pleased that the jail has to pay a hefty verdict because Lieutenant Hodgson wasn't given much credence. Might it even mean that Guard Shanahan would be made Lieutenant?"

"I am sure that you won't soon forget Jacques Lindstrom. Handsome fellow. Professional hockey player. Trusted Rover. Obviously devastated by what happened to Brad, he cried over it. Now, I'm sure that Mr. Wright is going to tell you that Sledgehammer has a reason to lie and deny his culpability, that he is at fault for Brad's suicide attempt. He may even point to the County's flying him in from Vancouver and putting him up in a hotel for three days as an additional impetus for him to lie. But, when you weigh his testimony against what B told you, with B's long history of dishonesty and duplicity, you will know what your verdict needs to be."

"As the judge will tell you, in order to return a verdict for monetary damages for the estate, you must find the defendant guilty of both deliberate indifference and that that indifference was the proximate cause of Brad attempting to hang himself. Now, proximate cause, as the judge will tell you, means that the estate demonstrates for you that the defendant's act, or lack of action, was a substantial factor in bringing about Brad's attempted suicide."

"Put another way, the judge will tell you, a proximate cause is a cause in a direct sequence, unbroken by a superseding or intervening cause, which produces the event, Brad's attempted suicide, and without which the attempted suicide would not have happened. So, if you find that the Jail was guilty of deliberate indifference, but you think that that deliberate indifference was not a substantial or real factor in causing Brad to try to hang himself. In that case, you can mark your jury ballot, which the judge will give you and explain to you, that you find deliberate indifference but no proximate cause or substantial factor. If you do not find a substantial factor, then you will return a verdict for no monetary damages. It is somewhat more than, but for the jail's deliberate indifference, Brad would not have attempted suicide, but not much. It is with your provence to decide whether Brad's attempted suicide was directly caused by the jail's deliberate indifference or whether there were other intervening factors."

Then, Fume launched into a long and involved discussion of the economic damages, which Sam's glance at the jury revealed left several jurors fidgeting in their seats. He partially tuned Fume out until he heard his name mentioned. Fume was nearing the end of his closing and said, "Now, I anticipate that Mr. Wright will make a subtle appeal to your compassionate nature, and even the most hardhearted will have to feel pity for Brad. But, as the judge will tell you in his instructions, you are not to allow pity or sympathy to influence your verdict. You are to decide the case solely on the facts."

"I will remind you that since Brad suffered his injury, so to speak, when he was in the custody of Coalton County, and therefore Coalton County is responsible for paying for his care for the rest of his natural life. Now, undoubtedly, Mr. Wright will tell you that a monetary verdict in his favor will allow him to reside in a top-flight nursing facility and allow for other bells and whistles, but it's important for you to recognize that Brad will be cared for for the rest of his life regardless of your verdict."

Because Sam guessed that Fume's closing was near its persuasive conclusion, so he shifted his psychic energy to psyching himself up for his imminent closing. When Fume was done thanking the jury for their rapt attention, which every trial attorney routinely did, whether it was accurate or not, he gripped his quad cane and shifted his weight. No sooner had Fume resumed his seat, and Judge Harris said, "Mr. Wright," than Sam struggled out of his seat and, losing his balance, plopped back down.

Then, with Steve's assistance, he got back once more, red-faced but no worse for wear.

"Ladies and gentlemen of the jury…"

CHAPTER 89-SAM'S CLOSING AND NICOLE AND BOBBY HAVE A DRINK TOGETHER

Unfortunately, Nicole was accosted by Bobby Blackmore when she was in line for the magnetometer and security. Unbelievably, he asked the person behind her in line if she would mind him "cutting," and a bewildered older gentleman said he was not. Consequently, she went through security, up in the elevator and into the courtroom with him. Now, he was seated beside her in the courtroom gallery.

She was constantly moving in her chair, trying, occasionally unsuccessfully, to put distance between herself and Bobby, who was continuously moving laterally in his seat and making an effort to make contact with her. Because of this seated dance macabre, she was distracted during Fume's opening statement, But she thought that overall, it was well delivered and made some sense.

She witnessed Sam's initial unsuccessful attempt to rise from his chair, which caused her to feel transient pity for him, and when he got up and began his opening, hopeful. Sam began his opening by thanking the jury and then moved to explain the difference between the burden of proof in a criminal case and it is a civil case. He said that, unlike a criminal case, in which the standard of proof was beyond a reasonable doubt, the standard in a civil case was preponderance of the evidence. Sam asked the jury to imagine lady justice and the scales which she holds, and, he said, if the scale tips ever so slightly in favor of the plaintiff, you must find a verdict for the plaintiff. Since Sam only had one fully operable arm, he struggled to demonstrate with his arms the tipping of the scales of justice.

He then went into the minutia of the economic damages which the estate was claiming. The only remotely interesting item about that component of the closing was Sam's reminder to Nicole that, although the County would be responsible for Brad's medical care for the rest of his life, there was so much more than a favorable verdict would permit Brad to get other than housing in a third-rate nursing facility. Those included a van to transport Brad home for weekends, modifications to any home that the administrator of the estate, Barbara, might purchase to allow easier access for Brad, and potentially cutting-edge rehabilitation for Brad anywhere in the country.

Sam next broached the subject of Brad's sexuality. He told the jury that the only reason that it was remotely relevant was the statement that Officer Shanahan said that Sledgehammer had made and the statement that B insisted that Sledgehammer had made. "And, as the judge has told you, every person stands on equal footing before the law, no matter what their defining characteristics may be, whether it be race, sex, national origin or sexual preference."

Then, Sam hoisted himself onto to counsel table and, sitting on the edge of the counsel table, looked at the jury and delivered what Nicole thought was the most consequential portion of his closing with nary a stroke-induced stumble, "Now, you have been presented with four versions of what occurred on the night that Brad attempted to take his own life. First, you heard from Brian Lowe, who likes to be called B, and he described how Sledgehammer and an inmate called Flake beat up Brad. Why? It was unclear from B's testimony, but he did hear Sledgehammer say, 'You better be careful, Gump, because I have permission to fuck you up like this every day.' And, I don't need to remind you that, in prison language, Gump means gay."

"Next, you heard from Jacques Lindstrom himself, also known as Sledgehammer. He claims that he was just trying to calm Brad down when Brad jumped him, and he might have left some marks on Brad's face, but they were purely defensive. You have to wonder why he didn't report the incident, or at least that the jail had a troubled new admittee named Brad to the Lieutenant Wasn't that his job as a Rover? Sledgehammer broke down on the stand. Was he crying crocodile tears? And, oh yes, he admitted that his backpack was in Brad's cell."

"Now, as Mr. Fume predicted, I would, and I wouldn't want to disappoint Mr. Fume, you might want to consider why Sledgehammer might not want to disappoint the County. But more about the reasons that Sledgehammer might not be honest later, I will mention one aspect of Sledgehammer's testimony which was verifiably false. He said that he didn't smoke, and Lieutenant Hodgson testified that he knew that Sledgehammer possessed a vape pen."

"Then you heard from Officer Shanahan, and I shouldn't need to refresh your recollection of his dramatic testimony. He implicated Lieutenant Hodgson directly. Officer Shanahan witnessed a face-to-face encounter between Sledgehammer and Lieutenant Hodgson wherein Sledgehammer sought the Lieutenant's approval to assault, in his words, the 'young faggot' for 'taking a drag off my vape.'"

"After securing the Lieutenant's approval, Sledge-hammer asks if he can tell him he'll get a licking every time he touches another person's stuff, and in a truly compassionate response says," and here Sam paused to allow for the full dramatic effect of his sarcasm to sink in, Nicole assumed, "I guess so, but I don't want him roughed up too bad.'"

"And then you heard from the Lieutenant himself, who denied that that conversation had ever taken place. But, again, he did say that he knew Sledgehammer possessed a vape pen."

"The judge will tell you that you should make every effort to reconcile the various versions of the facts which the witnesses have testified to. You can be very sure of five facts: number one, that Brad was arrested and incarcerated at the Coalton County jail; number two, that you have received undisputed testimony from both his mother and Officer Shanahan that he desperately wanted to smoke; number three, that Sledgehammer had a black backpack in Brad's cell; number four, that both Lieutenant Hodgson and Officer Shanahan were aware of the fact that Sledgehammer had a vape pen; and, number five, Brad's face bore bruises and physical evidence of an assault which were unrelated to the markings of the ligature."

"But whose version of events do you find most believable? I would suggest that you look to the person that doesn't have a dog in this fight, doesn't have a horse in this race, or whatever idiom you prefer, which means unbiased or most objective."

"Now, Sledgehammer's version could be quite obviously colored by him not wanting to admit that he had anything to do with Brad's attempted suicide. That, and the fact that he was brought into town and put up in a luxury hotel for three days with meals provided."

"Lieutenant Hodgson's version has a similar problem. He would not want to admit that he encouraged, or at the very least didn't stop, an assault by one prisoner on another. It could cost him his job."

"Now Officer Shanahan has multiple indicia of reliability. There is no allegation that he was directly involved with either Brad's hanging nor in dissuading or encouraging Sledgehammer to assault Brad. He was a totally uninvolved observer. But let's just say that you might be bothered by Officer Shanahan's disappointment at not being made a Lieutenant, and his letter expressing that disappointment to the jail's board."

"Now, who is the person that not only doesn't have a dog in this fight or a horse in this race but in fact, expressed a fear that his testimony might result in physical harm to him? Of course, it was B. B who told you that he was fearful that Sledgehammer might take his testimony out on him. B, who had nothing whatsoever to gain from sitting on this witness stand and telling you that Sledgehammer struck Brad multiple times in the head and heard him threaten, 'You better be careful, Gump, because I have permission to fuck you up like this every day.' Well, there is honor among thieves. You heard B say that he didn't think it was right. And what did he get for his testimony? Nothing except a cold hamburger for lunch. When you believe what B said, it makes eminent sense to believe Officer Shanahan's version of what transpired took place before B observed and heard what Sledgehammer did and said. And that requires you to return a verdict in favor of Brad."

Then, Sam explained the concept of proximate cause. Sam said there can be little doubt that Brad's attempted suicide was proximately caused by his encounter with Sledgehammer. Then he referred to what the judge was going to say in his instructions, "Proximate cause is that which, in a natural and continuous sequence, unbroken by any sufficient intervening cause, produces injury, and without which the result would not have occurred."

Sam said, "Put it another way, that the defendant's actions directly caused the plaintiff's injuries and losses." It sounded like a lot of legal mumbo-jumbo to Nicole.

Bobby leaned in and attempted to whisper something in Nicole's ear, and she shushed him, but not before the fruity smell of breath deodorizer assaulted her nostrils. When Sam concluded his closing, Judge Harris called a fifteen minute recess before he gave the jury their instructions. Nicole got up, stretched and told Bobby that she was going to walk around town because Steve would call her if, by some miracle, the jury returned a verdict today. She should have known that Bobby wouldn't be so easily disengaged.

"Do you mind if I come with you? In fact, I owe you a drink."

"No, you really don't, and besides, I need to get my steps in," she lied, hoping that it would cause his surrender. It didn't.

"Oh, come on. You don't look like you need to get your steps in, and besides, I was going to tell you what the guard who is in Protectors said."

Nicole weighed whether she should tell him that she wanted to hear Judge Harris' charge after all, but recognizing that he would undoubtedly follow her back in and continue his uncomfortably close seating assault, she consented to have a drink with him. Besides, she was somewhat interested in what the guard told Bobby.

"Well, okay, but we shouldn't go far in case the jury comes back. There's a bar in the US Steel Building that's only about a block from the Courthouse. It should be open for the crowd who drinks their lunch."

On their walk past the outdoor sign-holding crowd and up the street to the US Steel Building, Bobby prattled on about what he considered to be his ultra-liberal college professors and his belief that many "communist" courts were using the Constitution as "ass-wiping material."

After they had produced sufficient proof that they were of age, she was treated to an evaluative summary of his various romantic involvements, including a lengthy diatribe about his most recent one.

"That's a shame," she said as she finished her glass of wine, "I better get to walking. I'm somewhat obsessive about getting my steps in."

"I thought you wanted to know what the Coalton County jail guard who is in the Protectors said."

She let out a barely perceptible sigh, which he didn't catch, and acknowledged that she would like to hear what was said.

"Well, what was that last thing that your boyfriend's boss was talking about, approximate cause, proximal cause? I know that he had 'cause in it somewhere."

"I think the correct term is proximate cause, but go ahead."

"Well, I think what he overheard from your boyfriend's client might have been relevant to proximate cause. He swore he told another prisoner that he might want to do himself in, and it wasn't because of Sledgehammer. It was because of his fag friend and his mother."

At that moment, Nicole's phone played a guitar riff from Hendrix's Foxy Lady, and she said, "I've got to take this. It's Steve."

Steve told her the jury had a verdict, get here as quick as you can. She told Bobby that she had to return to the courthouse, and the jury had a verdict. Predictably, Bobby said, "Oh good, that probably means that the jury sided with the county, doesn't it?"

"Yep." Steve had told her last night that Sam had mentioned that the sooner the jury returned a verdict, the more likely it was that it was for the defendant. Made sense to her since the jury could take a long time debating how much to give the plaintiff, especially in this complex case.

They left the US Steel Building and made the short walk to the federal courthouse almost in silence. Bobby asked if she wanted him to continue with his story, to which she replied, "Maybe later."

Later never came, despite Bobby's numerous emails inviting her for drinks and dinner at her email address at the paper.

When she asked Steve that night whether he wanted to tell Sam about her conversation with Bobby, he simply replied, "What would be the point?"

CHAPTER 90-THE WEDDINGS

It was early December, and Franklin and Kim were on their way to the very same courtroom where Brad Moran's case was tried, except this was a much happier occasion. Not that Brad's case didn't ultimately turn out favorably. He suspected that that result was the inducement for Kim's question during their drive to the courthouse where Judge Harris would preside over the double wedding ceremony;

"Did you get the money for a two-week vacation in Paris over Christmas as a bonus for helping Sam try the Moran case?"

Franklin smiled and said, "That's a good guess. It's not often that an attorney gets a multimillion-dollar verdict."

He had in his breast pocket a quotation from Albert Camus that he intended to read before he and Kim and Sam and Becca exchanged vows, "In the midst of hate, I found that there was, within me, an invincible love. In the midst of tears, I found there was, within me, an invincible smile. In the midst of chaos, I found there was, within me, an invincible calm. I realized, through it all, that in the midst of winter, I found there was, within me, an invincible summer. And that makes me happy. For it says that no matter how hard the world pushes against me, within me, there is something stronger—something better, pushing right back."

Both Sam and Kim had helped him to realize these things.

ABOUT THE AUTHOR

Gary has been a lawyer for 43 years, and has tried over 40 cases to a jury. He specialized in personal injury law, including medical malpractice, products liability and civil rights cases. Since suffering a stroke eight years ago, he has been writing. He was the recipient of numerous honors during his years as an attorney, including being named a Pennsylvania Super Lawyer for 20 years and receiving a Lifetime Achievement Award for his pro bono work. He lives with his wife of over 25 years and various pets. Together, they have five children and seven grandchild.